HE IS HERE

JACK STAINTON

ALSO BY JACK STAINTON

This novel is entirely a work of fiction and any resemblance to actual persons, living or dead, is purely coincidental.

An imprint of Windmill Streams *Publishers*

He Is Here

For My Readers
Thank you, one and all…

1

THE OUTLANDISH INVITATION glowing on Ed Lawson's laptop stood out like a neon sign amid the never-ending drizzle; its intermittent flashes captivating any passer-by, inviting them to peer through the relentless curtain of rain.

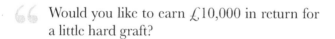 Would you like to earn £10,000 in return for a little hard graft?

The words mesmerised him, scared him even. Goaded him to make a choice.

At first, he welcomed the distraction, as the notification effortlessly slid from the right of his screen. It served as a break from unwavering hours of staring at a blank monitor; words failing him yet again. How many days had he sat forlornly at his desk, desperate for ideas to formulate inside his head and magically migrate via his fingertips? He needed to get another book published before the end of the year. He'd barely written a word for the past twelve months, his mind constantly distracted.

Ed Lawson was thirty-three and lived alone, and although his situation wasn't dire, money was becoming tighter by the month.

Sitting in his makeshift home office, he allowed himself a wry smile, and considered where life had taken him. Ed was far from ready to abandon his current way of living. He'd come too far, against all the odds. If only people realised what he'd been through to get to where he was.

He recalled his former English teacher, Mr McAlpine. An old-fashioned school tutor, set in his ways, never once allowing his students the opportunity to dream outside the status quo. But, deep down, Ed knew Mr McAlpine would have *loved* for one of his pupils to be sitting in a converted bedroom, overlooking the Atlantic Ocean, on the wild Irish Connemara coast, writing novels for a living. Full-time too. None of this '*I'll write a book in my spare time but never dare give up the day job*' nonsense. No. Mr McAlpine would have been so proud. But not once would he imagine the student to be Edward Lawson. The class clown, the chief protagonist behind all the tomfoolery, the constant disrupter and the bane of his life. The child who Mr McAlpine proclaimed, "Would never grow up."

The wind gushed, and the fragile wooden window frame rattled, instantly snapping Ed back to the present. His eyes returned to the screen. The neon sign was replaced by a resemblance to a fruit machine in the corner of a pub; its garish lights and melodic sounds gesticulating to the punter to dare to come over and play. An opportunity to throw away the last loose change in your pockets. *A metaphor for life?* Ed considered.

But this was a fruit machine like no other. It didn't *goad* someone to gamble. Instead, a one-arm bandit that ensured the player would win. The promise of a cash prize simply by taking part. A little graft, a fulfilled obligation, in return for thousands of pounds, which roughly translated to the same in euros. Enough to cover his modest rent for the entire year. Enough to allow Ed to peruse the fresh fruit aisle instead of surviving on tinned food.

Lured in by the assurance of living well for the foreseeable future, he clicked on 'Join Group' and waited impatiently for the screen to refresh. After what felt like an age, the page loaded, headed by an old black-and-white photograph of a grand-looking house. The turrets, perched atop each corner of the building, created a stately scene. An exquisite French château, albeit one in need of some refurbishment.

Clicking on 'About', Ed subconsciously read aloud. The entire experience was having its desired effect; enticing him in, bit by bit, word by word.

'Thank you for accepting this invitation to join my group. I hope you will now…READ MORE…'

Ed stared at the instruction on his screen, his hand trembling faintly as he clicked on the link.

'…agree to my promise of a small payment in return for your time in helping to rebuild my newly inherited French home.

'But why me, you will no doubt be asking. Please allow me to explain.

'I hope you will all remember me as soon as I remind you of who I am. My name is Joyce, but I know that will mean nothing. If

I said, 'Miss Young', would you be any the wiser? Miss Young, your History teacher from Ridgeview Grammar School'.

Miss Young. Ed couldn't help but smile, such was the incredulous notion that s*he*, of all people, was inviting people to her creepy-looking '*inherited French home.*'

'Now you remember, don't you, my dears? But I bet you are still asking, 'why me?' Well, each of you were, at one point, amongst my pupils at Ridgeview Grammar. Maybe in the same year, maybe not. Even so, I taught all of you during my career. I'm retired now, as you may have guessed, and I only taught at Ridgeview for four years, but that's of no consequence to you.

'But you, my friends, are the freshest students in my mind — the group of people I've become most intrigued by. You had the decency to 'friend' me when I initially invited you. Therefore, you have been 'hand-selected'.

Ed cringed at his ex-teacher's pathetic attempt at using buzzwords. *'The decency to* 'friend' *me?'*

'And I know, we all need money from time to time. I happen to follow you on social media and, as I am now in a fortunate position to help you out a little, what better way to become reacquainted? A reciprocal helping hand, shall we say? I want to know all about you, where you are, what you have done with your lives, and in return, I require your help. Don't be alarmed, it's as innocent as it appears. Call it perfect timing, no more, no less.'

. . .

4

Ed reread the contents of the mail several times over. He didn't remember accepting her 'friend request', but he forgot most of the people he interacted with on social media. He always assumed it was just a numbers game and the more followers you had, the better you felt about yourself. *A society of needing to be validated.*

So, Miss Young, or Joyce, had selected a handful of her ex-students to visit France and help restore her newly inherited château. All in return for ten thousand pounds each. She envisaged the work would take a month to complete. *'Mostly cosmetic'*, is how she described it. The package would cover travel expenses, food, and drink. Once accepted, Joyce would send further instructions.

However, the caveat was the one thing Ed couldn't divert his gaze from.

'Unless each of you agrees to sign up, the deal is off the table.'

It all appeared legitimate, a genuine invitation. The only issue Ed could see was the amount of money involved. Ten thousand pounds was ridiculous for a month's graft, but Ed had already considered nobody would agree to such a bizarre opportunity for less. He certainly wouldn't. The temptation simply *had* to outweigh the doubt.

Giving nothing else much thought, he calculated what the substantial amount of money would denote. In short, it would mean the world; a genuine lifesaver. An opportunity people wouldn't be able to refuse.

But then the inevitable negative thoughts hit home.

Why me? Why us? Surely that's what everybody is now thinking?

Joyce Young had selected a group of ex-students she hadn't set eyes on for years. But hadn't she made herself clear?

'*...And I know, as much as you, we all need money from time to time...*'

Ed's recollections of events at Ridgeview Grammar School were still regrettably fresh. Cursing himself for allowing such thoughts to seep back into his consciousness, he tried to dispel them as quickly as they arrived. Slamming his fist onto the table, he stood abruptly and paced the room, needing to concentrate on the positives instead.

Returning to his screen, he reread every word again, even though they were already ingrained in his mind. What was he looking for? Some kind of hidden agenda? Something which would cause enough doubt? But nothing leapt out. Did it sound like a hoax? Ed doubted it. The message was too personal. The group had been 'hand-selected' by a teacher who needed a favour in return for cash.

Half excited and half numb, his scrutiny of the situation stretched from one extreme to the other. He either counted down the days or hovered his finger over 'delete'. But whenever he considered the latter, the implications of not accepting made him cringe with guilt. *You have an obligation, Ed.*

The list of fellow invitees was deliberately left blank, so nobody would know who else had been selected. Ed realised that, because of the caveat, it would leave anybody who refused at risk. The reward – ten thousand pounds – would see to that.

Ed attempted to picture the others reading the same message, their faces, their reaction.

Will any of them actually say no?

2

———————

HAZEL DUNN SAT with her legs tucked underneath her, half-watching dreary daytime TV in the corner of her lounge. She played with a lock of auburn hair, which had fallen nonchalantly from her incredibly long fringe. Round and round her finger twisted and twirled, as if attempting to make it even curlier. The phone buzzing on the arm of her adjacent matching leather chair finally snapped her out of her trance. While casually retrieving it, she hoped it could be a job offer, but already knew that was unlikely. But Hazel was desperate, and within seconds of reading the headline, her heart sank yet again.

The subject had all the hallmarks of another scam. How many of those bloody things did she receive? On the cusp of sliding her thumb across the screen to delete, something caught her eye, forcing her to stop. So she read, her intrigue increasing, and Hazel soon tapped on 'Join Group'. The page loaded instantaneously.

She spent the following few minutes dissecting the content. Still, she continued to twist and twirl the lock of hair, but she had at least untucked her legs and sat perched on the edge of the chair, further enticed by an offer of what Hazel soon regarded as *free* money. Eventually, she stood with an enormous smile stretched across her face.

"Who are they kidding? I've grafted all my damn life," she said aloud, before emulating one of her favourite movie characters. "Show me the money!" She let her hair fall loose from entanglement.

Carrying her phone through to the kitchen, Hazel retrieved a bottle of white wine from the fridge she'd been saving for a *good news day*, before rummaging around the cutlery drawer for a bottle opener. She placed her mobile phone on the island, and as she opened the wine, she tapped the screen every few seconds to keep it active. Pulling carefully on the corkscrew, Hazel reread every single word of the email. She couldn't afford for it to be a scam. She needed the money. And if the stupid company she was supposed to work for would not come forward, then Hazel had to find the cash to pay for her mortgage somewhere else.

After filling a large glass almost to the brim, she downed half the contents before carrying it through to the lounge. Pausing to look at her reflection in the full-length mirror, she saw an onset of dowdiness staring back at her, despite it being far from the truth. She contemplated who the real Hazel Dunn was. The spontaneous, fashionable, trend-setting, Hazel Dunn, or one who was ready to give up on everything, even at the tender age of thirty-five. With a renewed bounce in her step, she returned to her favourite chair, thought *bollocks to the consequences*, typed 'I'm in', and hit '*Send*'.

Hazel Dunn had no ramifications from Ridgeview Grammar School. She couldn't even recall who the fuck Joyce Young was.

. . .

In stark contrast to Hazel's swish West London apartment, Oliver Ramsey's one-bed flat was something of a shit hole in comparison. The wooden sash windows were rotten and allowed rain to seep through, although at least the weather appeared to have finally brightened a little. Still, tiny puddles of water formed on the inside sills, and although Ollie noticed, he made no attempt to wipe them dry. He tightened his blanket to keep the cool breeze out and shivered exaggeratedly.

Oliver Ramsey, or Ollie as everybody knew him, was five foot eight and far too thin. Underneath his blanket, his T-shirt exposed scrawny arms covered in tattoos which were fading to a bluey green hue, leaving the naked eye unable to distinguish what any of them originally depicted. His short-cropped brown hair greyed at the temples, and both ears contained a small stud earring. Despite being in his mid-thirties, Ollie's neck bore wrinkles defying his age and crow's feet adorned both eyes, as if he'd spent far too long squinting into bright sunlight. Oliver was thirty-six going on forty-six. Losing his driving licence a few months prior, and his living wage, only added to his rapid decline in appearance. But he still carried an air of defiance. His chirpy cockney demeanour held him in good spirits, and even though his dilapidated flat wore him down, he remained hopeful for the future. Once he got his driving licence back, of course.

With the rain easing, he put the kettle on to make himself his sixth cup of tea of the day. Although he recognised his teeth were suffering with every sip of his beloved tipple, two heaped spoonfuls of sugar in each would invigorate him for at least another hour. But dentists were a thing for the rich in Ollie's world. If he got toothache, he'd get a mate to come round with a pair of pliers. At least that made him grin.

As the kettle boiled, he heard his phone ping from somewhere on the kitchen table. Pushing bills and take-away menus to one side, he eventually found his mobile. It was one of those old flip-style phones with a tiny LED square display on the exterior. Although Ollie really could do with his reading glasses, he at least distinguished an envelope icon on the flap, highlighting he had new mail. Ollie *never* got new mail.

Ten minutes later, he was back underneath his blanket, one skinny arm protruding so he could slurp on his hot sugary drink. He rubbed his tongue over his teeth and wondered when he last brushed them. They had a furry type of feel, *like felt*, he assumed. With ten thousand pounds coming in, maybe he should spend some of it on a visit to the dentist.

Then again…, he thought, smiling broadly.

"Twenty thousand pounds!" Charlie Green exclaimed, pacing the bedroom with just a towel around his waist whilst forever brushing his fingers through his wet high-lighted hair.

"Erm, ten thousand pounds *each*," his pretty wife, Mel, corrected him for the umpteenth time. "Ten thousand pounds… each."

Charlie glared at her as she stood in the bedroom doorway. She arrived upstairs a few minutes earlier, following her husband's squeals of delight. Mel too had a mobile phone in her hand, yet having read the same message as Charlie, her face remained sceptical.

"Ten thousand times two equals twenty in my books. Even you should be able to work that out, *darling*."

Melanie and Charlie Green had been at loggerheads for the past year, but their marriage somehow survived. The constant bickering resulted in them losing their two best sets of friends; two couples who they used to eat and drink with at weekends. But now, they formed their own friendships. Charlie had just returned home after his regular afternoon game of squash with his best *buddy*, Adam. Mel hated the word *buddy*, especially for a man of Charlie's age to use, as if desperately trying to hang onto his youth.

"Whatever," she replied, equally disdainful as the look her husband imparted upon her. "But you're forgetting one thing, *darling*." The last word dripped with sarcasm and she knew Charlie would realise exactly what she meant.

"Don't you dare say we're not going. Did you read it?" He held his phone aloft. "Unless we all agree, the deal is off the table. I'm guessing some people who have been invited need the money even more than us." Charlie altered his expression to resemble somebody sad and dejected. "We can't do that to them, can we, babe?"

Mel reluctantly walked into the room and sat on the edge of the bed. Despite Charlie being in great shape, she still wished he would put a T-shirt on. She didn't want him to get the wrong idea by joining him.

"And can't you read either? *Ridgeview Grammar School*. I know it must be around fifteen years since we last set foot in that place, but surely even you should remember that far back."

"Touché," Charlie quipped before accompanying her on the bed. Mel felt his wet towel brush against her hand, and she hunched herself away a few more centimetres, another thing seemingly not lost on her husband. However, he appeared to sweep it aside. She realised he would try every possible way to convince her to go along with whatever the thing in France was all about. "As you say, babe, that's all years ago. If anything bad was going to come out of all that, don't you think we would have heard by now?"

He was right. The rationale inside her mind told herself the same thing a hundred times over, so much so, until they received a message just five minutes prior, Melanie Green hadn't given Ridgeview Grammar School a single consideration for years. Even so, what she and Charlie did had still happened, and the very mention of that old place made her forearms break out in goose-bumps. Charlie wasn't finished, obviously irritated by her lack of enthusiasm.

"And we've spoken about it a million times." He turned and took her hand in his. Despite them being wet and feeling uncomfortably cold against her skin, Mel still appreciated the contact. "Besides, what did we do wrong? Nothing. Absolutely nothing."

"That's not entirely true, is it, darling?" But Mel was warming to her husband. Perhaps it was the sensation of being held. His enthusiasm and lack of guilt emanating through his fingertips and spreading through her veins, as if she'd popped a pill. Charlie sensed it too, and he leant forward to kiss her, lingering long enough to have the desired effect. He gripped her hand more firmly, but this time, Mel snapped back. "I'm still not happy," she proclaimed, and Charlie tutted his disapproval at her rejection.

"This has nothing to do with all that. It's, what's her name?" Charlie said, realising the fun and games were over.

"Miss Young. *Joyce* Young apparently."

"... yeah, Miss bloody Young. Our old geography teacher."

"History." Mel couldn't help but smile at Charlie's genuine lack of interest in anything connected to school. She doubted he recalled the name of the place until they just received the message.

"Yeah, history. What a load of old bollocks that was, too. I can barely remember her lessons. Can you?"

"But you do remember what we did?"

He tutted again. "Nobody ever knew it was us. If they did, why would we be invited to this?" Again, he held his phone aloft.

"But what if somebody knew it was us?"

Despite playing devil's advocate, Mel found it difficult to disagree. If anybody knew it was them, it would have surfaced years ago. "Perhaps she's angry because we were always snogging at the back of her class," Mel giggled, finally allowing herself to relax.

Charlie was the master of interpretations, especially where members of the opposite sex were concerned, and he took it as his cue to revisit one of those *snogs* from the rear of the classroom. Mel imagined Miss Young turning her back, writing some inane dates from the past on the blackboard, whilst she and Charlie had their classmates smirking at their juvenile love life.

And as they kissed, Mel knew she would accept the invitation. Twenty thousand pounds — or ten thousand each — was a lot of money. But Charlie's words were never far from her thoughts.

"...and what did we do wrong? Nothing. Absolutely nothing."

"That's not entirely true, is it, darling?"

3

SIX WEEKS LATER

The eight passengers crammed inside a makeshift taxi. A driver — who, given his strong accent, the group soon deciphered was local — and Joyce Young occupied the front seats. The invitees filled the rear, alongside a dozen bags and suitcases of varying sizes and weights. The trip would last a month, and because it was the final week in June, their time in France would stretch into the peak of summer. Ed Lawson prayed for sunshine and warm weather. Anything for a respite from the relentless wind and rain from home.

Prior to boarding the taxi, the group were greeted on the concourse at Nantes airport. Even though they had just flown in from Luton, it hadn't particularly dawned on Ed that they were on the same flight. Until they gathered outside the terminal, that was.

The minibus driver, roughly the same age as the travellers, held up a large sign reading 'Ridgeview Reunion', sprawled in hastily written letters. Once Ed stood beside their chaperone, he noticed his face contained an array of scars crisscrossing both cheeks. Upon closer inspection, his neck carried quite crude-looking burn marks, too. Figuring he must have been involved in a nasty accident or fire, Ed attempted to force himself to stop staring, albeit too late, and the guy offered him a disparaging glance in return.

After a few awkward moments of silence, one of the party impatiently asked the man with the scars what they were waiting for. He shrugged, counted the group by pointing at each of them, before dropping the makeshift sign to the floor. Taking a phone from his pocket, he turned his back and began tapping on the screen.

Undeterred, the remaining congregation made small talk, individually introducing themselves.

Feeling his hands perspiring, and his heartbeat hastening, Ed wasn't sure what he would say when his inevitable turn arrived. *Do any of them recognise me?* he thought. Thankfully, the others bore a similar apprehensive expression. The only couple amongst them were the first to speak.

"Hi," the same guy who just asked what they were waiting for cleared his throat before speaking. "I'm Charlie. Charlie Green." He turned to the beautiful woman beside him, smiling, although Ed couldn't help but notice she didn't appear to agree with his enthusiasm. "And this is my wife, Mel." Charlie beamed with pride, whilst her eyes narrowed with contempt, only offering a brief glance towards her husband. Despite her obvious annoyance, Charlie continued with his introduction. "You all probably remember her as Melanie Edmonds."

"They're not going to remember *us*, Charlie," she said, temporarily wiping the beam from his face. "I should think we're all different age groups, different school years. Jeez, you're not *that* fucking popular."

Ed couldn't help but smile at the immediate put-down, turning his face away to conceal his amusement. However, despite Mel saying nobody would recognise them, Ed certainly knew the couple standing before him.

It soon transpired Melanie Edmonds and Charlie Green were the youngest of the party, albeit one academic year below Ed. Mel was one of those girls who all the boys found attractive, but she dented everybody's dream by selecting just one. Equally handsome Charlie swooped in, and from the age of fifteen, they became childhood sweethearts, much to the annoyance of every boy who was dripping in testosterone.

As Ed studied her, standing reluctantly next to her husband, he noticed she had metamorphosed from a pretty little schoolgirl into a fine-looking woman. She stood around five and a half feet tall, had highlighted shoulder-length hair, striking blue eyes and a lovely smile — even if it only lasted a few seconds following her introduction.

Next, Ed considered Charlie. He had fewer recollections of him from school, but he knew who he was. Everybody did. Seeing them both together again, Ed recalled Charlie and Mel as *the* couple at school. And there they were, still together, all those years later.

There was no doubt he was a good-looking guy. A fraction over six feet tall, with wavy brown streaked hair, cut short at the back and sides and built as though he worked out regularly. Ed could just imagine the perfect male model body hidden beneath his sweatshirt and jeans.

Unsure if anybody else noticed, Ed watched as Charlie tried to take hold of Mel's hand, like a show of solidarity. But each time, she pulled it away. Charlie still fixed on a grin and ignored her rejection.

"Who's next?" he asked, as if wanting to deflect attention. "I don't recognise anybody."

"I'm Hazel Dunn, and I'm—"

"Hazel Dunn?" interrupted Charlie. "No, can't say I know that name."

Mel thumped her husband's arm, before speaking again. This time her voice was softer, understated and somewhat sultry, to Ed's discerning ears at least.

"Ignore him, Hazel. Charlie can be quite brusque, shall we say?"

Charlie said something under his breath, but not loud enough for Ed to hear. Mel ignored him before continuing to address Hazel.

"I thought I recognised you on the flight. It's that hair! It's amazing."

Sure enough, *amazing* was the only word to describe Hazel's hair. Long, curly and auburn, it reached down to her lower back and twirled forward in multiple strands from the top. She continually tucked it behind her ears so it wouldn't cover her eyes, leaving the fringe to hang like giant curtains at the theatre. Her cheeks, neck, and forearms were speckled with freckles, extending down beneath her rolled-up sleeves. She dressed the smartest of all, if somewhat unprepared for the sun that beat down from overhead. Hazel wore a black polo-neck jumper and tight-fitting dark jeans, inserted neatly into a pair of brown suede ankle boots. A large, expensive-looking matching handbag draped over her shoulder completed the look.

"Thank you, Mel," she said, with an air of authority. "I thought I recognised you too, even though I'm older than you. I'm thirty-five. You?" Mel confirmed she and

Charlie were thirty-two before Hazel continued, "Yes, I must have been in the sixth form when you and Charlie started seeing each other at Ridgeview. You were quite the couple, if I remember correctly."

Mel laughed, as Hazel air quoted 'seeing each other', which somehow helped to break the ice for at least one other guest.

"Okay. My turn," said the guy standing next to Hazel. The introductions followed the order in which the group stood. He spoke with a southern accent, even though Ed immediately recognised how exaggerated it was.

"Oliver Ramsey's the name. Everybody used to call me Ollie. Still do, actually. I live in London now." He talked at a hundred miles an hour and his leg jittered at roughly the same speed. "I was born there, moved to Lincolnshire when I was fourteen and went to Ridgeview Grammar for two years." He appeared to stall briefly at the very mention of the school. Ed thought it strange before Ollie recovered. "Got me own business. Think I'm the eldest by the looks of it. Thirty-six. I'm the bloody grandad of the group!" He laughed out loud at his own limited joke. Everybody smiled, unsure what to say, as he looked considerably older than his years. Ollie was a fraction shorter than Charlie and much thinner. So much so, Ed wondered if he'd been ill at some point. He noticed Hazel staring at Ollie's exposed arms, covered in faded tattoos. Ollie immediately became self-conscious and began rubbing his palms up and down each forearm. To divert attention, he clasped Ed on his shoulder and squeezed it a little harder than necessary. "Don't remember you though, mate?"

Ed cleared his throat, still secretly praying Ollie wasn't alone and nobody recognised him.

"No. I can't recall you either, Ollie," he replied, his

eyes flicking between his new *mate* and the rush of taxis behind him, urging a driver to step from one and call the group forward. "Can't say I particularly remember any of you," he added, turning his attention from Ollie to Hazel, then Charlie, before resting his gaze on Mel. Ed was finding it quite difficult not to stare at Mel. "I'm Ed. Edward—"

"Ha! Yes," Ollie piped up again, appearing to be high on nervous energy. "We were all kids back then. But look at us all now." He finally removed his hand from Ed's shoulder.

"Ed? Edward Lawson, did you say? Is that you?"

Ed had momentarily averted his gaze from Mel, mesmerised by Ollie's nerves, but now, Mel Edmunds, or should he say, Mel Green, reciprocated and stared directly at him. Indeed, all eyes were upon him, including the guy with the scars who had shown no interest in anybody else's introductions before then.

Why the fuck are you suddenly interested?

"Yes, it's me. How do you remember?" His involuntarily high-pitched voice only accentuated his self-consciousness. Feeling his cheeks growing warmer, he took deep breaths to compose himself; breathe in, count to four, breathe out, count to four. Something his mum taught him after he showed an onset of shyness at a young age.

"You've changed the most," Mel said, even though he prayed she'd shut up. "Weren't you quite the prankster at school? I knew about you despite you being a year older than us." Ed turned as Ollie laughed, again forcibly, but still Mel hadn't finished. She saved the most embarrassing line for last. "Quite the dashing author nowadays, if I may say so."

The muted laughter from the group didn't help, but it

had been the fact that Melanie Edmunds had called him dashing, and she knew he was a writer, which made Ed redden further. Even the guy with the fucking scars smiled.

"Oh, yes." An authoritative female voice from the back of the party thankfully averted Ed's unwanted attention, albeit only momentarily. "We have a famous author amongst us, don't we, Edward Lawson? Who would have thought it?"

More forced laughter ensued as the group parted to allow the older lady to make her way through. Ed noticed Mel glance at Charlie, who shrugged his shoulders in return, as if secretly asking, 'How should I know?'.

Joyce Young was small in stature but, unsurprisingly, immediately stamped her power upon the others. She was the reason they were there, after all. Standing at five foot two, her shoulder-length hair was completely grey and her face wrinkled considerably around her mouth and eyes. Even though they found out later that Joyce Young was fifty-eight years old, she could easily have passed as somebody a few years older. Life looked as if it had taken its toll on her since retirement from teaching.

The excitement of the host introducing herself finally allowed Ed to relax. It felt like being back at school; the teacher in command and everybody waiting on her every word. And Joyce was good, the old habits still installed in her demeanour. She was indeed in control, and everyone laughed nervously at her jokes and keenly agreed with each suggestion she made.

As the group finally collected their luggage and followed the man with the scars, Ollie stopped everybody in their tracks. "And who's this then?" he asked, in his already familiar chipper voice.

It appeared only Ollie had noticed the guy who stood

on the periphery throughout the entire introductions, although Ed had spotted him. An older man, roughly the same age as Joyce, maybe a year or two younger and incredibly sheepish. He had long grey hair, wore a baggy green jumper, khaki knee-length shorts and Doc Marten boots. He looked like a hippy, a throwback to the sixties, and unbearably hot in his overdressed and scruffy attire.

"Oh, of course," Joyce spoke on his behalf. "This is my ex-husband, Tony."

A look of bewilderment spread across the group. *What on earth is he doing here?* was the collective expression that nobody dared to ask. Joyce read their minds.

"He's very handy when it comes to DIY. It's the main reason you're here. Isn't it, *darling?*"

Her last word dripped with derision. Finally, Tony replied.

"Just here to help," he said, without taking his eyes off Joyce. His voice was gruff and melancholy. He looked as though he wanted to be there about as much as having an extra hole in his head.

"Yes, well, I'm sure you will be of *some* use," quipped Joyce, before turning and leading the group towards the airport car park.

Hazel walked alongside Joyce, whilst Ollie hung back to walk with Tony, already chirping away in his best cockney accent. But it didn't last long, as Ed overheard Tony say something before stomping off on his own. Ollie glared after him, bewildered.

Charlie said something to Mel, before tutting, picking up his holdall and trotting forward to join the man with the scars. Joyce had introduced him as Louis, and he would drive the minibus and stay at the château during the trip.

That left Ed and Mel. Mel bloody Edmunds. Ed

Lawson found himself walking from an airport in France, in the sunshine, with Mel Edmunds. Well, Mel Green. And he was going to be staying in the same place, a grand château no less, as Mel Green. And it hadn't been his choice to walk with her. She deliberately waited for everybody to pair up and stroll off so she could walk with him.

For the past six weeks, since the invitation from Miss Young arrived, the entire situation felt somewhat surreal and overwhelming to Ed. More than once, he'd contemplated saying no, telling himself he was doing the wrong thing. But as they walked towards the minibus on that fine summer's day, suddenly everything felt quite palpable in Ed Lawson's little world.

In hindsight, he should have stopped it there and then.

4

Hazel's initial impression of Joyce Young was both fascinating and annoying. To be fair, Hazel already identified the entire situation captivating yet unbelievably surreal. As she strolled alongside her host towards the airport car park, she attempted to probe her, a deliberate act after getting Joyce on her own. Following a little small talk, Hazel went for the jugular.

"So, what's this really all about, then?"

The pace at which her host walked surprised Hazel, especially given her outward appearance as somebody way past the peak of their fitness. It didn't help that Hazel had dressed inappropriately considering the unforeseen weather which greeted them.

"Why do you need to know such detail, my dear?"

Joyce's condescending reply irritated Hazel further. She felt tiny beads of sweat forming across her forehead as she tucked her hair behind her ears. Hazel was used to getting her own way. How else had she become so successful in her job? Ha! Job. She noticed her confidence evaporating in the stifling heat.

"Just curious, that's all. It's not something you do every day of the—"

"Aha. Here we are," Joyce interrupted, ignoring Hazel whilst turning to face the rest of the group. "Hurry along, you lot. I'm supposed to be the oldie amongst us."

Hazel glared at Joyce before finally following her gaze and facing the others, too. She wondered if any of them were bothered or the slightest bit intrigued by the real reason they were there. Upon receiving the invitation, Hazel felt an uncontainable sense of relief at the chance to deposit some much-needed cash into her bank account. *Free money* is how she'd perceived it. But now she was there, the reality was beginning to hit home. *If only my work hadn't dried up so suddenly.*

She'd had steady projects for twelve or more years, ever since leaving University and landing her dream job travelling the globe. Yes, maybe she was only a glorified hotel inspector, but visiting exotic places and reporting back on a broad variety of accommodations not only paid the bills, but allowed her to see a vast amount of the world too. Yet, six months previously, the assignments stopped, suddenly and unexpectedly. She landed one or two secondments around the British Isles, but they didn't pay the bigger bucks, and besides, Hazel perceived her homeland boring in comparison to arriving at an airport and flying off to yet another glorious destination. And so she found herself extremely frustrated. Not only did the agencies refuse to return her calls, but she was now on a trip without understanding what the fuck it was all about. Hazel Dunn needed to be in control, to know what each day would bring and why. She always dictated her life, never answered to anybody, and for most of her job, she picked her own journey around the planet. The freelance way of living was Hazel's passion. Her reason to wake up in the morning. Perhaps it's why she never married, never had a truly *serious* relationship, as in never actually living with anybody. She preferred her own company, to make her own choices and tell people what she wanted; not the other way around.

So when Joyce Young blanked her, in such a condescending manner no less, and then had the audacity to turn her back too, Hazel Dunn took an instant dislike to her purported host for the upcoming weeks.

Ollie liked geography. Well, the bit about maps and roads and stuff. He never liked all that shit about rocks and glaciers and 'human geography', whatever the hell that was. When Ollie put his name forward for the subject at Ridgeview Grammar, he thought it would all be about countries and continents and flags of the world, but within weeks, he'd lost all interest. And so it came as no surprise when he left school and ended up driving for a living. That was Ollie Ramsey's idea of *proper* geography.

So, when the minibus departed Nantes airport, picked up the E3, which appeared to circumnavigate the city, before joining the E60, Ollie stared between the road atlas and his adjacent window to take in as much detail as possible. He could see from the map of France, which Louis lent him, the dual carriageway would lead almost all the way to their final destination in southern Brittany. Ollie's brain was like a sponge as he soaked it up.

Eventually, following one impromptu toilet break, they turned off the major road and picked up signs for the D4 towards Pont-Aven. A small place, which sat at the mouth of an estuary in the Bay of Biscay. After they first boarded the minibus, Joyce had spun around and told the group the name of the town. Ollie heard Hazel allow a "pfft" sound to escape her lips, and he wondered why she was so pissed off. But Ollie was upbeat. He'd never travelled abroad before and he took in every road sign, every shop signage, everything he could to distinguish France from his homeland.

As the minibus meandered along the principal thoroughfare of Pont-Aven, he noticed, amongst the throng of tourists, so many galleries and artists' workshops. Even though he had no interest in such places, he floundered and forced his head sideways, away from any wandering looks on board the bus. Ollie's ex-wife loved art, and he knew she would have loved it there. He gulped heavily and felt tears prick at the back of his eyes. *Hold it together, you twat*, he repeated to himself, his neck now at an unnatural angle to the others. And wherever Ollie looked, he saw her reflection in the glass, smiling, her arms outstretched. By the time the bus trundled over a small bridge and a free-flowing river below, a solitary tear ran down each of his cheeks.

Minutes later, they arrived at a parking lot by the estuary, where Ollie noticed the town on the left and the sea on the right. The Bay of Biscay, according to the map, sitting on his lap. The only buildings were on the far side of the wide expanse of water, but none were château-like, even if Ollie didn't really understand what a château actually comprised.

Wiping his cheeks with the back of his hands, he looked at his fellow passengers for some kind of explanation of where the hell they were. He caught Tony looking at him. After telling Ollie to 'fuck off' at the airport, he'd taken an instant dislike to the guy. *Arrogant prick*, he thought. But there was something else about Tony. Something Ollie didn't like.

. . .

"Everybody out," Joyce called over her shoulder, already halfway out of the door. "Louis will help unload the luggage, so grab your own and make your way to that red boat over there."

Following further looks of bewilderment and a lot of shoulder shrugging, Charlie followed the group as they filed out of the rear of the minibus before Louis tossed the bags out onto the tarmac.

"Hey. Be careful," Charlie called, as his new Nike holdall landed at his feet. Louis stopped what he was doing and glared at him. Following a quick flick of his head and some kind of grunt, he returned to his task and continued to remove the luggage. Full of exaggeration, he carefully placed each item on the floor. Charlie nodded his approval, but not before his face was flushed with embarrassment.

"So where's this château, Joyce?" Charlie asked as they joined her at the edge of the quay. He was desperate to regain credibility, and what better way, in his opinion, than to lead the questioning like some kind of group leader? "And why are we getting into a boat?"

"Oh, you can't see it from here, my boy," Joyce replied. Charlie noticed Hazel roll her eyes. A 'just give us a straight answer,' sort of look. Joyce appeared to catch her and offered Hazel a wry smile in return. "Let's get on the boat, well, ferry, and once we're out to sea, you'll see the house in all its glory."

"But why a ferry? How far is this place?" Mel's face was full of concern and Charlie realised she was only echoing what the others were secretly thinking. The trip was getting more mysterious by the minute and he detected an edge amongst the group. Charlie thought he and Mel would stand out with their ongoing impasse, but Hazel had been in a gruff mood since boarding the minibus, even though she had been quite cheerful outside the airport. Ollie's original exuberance had diminished during the latter part of the journey, and Tony already seemed like the last person you'd want to be stuck on a desert island with.

After setting foot on the small boat, the lifejacket made Mel feel queasy and incredibly claustrophobic. Once everybody was seated, she tried again.

"I'm not good on boats, Joyce. I know it's all a secret and stuff, but can you please tell us where we're going?"

Joyce stood and instructed Charlie to swap places with her. She smiled as she took one of Mel's hands into her own before gently squeezing it. It had an immediate and desired calming effect.

"It's less than a mile, dear. The water is very calm today and as soon as we get out into the bay, you will see the island." Joyce raised her head and propelled her voice so all could hear. "We'll be at the château in thirty minutes, your home for the next few weeks." Mel observed more forced smiles and nods from the group.

"And we can catch the ferry back to the mainland whenever we want…" she asked, raising her voice yet barely audible over the engine as the boat spun around and picked up speed along the estuary. "… you know, if we want to look at some of those lovely art galleries and things?"

Joyce let go of Mel's hand before sitting back and letting out what can only be described as some kind of guffaw. "Oh no, my dear," she said, before shouting to ensure the entire congregation took note again. "This little ferry will drop us off and will return in exactly four weeks to collect us again. Your phones won't work and there is no internet."

Mel looked to Charlie, now sat near the front, for any display of compassion, but he shrugged his shoulders and widened his eyes as if to say, 'this is what we're here for'. *How can he be so bullish? No phones, no internet and now we can't even bloody leave.*

She then studied her fellow passengers, fear creeping up inside as the increasingly larger waves lapped against the side of the small vessel. But her comrades offered her nothing, either. No reassurance. No empathy. Just a look of acceptance. And to add to her misery, Joyce wasn't quite finished.

"Think of it as an adventure. The eight of us …"

Mel looked around and counted. Her, Charlie, Joyce, Ed, Ollie, Hazel, Joyce's husband Tony – who she had taken an instant dislike to – and Louis, the miserable scar-faced baggage handler. *What the hell?* she thought, her heart beating like a drum.

"… all stranded on our own little desert island."

Mel thought she might be sick.

"Oh yes," Joyce concluded. "It's going to be an experience none of us will *ever* forget."

5

THE GROUP's first glimpse of their temporary home came as the cramped boat left the mouth of the estuary and turned a slight right and made its way out to sea. The island looked small, and from their new vantage point, appeared to be covered in dense trees. As soon as Joyce pointed, Ed watched the others as they followed her outstretched arm and spotted a house perched in the centre at the highest stage. He studied them, speculated what they were thinking. *The same as me?* he considered. The property did indeed appear palatial; large, with a turret at either end. The quintessential French château. Ed recalled the invitation on his laptop screen, an old black-and-white photograph of a grand-looking house. *This is it*, he thought, half-smiling. *We're here.* Given the silence which had fallen upon his fellow travellers, he guessed they were having similar thoughts. The realisation of what they signed up for. The intrigue of the email finally turned into a reality. He wondered how everybody would react once ashore. Joyce's declaration there would be no phone signal or internet access had created a murmur, but nothing too untoward. Would they all feel the same as the days passed by?

Eventually, allowing his gaze to divert from the house, Ed's eyes rested on Mel. She appeared most apprehensive of all, and he wished he could somehow reassure her. However, given that all seven of them sat opposite one another in a line of three and four, he realised it was impossible to do so. Louis was sitting at the rear, talking to the skipper, and next to him was Tony. Ed caught his eye and offered him a brief smile, but Tony immediately turned his head and looked ashore instead. His manner was already grating on Ed and he recalled how gruff he was towards both Joyce and Ollie, back on dry land. He already suspected Joyce didn't want him there and Ed considered Tony's attitude could soon become a problem amongst the others too.

The boat grounded on a makeshift ramp and Louis, via some frantic arm gesturing, instructed everybody to remain in their seats. He climbed onto a step at the front before jumping ashore with an attached rope in his hand. Quickly, and rather impressively, he hauled the craft onto dry land before tying it securely to a large wooden stake protruding from the ground. Joyce admired his skills.

"Need any help?" she shouted. "I'm sure my Tony could make himself useful."

Joyce smiled as everybody turned to face her husband. But Tony didn't reply, he just glared at her. *If looks could kill*, she thought, still smiling.

"Non, merci!" Louis called, before waving his arms again, this time indicating for the others to join him. One by one, the group climbed onto the same step before he held out his hand to help them down. Joyce smiled her appreciation; Louis offered a solitary nod of his head in return before pushing the ferry back out to sea. The skipper shouted something and the vessel was soon on its return to the mainland.

Tony Young wanted to kill his ex-wife. He pondered if she had asked him to come only to ridicule him. He wasn't there for that.

Six months shy of his sixtieth birthday, Tony had been sceptical for weeks about Joyce's actual objective of dragging him along. Of course, they both knew he wouldn't refuse. How could he?

Collecting his holdall, he slung it over his back and gripped onto the cord handle. He wished he could remove his thick woollen jumper, but his T-shirt beneath resembled something moths had half-eaten. Tony had no intention of drawing any further unwanted attention upon himself. Reluctantly, he followed the group as they disappeared through a narrow opening into the trees just above the shoreline. And as one or two engaged in small talk ahead, Tony tried to convince himself he was doing the right thing. *Just keep your head down, do what's asked of you and get out of here.* After all, he probably needed the money more than most.

Spotting Joyce glance over her shoulder as she turned a sharp corner in front, she made eye contact with him, but she was too far away for Tony to discern her look.

Maybe she knows I would love to kill her. He caught himself smiling as he took in the surroundings of thick undergrowth and dense trees. *And what better place than a deserted island in the middle of nowhere?*

. . .

After a tough climb through the forest-like terrain, the group arrived at a small wooden gate. It hung nonchalantly by a solitary, rusting hinge. Ollie thought a stiff breeze would put it out of its misery once and for all. As he held it open for everybody to file through, Joyce stopped on the far side and noticed one or two observe the shabby looking entrance.

"That's one job on the list," she quipped, nodding at the gate. "Couple of new hinges and a fresh coat of paint, and it will be as good as new."

"I can do that," Ollie replied, half lifting and half pushing it closed. "I'm a dab hand with a tin of paint."

Joyce grinned sarcastically towards him before securing the gate with a piece of orange string, crudely attached to an adjacent broken post.

"This way," she said, retaking the lead from Ollie. He pulled a face behind her back, making Charlie laugh. Ollie watched as Mel punched her husband's arm and gave him one of her already familiar looks.

Mel's initial seasickness soon passed. Perhaps the firm ground beneath her feet steadied her nerves? However, once through the broken gate, she turned and studied the vast amount of water between the island and the mainland. "That's got to be more than a mile," she muttered under her breath. Quickly, she increased her step to catch up with the others.

The château was impressive, albeit in obvious need of a good spruce up even to the untrained eye. Mel remained at the rear as the group filed inside the grand entrance via the terrace and huge double wooden doors.

She was pleased to get indoors. The heat was stifling, and following the climb from the shoreline, it came as a relief to step into the cool building.

To concur with Ed's initial appraisal, the château wasn't too shabby. Sure, the paintwork needed attention, as did the exposed beams and skirting boards, but it was all cosmetic. Just as Joyce promised.

Standing in the centre of the huge foyer, he looked skywards towards the tallest ceiling he'd ever seen. Caught in his own thoughts, he ignored Joyce's latest order, calling the group through to another room. A separate voice soon beckoned him though, snapping him back to the present.

"Come on, mate," cried Ollie. He was standing in the doorway to Ed's right, grinning like a kid on a school trip. "Try to keep up."

Ed sighed at Ollie's annoying enthusiasm. "Yeah, okay. I'm coming," he replied, before turning his back and taking in his surroundings once more.

Still mesmerised by its enormity, he glanced up to the ceiling for further inspection. The house held him in awe; so grand, yet with a sense of some deep, fearful apprehension. Such a contrast to his humble little cottage on the Irish coast. *If only Mum knew I was here.*

"Yeah, I'll be with you in a minute…," he repeated to nobody in particular. Ollie tutted out loud, and Ed glimpsed him from the corner of his eye as he disappeared through the open doorway.

The mansion, and his own thoughts, captivated Ed, so he lingered a little longer. He realised that all the doors off the main foyer were closed, except for the one that Ollie had exited through. The only other route available, as well as the huge entrance behind him, was a giant stair-case directly in front. It stretched high; the steps narrowing the further you ascend. Ed's eyes followed the shiny banisters, reaching their summit, before continuing along the landing, both to the left and right in tandem. Cobwebs covered the balusters, intertwined between every opening. Hungry spiders waiting in anticipation for their next meal. Scanning both directions, Ed soon noticed the corridors descended into total darkness. It reminded him of a scene from an old black-and-white horror movie, and he imagined creaking floorboards and a rocking chair gently swaying by itself in a room beyond. A shiver travelled the length of his spine.

"*Somebody just walked over your grave*," he heard his mum say.

Brushing the sides of his jeans with the palms of his hands — an annoying trait he struggled to restrain from doing — a wave of sadness threatened to overwhelm him.

Ed's mum died of lung cancer when he was only four-teen. He moved to Lincolnshire shortly after. His foster parents were nice, but they could never replace Mum. Ed's real dad perished in a tragic car accident before he was even born, although his mum had *befriended* another man from the village before that fateful night. He discov-ered later that she'd been having an affair for a couple of years, and within months of Ed being born, she was preg-nant again. He couldn't say with any conviction who his *real* dad actually was.

But her new boyfriend didn't hang around either, and Ed never found out where he went. His mum assumed he moved abroad. "I'm not too sure," she told him when he was old enough to understand. "I haven't heard from him since the day he walked out of our front door."

I'm in France now, mum, he thought to himself, looking

skywards, his eyes full of tears, threatening to spill over at any moment. *But you know that, don't you?*

6

OLLIE PURPOSEFULLY LINGERED behind the open doorway and watched as Ed appeared mesmerised by the stairs and the long landing. He followed his gaze, but it looked just like any normal staircase to him, albeit much grander than anywhere he'd been before.

He didn't know Ed and wondered what Joyce was talking about when she announced they had an author amongst them. Did she say *famous* author too? Well, Ollie had never heard of him, but then again, Ollie couldn't be confident of naming any author. Books weren't his thing. He did like television, though. Ask him about his favourite game show or sitcom and he'd be on much firmer ground.

Ollie took a few steps backwards as Ed finally joined the rest of the group. He appeared lost in a world of his own and Ollie couldn't help but notice all the colour had drained from his face.

. . .

A solitary flute of bubbly sat on the silver tray, held aloft by a young girl. She looked a few years younger than anybody else. Maybe mid-twenties, Ed guessed. She wasn't unattractive, and her quintessential French accent somehow added to her appeal. He wondered who had organised her being there and where they could have found such a person willing to come to the island.

"Aha. You are the last one," she said as he approached. "Please, 'elp yourself to champagne."

With a nod of gratitude and a final glance over his shoulder, Ed accepted the glass and downed over half the contents in one gulp. It may not have been the most sophisticated way to sip the world-renowned fizz, but in the absence of something stronger, he craved the hit. Attempting to push the memories of his late mum to the back of his mind, he took a huge breath and wandered over to join the others. He knew he needed to fit in, make an effort, despite his introverted mannerisms.

The party had gathered underneath a large multi-paned window, which overlooked the front garden, awaiting their host to formally greet them.

Then Ed noticed Charlie Green staring at him.

Charlie studied Ed as he eventually stepped over and stood at the back of the group. He looked pasty white and his eyes red around the rim, as if he'd been crying. Charlie didn't understand grown men getting upset.

Just like his wife, he recognised Ed Lawson when they met on the airport concourse and he hadn't been impressed when she described him as 'quite the dashing author'. But who was Charlie Green to talk when it came to finding the opposite sex attractive? But it wasn't Ed's looks, it was more the recollections from Ridgeview

Grammar which held Charlie's attention. Mel was right. Ed Lawson was somewhat the rebel at school. He had a reputation in the year below and possibly in the year below that, too. Forever sat outside the head teacher's office, awaiting his next punishment, the child who the others were told not to copy. But Charlie recalled Ed only pranked around, nothing malicious, although wasn't he in the same school year as the notorious school bully? *What was his name?* Charlie's mind went momentarily blank. *Parry. Yes. Will Parry.* He felt a shiver wash over him as he remembered what had happened only recently to that particular boy.

So Charlie watched Ed a little longer than necessary. He noticed him neck his champagne in just two gulps. Was he nervous? He certainly didn't want to meet Charlie's, or anybody else's, gaze, and continually looked to the ground, only briefly peering back up. As soon as he caught Charlie watching, his eyes shot back to the floor.

It made Charlie think. They eventually expelled Parry from Ridgeview Grammar. Did Ed know him? And, more importantly, was he aware of what happened to him a few weeks ago?

Hazel watched their host intently as Joyce elevated herself by stepping onto a small pedestal underneath the large glass window. It acted as a mini-stage, perfect for somebody to perform a welcoming speech. Joyce tapped the side of her champagne flute with a metallic pen, ensuring she gained everyone's attention. Hazel found her all too patronising and still hadn't forgiven her for being so impolite on the quay.

"Welcome, all, to my château," Joyce exclaimed, her face beaming and flush from the drink.

Hazel heard a mock laugh from behind, like a muffled 'Ha!', but when she turned, everybody's expression remained blank.

Joyce summoned all to gather a little closer before formally introducing them to the previously undeclared attendee.

"This is Adrienne," she said, requesting the hostess to join her on the stage. "She lives locally and will be with us during our stay to cook and clean. I would imagine her English is far better than all of your French combined..." Hazel peered around as everybody laughed nervously, "... and she will ensure you are all fully fed to keep up your strength." More nervous laughter ensued.

Hazel discovered later, during informal chats, that Adrienne lived on the other side of Pont-Aven. An aspiring artist who responded to an advertisement Joyce had placed in the local town hall. She would carry out domestic duties in return for accommodation and a modest salary. Adrienne was much more welcoming than Louis, despite appearing nervous under the spotlight.

After the introductions, Joyce addressed the question that not only Hazel asked earlier, but she guessed was on everybody else's lips too.

"So," she stalled for effect, taking in each guest's expression. "Why you?" The subject brought a murmur of anticipation, alongside an apprehensive giggle or clearing of a throat. "Well, it's all quite simple really, and not the huge drama which appears to be etched across all of your faces."

Again, a ripple of laughter ensued, although Hazel was becoming impatient with Joyce's elongated hype.

Just fucking get on with it.

"Fourteen years ago, almost to the day, was my final year at Ridgeview Grammar School." She scanned the room before continuing. "And you, my darlings, are five of my pupils randomly selected from my time at the school."

"I didn't know you retired that year. That's when we left, wasn't it, darling?" Charlie asked Mel aloud.

Somebody tutted, but again, Hazel couldn't decipher who.

"Let her finish, will you?" Mel shot her husband a look, echoing everybody else's thoughts.

"Yes, Charlie," Joyce continued, "you wouldn't have known. Apart from the staff…" she paused, before looking at the back of the room. Everybody followed her gaze until their eyes set on Tony, standing by himself once more, "…and my husband, of course…", everybody turned back to the front, as though watching an imaginary game of tennis, "…nobody knew I would retire."

Unsure of where Joyce was leading with her announcement, Hazel watched on, still wishing she would cut to the chase.

"I'd had enough, had enough of teaching, and of my time at that school. Perhaps that's all you need to know." A slight murmur ensued. Hazel knew everybody was thinking exactly the same as her. *We want to know much more*. "My reasons were, and shall remain, quite private."

Hazel caught Ed's eye. He shrugged.

Joyce continued, "But that still doesn't answer my original question. Why you? The select five. Well, six, including Tony."

Once more, everybody turned in unison to face her ex-husband. Tony shuffled awkwardly and gave his ex-wife a look which Hazel couldn't quite decipher. However, he looked like a nasty piece of work and she found him somewhat scary.

"As you all appear so interested in him, I'll address

Tony first. As I briefly explained at the airport, Tony is quite the handyperson. Now, I doubt many of you follow in my ex-husband's footsteps. In fact, I doubt any of you know which end of the hammer to hold." A murmur broke out, people desperate to relax. "And how do I know that, you may well ask? Well, I am a big user of social media. As you all are. And I follow every one of you. And you, my darlings, were the only people to follow me back. Of all my ex-students who I befriended, you had the decency to reciprocate, and for that reason, you became my *chosen ones*," Joyce air quoted.

More shuffling of feet, muttering and forced smiles.

As Hazel tried to convince herself the entire situation could be as innocent as Joyce suggested, their host cleared her throat, indicating that she evidently wasn't finished.

"And I happen to know that ten thousand pounds is a lot of money. An amount that many people would find difficult to refuse."

The last few words caused the most fidgeting to date. Hazel noticed eyes scan one another, maybe for some kind of moral support. If Joyce hadn't held everybody's attention before, she certainly had now.

She knows I'm skint.

Suddenly, Hazel wanted the ground to open and swallow her whole. Feeling incredibly uncomfortable, she sensed she'd been invited on the pretence of being stalked on social media by her crazy ex-history teacher. But how much did she know? Taking in her fellow invitees, she wondered if they were all in the same situation. *We must be. Why else would we be here?* And however much Hazel wished she'd shut up; Joyce still hadn't finished.

"So why ten thousand pounds? Yes, for sure I could have got the work done much, much cheaper, and dare I say, much quicker." Again, Joyce allowed her sarcasm to sink in, as if trying to gain their trust, prove she was genuine and had their best interests at heart. "But would any of you have accepted for less? Come all the way to France to help an ageing ex-teacher you can't even remember? Of course you wouldn't. I needed to entice you, but not in a sinister way."

Hazel considered the question whilst glancing at one or two other faces. Ollie was slowly nodding his head, whilst Mel and Charlie looked at one another with a hint of acknowledgement that everything was okay. *Like some kind of fairy godmother.*

"I perhaps could have got away with a little less money, maybe five grand? Who knows? The thing is, I've come into a considerable inheritance and I wanted to help you guys out. Call me your philanthropic aunt, your knight in shining armour." Joyce paused again. "So, here's the offer. If you don't want to stay, I'm giving you all one last opportunity to leave. No questions, no quibble."

Another uncomfortable silence. Ollie shifted his weight from one foot to the other whilst Mel drained her already empty champagne flute for the umpteenth time. But one person spoke and Hazel recognised it had been Tony who laughed at Joyce's initial announcement.

"And who left you a considerable amount of money?" Everybody turned. Tony looked around the room, swinging his empty glass from side to side. "And this château? You don't know anybody with this kind of wealth."

The tension suddenly became tangible. The group reverted to face Joyce and Hazel realised her initial confidence had somewhat diminished. Still, she was the leader, the one person everybody was relying on in their quite surreal situation. Joyce *had* to grapple back control.

"There are many things you don't know, my darling,

and there are things I could tell this group right now which would make you even more unpopular than you've already made yourself."

Hazel noticed Ed's eyes widen, whilst Mel nudged her husband and a smirk stretched across Ollie's face. A collective undertone that Joyce really *was* in charge.

"Where was I?" Joyce continued unabated, her self-assurance returning much faster than it left. "Oh, yes. As I was saying, this is your last chance to go. I'll book you on tomorrow's flight, get Louis to take you back in the small dinghy, which is kept in the boathouse, and arrange a taxi to the airport."

Glancing around at her fellow invitees, Hazel wondered if anyone was tempted. But even if they were, Joyce's next words ensured that nobody took her up on the offer.

"Of course, there will be no ten thousand pounds for anybody who does decide to leave."

7

It did not surprise Charlie when nobody accepted Joyce's proposition. It made perfect sense to him once she explained herself. Of course, she had to entice them, and like she said, who would have gone for anything less? He doubted he and Mel would have. And as Joyce added, she'd come into money, despite Tony's doubts, and Charlie considered her offer extremely commendable. It pleased him they followed her back on Facebook now, even though he couldn't remember doing so.

However, as Joyce explained how events had unfolded in her life, Charlie became convinced Mel might say something. The way she'd been acting since getting off the minibus made him angry. What was all that regarding not liking boats and continually asking Joyce what the trip was *really* about? He noticed how queasy she looked once they stepped foot on the island and when she stared at the mainland, as if she might contemplate swimming home. Why couldn't she relax, enjoy it and think of the money? How had Joyce described it?

'*Think of it as an adventure. The eight of us, all stranded on our own little desert island*'.

What's not to like about that? Charlie thought as he helped himself to another glass of champagne from Adrienne's silver tray. The bubbles were rapidly going to his head, and he wished his wife would drink too. *Twenty thousand pounds for a month of this. Ha! Easy.*

Moments later, he smiled at Adrienne as he replaced his flute before swiftly collecting another. Charlie thought she was very attractive. An aspiring artist, no less. He considered she must be in her mid-twenties, maybe six or seven years his junior. Her dark brown bobbed hair shone as the light filtered through the huge window where Joyce made her speech. Freckles dotted across the bridge of her nose and underneath her pale blue eyes. Adrienne stood around the same height as Mel, a good six inches shorter than him, but Charlie liked petite girls. *Yes*, he told himself as he took another large swig of champagne, *this could be an adventure of a lifetime.*

Look at him ogling that poor girl, Mel thought, standing alone whilst observing her husband drinking champagne like it was going out of fashion. She was still angry he had shown no kind of loyalty when she was obviously struggling at the quayside. And then he walked up ahead on the climb to the château, leaving her to wrestle with both the weight of her luggage as well as the internal emotions doing somersaults inside her head.

She wondered if Charlie panicked when Joyce offered them all a get-out clause. She wished she said something or coughed to clear her throat, just to gauge his reaction. He would have been beside himself. However, she wasn't at all shocked that nobody accepted. And Joyce did explain herself. She'd come into money and she followed them all on social media. Mel realised it wouldn't take Hercule Poirot to realise how desperate they were for cash. Besides, who the hell would get that far and then back away? Joyce knew that, too. If she'd offered the same get-out clause at the airport or on the quayside, then Mel may have said okay and rescinded. But the sensation of being trapped on a desert island made it nigh on impossible for anybody to opt-out. No phone signal, no internet. *Is there a landline?* And what did Joyce say, *"I'll get Louis to take you back in the small boat"*? Small fucking boat? You've got to be kidding. It took all of Mel's effort to get into the bloody ferry thing, and that had a proper engine and life jackets and was made of sturdy material. She could only imagine what this *small boat* looked like. She had visions of an inflatable kid's toy bobbing on breaking waves at the seaside, all of five metres from the beach.

Finally, the champagne and informal inauguration ended, and they regathered in the foyer to collect their bags before being taken, two at a time, upstairs to their respective rooms.

Mel and Charlie were called last as Louis beckoned them forward to follow him and she felt a fresh wave of apprehension wash over her. Louis hoisted her larger bag onto his back whilst she clung to her hand luggage. Ignoring the grumpy baggage handler, her eyes instead became transfixed on the dark corners of the elongated landing.

"Go on, love," prompted the ever-charming voice of her husband. "We'll be here all day if you don't get a move on."

Glancing over her shoulder, she noticed Charlie

smiling and his eyes glazing over. He was pissed after drinking five or six goblets of champagne in less than thirty minutes. Joyce had parted with explicit instructions for all to meet for dinner at seven o'clock sharp, and Mel wondered if Charlie would even make it.

A noise from what she presumed was the kitchen momentarily distracted him, so she followed Louis up the stairs. Anything to put some distance between herself and her husband. Halfway, she noticed Ed standing on the landing outside an open door, which she surmised was his room. She offered him a brief smile, and he briefly returned the gesture.

Once at the top, Mel spotted Tony further along the landing too, and although she smiled at him, unlike Ed, he didn't reciprocate. Instead, he stared at her. She felt uncomfortable as his eyes shifted up and down her body and she involuntarily crossed her spare arm over her chest. With a smug grin, he returned to his room. *What the hell is wrong with him?*

Louis called after Charlie, who was still standing in the hallway looking lost but not at all bothered.

"Suivez-moi," Louis ordered abruptly. Without understanding what he meant, Mel cleared her throat and Charlie eventually looked up. He slung his new bag over his shoulder and began the ascent, the grin not once leaving his face.

Their room was enormous. A four-poster bed appeared both grand and extremely comfortable in equal measure. The ensuite was twice as big as the main bathroom in their house and came complete with what looked like a brand-new fitted shower unit in the corner. An old-fashioned roll-top iron bath completed the scene. The bedroom had a large window that provided plenty of light and overlooked the rear of the property. She strolled over for closer inspection.

The garden needed attention, even though a large patch of grass had been freshly mown. Beyond the lawn, the grounds eventually reached a row of newly planted trees, which she surmised must be the property's boundary. In the distance, she recognised the small wooden gate hanging off its hinges, the way they arrived, and the pathway beyond which led towards the much thicker covered woodland, the shadows quickly descending into total darkness.

After Louis left the room, Mel unpacked. Immediately, she heard the distinctive sound of Charlie outside on the landing. His constant chatter interspersed with the occasional word and deep French accent of Louis.

"Is this us, love?" he finally enquired, his voice slurred. Mel watched as he left his bag in the middle of the room before falling backwards onto the bed with an exaggerated 'ahh'. She made no effort to reply, and within seconds, he appeared to be drifting out of consciousness. Mel imagined grabbing one of the plump pillows and pushing it over his head until he stopped breathing altogether.

The knock on Ed's bedroom door woke him with a start. His initial observations had been correct, the four-poster bed was indeed extremely comfortable. He must have fallen asleep within minutes of laying down.

"Yes, who is it?" he enquired gingerly, slowly shifting his body to the edge of the bed.

"It's me. Mel." She spoke just above a whisper.

"Oh, hang on," he replied, wondering what on earth she could want.

Standing a little too quickly, he felt momentarily light-headed. Giving himself a moment, he straightened his T-shirt and pulled his jeans into some kind of semblance.

As soon as he opened the door, he noticed Mel had changed. She looked much fresher, and dare he think, even prettier? With a quick glance over her shoulder, she asked if she could come in.

"Yeah, sure," Ed replied, opening the door wide enough for her to pass. With a peer along both sides of the landing himself, he purposefully left the door slightly ajar and turned to face Mel.

She wore a pale yellow linen blouse and tight-fitting white jeans. Her hair was tied in a ponytail. He thought she looked younger than his first impression, and thankfully, much less solemn.

"Everything okay?" he asked, not really knowing what to say or whether to sit or stand. Mel suddenly looked as uncomfortable as he felt.

"Yes. Yes, I'm fine," she stumbled. "Charlie's asleep. Too much bubbly." She forced a smile.

"Yeah, I noticed him helping himself to a few."

Desperately trying to keep the conversation light-hearted, Ed rolled his eyes to imitate a drunk. Mel laughed unnaturally. After another moment's awkwardness, Mel spoke again.

"We're not getting on great. You know, me and Charlie." She pointed nervously to the wall to where Charlie slept in the adjacent room.

"Oh, okay." Ed walked over to the vast window and glanced outside. "Not really my business, Mel," he added. He wondered why on earth she was telling him so much after they only met hours earlier.

"Oh no. I didn't mean to make you feel uncomfortable. It's just that I thought it was pretty obvious and you may have noticed."

Is that what she's really come to tell me?

"As I say, it's none of my business."

But Mel hadn't finished. She wanted to offload on someone, and for some reason, she had chosen Ed.

"I think he's having an affair."

All Ed could do was watch as a wave of emotion washed over her. She looked close to tears. He stepped back across the room, but once they stood a foot apart, he didn't know what to do again. "What, back at home?" Kicking himself, he realised how stupid his question was before he'd finished asking. At least Mel had the decency to ignore his blushing.

"Yes. He's been coming home later and later. He says it's business, but he never used to come home so late."

"What does he do?"

Is that all you can think of?

"He runs a print firm. It's our small company, you know, we're both directors." Nodding his head, Ed thought it best if he remained silent. Mel looked at the wooden floor as she continued, now appearing unsure whether she should be there at all. "It's true. Business has been tough for a while. Everything seemed to dry up a few months ago. Our largest customers dropped us like a brick for no apparent reason. Sheesh, Charlie makes no secret of our struggles." She looked back at Ed. "He's always banging on about it on the phone or on social media. That's how Joyce must know. But for the past few months, he's been staying behind, trying to drum up new business." Mel air quoted 'staying behind.'

"Could he be?" Ed asked, noticing his heartbeat inadvertently going up a notch. They remained within touching distance, neither particularly interested in taking a step back. "You know, could he be trying to save the business?"

"Well, there's been no new orders, no new customers, despite him staying in hotels and using up even more of what little cash we have left. It's got to the stage where I have started job hunting. I haven't worked for years." As if reading his mind, Mel answered the obvious question. "I'm not really in a position to go out working. My mum is disabled, you see. I'm her carer. It's pretty much full-time. I've only come here because Joyce is giving us twenty grand. Mum has gone into a home, which is costing a small fortune, but we're still making a good sum of money out of this."

Charlie and Mel were obviously going through a difficult period, not just their marriage, but also financially. Ed spoke to reassure her.

"It's the same for me where money is concerned," he replied. "I guess Joyce really does know we're all struggling." Another awkward silence ensued. "Sorry to hear about your mum," he eventually added.

Mel reached out her arm and brushed her hand across his. It took him by surprise. "It's okay," she said. Instantaneously, she attempted to lift her voice and reverse the gloom, which had begun to suffocate the room. "Hell, you don't want to hear my problems." She smiled. "We've only just arrived. What must you think of me?"

Brushing the sides of his jeans with the palms of his hands, Ed grinned nervously. She was right. It was too soon for her to be sharing her secrets with anybody, let alone with him. "Hey, it's fine. Anytime."

Without warning, Mel took a step forward, and they embraced. Her arms reached around him and pulled him in tight. Feeling totally devoid of his own response, Ed clumsily reciprocated, his hands motionless but firmly in the middle of her back. It felt good, yet so wrong. Her husband was asleep in the very next room.

Finally, Mel's grip relaxed, and Ed took it as his cue to let go, too. She didn't leave his side, though, holding her stance just inches away. He became transfixed, unable to move, as if the hug had somehow tranquillised him.

Mel smiled before kissing him on the cheek. It was only brief, but Ed still sensed the full softness of her lips against his skin. "Thanks for listening, Ed."

As he struggled to think of a reply, a noise from outside on the landing made them both jump. Instinctively, they backed away from each other. Mel turned her head and noticed the door was slightly ajar. She mouthed to Ed, "fuck".

Putting his finger to his lips, he tiptoed over towards the opening. Inevitably, the door resisted with an annoying squeak; the hinges objecting to being moved so painfully slow. Following a quick glimpse at Mel – she had placed her finger between her teeth and was biting on it so hard Ed thought she might draw blood – he took a tentative step out onto the landing.

Looking right and left, he involuntarily let out a sigh of relief before hearing another sound. Quickly finding his bearings, he looked to his left as he heard a door bang shut along the landing, three rooms from his own.

Shit.

His mind raced. Tony's room.

With his thoughts recoiling, he flinched as Mel joined him, her bare arm resting against his as she too gripped the balustrade. With adrenaline already gushing, her presence sent another jolt of electricity surge through him.

"He was glaring at me earlier," she whispered. "I really don't like him, Ed."

Not only had Tony pissed off most of the group within hours of arriving, but now Mel appeared positively spooked by him.

Contemplating what to say or do next, they both jumped again as they heard the distinctive sound of another door. But this time, it came from directly behind them.

8

BARELY DARING TO BREATHE, Ed slowly turned. Mel followed his lead and steadily moved her head in unison. They gasped simultaneously as Charlie stood in his open doorway, dressed in only a pair of boxer shorts. He yawned, stretching his arms wide as if to exaggerate his tiredness. Quickly, Ed took a step away from Mel.

"Hey," Charlie said, his voice elongated and equally annoying as he feigned a second yawn. "What's with all the banging out here?"

Mel couldn't help but stifle a laugh, and Ed instantly felt himself redden. Her giggle perked Charlie's awareness, apparently noticing his wife for the first time.

"What are you doing here?" he belatedly asked. Glancing over his shoulder into his room, he looked sceptically at his wife, before finally focussing his attention on Ed. Fortunately, Mel thought on her feet.

"Look at the state of you," she said, hurrying to her husband's side. She placed her hand on his shoulder and spun him around. "Get back in there, will you? I'm sure nobody wants to see you in your underwear."

She gave Ed an awkward smile before closing the bedroom door while leading her husband inside.

As Ed turned, he flinched as he noticed Hazel on the landing too. She stood on the far side of the central staircase, again outside her own room. Offering him the briefest of smiles, she turned and stepped back inside.

Fucking hell, Ed thought. *Tony, Charlie and now Hazel. Did* everybody *see Mel leave my room?*

The door banging loudly had awoken Hazel from her afternoon siesta. She wasn't the best of sleepers and the slightest noise often stirred her. Ironically, given her job, hotels were the worst, and she cursed herself for not packing earplugs.

Still wearing the same polo-neck sweater and jeans, Hazel reluctantly swung herself off the bed and made her way to the bedroom door. Looking over the banister, she tried to establish where the noise had originated from, but she soon became bored and turned to step back into her room. But then she caught sight of Charlie, in his underwear, no less, until his bloody wife escorted him through their open door before she could get a proper look. But that wasn't all. Ed was standing on the landing too, intently watching the married couple before Mel offered him a brief glance and a smile. He spotted Hazel, looked incredibly sheepish, before disappearing inside his own room and closing the door with a loud click.

Hazel looked from Ed's door to Mel's door. *Hmm*, she thought, allowing herself the slightest of smirks.

. . .

"Aha. Oliver Ramsey. Late as per usual," quipped Joyce, seated at the head of the table. Everybody laughed, whilst Ollie took the only remaining seat next to Mel.

"Hold your glass up for me, Ollie."

Prior to even sitting down, Hazel stood opposite, holding a carafe of red wine aloft before him. The thought of drowning himself in alcohol suddenly felt very appealing, but Ollie refused the offer.

"No thank you," he said, whilst awkwardly scraping his seat forward an inch or two, then back again before pulling it all the way under the table. He knew he was being stared at, but it was one of his traits he couldn't help. "I don't drink. Never have touched the stuff."

Ollie swore he heard somebody laugh – more of a brief 'Ha!' underneath their breath – but by the time he looked up, he couldn't decipher who it emanated from. It made him feel extremely uncomfortable, and Ollie was normally the kind of guy who wasn't easily phased.

Does somebody know what happened?

Nodding a brief 'hello' to Joyce, he noticed Hazel still gazing at him. Was it her who laughed? She looked from Ollie to Joyce and back again. Quickly, he attempted to shift the focus.

"So, Hazel," he said, helping himself to a glass of cold water instead. He tapped the side of the glass three times with his forefinger before taking a drink. Hazel watched him, mesmerised. "What have you been up to since Ridgeview?"

The indistinct murmur of chat between one or two of the others abated, and all eyes fell on the wild-haired lady who sat opposite Ollie. Anybody normal may have felt a twinge of guilt for making her the centre of attention, but not Ollie. Sensitivity was never at the forefront of his mind and sometimes he needed to shift the scrutiny away from himself.

Just as at the airport, Hazel had made an effort with her attire. She wore a stylish cream blouse and a dark blue bandana, holding the mass of hair from her face. The blusher on her cheeks hid the freckles underneath, giving the appearance she'd been out in the sun. Although not quintessentially attractive, Hazel oozed class, which Ollie imagined would draw attention wherever she went. Her outfits looked expensive, chic, and sophisticated. Ollie considered that even if she dressed drably, her amazing hair would still turn the eye of any passing daydreamer. She was a far cry from his ex-wife.

"Well, I stayed local," she replied confidently. "Still am actually."

"You stayed in Lincolnshire? Wow, you must be mad!"

Ollie had a habit of speaking his mind, but his chirpiness often put people at ease. He liked to make others laugh, and it pleased him to see smiling faces around the table. Until then, everyone appeared nervous, as if they were all treading on eggshells.

"Hey, it's not so bad, Ollie," Hazel jested in response. "Anyway, I left school after sixth form, and went onto Liverpool Uni. That's where I studied business——"

Ollie faked a yawn, again making everybody laugh. Everybody that was but Joyce. But Hazel didn't appear to notice, to begin with at least, and continued chatting with Ollie, enjoying their little bit of banter.

"You may mock Ollie, but after getting my boring degree," she said, air-quoting, "I went to work for a travel company in Peterborough. I'm still there now, as it happens."

"What do you do, Hazel?" Mel asked, also appreciating the lifting of tension in the room. One or two people glanced at her before turning their attention back to Hazel. Ollie thought it was like some kind of nervous trait, an exaggerated peek from one person to the next. Even though they were slowly getting to know one another, it felt stifled and unnatural.

"I visit holiday destinations. You know, inspect hotels, self-catering properties. See if they come up to scratch for our company. I get to travel, so it's okay."

"Okay? That sounds amazing." Charlie joined in, placing his now empty wine glass on the table.

"Well, it pays the bills."

"Come, now." Everybody turned to Joyce. Unlike the others engaged in the conversation, she showed no emotion. "You're being modest, Hazel. You're quite the high flyer, and I don't just mean using aircraft."

Just as when Joyce gave her inauguration speech, the laughter felt feigned. Ollie noticed the way Hazel looked at Joyce, a definite degree of hostility attached.

"I've done okay for myself. If that's what you mean?" Hazel was resolute in her reply and Ollie already realised she didn't suffer fools.

"Hmm, okay. If you say so," replied Joyce.

Before Hazel could respond for a second time, Joyce quickly changed the subject. Her apparent melancholy mood shifted like the click of a light switch.

"Who's hungry then?" she asked, before calling out to Adrienne, instructing her that they were ready to eat.

Ollie couldn't help but scan Hazel's face. She gave the impression of being both confused and embarrassed by Joyce's comments. But then it appeared to turn to anger. Her hand gripped the wine glass until the whites of her knuckles protruded, so much so, he thought it might shatter underneath. Within hours of arriving, he knew Hazel didn't like their host. He remembered the minibus journey, when Joyce turned and told the group the name of the town they would be staying near. Hadn't Hazel allowed a "pfft" sound to escape her mouth then? *Great,* he thought. *How the hell are we going to get through four weeks of this?*

Tony watched and listened as the pathetic charade unfolded before him. Everybody striving to coexist, the false laughs, the nervous interactions. He didn't know whether to laugh or cry.

He glanced towards Ed and Mel and noticed their eyes occasionally flick to one another. But instead of feeling content that he knew of their little secret, he found himself incredibly jealous. Tony didn't like people, but he despised Ed Lawson the most; well, not quite the most, but *he* wasn't there. And now the prettiest girl had been to Ed's room, on the very first day, no less. Should he tell Charlie? That would certainly stir things up. However, Tony had been warned not to ruffle any feathers. "Keep your head down and do as you're told," were his strict instructions. But Tony was already bored, and Tony had been bored before.

And look at him, he thought, watching Ollie. *What's wrong with him, tapping his glass three times, dragging his chair forwards, backwards, forwards? Has he got that thing? What do they call it? OCD? Fucking mental, more like.*

Standing abruptly, everyone turned to face him. He could stand their company no longer and needed to stop himself from saying something he shouldn't. That could wait for another day, but for now, he had to make himself scarce.

"I'm not hungry," he declared, to everybody's obvious astonishment. "I'm going to my room."

9

_____

BREAKFASTS WERE CONSIDERABLY MORE informal than evening meals. The group would gather at eight o'clock each morning before helping themselves to croissants, pain au chocolat or other pastries, as well as the strongest coffee some of the party had ever drunk. The idea was for the guests to mingle and chat amongst themselves; much more relaxed than the two suffocating dinners had been to date.

On Monday morning – the first 'working' day and two days after arriving on the island – Tony emerged, and Joyce noticed how the room suddenly dropped silent. Not a single person had mentioned or seen him after he left dinner on the first evening, and Joyce was already cognisant of the fact that her ex-husband was not popular. _Good_, she thought. _They already appreciate what a conniving little shit he is._ She wanted to tell them more, but that wasn't part of the deal. Joyce was the host, and her remit was just that.

With all eyes set upon him, Tony picked up on the vibe, and after grabbing himself a coffee, he skulked away to sit alone. Joyce observed Charlie nudging Ollie, who in turn stared at Tony.

Finally, Joyce spoke, realising she was compelled to give everybody something positive to focus upon. "Morning, all." Her bright tone surprised herself given her own solemn mood. She needed to keep herself upbeat and caught Ed watching her with sudden interest. A chorus of muted 'mornings' echoed in return. "Okay, let the work commence." Everybody gathered and listened intently as she listed some of the jobs to complete during the stay.

First, everybody would paint their own bedrooms, with the remainder of the rooms to be delegated amongst the group. There were pictures to be mounted, shelves to be erected, wallpaper stripped, floorboards sanded, light fittings fitted, as well as a 'general spring clean' of every nook and cranny the grand old house offered. The heavy-duty DIY jobs would be given to Tony and Louis, whilst the more menial tasks would be split evenly.

"And, to keep you all on your toes, the garden will need to be completely overhauled too," Joyce finished, with a smile etched across her face. "Once a teacher, always a teacher." At least that made everyone laugh.

After eating, she instructed the group to gather in the barn, which was located roughly halfway along the large back garden. "Towards the footpath where you arrived on foot," Joyce added. They all traipsed after her, like lost sheep on the moors.

Once inside, Louis waited impatiently for everybody to be quiet. There were all sorts of materials stored away in the outhouse; a ride-on mower, hedge cutters, saws, an array of gardening tools, paint, brushes; everything neatly kept along two adjacent walls. She caught Charlie looking at some petrol canisters near the mower.

Louis handed everybody a tin of paint, as well as a

roller and a brush. They were all individually labelled. Finally, Joyce gave each of the party their own set of dungarees; the 'work clothes' for the duration. Ollie suggested they all looked like prisoners equipped for boot camp. Joyce couldn't help but notice even Tony allowed himself a slight smirk at that comment.

At eleven o'clock, a bell rang from downstairs. Voices and footsteps followed, so Tony stepped out onto the landing to see what the commotion was about. Leaning over the banister, he spotted Adrienne in the lobby, holding a brass bell. He considered it far too heavy for her. She rang it again; the sound reverberating around the foyer.

"Yes, what is it?" Ollie shouted from Tony's right.

"Drinks," Adrienne announced before disappearing into the dining room.

Tony watched as Ollie perched himself over the banister. He was still holding his paintbrush, dripping tiny splashes onto the wooden floor beneath him.

"Oi, you idiot," Tony called to him. Ollie peered over his shoulder, and Tony nodded to the ground.

"Alright," Ollie replied, following Tony's eyeline whilst still dribbling paint. "Can't you be any more civil?" Ollie scampered into his room, one hand placed underneath his dripping brush, although his focus remained on Tony. "Prick," he said as he disappeared from view. Tony smiled to himself.

"I'd hate to think what a mess he's making in there if that's what he's doing out here."

Tony hadn't noticed Mel further along the landing. He knew she was trying to be friendly.

"Yeah," he replied. "Still, I'm sure he's only doing his

best." Mel's smile appeared more genuine. She'd misread him, though. "Useless twat that he is."

The heat became more and more relentless as the day progressed, and at around three o'clock, the bell rang again. This time, Joyce stood halfway up the staircase, waiting patiently for everybody to appear above. Her bright T-shirt and knee-length khaki shorts presented a more relaxed facade, a far cry from the drab clothes she'd worn to date. Mel noticed numerous liver spots dotted along her bare arms and legs. In places, they threatened to amalgamate and form giant patches.

"Well done, all!" Joyce exclaimed enthusiastically. "You're free to finish for the day now." A general murmur of acceptance circulated amongst the group. "Not only is it too hot," she continued, "but it will allow the paint time to dry sufficiently so you can sleep in your own rooms tonight. I expect another coat tomorrow should be enough. So, if we get an early start, your first task will be complete. And to think, you've only just begun and one job is out of the way. If only you had all been so efficient with your homework."

Joyce's constant referrals and comparisons to school appeared to put everybody at ease, on the exterior at least. Mel watched the others as they returned to their rooms to clean up and as the landing cleared, as earlier, Tony remained on the far side. She recalled his tirade towards Ollie that morning.

He stood perfectly still, ogling her again. Again, Mel felt vulnerable as his eyes drifted up and down her body and he eventually licked his top lip. Quickly, she turned and disappeared into her own room, searching for her husband.

. . .

After opening his window to allow some fresh air to circulate, Ed cleaned his brush and roller and, as promised, he was free to do as he pleased until dinner. Promptly showering, he thought it would be the ideal opportunity to stroll around the island. Not only did he crave his own company, but he also wanted to spend time in his new surroundings.

With the foyer deserted, Ed hastened his step to reach the large double doors.

"Hey!" *Shit.* "Going anywhere nice?"

Spinning, he spotted Hazel leaning over the banister. She had changed too and wore a smart T-shirt and dark blue shorts, her hair held from her face with a brightly coloured band.

With an inward sigh, Ed suggested Hazel join him, which she did without hesitation. The cynic inside him suspected she'd been waiting in the wings all along.

After walking to the end of the rear garden, they found themselves at the edge of the dark tree line and footpath they had climbed on the day they arrived. Lifting the broken wooden gate, Ed accompanied Hazel into the welcoming shadows. They followed the trail for a few minutes before the expanse of the bay opened up before them. They went a different way, the narrow pathway dividing at various points. Once out of the dense trees, it was a beautiful spot; secluded and tranquil. An even better-trodden footpath ran both ways down towards the shoreline, and they turned left. With the path only wide enough for one, Ed led the way and Hazel dropped in behind. Soon, he became lost in his thoughts, watching the small fishing boats bobbing on the water in the distance.

"She's very pretty, isn't she?"

The sound of Hazel's voice made Ed jump. He'd momentarily forgotten she was there.

"What? Sorry?" he replied, acutely aware of whom she was referring to.

"Mel Green. She always was quite the looker. I remember her after she left school."

"Yes, I guess so."

Hearing Hazel chuckle to herself, he hoped she'd finished probing. No such luck.

"Do you think Charlie's having an affair, Ed?" Hazel asked nonchalantly, as if asking about the weather or his favourite colour.

Not wanting to engage her in conversation, Ed continued to pace ahead, whilst doing his utmost to sound uninterested. "I've really no idea. I've only just met him. Only just met the pair of them." Ed realised that Hazel must have spotted Mel leaving his room. Her next comment confirmed his suspicions.

"Mind, when I saw him in his boxers shorts, I thought I wouldn't object to a bit of that myself." She tapped Ed on the shoulder, catching him off-guard once more. "We could be swingers," she added with a giggle. But Ed didn't want to discuss it and he increased his pace to put distance between them.

"How's work, Hazel?" he asked as he realised she'd matched his stride. "Was Joyce trying to wind you up on the first night?"

After a few second's silence, Ed turned around, still smiling at his question. But Hazel had stopped, now several paces behind. "Hazel? You okay?"

"Erm, yes. I'm fine."

Allowing her to catch up, he knew he'd hit a nerve.

Her normal rosy complexion had faded. "You sure? You look like you've seen a ghost."

"No, it's okay. I'm fine." She attempted a smile.

"Sorry. Ignore—"

"No, no," she interrupted. "It's okay. You're fine to ask."

Deciding to give the impression he was giving her some privacy, Ed walked ahead again, but silently hoped she would say more.

"The thing is, work isn't fine." Hazel continued, whilst Ed hid the knowing smile on his face. "I didn't quite understand what Joyce was alluding to, but it became obvious she knows something." She tapped Ed on the shoulder for a second time. He stopped and faced her. Initially, he'd wanted a while alone, but he found himself intrigued by Hazel's disclosure. "The thing is, I haven't had any proper work for some time. About six months ago, it all kind of dried up. Completely out of the blue."

"Hey, I'm sorry," Ed replied. "Me and my mouth—"

"No. It's not your fault. It was bound to come out, eventually. I'm just surprised that Joyce appeared to know. I can't think how."

"Social media," Ed tried to help with her confused expression. "Didn't she say she follows us on there?"

Hazel blushed at her own stupidity. "Of course! Shit, she really does know."

As they began walking again, Hazel told Ed about her job and how the assignments suddenly stopped. Apparently, she openly shared it online, and Ed recalled the similar story Mel had told him.

'It's true. Business has been tough for a while now. Sheesh, Charlie makes no secret of that. Always banging on about it on the phone or on social media…'.

Hazel went off at a tangent and into too much detail

of how high her mortgage payments were and how she was considering putting her house on the market if the offer in France hadn't materialised out of the blue. "The timing couldn't have been better," she concluded. "Even if it doesn't feel quite right."

10

As she heard the distinctive sound of the broken gate
squeak shut, Mel looked up and felt a strange pang of
jealousy. She watched intently as Ed and Hazel walked
along the garden path from the woods. But she kicked
herself for being so stupid. They had only just met, and
she was there with her husband, however poorly they
were getting on. But Mel found Ed attractive, albeit in a
non-conventional way compared to Charlie, and wished
she had been on a walk with him, and not that surly bitch
with the crazy hair.

She studied Ed through her sunglasses. Standing
around six feet tall, an inch or two smaller than Charlie,
his dark brown hair was cut short, although in no particular style. Complete with a side parting and cropped a
little shorter at the edges, it was nothing compared to her
husband's long, wavy, highlighted hair, shaved close at the
back and sides. Charlie was clinging to his youth, and
he'd never changed his appearance in all those years. But
Ed Lawson was different. Perhaps that was the attraction.
She recalled him being skinny at school and coming

across as relatively unkempt; dirty knees from playing football on the field, and memories of his school jumper forever tied around his waist. However, his freshly ironed T-shirt and dark blue shorts showed him in a different light, laughing and joking with Hazel as he strolled towards the house. Mel noticed his blue eyes at the airport and how he'd filled out during the past decade, broad shoulders and muscly arms. It's why she'd called him 'quite the dashing author', but that was mostly an attempt to piss her husband off. However, there was genuine intent in her observations, and as she watched him with that Hazel woman, it made Mel feel quite nauseous. *Why didn't he invite me for a walk?*

To make a point, she stood abruptly, dropped her magazine onto the sun lounger, and strode purposefully to the far side of the property.

Charlie helped himself to a glass of red as Adrienne carried a tray of drinks around. Because it was such a lovely evening, Joyce suggested pre-dinner aperitifs would be taken outside. Charlie needed alcohol and was still fuming after Mel told him of Tony ogling her earlier. *Licking his lips at my wife? Fucking creep.*

"Careful how much you drink tonight," Mel said under her breath, nodding her appreciation towards Adrienne whilst taking a smaller glass for herself. "We don't want you saying anything untoward, do we?"

Although Charlie looked at his wife as if she was suggesting he might commit a murder, deep down, he knew she was right. He could say things he later regretted. Several glasses of the delicious vino may just tip him over the edge. But Charlie Green had other matters on his mind, as well as bloody Tony.

To begin with, he would love to learn how acquainted Joyce Young was with their business and the financial trouble they were in. His suspicions were intensified ever since that opening speech on the mini-stage underneath the large paned window.

'And I happen to know that ten thousand pounds is a lot of money. An amount that many people would find difficult to refuse…'.

Charlie realised he said too much, especially on social media and more so after a few drinks. He once pleaded for business online after a skinful of whisky, something Mel instructed him to delete the next morning. "How will that appear to prospective clients?" she scorned. "You look bloody desperate."

He looked around the group and wondered if his wife's intuition had been correct all along. However, he also knew she was so damn apprehensive, and although he hadn't admitted to it, he realised they were both extremely relieved that the *boy* wasn't there. Further still, nobody had mentioned his name.

So, Charlie, it can't be about him.

He emptied his glass and summoned Adrienne over for a refill. As he sipped, desperate not to drink too quickly, Tony arrived, so Charlie soon drained that one too. He noticed Adrienne stare at him, open-eyed, as he helped himself to yet another.

Tony hated dinner time more than any other. Breakfast he could cope with. He could always keep his distance outside on the terrace. Work on the first day had been fine, too. He spent it alone in his room painting and he knew he would mostly be grafting by himself going forward as he was the only do-it-yourself expert there.

But at dinner time there was no escape. Polite conversation had never been Tony's strong point, but this was taking things to an entirely new level. His ex-wife giving out orders, the gullible invitees hanging on her every word and all eyes seemingly focusing on him when all he wanted to do was disappear to his room with a tray of food.

Helping himself to a glass of red — he only ever sipped it as he didn't even like it — he once again stood on the periphery. He noticed Charlie watching him as he drank his wine far too quickly.

Ed thought it a good idea to have aperitifs outside. It suited him to be outdoors anyway, as he always felt stifled and claustrophobic when forced inside with people he didn't particularly want to be with. It was why he was so shy at school in the classroom, yet out on the fields, he became a totally different person. He knew that was why he got into so much trouble. Messing around was the only thing he could do, conversely attempting to shift the attention from himself onto his latest victim. A teacher once told his mum at parents' evening that he thought Ed did it to make himself more popular. The class clown. Everybody loves someone who can make you laugh.

He thanked Adrienne for the wine and stepped out onto the lawn to escape the shade of the canopy which covered half the terrace. The sun felt warm on the back of his neck and he regretted not bringing his sunglasses from his room.

Studying the others, he noticed Mel take a glass from Charlie and place it on a table. Was he drinking too fast again? Tony stood at the rear, fully in the shade, his back pressed up against the wall. He sipped at his wine and looked as though he wasn't enjoying the situation at all. Ollie was full of his usual chatter, Hazel his latest victim. At one point, she glanced over his shoulder and mouthed something to Ed before smiling. Perhaps a plea to rescue her. Ed considered Ollie *too* hyper, either trying too hard or unable to control himself, maybe a bit of both. He wanted to speak to him, get him to talk about his own plight and why he'd been summoned to the château, even though he already knew the answer.

"Okay, everybody," Joyce announced from inside the gigantic doors. "Adrienne will serve dinner in ten minutes. If you could all make your way through to the dining room, you will find a little surprise on the table."

A murmur of excitement pursued, and they filed through. Joyce remained in the doorway and Ed realised she was waiting for him.

"I hope you don't mind, Edward, but I thought your fellow guests should become acquainted with your work."

"What? What do you mean?" he asked, confused. But Joyce just smiled, took a step back, allowing Ed to pass before following him to join the others.

As he stepped into the dining room, everybody was standing at their seating place, and each one of them held a brand-new book. Ed wanted to run. What kind of *game* was this? He glared at Joyce.

"It's Edward's debut novel," she announced, ignoring him. "The one which set him on the road to become a full-time author."

Joyce was in full flow, although nobody appeared particularly pleased that the *surprise* was a book. Ollie looked as though he didn't know which way up to hold it, and Tony had already discarded his copy.

"Where did you get them?" Ed asked, frozen to the spot, his hands gripping the back of his chair.

"I ordered them before we left and brought six copies over with me."

Ed continued to stare at her. *Why is she doing this?* "But why? Nobody wants to read it."

"Ah, come, Edward. Don't be modest." Joyce stepped over to her own seat at the head of the table before gesturing with her arms for everybody to sit. As always, the guests did as they were told and, much to Ed's annoyance, she now had their full attention. "There are two reasons I've given you all a copy." Ed felt himself swallow hard. "First, I believe your fellow companions will find the subject quite entertaining…"

She allowed her words to hang. *Shit*, Ed thought, *does she know who it's about?*

"… and second," she smiled broadly at him, "I expect you'll be pleased with the commission."

11

THE PIERCING SCREAM woke Charlie from his deep slumber. He'd drank too much again and his head throbbed the moment he opened his eyes. *Am I dreaming?* A subsequent shriek and running footsteps somewhere in the distance informed him otherwise. Disorientated, he rolled onto his back and pulled the duvet tight to his chin.

Mel turned over and clung onto him underneath the cover. "What the fuck was that?"

Before Charlie could reply, he heard further footfall. This time, directly outside their room. Were they on the landing or on the staircase? It was difficult to tell. His heart thumped rapidly as Mel grabbed him tighter still. He wanted to tell her to get the fuck off, but even Charlie felt some compassion, as he was just as scared as her. *That scream.*

More footsteps, doors banging and finally voices. Straining his ears, he tried to decipher who it could be. His hideous hangover wasn't helping, and he found it difficult to differentiate between reality and the hammering inside his skull.

"It came from her room, I'm sure. Hazel's room."

That's Ollie's voice. Thank fuck. Charlie allowed himself to breathe.

"You should go," Mel spoke again, sounding slightly more relaxed, too. Her palms gently pushed his arm rather than clinging on for dear life.

"You're the female," Charlie replied. "You heard Ollie. It came from Hazel's room. I can't go barging in there." Even in the dark, he could just imagine the look on his wife's face. Her silence and lack of movement confirmed his suspicions.

Tentatively, he climbed out of bed before putting on last night's shirt and shorts over his boxers. Hearing Mel clambering around on her side of the bed too, Charlie felt a little confidence build inside, and as he guardedly opened the door, the familiar sights and sounds of his fellow guests allowed the fear to wane further.

Ollie was talking to Ed while Joyce climbed the staircase. Adrienne and Louis followed close behind, talking in French. Unsure why it was the first thing he thought of, but Charlie couldn't understand why Louis would follow Adrienne up the stairs. His bedroom was the next one along from Hazel.

As Charlie stood reluctantly in their open doorway, Mel nudged him to one side. She noticed his initial alarm had diminished, replaced with a smile as he took in the circus-like performance before them. People running, chatting, pointing. She might tell them all later what a nervous wreck he was when they first heard the scream. Not that she could talk.

Joyce came to a halt as she reached the top of the stairs. Mel waited a few seconds for her to take charge of the situation, or at least summon Louis forward to investigate where the yell had originated from. But she stood still, as if unable to find the words or actions on what to do next.

Perhaps Charlie was right. It should be a woman who checked on Hazel, and with Joyce not moving and Adrienne tucked in behind her like a frightened mouse, Mel took an exaggerated gulp before looking up towards Hazel's door. She noticed Ed standing outside his own room alongside Ollie, his hand firmly gripping the door handle, and she offered him a tentative smile.

"What's going on?" she asked him.

To Mel's annoyance, Ollie replied on Ed's behalf.

"Didn't you hear it? The scream? And look, Hazel's door is open."

After a further glance to Ed, Mel saw that sure enough, Hazel's door was slightly ajar. A glimmer of moonlight escaped through the tiny crack. Mel looked back to Ed, surprised at his silence and reluctance to let go of his door.

"Let me pass," Joyce unexpectedly intervened, barging her way through. Her sudden aggressive nature made everyone stand on guard. All but one person, that was.

"And who put you in charge?"

Tony was outside his room, wearing a dressing gown, crudely tied with a dishevelled belt. His hair stood on end. He carried the appearance fitting of his demeanour; scruffy, miserable, downright horrible.

"Oh, look. It speaks." The animosity between Tony and Joyce was tangible. Tony wasn't finished.

"Always sticking your nose in where it isn't wanted. Always the one who has to be in charge. Perhaps these people should know the *real* reason you had to leave that school."

The tension was crackling, and Mel glanced towards Ed again. Why did she continually look to him for comfort or reassurance? Her husband stood only two steps away. Ed still averted her gaze.

"Just go back to bed, Tony," Joyce replied. Her tone had changed, though, her authority questioned by her ex-husband again. "You know why you're here, and you know not to mess up."

Everybody's eyes darted from one to the other. Nobody dared speak or even move. It felt like an adult version of musical statues, yet there was no music, no laughter, no fun. To Mel's side, Charlie summoned the courage she had rarely witnessed before.

"Why can't you just piss off, Tony?"

Tony's eyes left Joyce's and instead glared directly into Charlie's. Mel felt her husband flinch and involuntarily take a step backwards.

"Yes," another voice said. "Just fuck off, Tony. Everybody hates you."

Mel couldn't believe what was happening. Ollie stood firm; his tiny chest puffed out. She took it in turns to study the group and each one of them appeared to hold the same contempt towards Tony. A built-in disgust for the man none of them could stand being in the company of any longer.

"Hadn't we better check on Hazel?" Mel asked, breaking the silence and recalling the reason they had gathered on the landing in the middle of the night.

Joyce stopped glaring at her ex-husband and instead looked at Mel. "Yes, Mel, yes. Stand back. I'll go."

Mel stepped aside as Joyce moved purposefully forward, her eyes now set back to Tony. If looks could indeed kill, then surely he would have been struck down dead there and then. Despite holding her glare for a moment or two, he backed off into his room. The slam of his door was the last time Mel would see him.

Feeling a mixture of relief and annoyance, Charlie followed Mel to their room. He paused as everybody shuffled along the landing whilst Adrienne quietly descended the stairs. Before he shut their door, curiosity made him peek out one last time. He noticed Ollie and Ed were still chatting over to his right, their eyes fixed on Tony's closed bedroom door.

He's pushed it too far this time, he thought.

The following morning, all attention fell on Hazel as she joined the others for breakfast. She was ashen-faced and Ollie thought she looked as though she'd had about as much sleep as him.

Everybody offered her a smile, a recognition, but nobody dared to speak. She poured herself a coffee, omitting the generous amount of milk she normally added.

Finally Ollie broke the silence, but didn't have the nerve, or the words, to say anything to Hazel. He had been talking to Charlie before she arrived, and they resumed their stifled conversation. It acted as some kind of trigger and Mel spoke with Joyce again, albeit strained and typical boring British chit-chat about the weather.

"Is Tony not joining you today?" Adrienne directed her question at Joyce, although everybody stopped talking at the very mention of his name. With everyone waiting for her response, Joyce cleared her throat, surprised at the amount of loose phlegm, and she immediately wished she had a strong cup of coffee to hand.

"I think Tony has decided to leave us," she announced in a somewhat faltering voice. She cleared her throat for a second time. "He came to see me after our altercation last night, once I'd seen to Hazel, of course." Everybody glanced at Hazel before refocusing their attention on Joyce. She realised Hazel's scream had already lost significance with the group. "He said he wasn't happy. I've just checked his room and most of his clothes are gone. His holdall too. I am surprised he didn't wait until morning, though."

Joyce noticed one or two shuffle on their feet, not dissimilar to the day they arrived.

"What else did he say?" Mel asked, shifting in her seat, her eyes darting around the room.

"Not much," Joyce replied, some confidence finally returning. "I did warn him he wouldn't be getting a single penny of his entitlement if he left, though."

Joyce gained further strength when the group fell silent. She still held the ace card. *It's the only reason they're here.*

"Why would he go?" Charlie spoke next. Joyce had been expecting a barrage of questions.

"He told me he wasn't enjoying it and felt he wasn't fitting in." Joyce paused for effect. "Well, he's not wrong, is he?"

Joyce studied their faces individually. She was looking to see if anybody didn't appear shocked by the news. She'd laid awake after seeing to Hazel, and in the still of the night — she checked her watch at two-thirty-five — she thought she heard footsteps on the landing above the main reception room. It sounded like mice in an attic, scurrying around searching for scraps of food.

"But where would he go?" Ollie asked. Joyce was surprised it took Ollie to ask the obvious question. It immediately introduced a murmur amongst the group and a solidarity nod of heads broke out.

"That I don't know, Oliver. But I do know there used to be the odd boat moored up around the island. I haven't seen one myself, but perhaps Tony found one and rowed himself back to shore."

"Has he taken the one from the boathouse?" Mel asked next, her face still ashen.

"No, my dear. Louis has already checked."

"Well, I haven't seen any," Mel replied, sounding even more exasperated.

"There are one or two." Joyce was pleased to hear a calming voice amongst them. She followed the others as they turned to Ed. "We saw a couple on our walk, didn't we, Hazel?"

Hazel nodded, noncommittal, but at least it ensured Mel calmed down a little.

A few moment's silence ensued as everybody scrutinised the news.

"Still," Hazel spoke for the first time that morning. Joyce had completely forgotten about her nightmare. "It's a surprise he would give up on that amount of money."

"You tell me why he has," Joyce retorted in her usual derisory manner towards Hazel. She realised she was making her feelings too obvious. *I don't really like any of them*, she thought. *Why am I picking on her so much?* "But he did tell me none of you made him particularly welcome." Joyce struggled to contain her smile. She'd hit a nerve as she watched every one of them squirm.

"Well, he is a bit of a twat," Ollie finally responded,

breaking the silence in his chipper cockney tone. Joyce noticed Hazel nudge him whilst everybody else attempted to stifle a laugh.

"Perhaps you are correct, Oliver, although I do find your language rather brash." She raised her voice once more and sounded the most upbeat to date. "Now, you are all free to take the day off."

Adrienne waited and watched before putting down the food tray and leaving. Hazel wondered what she made of it all. An eccentric ex-teacher inviting a strange set of English folk to an island in France. And now, after only a few days, one had upped and gone because 'he doesn't get on with the others'.

Hazel stood to one side, nursing her second caffeine hit of the morning. She watched as Ed poured one of his own before stepping towards the garden. He hesitated when Hazel took a small step forward, making it obvious she had something to say.

"I need to speak to you," she whispered in his ear. "In private."

Without giving him an opportunity to reply, Hazel wandered off, carrying her coffee inside and into the coolness of the foyer.

12

IT PLEASED Charlie when Joyce gave everyone the day off. The news of Tony leaving had taken them by surprise, even though Joyce was correct in her assumption that everybody was secretly happy. She said she would meet with Louis to reschedule the remaining tasks she had put to one side for Tony to complete, but Charlie didn't believe her. Joyce wanted time to herself just as much as everybody else. A day away from more inevitable questions and prying eyes.

He guessed everyone would ask themselves the same question; why would Tony give up when he only needed to keep his head down for a few weeks and take the ridiculous amount of money on offer? The work was lightweight, and they all enjoyed plenty of spare time to themselves. *No more than a working holiday*, Charlie thought, *so why leave?* But Joyce was right. Nobody liked Tony, and nobody made him feel welcome. He hadn't helped himself, but surely he could stomach being an outsider for a while longer?

. . .

After breakfast, once Joyce excused the group for the day, Ed returned to his room. All he wanted was to be alone. He still hadn't forgotten Joyce handing out copies of his book. Why would she do such a thing?

Trying to dispel any ulterior motive, Ed lay on his bed and thought of Tony leaving. He was pleased he had gone. He knew everybody was. Apart from the obvious questions regarding money, nobody had baulked at the idea he was no longer with them. But now Hazel wished to see him *in private*. What the hell could *she* want?

Ed wanted to avoid being the unelected confidant of the group, caught in the middle of everything. First, Mel disclosed her and Charlie's business and marriage woes, before Hazel conveniently asked if she could walk with him and divulged her job was also in trouble.

Even so, the book occupied his thoughts.

"I believe your fellow guests will find the subject matter quite entertaining…".

Why make a thing of that? And why would they find the subject entertaining? There was nothing there for any of his fellow guests to get excited about, only if someone pointed it out. Ed was fuming with Joyce, and he would have to confront her about it. Yet more shit thrown in his direction and from the one person he thought he could trust.

However, Ed was confident Joyce wouldn't say anything. It wasn't in her interests to do so. Besides, Ollie would never read it and he knew his and Tony's paths wouldn't cross again. That left Charlie, Mel and Hazel. Even if Hazel did read it, she left school two years before Ed and they had never met before the impromptu meeting outside the airport. Surely she wouldn't understand who it was about? However, Mel and Charlie remained.

A light tapping on his door made Ed spring to his feet. His heart thumped, and he instantly felt his palms become sticky as he wiped them down the front of his shorts. Once he opened the door, both he and Hazel looked both ways before she slipped into his room.

"What the fuck is wrong, Hazel?"

Although he hadn't intended his words to escape so forcefully, Ed needed to show some kind of authority. He didn't want Hazel walking all over him, a trait he'd always allowed in his life. His mum continually told him people would take advantage if he never grew a backbone. Ed missed his mum so much. If only she could help him now. Would she have advised him not to go?

"It's about last night." Hazel appeared unperturbed by his welcome. "Something isn't right about us being here."

She sat uninvited on the edge of his bed, and although it pissed Ed off she was making herself at home, he followed her lead and grabbed the only chair in the room. Spinning it around to face her, he sat down, suddenly feeling extremely uncomfortable. He hunched himself forward before shuffling his backside into the shallow recess.

"There was a boy at Ridgeview," Hazel continued, ignoring his awkwardness. Ed noticed bags underneath her eyes. "A boy around your age, I guess."

"There were several, Hazel," Ed replied sarcastically. "What's your point?" He glanced to his right and out of the window. It was another fine day, and he suddenly wished he was outdoors, alone. Again, Hazel disregarded his ambivalence. She had gone to his room with a purpose and would finish what she had to say.

"A couple of years after he left school, he wrote to me, asking for a job. I didn't know who he was or where he got my details from, but I do remember his CV having Ridgeview Grammar on it." Ed belatedly looked back at Hazel. "It's what brought it to my attention. He even mentioned going to the same school as me in his covering letters. At first, I ignored them, but more letters arrived, week after week. He pleaded with me to give him a chance, said he'd do anything and he was mad keen on travelling. Although I found it quite creepy, not to mention invasive, I also admired his tenacity. So, a few months later, when the company needed new staff, I asked my boss to interview him."

Ed rubbed his hands up and down his shorts.

"When he got the job, my supervisor asked me to show him the ropes. She introduced me on the day he started, but I didn't recognise him. However, he was a few years younger. As I say, around your age."

Stop fucking saying that.

Even though Ed didn't particularly want to listen, she was drawing him in. Hazel had a way with words, dwelling on the parts which made the hair stand up on the back of his neck. He imagined her telling ghost stories around a campfire, scaring the little kids to death, maybe the odd adult too.

"And boy, was he keen? He told me he was prepared to start at the bottom as long as there was an opportunity to progress. I thought he came across as a bit weird, geeky, but what could I do? He was nothing to do with me, or so I assumed."

Ed knew he had to ask something. He'd sat there gawking at her and now Hazel paused, needing clarification he was listening. "So, what was his job? What did he do exactly?" he asked, his voice slightly higher pitched than intended.

"To tell you the truth, I don't really know." Hazel

smiled as she reflected. She sat upright, placing her hands behind her on the bed. "After the first few days, I saw little of him. He was a bit of an odd-job man, I guess you'd call it. He made tea, cleaned up, collected and delivered mail. All sorts I believe."

"But I thought you travelled?"

"Yes, yes, but I also spent a lot of my time in the office, writing up reviews, preparing trips. It wasn't all champagne and skittles."

Although Hazel laughed, Ed knew she was still traumatised from whatever made her scream out in the middle of the night. The part he inevitably realised everything was leading to.

She went on to reveal that after the initial few weeks, she barely saw him. As she'd already explained, over fifty percent of her job was travel, and although the guy occasionally asked if he could join Hazel, she said he wasn't too perturbed when she pointed out she travelled alone and there was no need for two people to do the inspections. One day, Hazel told him to remain patient, even though she knew they would never trust him for that side of the job. She had every intention of mentioning him to her boss, explain he had obviously got the wrong end of the stick, but with her extremely busy schedule, she completely forgot.

And then, one day, after around a year in the job, he sent her an email demanding to see her. He told her he wasn't progressing and Hazel wasn't keeping her side of the bargain. "It came as a total shock. I'd totally forgotten about him."

Ed's patience was wearing thin. "Where is this going, Hazel?"

Hazel stood and walked to the long window. She stared outside, gathering her thoughts, or so Ed guessed.

Suddenly, she turned to face him, catching him off-guard. Her expression had changed.

"He became a nuisance. A pain in the arse. He would wait for me in the car park and when I ignored him, he sent more emails, insisting he travelled with me on my next trip abroad, stipulated he wanted his own office. He even threatened to take me to a tribunal for breaking my side of his employment. He was a fucking nutcase, Ed."

Ed could feel his heartbeat rising. He scratched the back of his head, even though there was no itch. "What happened?" he finally asked.

Hazel stepped back to the bed and perched herself on the edge once more. She was becoming agitated too, as the story reached its crescendo. Ed noticed red blotches around her neck. She kept pulling at the collar on her pretty cotton shirt.

"I told my boss to fire him. She said okay, but she instructed me to do it. Perhaps I took it too far the way I sacked him in front of everyone, but he scared me. I had to get rid of him." Ed wanted to say something, but bit his lip. "And that's when it started," Hazel concluded.

"What started?"

It was Ed's turn to stand and pace the room. To the large window and back before sitting down once more. He rubbed his hands down the side of his shorts, the stickiness of his palms making them catch.

"He started writing to me again. You know, proper letters, not emails. They got worse, more intense. He even threatened to take his own life. He sent one with pretend splatters of blood on it, like ink on blotting paper."

Holy shit.

"Did you tell anybody?"

"No. In the end, I didn't need to. It just stopped. No

more letters, no more waiting outside of work for me. Nothing."

"So, what's the problem? He's gone. Why bring him up now?"

Hazel sat perfectly still, wide-eyed and staring directly at Ed.

"Because that's why I screamed out in the middle of the night. I woke up, and for a brief moment, I'm sure that same boy was there. In my room. Standing at the end of my bed…"

13

————

ALTHOUGH CHARLIE CONSIDERED his marriage a convenience, a means to show off his beautiful wife to his mates down the pub or when they were on holiday, he also had an inner male machismo installed into him by his father at an early age. A duty to protect her from prying eyes. But the way Ed kept looking at her that day made the hairs on his arms stand on end. He hadn't noticed it before. Perhaps Ed hadn't looked at her in that manner before. But Charlie noticed little. Often lost in a world of his own, dreaming of fast cars or lying around a swimming pool watching scantily clad ladies sunbathing. Just like his own father and his father before that, Charlie was a throwback to male chauvinism. Days long gone, but not in his world. Mel often told him to stop living in the nineteen-seventies, but he shrugged her off before asking what time dinner would be ready or if she had ironed his shirt for the following morning.

Does he think he stands a chance with her? Charlie thought, still peering at Ed out of the corner of his eye. He took a step back so he could watch his wife, too. Was she looking at Ed in return? But instead, Mel studied each of the group, one by one, paying no particular attention to Ed Lawson.

Perhaps it's my imagination, Charlie finally assumed.

Part of Mel found her husband's protective nature quite redeeming, but she wished he could show such loyalty in far more important aspects of their relationship. She always wondered if he'd had affairs, was possibly even in the middle of one right then considering the phone call she overheard the day they left for France. Whatever. She knew she would leave him when they returned home. The ten thousand pounds would come in very handy to pay removal fees and a deposit on a rented property until she found her feet again. Her mother's inheritance would be due soon too, given her deteriorating health.

But it wasn't just Charlie's affairs, it was his chauvinistic ways. He'd never used a vacuum cleaner, never used an iron. She doubted he could operate the washing machine or know how to hang clothes on the line. However, deep down, she loved him. They'd been childhood sweethearts, after all. Meeting at fifteen years of age at Ridgeview Grammar, they quickly became inseparable. Skipping lessons to bunk off down by the river. Spending hours in her bedroom whilst pretending to be doing homework. And boy, were they the envy of the school? Every boy wanted to be Charlie Green, and every girl wanted to be Melanie Edmunds.

As everybody gathered that evening on the terrace, Mel caught Ed watching her. And out of the corner of her eye, she knew Charlie noticed too. Her husband took a small step backwards and she could feel his eyes boring into her own. Trying her utmost to ignore Ed, she attempted to focus on anybody and everybody instead, a way to put Charlie off his scent.

After a few moments, she took her husband's hand in her own. A show of solidarity for him, not for Ed. She wished she didn't have to do it and was convinced Ed looked slightly forlorn once he spotted them. Finally, she felt Charlie relax, his fingers no longer gripping her own. But although pleased she'd placated her husband, she so yearned she were holding Ed's hand instead.

Hazel had almost had enough. It felt like walking through a minefield. An unbridled air of tension remained amongst the group when they reconvened at dinner. She wondered when the emotional strain really began; the day they arrived or now Tony had departed? Hazel considered whether any of them had contemplated not going at all after receiving the invitation. It never crossed her mind. Ten grand saw to that. Mind you, Tony didn't believe the cash was worth hanging around for. *Perhaps he was right?*

Hazel's experience in the middle of the night still played heavily on her mind. Ed was convinced she'd been dreaming, as had Joyce, when she came to see to her following the scream. And although a nightmare made sense, she wanted clarification of one thing at least.

Watching Joyce, who yet again arrived last for dinner, like some bloody entertainer taking to the stage once everybody was seated and desperate for their entrance. Hazel remained patient and waited until Adrienne placed the food in the centre of the table. Helping herself to roast potatoes, she tried to stay casual, a matter-of-fact remark, an attempt to keep things neutral.

"Erm, Joyce." Her plan backfired immediately. The

others fell silent, as if Hazel was some crazy woman who dared take on their leader. She took a deep breath and spoke as indifferently as she could muster. "There's nobody else living on the island, is there? No other houses, I mean?"

All eyes swung to Joyce at the head of the table. Hazel noticed two slices of chicken on the end of her fork, hovering over the meat platter which contained three different dead animals. Hazel was a vegetarian and was pissed off that nobody had asked if she cared about having a serving dish dripping with blood before her at each mealtime. At least Adrienne cooked her a separate meat-free alternative.

"Of course not, dear," Joyce responded, lifting the meat onto her plate after recomposing herself. "This is the only house on the entire island." She looked up at Hazel, her demeanour light and breezy. "Is this to do with your apparition in the middle of the night again?"

Ollie laughed a little too forcibly, but Hazel knew it was down to his nerves. She'd noticed how his right leg would jiggle up and down whenever they were all seated. All the others returned their glare to Hazel, daring her to respond.

"Partly that, yes…" Hazel deliberately left her sentence hanging and helped herself to some vegetables.

"Well, what else, dear?" Joyce intervened impatiently. Hazel enjoyed making her host grovel for a change.

"It's when you said there might be some boats sporadically moored around the island." She had Joyce's, and everybody else's, full attention. "Who would they be for if nobody else lives here?"

Joyce stopped what she was doing, put the meat fork back onto the platter and placed both hands face down on either side of her plate. She looked as though she would stand, but remained seated, pushing her chest forward instead. "Hazel, my dear. This house is ancient. There have been generation after generation of families living here. Some could have had servants. Perhaps they used to trade garments. Who knows? But they would need boats to get to and from the mainland."

Hazel looked around the table at her fellow guests. All eyes were back on her and she suddenly felt uncomfortable. But Joyce's voice had been hesitant.

"So how old is this place, exactly?" Hazel asked, wanting to know more but doubting their host knew the answers. And Joyce definitely *was* faltering. She looked at one or two of the others before resting back on Hazel.

"Two, three hundred years. Why do you—"

"And who did you inherit it from?" Hazel recalled Joyce's indecisiveness when Tony asked the same question. "A relative? A friend?"

A suspended hush engulfed the room. Not only was everybody deadly quiet, but no longer did anybody help themselves to food or sip their drink.

"Wow, so many questions, my dear," Joyce said, lifting the meat fork once more and finally dropping the slices of chicken onto her plate. "I said before. My reasons for leaving that school are personal and my financial information should be respected as private."

Now wouldn't be the time to push her luck, but Hazel knew she'd hit a nerve. She glanced around the table. Had any of them noticed too? Ollie stared into his empty plate whilst Charlie broke the silence and asked Mel to pass him a bottle of wine. Louis called over to Adrienne, said something in French, and she immediately left the room, probably to fetch something from the kitchen. Ed eventually ended the impasse between Hazel and Joyce.

"It's been a long day," he said, doing his utmost to

force a smile. "Last night was a long night, too. Especially for you."

Charlie, Mel and Ollie nodded in agreement before Mel placed her hand on the back of Hazel's. Ollie stood, picked up the wine bottle, and filled Hazel's glass. *They're all in it together*, she thought.

"It was just a bad dream," Ollie said, his voice the calmest she'd heard since the day they arrived. "And Tony has left us by whichever means he could." He looked up at Joyce before returning to Hazel. "New boat, old boat, who cares? He's gone." Ollie raised his glass of water to the centre of the table. Mel, Charlie, Ed, and finally Hazel reciprocated, and they all clinked their drinks. "And I, for one, am very pleased," Ollie concluded, back in his chirpy cockney accent.

Joyce smiled contentedly in the background and helped herself to more meat. She piled so much on; Hazel knew it was an attempt to wind her up.

And it was definitely working.

14

_____

WHILE LYING in bed and staring at the chandelier, Ed considered Hazel's nightmare and their conversation after dinner. She'd asked Joyce if anybody else lived on the island, quizzed her about abandoned boats and once out on the terrace, she'd spoken to Ed once again.

"And you're a hundred percent certain you saw somebody?" he asked, recalling her original recollection.

"*… for a brief moment, I'm convinced that same boy was there. In my room. Standing at the end of my bed…*"

Hazel had hesitated, as if hearing her own words had put significant doubt into her mind. "I thought I was sure. Well, ninety percent. And now I don't know." Hazel's eyes didn't leave Ed's for one moment. A nervous energy enveloped her. "But where else could I have dragged his image from?"

"One hundred percent?" he reiterated.

Ed studied her as even more uncertainty etched across her face.

"I don't know. This place," he reasoned, looking around the garden. "Just being here with all the mentions of Ridgeview Grammar. Joyce quizzing you about your job, you telling me about it during our walk. Even I had a dream about that bloody school last night."

"Did you?" Hazel asked, a glimmer of hope in her eyes. "Maybe you're right. I'm agitated. Perhaps it *was* a dream." She paused again. "However, I stick by what I said about something not being quite normal."

A few minutes later, Hazel left Ed alone. She thanked him for listening again and at least a little colour had returned to her cheeks.

After returning to his own room, Ed sat on the bed. He'd lied to Hazel about his dream. He hadn't dreamt of Ridgeview at all. He did it to protect her from her obvious vulnerabilities. She'd been on edge since they arrived. Joyce was getting under her skin and now an awful dream threatened her mental health further.

Lying flat on his back, staring at the chandelier, Ed contemplated his last question to Hazel after she thanked him for listening.

"What is it?" she asked, clearly wanting the sanctuary of her own room and the conversation to be at an end.

"The boy," Ed replied.

"What about him?"

"You never did tell me his name."

That night, Ollie barely slept. It wasn't only the rising temperature; it was the apprehensiveness growing amongst the group too. Tony left without saying a word to anybody, apart from Joyce. The continual disagreements between Charlie and Mel, Hazel screaming out in the middle of the night, followed by her and Joyce's snide remarks across the dining table. And on top of all that, just to add to his discomfort, the weather in Brittany was predicted to reach record levels. Ollie didn't like hot temperatures, despite not carrying an ounce of fat on him.

At four in the morning, he retreated to the bathroom and splashed several handfuls of cold water over his face and neck. But within minutes of returning to bed, he was boiling and sweating profusely again. Ignoring Charlie's suggestion at dinner, he decided to open the enormous window in his room. Charlie had explained to everybody it was counterproductive to open your window during the night, as more heat crept in, rather than the expected result one would expect. Everybody else nodded their approval at his newfound wisdom, all apart from Mel, of course, who tutted her annoyance. But Charlie's theory made no sense to Ollie, and he intended to do the exact opposite.

Leaving his light off — feeling self-conscious whilst walking around in his unstylish underpants — he drew back the heavy curtains. The first thing he noticed was the stunning, clear sky. Stars shone vividly and formed the perfect accompaniment to the jet-black canvas beyond. They appeared to go on forever, reaching the very edge of space itself, and Ollie briefly considered what it would be like to be an astronaut. The moon rose brightly on the far side of the house, and a giant shadow tumbled across the lawn below. Even the shape of the turrets were distinct at each end, *like two pointed 'Dunces' hats*, Ollie thought, smiling.

After pulling the rusty latch towards him, Ollie heaved open the huge sash window. But instead of being greeted by an anticipated refreshing breeze, warm air encircled his bare legs, like a blanket slowly wrapping itself around him. Barely able to bring himself to admit it, Ollie realised Charlie had been right all along.

Adamant his room would soon cool down – probably more an act of defiance against his fellow traveller – he left the window ajar, and the curtains parted, before wearily making his way back to bed. As he lay still, desperate to fall off to sleep, the sound of footsteps from somewhere outside startled him. It was quite distinct, footfall on gravel.

Checking his watch a second time, he remained perfectly still, apart from his right leg jigging at the knee. Feeling his heart beating hard in his chest, a torch light shone outdoors, illuminating his room and making Ollie feel even more vulnerable.

Instinctively, he crawled sideways, hunching his body in sporadic movements to his right; away from the window. Without concentrating, Ollie knocked a glass of water from his bedside table and it crashed to the wooden floorboards below. *Shit.*

He lay statue-like once more, even his knee somehow understanding the importance of the situation. His room then plunged back into darkness. Once more, he heard the distinctive sound of footsteps on gravel and held his breath until they disappeared.

The last sound Ollie heard was the creaking of the broken gate at the end of the footpath being lifted open and closed.

With his heart still pounding, he didn't even contemplate venturing over to the window to look. Instead, Ollie left his curtains apart and the window wide open for the remainder of the night.

The following morning, everybody congregated outside for breakfast. Charlie welcomed the cool air. He guessed he got roughly three hours' intermittent sleep in total and felt thoroughly drained, but looking around at his fellow guests, he realised he wasn't alone.

Not only did everybody appear washed out, but they were also on tenterhooks, glancing from one another, barely saying a word. Charlie studied Ollie in particular. His eyes somehow transfixed on the broken gate at the end of the garden. He detected a slight tremor in his hand as he held tightly onto his morning coffee.

"Did anybody hear anything in the night?" Ed asked without warning. The muttering of chat abated.

"Not you as well," Hazel replied. Charlie noticed Ed glance towards Hazel. She smiled in return. A gratuitous smile.

"Yes, I did." Charlie spun to his wife. "I thought I heard a glass or bottle being dropped." He had heard it too but hadn't realised Mel had been awake.

"Yeah," Ollie replied sheepishly. "That was me. Dropped my glass of water, didn't I?" He grinned, showing off his yellowing teeth. Charlie thought he looked ill, malnourished even, and realised he knew little about him. Ollie tapped the side of his cup three times before taking a huge swig of coffee. His leg began twitching, and his eyes darted around the group. "Sorry," he eventually said. "I've always been a little clumsy."

Unlike Mel, it wasn't the dropping of Ollie's glass that woke Charlie. Instead, he was wide awake at the time anyway, sat up in bed, reading his copy of the book Joyce had handed out. Charlie rarely read books, but he couldn't sleep and it gave him something to do in the still of the night.

But that wasn't the main reason he decided to give Ed's novel a chance. He hadn't liked the way he looked at his wife and Charlie had also picked up on how Ed glanced at Joyce when she left a copy of the novel for everybody to read. Charlie could understand embarrassment, but he hadn't appeared self-conscious. Instead, he looked angry with Joyce, but then his expression changed. He became anxious, looking at each guest as they collected their own copy and flicked through it from front to back. And that wasn't all. Charlie still wanted to know how well-acquainted Ed was with Will Parry.

I still haven't asked him.

So Charlie's mind went into overdrive. Could there be something in the story Ed didn't want people to know and could there be a mention of Parry and his mates? Charlie doubted Ed would write a story about such things, but his interest was still piqued. Besides, that night, he wasn't able to sleep, and with his wife continually showing him a cold shoulder, what else was there to do?

However, given how slow a reader he was, and only being a few chapters in, something about that book was making Charlie feel extremely uncomfortable.

15

FOLLOWING BREAKFAST, Ed worked outside with Ollie. Ironically, Joyce asked the two of them to fix the gate at the end of the garden. Even for novices, she said it would be quite a simple task; remove the broken panels, and replace them with new ones from the barn, before fixing fresh hinges. Louis had already repaired the posts, so the hard part was complete, according to their host. The biggest problem would be working in the heat, but again, Joyce informed everyone she only expected them to work until lunchtime.

"So, how's the world of writing?"

Although Ollie had a smile on his face, Ed recognised how nervous he appeared. He wasn't his usual hyper self and seemed anxious about something. Ed recalled his expression when admitting to knocking his glass of water over in the night, and couldn't help but smile at his uneasiness as he realised his question was a red herring. A way of making conversation, and he was aware Ollie wasn't the slightest bit interested in his reply.

"Yeah, not bad, thanks. Up and down, if you know what I mean?"

Ed had told nobody how poor book sales were, even though Joyce hinted at it. He wondered if anybody picked up on that, although probably Ollie would be the last of the group to ascertain any connection.

"I know exactly what you mean, mate."

Mate? Is that your term of endearment?

Ed considered Ollie's job situation. He was the only one he didn't officially know about. "So, what about your business, Ollie? Didn't you say you work for yourself in London?"

The colour appeared to drain from his face before Ed even completed the question. Ollie stopped whatever he was doing.

"Yes, well, that was all front, wasn't it? You know, to make an impression."

No shit.

"I don't understand," Ed replied, showing a genuine interest.

"Went out of business six months ago, mate." Ollie desperately tried to regain his pride and positivity. "Haven't worked since, you know, apart from a bit of this and that?"

"I'm sorry to hear that," Ed said. "I guess the money will come in handy?"

"It's why I'm here, mate. Ten bloody grand. Can't turn that down, can you?"

"No, I guess not," Ed replied, returning to his original task.

Following a few more moments of awkward silence, Ollie stood and faced Ed. He knew he had something to get off his chest.

"It's been a pretty shit year, to tell you the truth."

As Ollie explained how his wife was killed in a hit-and-run incident, Ed stood and patiently listened. It was around nine months ago, following an art exhibition in a local town, as she walked to her car. "It was night-time, no street lamps," Ollie said, his voice faltering as each word escaped. "Even the police said she would have been difficult to spot, given the dark clothing she was wearing. Still, makes little sense why the driver never stopped."

After recalling the awful incident, it took Ollie a few minutes to compose himself. Ed didn't know what to say, apart from the obligatory *sorry*, a thousand times over. Ollie described how much his wife loved art and how much she would have loved to have visited the town on the mainland, the name of which had already eluded him. He said she lived for it, and would forgo new clothes or fancy stuff for their flat just to buy more paints and canvases. Ed wondered why such a person would even be with somebody as stupid as Ollie, but he had shown a kind side, so perhaps they'd been the perfect match after all?

Ollie fumbled in his pocket and removed his wallet before retrieving a photograph of his wife.

"Right," Ed said, with no real conviction. "She looks nice. Where did you meet her?"

The question appeared to catch Ollie off-guard, and he quickly put the picture away. "Come on," he said, the nervousness returning to his voice. "We need to get on with fixing this damn gate." He punched Ed in the arm, a little too firmly.

Ed knew he'd hit a nerve, but decided not to pursue it. Instead, he bent back down and put his efforts into a nail that refused to budge.

"Give it here," Ollie said, pushing him aside and grabbing the hammer from his hand. Ed watched as he removed the nail with one swift yank. Ollie laughed, pointing the hammer at Ed's face. "No wonder you're a writer. Do you just sit around all day daydreaming? No muscles sitting at a typewriter, mate."

Ed watched as Ollie walked towards the outbuilding to fetch the new gate panels. He whistled some indecipherable tune, his confidence reinstalled. But instead of feeling any hostility towards him, Ed thought of Ollie's ex-wife and the photograph he'd just shown him.

Ollie smiled to himself as he headed towards the barn to collect the new panels. His show of strength gave him a sense of one-upmanship. He knew he wasn't as smart as Ed Lawson, but successfully removing the nail made him feel good about himself.

Glancing over his shoulder, he noticed Ed looking, deep in thought. "Did I tell him too much?" he asked himself aloud. It was no secret about his wife and it actually felt satisfying to offload on someone, but Ollie realised Ed wasn't much of a talker. And then Ed asked him how they met. *What business is that of yours*, he wanted to say. Instead, he excused himself and returned to the job they had been assigned. Anything not to talk about *him*, of all people.

But then, Ollie could have kicked himself, because he'd really wished to discuss the footsteps on the gravel, and Ed was probably his best option. He was the most sensible, and Ollie had made a fool of him by yanking out the nail. *Who else can I talk to?* he considered, whistling some random song that entered his head.

"Good evening, Mr Lawson."

Spinning around in his chair, the sight of Joyce's silhouette in his bedroom doorway forced Ed to jump. He hadn't heard a sound.

"Shit. I didn't hear you. You nearly gave me a heart attack," he said, holding his chest.

Without invitation, she stepped into his room and meandered her way over to the window. Quickly, Ed closed his laptop lid. It made her smile.

"Top secret is it?" momentarily glancing over her shoulder.

"I never share my work in progress. Just one of my things."

She continued to speak with her back to him, her arms folded. "Your first book was excellent, Edward."

He didn't like her tone of voice, calm yet condescending. "Why did you give everybody a copy? Why would you do that?"

Still, she looked out of the window.

"And how have sales been going recently?" Joyce asked, completely ignoring his question. Without warning, she turned to face him, her arms tightly bound across her chest, like someone trapped in an imaginary straight jacket.

The look of self-satisfaction made his blood boil. Surely she wouldn't take such joy in *his* demise, too?

"Not so good. But I get the distinct impression you already know that."

Her expression didn't falter.

"Everybody puts too much information on social media, Edward. You're all as easy to read as one of your books."

Ed counted to four, breathed in, one-two-three-four, breathed out. The last thing he wanted was a stand-up row with his host. Fortunately, Joyce side-stepped any such quarrel and changed the course of the conversation altogether.

"Be careful getting too close to Melanie. She's vulnerable and not in a good—"

Ed stood, his chair catching against the wooden flooring, making an annoying scraping sound.

"Stop interfering, Joyce. It's none of your—"

Joyce raised her hand to stop him mid-flow.

"Oh, but it *is* my business, Edward. You're a guest at my property." Ed opened his mouth to interrupt once more, but Joyce raised her hand for a second time. She stepped to his open doorway and turned to face him. "Keep your head down. Do what you're here to do and don't get involved with any other guest."

Her expression appeared genuine, yet irksome. Ed sighed.

"Don't worry, I won't."

He wanted to avoid confrontation, and he knew Joyce had all their interests at heart. However, as he watched her leave, Ed uncrossed his fingers from behind his back and smiled confidently to himself.

"Who did it?" Mel exclaimed, waiting impatiently until she had gained everybody's attention. She was already late for dinner as the others stood on the terrace.

"Whatever's wrong, darling?" Charlie was the first to speak. He stepped over and attempted to embrace her. "You looked freaked out." Mel brushed her husband's hand away and took a further step forward.

"Which one of you wrote it?" Mel asked, her voice even more animated. Her hair was wet, and she had a towel wrapped tightly around her body. She noticed

Hazel glance at Ed. "Was it you?" she asked, glaring at her.

"I don't know what you're talking about," Hazel replied. Ed said nothing, a look of bemusement as he waited patiently for Mel to explain herself.

"What's all this about?" Joyce spoke next. Even amid her anger, Mel couldn't help but notice how Joyce constantly seemed to appear out of nowhere.

"Mel has just come out of the shower and—"

"I'm more than capable of speaking for myself." Mel shot her husband a look. He held the palms of his hands aloft. She addressed the others once more. "When I got out of the shower, the mirror was steamed up." She paused. "And there was a message written on it."

"A message?" Joyce asked condescendingly, stepping froward before helping herself to a small glass of wine from the table. "What kind of message, darling?"

Mel fumed at her host. *Why is she doubting me?* "Come and look for yourself."

Whilst Joyce and the others contemplated going to see what the fuss was about, Charlie stood and sprinted upstairs.

She ran after him before waiting impatiently for the remainder to catch up, suddenly feeling quite exposed, her hair dripping and only a towel hiding her modesty. Infuriatingly slowly, Joyce led the group up the steps, a mixture of curiosity and disbelief written across their faces.

"This had better be good," Joyce said as she reached Mel, slightly out of breath.

Once in the bathroom, Mel instantly felt her face redden. Acutely aware that six or seven people were congregated in her doorway, no doubt peering over each other's shoulder to get a proper look, Mel stared at her blank bathroom mirror. Quickly, she strode over, leant forward and breathed on the glass. A murmur broke out between one or two of the guests. "It's gone," she declared, feeling both deflated and stupid. "It's gone."

Charlie stepped forward from the back of the huge bathroom. "What's gone, darling?"

Mel glared at him. His voice was more patronising than Joyce's. "The fucking message you imbecile!" she shouted at him. Joyce pushed Charlie to one side and took a step closer to the mirror. She moved her head from one angle to the other. Eventually, she wiped the mirror with her palm before turning to face Mel.

"Nothing there, dear. Did you imagine it when the room was filled with steam?"

Finally, Mel detected some compassion in Joyce's tone before their host indicated for the others to leave and go back downstairs. Once they departed, Joyce told Mel to take her time and asked if she would like Adrienne to bring dinner to her room instead. Mel caught herself nodding.

A few moments later, Joyce left her alone, and she sat on the edge of the bed clinging tightly to the towel still wrapped around her body. Slowly, she stood and gingerly made her way back to the bathroom. Watching from the doorway, Mel stared at the mirror, already doubting her own mind. *Could it have been your imagination?* She even had to think hard to remember what the message said; or what she *thought* it said.

I know what you did

16

AT LUNCHTIME THE NEXT DAY, Joyce agreed to give the group the afternoon off. "No rush," she said, as they ate on the outside terrace.

"Suits me," Charlie said, necking what remained of his second bottle of beer. "Think I'll top up my tan on one of those sun loungers." He stood with a renewed spring in his step. "Just going upstairs to change into my shorts."

Without a hint of acknowledgement towards his wife, Mel felt both anger and embarrassment with his conduct. She didn't know which irked her more, the fact he still hadn't spoken to her about the hidden message in the mirror, or his complete disregard for his fellow guests.

"I'm sorry for Charlie's behaviour," she said quietly. "He can be rather selfish at times."

"Well," Joyce replied on everybody's behalf whilst standing and helping Adrienne to clear the plates. "That's none of our concern, Mel." Mel nodded a brief *thank you* before Joyce spoke again, allowing Mel some much-needed respite. She was warming to Joyce and could sense some kind of affinity between them. She felt an underlying kindness in her when they held hands during the boat ride, despite her assertive personality. "What does everybody else plan to do on this beautiful day?" Joyce asked.

Mel looked around the group, hoping they all had plans because suddenly she had one of her own.

"I'm going to take a nap in my room," Hazel said. "Didn't sleep too well again last night."

Mel noticed Hazel glance at Joyce as she spoke. She sympathised with her, recalling the lack of support she received at dinner a couple of nights before. Now Mel had gone through a similar experience, she could empathise with Hazel, despite neither of them having any concrete evidence it wasn't their wild imaginations at play. Could Joyce have been right? Had Mel imagined the message and did Hazel just have a frightful nightmare?

"Good idea, Hazel," Ollie said. "This heat makes you knackered. I'm going to grab forty winks too."

With three of the guests gone, Mel lingered until Joyce and Adrienne disappeared into the kitchen. Louis stood and mumbled something in broken English about the barn as Mel waited impatiently for him to finish his coffee before eventually leaving.

Once satisfied everybody was out of earshot, Mel looked over to Ed, who was still finishing a cold beer and appeared in a world of his own, gazing across the lawn and to the sea beyond. She cleared her throat. "Fancy a walk?" she asked, before standing and stepping onto the garden path without waiting for a reply.

Ed regarded Mel's presumptuous invite something more akin to her husband's behaviour, and for a brief moment, considered telling her he had plans of his own. However, watching her walk along the footpath, he couldn't resist the prospect of an afternoon stroll with Melanie Edmunds in the shade of the woods. With a quick glance around, he put his empty bottle on the table and scooted after her.

Following a brief nod of his head, Ed opened the gate at the end of the garden, now fixed, painted and pristine after his and Ollie's work, and he followed Mel along the same path he and Hazel walked days before. Eventually, they reached the same opening, but instead of turning left, Mel allowed Ed to lead as he stepped in the opposite direction. They still hadn't exchanged a word, and Ed realised how content they were in each other's company, so much so, it was as though they'd been friends for years.

Soon, they came across a wooden bench overlooking the sea and towards the undulating green hills on the mainland. Taking a seat, he allowed Mel plenty of room without the need to be too close. Suddenly, he felt quite exposed and unsure if he should be there. Why had he led her so far from the house?

"Everything okay?" he asked, remembering it was Mel who purposefully chose him to walk with her.

"I'm leaving him."

Despite the shock announcement, Ed experienced a pang of guilt followed by a surge of excitement coursing through his veins. Joyce's words immediately echoed inside his skull.

'Keep your head down. Do what you're here to do and don't get involved with any other guest …'.

"What? I mean, why?" Ed stared at Mel as her eyes flicked between his and the clear blue water in front. The bank rose sharply on the far side and he noticed a red tractor meandering its way high on the hillside. It looked like a toy, small enough to push.

"He took a phone call the day we left for France. I was in the ensuite, although he didn't realise. He thought I was downstairs somewhere."

"Who was it?"

"Whoever his latest flame is, I presume." She managed a stifled laugh. "It was all, 'can't wait to see you', and 'I won't be gone for long' and 'we'll get together as soon as I get back'. I just stood there; my ear pressed against the door. I swore he would hear my heart thumping on the far side."

Ed didn't know what to say. They had only arrived a few days ago, and Mel had already shared their failing business, and now she was confiding in him about leaving her bloody husband. However, it was pleasing she chose him to open up to. "Did you ask him about it?"

"No way! I wouldn't give him the satisfaction. I just waited for him to finish the call and leave the room. Later, he said he tried to find me and asked where I'd been. I said for a walk, but I'm not sure he believed me. He made an effort to be nice to me on the flight over, even at the quayside, when we all made our introductions. But he's soon dropped into his usual ways. Didn't you notice when he said he was going sunbathing? Totally ignored me. And he thinks I'm a fool about the message in the mirror."

Relationships weren't Ed's thing. He'd had two fairly long-standing girlfriends in Ireland, both local. He met each of them in a pub – he guessed the most frequented meeting place in Ireland – but after a year, both fizzled out. The timing of each coincided with reaching the long-term commitment stage and both romances ended amicably. There were no scenes, no tears, and no regrets from either party. Mel continued.

"It's not just this one, though. I'm sure there have been others over the years." After a few moments of awkward silence, Mel caught Ed completely off-guard. "Will you give me a hug, Ed? I'm feeling pretty low at the moment, believe it or not."

She endeavoured to force a smile, but looked agonisingly close to tears. Ed suddenly felt uneasy about the situation. They'd only been in France for five days and he found himself in the middle of a personal crisis. However, resistance was futile and his willpower non-existent. As in his room the day they arrived, Ed reached over, Mel shuffled closer and he put his arm around her. They sat motionless for several moments, both looking out to sea. Intentionally, Ed tried to focus his mind on something else; the tractor and then the small waves lapping against the bank.

Eventually, Mel slid her arm around his waist, and pulled herself closer still. Glancing at her, their faces were only inches apart, and Mel removed her straw hat and slid her sunglasses onto the top of her head. Ed felt his heartbeat rising rapidly.

Without warning, and not unlike their encounter in his room, Mel kissed him. However, rather than a peck on his cheek, she kissed him full on the lips. She lingered long enough for Ed to realise there was true feeling behind it. He didn't know how to reciprocate. Everything felt so wrong, yet he couldn't stop himself. Instead, he concentrated on the sound of the waves and the leaves rustling in the gentle breeze.

Mel pulled herself away, but clung to his hand. He noticed her neck was flushed, small red blotches along each collarbone. She stood, not letting go, and led him into the trees as they followed the faintest of footpaths. Still, he didn't object, even though every ounce of common sense screamed at him otherwise.

After a few moments, they came to a clearing, and she stopped before turning to face him. This time she kissed him harder still. She had Ed totally mesmerised, completely under her spell.

She's using you, Ed. A way to get back at her cheating husband.

Her hands reached under his T-shirt, her nails gently caressing his skin.

Get the fuck away.

Mel moaned, ever so lightly, as they both became lost in the moment.

Ed!

Charlie's mind worked overtime as he lay on his bed in the early hours. Ed's book remained open on his bedside table. He knew Mel still hadn't picked up her own copy. *Probably best that way*, he thought.

She had returned to their room that afternoon, implying she'd been for a walk in the woods alone and had discovered some clearing in the trees. She even offered directions and something about a bench overlooking the sea. But Mel was agitated, her behaviour restless. Was it still the message in the mirror or an entirely different matter? He caught her rubbing her ear and could see she had a missing earring. But Charlie said nothing, just let her stew in her own discomfort. He liked to play her like that.

It was the sight of the book which got him thinking about Ed Lawson once more. He was still at chapter four, unable to pick up from where he left off. But it wasn't the subject which played on his mind. Charlie just couldn't recollect whether Ed hung around with Will Parry at school or not. There had been no mention of any such character in the book to date, so why did it trouble him so much? He never bothered Charlie or Mel at school, but he was a year below Will, and besides, Charlie and Mel only had eyes for each other, not a problem for the school bully.

Wide awake, he grabbed his holdall and went to the bathroom so not to disturb his wife. Sitting on the edge of the bath, he unzipped the side pocket of his Nike bag and pulled out a couple of magazines, as well as a copy of his local Lincolnshire newspaper. Charlie had slid the paper in with his favourite magazines out of curiosity, even though he wasn't sure why he brought it. *Something to read if I get bored*, was all he could recollect.

But the local rag, now crumpled and torn, was the real reason he hadn't been able to shake Will Parry from his mind. Even though he'd read it a hundred times before, the front-page headline still made him jolt. He finished reading, stood too hastily and knocked over a can of deodorant sitting on the edge of the bath. It clanked loudly on the tiled floor in the dead of night. Cursing, he bent to retrieve it and heard Mel stir on the other side of the door.

"Is that you?" she asked, her voice laced with sleep.

"Yeah, sorry. Needed a pee."

Charlie did in fact take a pee, but as soon as he finished, Charlie read the article twice more, the words ingrained in his head. He double-checked the date.

One month ago, almost to the day, someone killed Will Parry in his own house. His throat slit in the middle of the night as he slept alone. And as far as Charlie could decipher, the murder enquiry was still ongoing. Nobody had been caught.

17

THE FOLLOWING MORNING, Mel found herself on decorating duties once more. Joyce requested her and Hazel paint the guest bedroom doors. The group were becoming accustomed to being partnered up with different people. It made sense to Mel, everybody mixing, but she secretly wished she was working with Ed. She was struggling to push him out of her thoughts since their rendezvous in the woods.

But perhaps she needed to keep herself in check. The day before, after returning to her room, Mel realised she was missing an earring. Out of habit, her hand rubbed against her empty lobe and, once or twice, she caught Charlie watching her from his side of the bed. *Shit, shit, shit,* she thought, glancing at her husband and smiling, realising her face must be riddled with guilt. But Charlie said nothing. He rarely did anymore.

In the middle of the night, he thought he had woken her after dropping something onto the bathroom floor, but unbeknown to him, Mel was already wide awake. She watched his silhouette as he walked across the room before picking up his holdall and sneaking into the bath-room. *What the hell is he taking that in there for?* she thought. *Perhaps looking at those filthy magazines he keeps in the side pocket?* But something else played on Mel's conscience, and she had no time for Charlie's overactive testosterone. A couple of days before, she noticed him reading a copy of Ed's book. Mel couldn't recall the last time he read anything, apart from his stupid magazines. But he appeared to be taking a keen interest in the novel and she wondered what he found so fascinating. Maybe she should read her own?

And that wasn't all. The message in her mirror still played heavily on her mind, and she considered if Charlie was the culprit. Had he sneaked into the bathroom whilst she showered? And then, once Mel told the group, he sprinted upstairs before anybody else moved. Why move so fast? To wipe the mirror clean? But why? *I know what you did.* Charlie was the only one who knew, wasn't he? But even if that boy also knew, he wasn't even on the island.

Was he?

As she painted the door frame, her mind gratefully distracted by the banter from Ollie and Charlie below – they were tasked with painting the downstairs doors – Mel sensed Hazel shuffle a little closer. With a quick peek over the banister, she stepped closer still. *Oh shit, not her. Not now.*

"I've been meaning to get you on your own, Mel."

Mel wondered what she could want. Surely she didn't know about her and Ed? "Have you?" Mel replied evasively, returning to her painting whilst fearing the worse.

Hazel ignored the frosty response and continued, regardless. "I followed Joyce yesterday. Later in the afternoon." Her voice dropped to a whisper. "But you must promise to keep this between us two."

Although Mel's interest heightened, she was unsure she wanted to know where the conversation may lead. "Of course I will," she replied. "But why did you follow her?"

Hazel looked at her incredulously. "Because I don't believe her. I don't believe she's into social media and I'm not even convinced she owns this property."

Mel couldn't help but stop what she was doing and stared at Hazel. "Why don't you believe her? What other reason could she have for getting us all here?" Mel's second question scared herself. *I know what you did.* Hazel lowered her voice further still.

"Call it a hunch. There's no—"

"A hunch? It's not some cop show, Hazel." Mel's pulse quickened and her jaw tightened, but knew it was through fear rather than anything Hazel was actually saying.

"Come on, Mel," Hazel replied, her face scornful towards the one person she'd chosen to confide in. "This isn't right. Ten grand for painting a fucking house. We must all be off our heads to accept it."

"So, why did you?" Mel dipped her brush back into the paint pot, but Hazel reached forward and gripped her wrist.

"Because I believed it, at first. Like you did. Like Ed, Ollie, Tony even. It *looked* real, and Joyce *is* convincing."

Mel wasn't enjoying the exchange in the slightest.

"And what's changed for you not to believe it? Is this to do with you asking Joyce if anybody else lives on the island?"

Hazel shook her head. "No, not that. It's when I probed her about the house, how old it is, who it belonged to, who she inherited it from. Didn't you notice, Mel? She didn't answer any of those questions. Side-stepped the lot." Hazel was on a roll and struggling to keep her voice in check. "And can you remember the invitation?" Mel shook her head even though she remembered it like the back of her hand. "She said she wanted to know all about us, where we are, what we've ended up doing with our lives. She hasn't asked any of us one question." Mel resisted the urge to nod in agreement. "I don't believe she has any particular knowledge of us or even about this place. Especially now."

Hazel explained she had been sitting in the garden the previous afternoon when she saw Joyce return from a walk. Mel wanted to ask what direction Joyce had come from, but didn't want to alert any unwanted attention to why she might ask such things. Hazel told her she followed Joyce into the château via the back doors.

"Her room is down there." Hazel pointed below. "One of those doors off the main foyer. It leads down a corridor."

The animated expression on Hazel's face had the desired effect, and Mel's interest piqued further. "And did you follow her, you know, down the corridor?"

Hazel appeared pleased she'd finally grabbed Mel's full attention. Her eyes widened, and she took a deep breath before continuing. "No, not at first. It would have been too obvious, as there's nowhere to hide. Instead, I came upstairs and waited in my doorway, watching and listening. It wasn't long before she returned and disappeared outdoors. I assumed towards the barn."

"Go on," Mel said.

"Well, the corridor is long. Longer than I imagined from the outside. It's full of rooms, maybe five, six. I was about to give up when I noticed the door to one of the last rooms was slightly open. I peeked through the gap and I saw her cardigan on the bed."

Mel couldn't believe Hazel had taken it upon herself to find their host's bedroom. What had she hoped to discover? "Did you go in?" she asked.

"Yes," Hazel replied, the excitement in her voice rising. "And I found something."

Do I want to know?

"What, Hazel? What?" Mel couldn't help herself.

Hazel once more peered through the banister before continuing in a hushed voice. "I found a notebook. And I looked inside."

Mel suddenly felt guilty. She liked Joyce, and no longer wanted to be part of whatever Hazel discovered.

"Shit, Hazel. You shouldn't do that." Mel considered how she was breaking the line of privacy. It was one thing to go sneaking into her room, but going through her personal things was another matter altogether.

"Bollocks," Hazel retorted, obviously taken aback by Mel's defence of Joyce. "She wants us here for some other reason than what she's letting on. I didn't have long, but her notebook contained loads of scribbles and names." Mel dipped her brush into the paint pot, desperate to bring the conversation to an end. She didn't want to know. No, she didn't want to hear. "Don't you want to know what I saw?" Hazel asked, her voice raising, so much so, Mel knew it was deliberate to gain the attention of others in earshot.

"Shh," she conceded, pushing her finger to her lips. "Whose names?"

Hazel lowered her tone once more. "Our names. And we all had the year we attended school next to them. There was one with a line through it..."

Mel's heart began beating faster still. There were

secrets she never wanted to resurface from that school. "Who was it?" She realised her voice had gone up an octave or two.

"Somebody called William Parry." Hazel waited for Mel to respond, but her impatience soon kicked in. "Do you know him?"

Mel recognised the name. *Wasn't he expelled?* "I've heard the name, but can't really recall him. Anything else in the book, or the room?"

"I ran out of time. I heard someone coming, so I put it back. I was shit scared it would be Joyce. However, I managed to get out of her room in time. Like I said, that corridor is long, and her room is the second from last. I quickly tried the end door, and it was unlocked, so I sneaked in there to wait."

"Shit. How long were you in there for until Joyce came back?" Mel realised she was getting louder, and she too peered below to check on Charlie and Ollie.

Hazel was struggling to quell her enthusiasm. "No, no. It wasn't Joyce I heard. It was someone else. I couldn't see who, though. I only had a tiny crack to peep through. But whoever it was, they made their way so quietly along the corridor. Sounded as though they were walking on tiptoe."

"How do you know it wasn't Joyce, then?"

Hazel tutted. "Because, if you let me finish, once whoever had gone into her room, I listened until they closed the door. Then, gingerly, I opened my door and made my way back out and eventually into the foyer. My heart was thumping so loud. I can't believe I got out of there unnoticed."

"But it wasn't Joyce?" Mel asked impatiently.

"No. I went straight outside. I needed some air. Shit, I was sweating like a pig." Hazel laughed, but neither of them found Hazel's experience amusing. "I thought about telling Ed, but I'm not sure how much he believes me…"

Oh yes. Me and Ed. Our time in the woods…

"… which is why I wanted to talk to you alone." Mel didn't know whether to feel flattered or angry that she was Hazel's latest confidante. Still, Hazel continued unabated. "So, I doubled back on myself, towards the barn. And, without paying attention to where I was going, I bumped straight into Joyce as she came out."

"Bloody hell. So it wasn't her in her room?" Mel's fervour reached new heights. "What did she say?"

"Nothing at all. She appeared just as shocked to see me. I realised I must have looked flustered, but she looked twice as bad as I felt. She was sweating, like she'd been running. I know yesterday was a particularly hot day, but not that bad."

Mel's mind flash-backed to the day before. She, too, had been particularly flustered, but for an entirely different reason. She tried to banish such thoughts, for the time being at least.

"So, what are you thinking?" Hazel asked, snapping Mel out of her trance. At first, she thought Hazel had read her mind. Fortunately, she soon dispelled that theory. "You know, going into Joyce's room?"

Mel dipped her brush into the pot for the umpteenth time, still not applying any of the paint to the door. "Oh, well, I don't know. Could have been Louis——"

"No. He was in the barn too, fixing something or other."

Mel couldn't think straight. Too much was going on and none of it made any sense. "I guess we'll never know," was all she could muster, much to Hazel's instant disapproval.

"Maybe *you* won't, Mel, but I'm determined to find—"

"Leave it, Hazel," Mel interrupted, reading the intent in her voice. "There's obviously a simple explanation. You shouldn't go prying."

Hazel nodded before finally returning to her original task. As she casually painted up and down the wooden door, Mel heard her say something under her breath, and it sounded uncannily like "*we'll see.*"

18

AFTER NEARLY A WEEK at the château, Charlie was desperate to discuss the newspaper article. However, the following morning, when Joyce paired him up with Ollie, he felt uncertain about placing any trust in him. Charlie believed Ollie was like a cat on a hot tin roof, forever bouncing around, talking far too quickly and trying to make light of everything. To allay his initial suspicions, Ollie started jabbering in his typical incomprehensible manner and Charlie realised he wasn't the person to confide in.

Before the trip, after he first read the article, he contemplated notifying Mel but doubted she remembered who Will Parry was. Besides, she was already a bag of nerves and any further negative connotation would have made her say no before the excursion had even begun. He again contemplated discussing it in the middle of the night, after he knocked over the can in the bathroom and woke her, but he soon dispelled that idea too. After the message in the mirror, how could he break the news that someone closely linked to Ridgeview was killed a few weeks before their trip?

Instead, Charlie returned from the bathroom and didn't sleep at all. Surely the killer of an ex-pupil at their former school couldn't be connected with where they were? They were in a different country, and what did Will Parry have to do with decorating an old château in France? Although Charlie laughed at his own stupidity, he still needed to talk to somebody. He had to offload before he burst.

As he worked silently next to Ollie, he overheard Mel and Hazel chatting in hushed tones above. Now and then, one would raise their voice, or peer over the banister, but he couldn't decipher what they were discussing. It didn't help that Ollie only appeared to stop talking whenever he needed to breathe in.

Charlie remembered Mel rubbing her ear and the missing earring. Didn't she say she'd been out walking alone in the woods? A clearing near a bench? *"Turn right at the end of the path and follow your nose,"* she'd said.

As Charlie contemplated his next move, Ed stepped into the hallway from outside. He was sweating profusely, and Charlie couldn't remember what task Joyce had given him. But that didn't matter. As soon as he saw him, Charlie glanced up at his wife, and he knew he was the one. He had to speak to Ed Lawson. Alone.

Ed desperately needed a shower. Joyce asked him to cut the lawns, and he hoped to use the ride-on mower. It even sounded fun, as he'd never used one before. However, when he arrived at the barn, Louis instructed him to wait outside before unveiling a petrol-driven push mower instead. "I can't cut all the damn grass with that," he protested, but Louis smiled and disappeared back inside the barn. Seconds later, he returned with a canister of petrol and held it aloft, leaving Ed no choice but to take it.

Around three hours afterward, Ed was drenched and his T-shirt clung to his back, freezing cold to the skin. He walked with a straight spine and kept his arms to his side, like some kind of robot.

"Bit of a strange walk, Ed." Charlie laughed as he stepped into the welcome shade of the entrance hall.

Charlie caught Ed off-guard. He hadn't spotted him working in the shadows. Then he spotted Mel and Hazel on the landing, paintbrushes in their hands, and Mel smiled at him. But Ed couldn't smile back, not with her husband a step or two away. Instead, he averted Mel's gaze and pulled at his shirt to show Charlie how wet he was. "Just going to grab a shower. Bloody lawns have taken hours."

Charlie stood and Ed couldn't help but notice how friendly he appeared, a smile imprinted on his face and a manner he hadn't witnessed before.

"Why didn't you use the ride-on mower?" he asked bullishly.

"That's what I thought," Ed replied, desperately trying to avoid looking at Charlie's wife as he addressed him. "Louis gave me the bloody push one. Never said a word, but just passed me a canister of petrol."

"He's stitched you up, mate. There's a bloody great machine in the barn. A trailer too." Although Charlie was being overtly friendly, Ed's anger grew at how he'd been led on by Louis. Why would he do that? Charlie spoke again. "Grab yourself a shower, mate. I'll wait here for you. I need to pick your brains and thought we could go for a walk?"

Ed's eyes widened. He forgot Louis in an instant and

instead glanced above, but Mel had her back turned. Surely Charlie didn't know about their encounter in the woods? Why not just have it out with him there and then? Whatever the reason, Ed knew he had no choice. Reluctantly, he nodded, told Charlie to give him half an hour and they could talk outside.

Ollie wanted to be paired with Hazel that day. He had to speak to someone about the footsteps he heard on the gravel, and Hazel seemed his best option, especially since Ed was too damn full of his own importance. Hazel was already sceptical about the entire arrangement anyway, so who better to confide in than somebody who would be on his side to begin with?

Following his disappointment at having to work with Charlie, Ollie tried to keep up the pretence that he didn't have a worry in the world. He was good at that. So, he spoke about everything and nothing. He could see Charlie wasn't interested and caught him trying to listen to Mel and Hazel's conversation instead. *Ignorant prick*, he thought, so changed tack and talked about football. Ollie knew Charlie didn't like football from previous conversations around the dinner table, so what better way to piss him off?

He just needed to remain patient though, something he wasn't renowned for, and wait until he could get Hazel alone. He glanced up at her through the balustrade and smiled to himself. *Yeah*, he thought, *we'll make quite the team, me and Hazel. If anything is going on here, we'll soon get to the bottom of it.*

. . .

Hazel's story resonated with Mel all morning. If she could be believed, and somebody had ventured into Joyce's room, it obviously ruled out Hazel herself. So who else? Well, she knew it wasn't her or Ed and Joyce and Louis had been in the barn. But with everybody else, she couldn't understand why Ollie or Charlie would go sneaking around, assuming somebody was actually *doing so*. To satisfy her own curiosity, Mel convinced herself it must have been Adrienne. She would have the most reason to be allowed to go into Joyce's room. Clean, change bed linen or bring fresh towels; any manner of chores sprang to mind. But why tread so carefully along the corridor and why close the door so quietly behind her?

As lunchtime approached, Mel heard Charlie's raised voice. "Bit of a strange walk, Ed," he said. Ed! Mel felt her heartbeat increase at the very mention of his name. She peered over the banister and their eyes briefly met. Mel smiled, hoping he would reciprocate, but Ed immediately avoided her gaze and focused his attention on Charlie instead. She strained to listen, but her husband lowered his voice before Ed eventually trudged upstairs and vanished into his room. His T-shirt was sodden and Mel realised he would be taking a shower. All kinds of thoughts echoed around her head, and she forced herself to concentrate on more mundane issues.

With the heat rising, everybody could do as they pleased in the afternoon. Mel desperately wanted to get Ed on his own and relay Hazel's story. She needed to confide in someone, somebody more neutral, somebody she trusted. She tried very hard to convince herself all was fine, but couldn't shake a nagging feeling deep inside. Hazel's story had brought all her initial fears racing back to the surface.

But getting Ed on his own because she depended on him wasn't the main reason. What they did in the clearing was never far from her thoughts and she needed to gauge his reaction, see where they stood. Hoping he hadn't taken advantage of her; Mel knew that her feelings for him were growing stronger by the day.

Forty minutes later, as she sat in the garden, hoping to catch Ed leaving the house alone, her plan soon backfired when she spotted him and Charlie step outside together.

Where the hell are they *going?*

They made their way along the footpath and towards the newly fixed gate.

Does Charlie know? Is that what they were talking about earlier?

Mel's hopes were raised slightly when Ed stalled at the beginning of the woods, turned and offered her a brief smile. He followed with a shrug of his shoulders towards her husband.

He doesn't know where they're going either. Shit. What should I do?

As soon as they disappeared from sight, Mel detected her panic rising. Should she follow them? Try to find another way and beat them to the clearing?

Instinctively, she reached for her earlobe and rubbed where the missing earring should have been.

19

Ed couldn't believe Charlie was leading him across the lawn towards the gate and into the woods. And he strode briskly, as if determined to get Ed alone as quickly as possible. Once through the small opening, Ed stalled and offered Mel a brief smile. He followed with a shrug of his shoulders towards her husband, hoping she realised it wasn't his idea at all. She looked as worried as he felt.

As they reached the end of the initial footpath, Ed called for Charlie to turn left, but he had drifted too far behind and instead, Charlie turned right. He glanced over his shoulder and offered Ed the briefest of smiles. *He did hear me.* They hadn't spoken a word since leaving the house, and Ed's suspicions were growing by the second. He considered feigning a headache, but Charlie would never allow such a thing. This was on his terms and Ed was following like a lost sheep.

Eventually, they reached the bench where Ed and Mel first spoke. He recalled how relaxed he'd been only twenty-four hours earlier, a stark contrast to the discomfort that washed over him when Charlie sat down and patted the seat beside him.

Charlie could tell how uneasy Ed was feeling. He wasn't a great observer of people, but he could quickly decipher when somebody looked *that* ill at ease. Ed continually glanced over his shoulder. He watched as he shrugged his shoulders towards Mel, who was sitting in a deckchair on the lawn. Why would he seek clarification from her? But Charlie had no time for any of that and he promptly scooted off.

As they reached the end of the footpath, Charlie heard Ed tell him to turn left. But why would he do that? Mel had given him directions to a so-called clearing she'd been to the day before, and he wanted to kill two birds with one stone.

Once seated on a bench overlooking the sea, Charlie tapped the space next to him, and Ed reluctantly joined him.

"What do you want, Charlie?"

Ed's voice wasn't natural; higher pitched and hesitant. With a quick glance around, Charlie got straight to the point.

"You knew Will Parry at school, didn't you?" Charlie faced him. He watched as Ed began rubbing his hands up and down his shorts.

"Will Parry?" he replied, obviously stunned by the question. Ed looked from Charlie and back out to sea. "Why would you mention him?"

Charlie had hit a nerve, but it wasn't the response he'd been expecting. He thought that would be the simple question, with a straightforward '*yes*' as a reply. Already, Ed was on the defensive. He watched as he gawped out to the mainland, his eyelids rapidly flicking open and shut whilst his right leg bounced up and down at the knee. It reminded Charlie of Ollie's annoying trait. *Why is everybody so bloody nervous?* Charlie needed to keep things neutral as he feared Ed might up and leave before he got the chance to talk. "Hey, it's okay. I'm just asking as I thought you hung around with him."

Finally, Ed turned to face him. His complexion was pasty white and tiny droplets of sweat formed across his forehead, like he was carrying some kind of fever.

"Yes. I knew him, but he was no friend of mine. I haven't seen him since the day he got expelled."

Exactly what Charlie wanted him to say. "Yeah, why was that? The rest of us kids never were told why he was thrown out of school."

Ed stood up and paced to the edge of the bank, which dropped steeply into the water below. Charlie watched as he swatted at a fly on the back of his neck, his hand remaining in place before rubbing it back and forth. Before their meeting, Charlie considered Ed to be the one in control, the mature member of the group. But there he was, literally having palpitations in front of him, just at the mere mention of someone from Ridgeview Grammar.

During the silence, which felt like an eternity, Charlie also reminisced about school, and not unlike Ed, he could sense the discomfort that came with those memories. *What is it about that place?* He already knew what Mel thought and Charlie had picked up vibes from Hazel that she wasn't comfortable about the past, either. *What about Ollie?* he considered. *Does he have similar concerns?* Finally, Ed turned to face him.

"I can't remember exactly," he stumbled. Charlie recognised he was lying, but didn't have to probe any further as Ed continued by himself. "He bullied some kid. Took it too far one day. He was hauled in front of the head teacher and never set foot inside the school again."

Some kid?

Charlie knew he needed to speak to Mel, but how could he ever broach the topic and mention that boy's name? Their *taboo* subject. Instead, he concentrated on Ed, not believing how quickly he was talking. It was obvious he knew much more than he was prepared to divulge. However, the crux of his statement made sense and wasn't dissimilar to the rumour, which escalated around school. It was big news, primary gossip for fifteen and sixteen-year-olds, and although the stories became more and more exaggerated, Charlie definitely remembered the bullying narrative.

"And you say you haven't seen him since?"

Ed looked to his left and into the trees. "No." He turned back. "Why?"

"Because he was in the local Lincolnshire newspaper last month." Again, Charlie paused to watch Ed's reaction. But he just continued to glare at him, as if desperate for him to finish what he had to say. "And a few weeks ago, somebody killed him." Ed looked as though he'd lost the ability to speak, and Charlie couldn't recall the last time he had seen him blink. But Charlie didn't hold back. He'd come this far. "Actually murdered him, Ed. Slit his throat, apparently."

Charlie slid his finger across his neck to mimic the act. Was he actually enjoying himself?

Ollie knocked lightly on Hazel's door. He didn't want to alarm her; especially given the way she'd screamed out in the night. "Who is it?" he heard her ask faintly. Was she asleep? *Shit.* It wouldn't be the best time to chat if he'd just woken her. Ollie had already deciphered Hazel could be quite moody, and he needed her in one of her better frames of mind. "It's me. Ollie. Is it okay if I come in?"

"Doors open," Hazel replied, noncommittal.

Ollie pushed it gently open, his eyes following the edge until Hazel eventually came into view. She was perched on the end of her bed and didn't appear sleepy. She wore grey jogging bottoms and a yellow T-shirt. Ollie noticed both contained a well-known brand logo and knew they wouldn't be cheap. His ex-wife was never able to afford such luxuries, and he felt a sudden pang of sorrow.

In contrast, Ollie donned an old green vest and long white shorts which covered his knees. When he bought them online, they were above the knee in the photograph, but once they arrived, they drowned him and he knew he looked stupid. But Ollie could never be bothered to return things and instead he wore them in the hope they might shrink in the wash. They never did, and he still looked stupid.

"Got a minute, love?" His words slipped out, and he could feel the heat rising in his cheeks as he realised his own overfamiliarity.

Hazel sighed — this wasn't going well — before fixing on a smile and looking Ollie in the eye. "Of course. Something wrong?" She tugged at her wide headband, readjusting the hair beneath until she removed the last strand from her face. Ollie gave himself time and tried to regain some of the confidence he originally felt when painting.

"Your intruder," he said, and noticed Hazel baulk. *Keep her calm, you bloody idiot.* "Well, not intruder. The person you thought you saw the other—"

"It's okay, Ollie," she interrupted. "You can call it an intruder. Now, what's wrong?"

Ollie appreciated her sensitivity. He couldn't believe how flustered he was. Normally, nothing phased him and he could usually say what he wanted to say and suffer any consequences later. "Well, the night after your intruder, erm, visitor…" Hazel smiled. "… I heard someone outside. Walking on the gravel." Hazel's interest perked, and she sat forward on the edge of the bed, the palms of her hands pushed against the soft-looking flowery duvet. "And they had a torch."

Hazel stood and stepped over to the mini fridge in the corner of her room. Retrieving two bottles of water, she held one aloft to Ollie. He nodded and waited for her to step back over and hand it to him.

"Could have been anybody," Hazel spoke as she walked across the room. "Louis, Adrienne——"

"They went through the gate at the end of the footpath. I heard it open and close," he interrupted, unable to control himself. Thankfully, Hazel nodded.

"Have you told anybody else?" she asked, passing Ollie a bottle before twisting the screw top off her own. She took a small swig before replacing the blue plastic lid.

"No. No, nobody. I saw the way Joyce spoke to you, and then when you asked her if anybody else lived on the island, she, well, don't take this the wrong way, but she kind of took the piss, didn't she?"

Again, Hazel smiled. Did she like the fact Ollie was confiding in her or more his observations about Joyce? It was quite common knowledge Hazel didn't like their host, so maybe she just wanted some camaraderie.

"Forget Joyce," Hazel said dismissively, instantly disproving his theory. She flicked her head as to prove her point. "She'll get her comeuppance one day soon…"

Ollie glared at her. *What does that mean?* "… but now you've told me this, I'm convinced there's somebody else who we haven't yet met."

Shit.

"Yeah, me too," Ollie replied too quickly, sensing his right foot jigging on the spot. He hadn't really considered anybody else was on the island, but now she'd suggested it again, Ollie became quite scared of the can of worms he might be opening. He briefly contemplated questioning Hazel what the person looked like who she believed she had seen in the night. However, he promptly dismissed the idea, realising he may have to divulge things he didn't want to bring up himself. "By the way," he said, desperately attempting to keep his voice level. "I overheard you tell Ed you wished to speak to him, too. One morning at breakfast." He waited for his words to sink in, hoping it did not offend Hazel that he'd been eavesdropping. "But I don't trust him, and you shouldn't either." Another moment's silence ensued, and Ollie felt awkward. He was on a roll, and wanted to grab the opportunity, but was also conscious he could be overstepping the mark. *Why isn't she replying?* "Do you want to pair up, Hazel? You and me. Nobody else wants to listen, but something weird is going on and I think we can get to the bottom of it."

Hazel almost laughed at Ollie. He was like a child. But maybe not a totally useless little boy. Ollie was right, she did want to talk to Ed, but he didn't back her around the dinner table and Hazel felt let down. She also confided in him about her job situation, but again, Ed offered little in return. Besides, he couldn't take his eyes off Mel and she too told Hazel she thought she had gone too far by sneaking into Joyce's room.

She unscrewed the lid of her bottle and took another small swig of water, her eyes not leaving Ollie. He looked like an excited schoolboy. Perhaps she could use him? He would do anything she asked. Gullible little fool that he was.

"Yes," she said, and Ollie's face lit up like a beacon. "I think we could be quite the team, young Oliver."

20

_____

ED EXPERIENCED an ice-cold shiver course along his spine and immediately felt queasy. The way Charlie slid his finger across his throat had the obvious and desired effect.

"Why haven't you said anything before?" Ed asked, trying to keep the conversation as light as the subject matter allowed. Did Charlie believe that Will Parry's death and the island reunion were connected? Surely not. He recalled the email Joyce sent out and remembered the list of names had been intentionally left blank, but there was no way Parry's name would have been amongst them. Did Joyce even teach him?

"I only read it last week, thought nothing of it. Until a few days ago."

Charlie paused and looked at Ed. His expression suggested he had another question in mind, and Ed couldn't shake the sinking feeling about what it might be.

"It's just being here," Charlie eventually replied, standing and slowly walking away from the bench. "It's brought back memories from Ridgeview..." Charlie stopped and turned to face Ed, "... and to be honest, mate, they're not good memories. Things I thought I'd left behind years ago." He turned and walked again, towards the clearing where Ed and Mel were the day before. *Why is he going that way?* Charlie continued to talk as he wandered, leaving Ed no choice but to scurry after him.

On the cusp of asking him to expand on his *bad memories*, Ed soon dispelled such a stupid notion. Although Charlie's admission intrigued him, he needed to change the subject.

"Where are you going now? This isn't the way back."

Charlie turned again, brushed his hand through his thick hair and spoke, walking backwards. Ed noticed a slight smile etched across his face as though he was suddenly beginning to enjoy their excursion into the woods.

"Oh," he said, his eyes fixed on Ed's. "Mel lost an earring yesterday, and she told me she was down here…" he nodded towards the exact spot where they had been, "… in this clearing." Ed could feel the heat rising. He said nothing, the words stuck in his throat, even if he wanted to. Yet Charlie had no problem finding something else to say. "Mind you, I've absolutely no idea what she was doing down here." He paused for effect. "Have you, Ed?"

Ed left Charlie alone to look for Mel's earring. He couldn't take anymore. No more questions, no more of his company, and no more of his cryptic accusations. But it wasn't just Mel's earring and how she may have lost it, it's what happened to Will Parry too. Did Charlie believe it to be a freak happenstance? A twist of fate? And what about Mel's message in the mirror? Ed never did ask her what it said. Should he have done? He pondered as he walked, his eyes continually drifting to the mainland, which incomprehensibly looked a little further away.

Meandering through the woods, his mind caught up in his own thoughts, Ed deliberated what to do next. For over an hour, he wandered on footpaths that no one had trodden for years. Overgrown but passable with care. But Ed barely took notice of the vegetation or the direction in which he ambled.

The sound of his stomach rumbling finally forced him to check his watch. Less than an hour to dinner. Standing still, he gathered his bearings. The château was in the centre, at the highest point of the island, which made navigation quite easy. He noticed a track to his left. By now, Ed realised the woods contained a myriad of trails meandering throughout the trees, down to the shoreline and, in return, back up to the property. But as he stepped onto the pathway and began his latest uphill climb, he noticed a wooden construction over to his right, at the foot of the hill, adjacent to the waterside. He squinted his eyes, trying to establish exactly what it could be. Was it a shed of some description? *Of course,. The boathouse.* He recalled Joyce telling them of a small dinghy kept inside. *The way out of here?*

Ed's stomach gurgled again, and he knew he had to get back, not to quell his hunger, but to ensure no unnecessary focus lay upon him. The last thing he needed on top of everything else was for anybody to question where he'd been or why he'd been missing for a sizeable chunk of the afternoon. With one final look at the wooden outbuilding, Ed rubbed the palms of his hands along his shorts and began his ascent.

Once back, he breathed a sigh of relief as the garden lay empty, just deckchairs sporadically left abandoned across the freshly cut lawn. Quickly, he scooted upstairs, craving to remain alone, at least for the extra few minutes before dinner.

But as soon as he opened his door, he noticed a copy of his book on his pillow. *His* novel. And as he tentatively stepped closer, he could see something attached to the cover. Following a quick glance over his shoulder – Ed was becoming paranoid about being watched at all times – he sauntered to his bed. Something indeed was stuck to the cover. One of those sticky notes, pale yellow with crude handwriting scrawled across it.

Allowing himself another peek over his shoulder, he gently peeled the *post-it* from the book and read the barely legible writing.

I know who this book is about...

Ed's heart thumped as he strained his eyes and reread the note over and over. The sound of Adrienne ringing the bell made him jump from his skin. Spinning quickly, he saw something through the crack in his door. A flash of a shadow, maybe? He ran to the opening and looked both ways along the landing, but nobody was there, to begin with at least.

One by one, his fellow guests surfaced from their respective rooms. First Ollie, who only offered Ed a brief nod of his head before taking the grand staircase down to the foyer. The door swinging open next to him made him spin to his left, only to see Mel and Charlie vacate their room. Charlie gave him a look he couldn't quite decipher, whilst Mel said "good evening" accompanied by her usual lovely smile. Charlie told his wife to hurry, as he was desperate for a pre-dinner drink. As Ed watched them descend the steps, Hazel appeared and nodded in his direction as he clung to the handle of his door. "Come on," Joyce called after him, standing at the foot of the stairs. Ed hadn't noticed her before. She turned her back, still speaking, as she strolled outside. "You must be starving after all that walking, Edward." Ed glanced at the book on his bed and the *post-it* note, which lay crumpled by its side.

Following dinner, he joined the others on the terrace for a drink, in no particular hurry to return to his room. He spent the entire meal studying each person, looking for any tell-tale clue that they were behind the note. But nobody looked at him for any longer than a brief glance or to acknowledge him in conversation. Whoever it was, they were an excellent actor. Only Joyce appeared to be showing him overt attention, glancing towards him throughout. *Was it her? Was Hazel right? Is there someone else on the island?*

Ed was the last person to retire upstairs, apart from Adrienne, who was busy collecting glasses. Begrudgingly, Ed returned to his room and slowly opened his bedroom door. Instinctively, his eyes focused on the bed and he couldn't believe what he was seeing; or not.

The book was gone, and the note too. Ed scrambled to his bed, pulling back the duvet, tossing the pillows onto the floor before getting down on his hands and knees and searching underneath. He stood again, checking the tops of furniture before staring at his open door.

But everything remained deathly silent. The only sound was the ticking of the enormous grandfather clock echoing in the hallway below.

. . .

The following morning, Joyce watched Ed as he finally joined the rest of the group for breakfast. She couldn't believe how ashen he appeared, as though he hadn't slept in weeks. His eyes were red around the rim and flickered from person to person. Was he looking for anybody in particular? She recalled how quiet he had been at dinner the evening before, too. At first she presumed it was because he'd walked so far during the afternoon — Joyce had seen him whilst out exercising herself — but Ed was fit, and a little exertion wouldn't leave him that exhausted. Eventually, he stepped over to the coffee percolator and poured himself a cupful of the dark brown liquid. Turning, he sipped at the drink, again his eyes taking in every one of his fellow guests. He was definitely looking for someone.

She then noticed Charlie watching Ed, too. He appeared just as transfixed as Joyce was herself. She resumed her focus on Ed. He finished one cup of coffee before pouring himself a second. She knew how hot it was straight from the machine and couldn't believe he could drink one so quickly. *It must be burning his throat*, she thought to herself. *Something's happened. Why else would he be acting this way?*

Charlie couldn't take his eyes off Ed. He looked different from the day before; pale and rugged. He presumed Ed wasn't particularly concerned with his personal appearance, especially compared to himself. However, that morning, it seemed as though he had made no effort at all. His hair stuck up at angles and his T-shirt hung loosely at the neckline, creased and ill-fitting. Was it Will Parry's death that caused him such a sleep-deprived night?

But Charlie had other things on his mind. The previous day, after Ed left him in the clearing, he spent the next ten minutes searching for his wife's missing earring. She'd told him roughly where it could be, so Charlie knew he was in the right area. He noticed how red Ed went when he explained what he was looking for and he soon made his excuses to leave. Perhaps Ed found his wife attractive. Charlie couldn't blame him. Everybody found her attractive.

As he was on the cusp of giving up, he heard footsteps approaching from the same direction he'd walked in – from the bench. He stood perfectly still, believing there was nowhere to run or hide. The person fell into view and Charlie let out an exaggerated sigh of relief.

"Shit. You nearly gave me a heart attack."

"Sorry, I came to find you."

Charlie detected an air of disappointment across his wife's face as her eyes darted around. Was she hoping to see somebody else? "Why, what's wrong?" he asked, pissed off.

"Just wondered if you've found it?" Mel retorted, quickly stepping past him into the clearing, her eyes searching the ground below.

"No, I haven't," Charlie replied. "Perhaps you should take more care."

He noticed her looking at him as he left her alone to continue with her search.

21

HAZEL BELIEVED she knew most of the party better than others. *Look at him now,* she thought as she watched Ed helping himself to copious amounts of strong coffee outside on the breakfast terrace. *He's got secrets.* However, he had divulged nothing to her during their walk and she didn't believe he said much to anybody else either. Possibly Mel, as he so obviously liked her, another thing Hazel had picked up upon.

Hazel then glanced at Joyce, who was also studying Ed from the corner of her eye. She needed to get back into her room, find the notebook, and see what else she could discover. *There's something she's not telling us.*

Next she looked at Charlie, who too appeared mesmerised by Ed's strange antics. Mel was her usual nervous self, and Hazel couldn't help but smile when she glanced at Ollie, who also couldn't take his eyes off Ed. *What a bloody idiot.* But Hazel's intuition informed her that Ollie had a secret too. Slowly, she stepped around the periphery of the group to speak to her new comrade. *Holy shit,* she thought, *every damn one of us has a skeleton in the cupboard.* And then she recalled the boy at the end of her bed.

It disappointed Ollie that Hazel only appeared to have eyes for Ed bloody Lawson that morning. He'd been so excited since their impromptu meeting and wanted to get her alone again so they could continue to build a plan of action. Patience wasn't Ollie's strong point, and he forced himself not to march over and talk to her right there and then.

So, instead, his eyes followed hers. She couldn't stop staring at Ed. Ollie took little interest in the author, but now, he could see how rough Ed actually looked. Was he ill? If so, should he be mingling with the rest of them? *Why don't you go upstairs and write a bloody book?* Ollie became so lost in his thoughts, he didn't even notice Hazel had stopped glaring at Ed and almost jumped out of his skin when she tapped him on the shoulder.

"Morning," she whispered. Ollie composed himself quickly and grinned ear to ear, something Hazel picked up on before he had a chance to speak. "Calm yourself down, Ollie," she said, even quieter than before. Ollie spotted Joyce peer over and he felt himself redden.

"Sorry," he replied. He continued to look forward to nobody in particular and secretly praised himself for his ability to look inconspicuous.

"Have you noticed who isn't here?" Hazel asked, her face now turned sideways so Ollie could feel her warm breath in his ear. Ollie blushed further as he desperately tried to search who was missing. *What kind of fucking private detective misses something as obvious as this?* His eyes darted everywhere, individually clocking who was, and who wasn't, outside on the terrace.

"Adrienne," he announced with pride, a little too loudly. Joyce looked over again.

"No, you fucking idiot," Hazel retorted under her breath. Ollie felt hurt. *Would one of those detectives on the cop shows he loved to watch talk to their partner in such a way?* "She's cooking breakfast, isn't she?" Ollie nodded like a schoolboy. "It's Louis. He isn't here."

Ollie's eyes darted again to confirm Hazel's observations. She was right, Louis wasn't there. But then she ridiculed him further. "He's in the barn. I watched him take his coffee out there." With that, Hazel took a step away before turning to face him for the first time. She kept her voice to a whisper. "If you want to be my partner, you really need to be more observant, Oliver."

He watched as she walked away, her mass of auburn hair swishing in unison with each step. Ollie was already going off his new associate, and he wondered if she was taking the piss out of him. He hopelessly wanted to ask his wife what she thought. She was always his go-to person, his lookout, his soulmate, and now he desperately craved her. In fact, Ollie realised that since they arrived on the island, he was missing his wife more and more as each day passed by.

"Penny for your thoughts?" Mel waited patiently for Ed to help himself to his third coffee of the morning before walking out onto the lawn. He placed a plate containing a solitary croissant on one of the circular metal tables. She noticed a slight tremor in his hand as he sipped at his coffee.

"Oh, hi, Mel," Ed responded, unenthusiastically. It

immediately dampened her spirits. It was the first time they'd been alone since their infamous meeting in the woods, and she, for one, hadn't been able to stop the butterflies from fluttering deep inside the pit of her stomach. She prayed Ed felt the same way. But that wasn't all. Mel wondered what on earth her husband wanted with him the day before.

"Everything okay?" she probed. "I saw you and Charlie walk into the woods yesterday."

Ed looked at her, and she noticed the bags under his eyes. They definitely weren't there before. *Shit, something's happened*.

"Did Charlie find your earring?" Ed eventually asked, his tone evasive.

Mel instinctively felt her lobe. "No. How do you know he was looking for it? Is that why he took you off yesterday?"

She listened intently as Ed belatedly opened up and explained about his and Charlie's venture into the woods, down to the bench, and finally into the clearing. "Yes. I told him where I thought I lost it. I wanted to cover my tracks. You didn't say anything about us, did you?" She watched as Ed took in her question. A little colour returned to his cheeks.

"Of course I didn't," he replied, his mood lifting slightly. "I just left him looking and went for a long walk." He eventually turned his head to face her. "But I thought he knew about us, you know, in the clearing?"

Mel sighed, and the butterflies threatened to return. "Me too. That's why I told him what I did. I had to know if he suspected anything." She paused. "Charlie doesn't know, Ed," Mel concluded, shaking her head slightly. "There's no way he could keep quiet about something like that."

The sound of Joyce's voice from underneath the shade of the terrace made them both look up. Ed collected his plate, and they strolled back towards the house.

"What else did Charlie want with you in the woods?" she asked, keeping her focus ahead and trying not to make too big a thing of it. Mel knew her husband hadn't got Ed on his own just to look for one of her earrings. Charlie's mind didn't work like that.

"Sorry?" Ed stumbled. "Oh, yeah, just catching up. Nothing important." Mel instantly knew he was lying, and she slowed her pace as they reached the terrace. Ed looked at her.

"Tell me the truth, Ed. I can't stand any more secrets."

Ed nodded. "I'll tell you later." He stopped himself from saying something else.

"What is it?" she asked. His next question threw her completely.

"Did you leave your copy of my book in my room last night?"

Ed couldn't help but smile when he asked Ollie if he'd read his book yet. He waited until Joyce gave them their list of jobs for the day before stepping over to him. He stood alone at the back of the group. Mel had shaken her head when he asked her the same question, and Ed knew she was telling the truth. Ollie told him he'd sooner eat his own shit than read one of his novels and immediately walked away. Although Ed was taken aback, he had to laugh. *Of course he hasn't read it.* He doubted Ollie had ever read a book in his life. But Ollie didn't like Ed. There was something about his mannerisms. He doubted Ollie liked anybody much. He shared nothing with any of the fellow guests, apart from the school they all attended, of course. *The only common denominator between all of us.*

"No, mate, but I think my missus has been reading it." Charlie lied as he glanced at Ed. "But you probably already know that."

Why was he asking him if he's read his book? Charlie was more concerned about Will Parry being murdered just weeks before.

Ed shrugged his shoulders, but just as he hoped he would leave him alone, he faltered before speaking again.

"Yesterday, down in the woods, you said something."

"Did I?" Charlie tried to recollect their conversation.

"Yeah. You said something about Ridgeview and being here. Didn't you say it's brought back memories and they're not good memories?" Charlie hesitated as Ed finished what he had to say. "Things you thought you'd left behind years ago. What were you talking about, Charlie?"

Brushing his fingers through his hair, Charlie stalled whilst he considered a reply. It wasn't what he'd been expecting. "I don't know," was all he could think of. "I guess it's this reunion. Hasn't it sparked memories for you, too?"

Ed smiled weakly and offered Charlie a knowing nod of his head. He bid him farewell, and Charlie watched as he walked nonchalantly back indoors. He breathed a sigh of relief, pleased Ed didn't quiz him further, before looking around to see if anybody had witnessed their encounter.

As he slowly followed in Ed's footsteps, Charlie wondered how much he should disclose if he pressed him further. He had always believed their secret was secure, and even though he had expressed no sympathy to Mel about her alleged message in the mirror, he found it difficult to banish those words from his mind.

I know what you did…

22

ED ARRIVED at the gate first. He momentarily paused; suddenly aware he was running directly towards somebody screaming. However, before he had time to think, it happened again, another ear-piercing shriek. The sound of footsteps from behind made him jump, but the sight of Ollie sprinting across the lawn allowed him some temporary relief. A familiar face, whatever they thought of each other, at least informed him he didn't have to go into the woods alone.

"What the hell was that?" Ollie asked, staring over Ed's shoulder and into the trees beyond.

"No idea. It came from—"

Yet another scream. Or on this occasion, more of a wailing noise. The sound of grief.

"Come on," Ollie instructed, before bolting off ahead without hesitation. Ed had to hand it to him. He appeared to hold no fear, whilst inside, Ed was secretly shitting himself.

The cry of pain subsided to weeping by the time they reached Hazel. She stood motionless, apart from an occasional shrug of her shoulders in unison with her convulsive sobs. Ollie and Ed followed the trail through the dense woods, before reaching the pathway which spilt both ways. The pitiful sounds led them to the right and when they arrived at Hazel's side, Ed couldn't help but notice where he was again; the bench near the clearing. *Why does everything lead here?*

Ollie put his arm around Hazel's shoulder, making her simultaneously scream again.

"Hey, it's okay, it's okay. It's just us, Hazel." Ollie nodded towards Ed. "Just me and Ed."

Hazel turned to face them. Her expression contorted. Long strands of black eyeliner ran from the corner of each eye. The contrast against her bright red lipstick looked surreal, like a poorly made-up clown. Slowly, her head turned back towards the water and, in slow-motion, she raised her right arm before extending her finger.

Ed couldn't believe neither he nor Ollie had spotted it before. Floating against the rocky shoreline was a body. Face down. Bobbing up and down over the repetitive lapping waves, its arms and legs splayed out like a starfish. Ed immediately recognised Tony's light blue T-shirt. It ballooned upwards, full of trapped air, and Ed thought he might be sick.

The first thing Ollie thought of was his last meeting with Tony. Ironically, it was the night when Hazel screamed out and everyone gathered on the landing before Joyce eventually went to see to her. But Joyce and Tony argued and everybody's loathing towards her ex-husband spilled out into the open. Ollie didn't hold back either. *"Just fuck off, Tony. Everybody hates you anyway."*

But Ollie hadn't finished. He wanted to understand

the reasons behind Tony's abhorrent behaviour, so he waited for Joyce to attend to Hazel, and for the others to retreat to their respective rooms.

"What the hell is wrong with you?" Ollie enquired sharply, walking directly into his room without waiting for an invitation. Tony laughed and told him it was none of his concern. "Unless you're going to beat it out of me?" he teased. Ollie could sense the heat and hatred rising inside and he so wished he could put a stop to Tony once and for all. *Everybody would be pleased with me. Nobody likes the guy. Perhaps I would become some kind of hero in the team if I could make Tony disappear?*

"You need to watch your back," Ollie said, stepping away, his mind full of schemes and tricks to get Tony off their case. However, Tony appeared bigger and stronger once they were alone, so Ollie retreated further. "One of these days, somebody is going to make you regret the way you talk to people, the way you treat them."

Tony laughed, more of a guffaw, another ridiculing. "And how are you going to do that, you little piece of shit?" he called after him as Ollie left his room and shuffled along the landing.

And so Ollie watched the lifeless body floating upside down in the sea. He wondered what Tony would look like if they turned him over. Would his skin resemble the wrinkles that form when you stay in the bath too long? Would he be pale or blue? Ollie didn't know how long it took for a person to decompose or if the fish would have begun to nibble away. Part of him wanted to wade in and flip him over, whilst his other half preferred to turn and run.

"You okay, Ollie?" He looked up and saw Ed leaning over him. He couldn't remember bending down, his hands on his knees as though he might be sick. Gradually, he stood upright, his eyes not once leaving the floating body in the water.

"I'm glad he's dead," Ollie declared, wiping his mouth with the back of his hand. "And I'm pleased I called him a twat in front of everybody," he added. Ed glared at him. "Oh, come on, Edward," Ollie smirked, "I know for a fact you hated him too."

Last to arrive at the sorrowful scene were Mel and Charlie. Joyce sent Adrienne to fetch them from their room after they had followed the screaming down to the shoreline, too.

"What's going on?" asked Charlie, as they stepped from the shadows near the clearing. He cursed when Mel bumped into him as he abruptly came to a halt. Joyce mouthed something to Louis, who appeared pleased to be dismissed from the commotion. He quickly dashed off, not once looking back.

"Oh my God!" Mel exclaimed, stepping around Charlie and clamping her hand over her mouth. Charlie knew he should have protected her, but the floating body mesmerised him too.

"What the hell happened?" he asked nobody in particular.

"I've just sent Louis to take the dinghy to the mainland. The police will soon be on their way." Joyce informed the group. "But before they arrive, who discovered the body?"

. . .

Ollie cleared his throat and Ed noticed he still appeared quite upbeat by the situation, despite almost vomiting at the scene. He couldn't believe how he was acting. Was it nerves or did he know something?

"I heard a scream," he began. Ed noticed the look on Joyce's face. Was she expecting some kind of confession? "I'd been in my room," he continued, "you know, lying on my bed. I'd been reading Ed's book as it hap—"

"Just fucking tell us, Ollie." Charlie interrupted. Finally, Mel's vacant expression turned to anger, and she glared at her husband.

"Charlie!" she shouted. "Give the man a chance, for fuck's sake!"

A look of disbelief spread between the group. Even Hazel appeared to momentarily recover from her shock. She sat on the bench, Adrienne's arm wrapped around her, desperate to offer some kind of comfort.

"As I was saying," all attention fell back onto Ollie. "I sprinted to the bottom of the garden, you know, following the scream. I saw Ed at the gate …".

His pause unsettled Ed, not helped when everybody turned to face him.

"… yes, anyway. Ed and I ran through the woods to the edge of the sea, erm, the water thing, the—"

"The shoreline," Ed completed his sentence. Ollie's talking was frantic. He hopped from foot to foot, his hands rubbing up and down each arm as if he was freezing cold.

"Yes, yes, the shoreline. I know the word. Such a clever twat, aren't you?"

Ed wanted to shut him up, not confident how far Ollie might bend the truth. He appeared capable of saying anything and his rambling was out of control.

"And we found Hazel," everybody turned towards her.

She attempted a smile, but faltered and soon became lost within herself once more. "Yes, yes. She spotted him." Ollie took over once more. "Well, she found a body. You know. In the water."

Mel gasped again, and Ed noticed how Charlie ignored her. He desperately wanted to step over and hold her.

"And who the fuck is it?" asked Charlie, showing no remorse. Everybody stared at the bobbing body once more. Ed couldn't believe Charlie was even asking the question. Wasn't it obvious? The silence became unbearable despite it being only seconds.

"It's Tony, you jerk," Ed confirmed. Ollie shot him a look as if to ask, *how dare you finish my story?*

"Tony?" Charlie stepped closer to the water, quickly followed by Mel, who put her arm on his shoulder. Ed wanted her to back away, or better still, push the idiot in to get a better look.

"Yes, Tony," Joyce spoke at last, her voice unbelievably melancholy. "He must have drowned."

Everybody went quiet. Even Ollie stopped jigging his legs. Despite their obvious hostility towards each other, he *was* her ex-husband.

"It's just a terrible accident, Joyce," Adrienne replied. She left Hazel on the bench and stepped over to their host, her employer, and held Joyce's hand with both of her own. Joyce smiled affectionately at the girl who had barely spoken before. She nodded her gratitude before looking back down at the body.

"Do you think he jumped?" Charlie asked, a glimmer of joviality in his tone.

Ed could no longer contain himself. "Shut the fuck up, Charlie."

Charlie stopped staring at the floating corpse and

instead turned to face Ed. Ed needed to keep up the pretence, but was secretly delighted when Ollie stepped between them.

"Come on, come on," he said. "This isn't helping. Back away, the pair of you."

They both did as instructed and Ed thought Charlie looked as pleased as him that the situation didn't escalate.

"We don't know anything, Charlie." Joyce broke the silence, as if oblivious to the stand-off between them. "It's why the police are on their way." She looked at Hazel before finishing. "They'll soon sort this out, dear."

23

MEL AND CHARLIE were the last to arrive again that evening. Adrienne prepared a cold buffet, which Mel thought considerate, given nobody would be in the mood for a formal gathering around the dining room table. Also, Adrienne spent most of the day seeing to Hazel. She explained she'd eventually dropped off to sleep, albeit with the help of a couple of pills and a powerful shot of brandy.

Two police officers questioned everybody at the château. It was quite informal, and they were soon content it was a tragic accident or possibly Tony took his own life. Joyce certainly didn't hold back and painted a very sad picture of Tony's recent years. She said he was practically out on the streets leading up to the trip, sleeping in hostels and receiving counselling for his drug addiction. Mel could feel the guilt rise inside at every step of Joyce's story and remonstrated with herself for ever wishing Tony ill. Finally, the police left with the strict instructions nobody else should leave the island until a full post-mortem was complete.

Mel helped herself to a couple of sandwiches plus some cold quiche before carrying her plate out onto the terrace and into the welcoming cooler air.

"Fancy one of these, too?"

Ed sat at a table at the rear of the patio, under the shade of a huge wisteria, which looked splendid in full colour. It was more than she could say of Ed. The glass of red wine he held aloft at least made her perk up a little, though.

"Hell, yes. The biggest glass you've got, please." She was pleased to see Ed smile.

As he poured her a drink, she sat next to him and pulled her chair closer.

"You okay?" he asked solemnly.

"Yeah," Mel attempted a smile. "I'm okay. It's just, well, it's all such a shock, isn't it? I can't imagine what it was like to actually find the body." She involuntarily shivered.

Ed appeared to check they were out of earshot before dragging his chair closer still.

"Mel, can I tell you something?"

Although pleased he wanted to confide in her, she was equally afraid of what he might say. She couldn't handle many more secrets. "Sure, Ed. What is it?"

Ed explained about the note on the book left on his pillow. He'd asked everybody if they had read his novel, in a roundabout way, and once satisfied none of the group had left the post-it, it rendered him devoid of ideas.

Mel stalled, deliberating whether to ask the question on the tip of her tongue. "And the note definitely said they know who the book is about?"

Ed looked at her, and she noticed how anxious he'd become, as if realising what was coming next. He nodded, and she had to ask.

"So, who is it about?"

Ollie felt nothing but relief when the police finally departed. They only asked general questions, nothing too personal, but he didn't want to mention his argument with Tony. He was equally pleased Ed didn't repeat what he'd said about wanting him dead. Joyce's story of Tony's drug addiction and near homelessness appeared to appease the gendarmerie. It all tied in with his hostile and anti-social behaviour since they arrived. Ollie knew many people like that back in London. He smiled that he'd worked it out for himself.

However, Ollie couldn't allow himself to get bogged down with how Tony may have topped himself. As far as he was concerned, he was a pest and the rest of them were better off without him. He was more worried about Hazel, upstairs in her room, sleeping off the shock of finding a body floating in the water. They still had to put their plan into practice, and now, more than ever, Ollie wanted to find out more about Joyce Young. Something wasn't right and he didn't trust her. Even talking with the police, she had all the answers, as if her script was ready-made.

Charlie considered it as some sort of relief when Joyce faltered once or twice as she spoke about happier times with Tony. It proved she could be human after all. They met at Ridgeview Grammar of all places. The school employed him as a general handyperson, or caretaker, as the title went in those days. She explained he already suffered from depression, something Joyce thought she could help with, and Charlie found himself sucked in by her recollections.

But then Joyce moved her personal story onto much harder times between them. Times she didn't want to go into great detail about, even though she clarified that domestic violence had crept into their relationship. "The beginning of the end," she called it, and how frightened she became to go home after work. "I finally met somebody else," she said, looking to the floor, lost in her own world. "Somebody younger. But at least he made me happy."

Charlie glanced at Mel and noticed how white she'd gone. He experienced the exact same emotions as her appearance conveyed and suddenly yearned to be anywhere but in Joyce Young's company.

The next morning during breakfast, Joyce announced she didn't expect anyone to do any work for the rest of the day, given how visibly shaken they still were.

Hazel had slept little, despite whatever Joyce instructed Adrienne to drop in her brandy, and was pleasantly surprised that Joyce took the horrible experience into consideration. It equally staggered her when Joyce made a similar offer to the one the day they all arrived.

"If it's all too much for any of you," she announced, "I completely understand and you are welcome to leave. Once the police have carried out their post-mortem, of course."

Hazel looked around at the others to gauge if anybody appeared as tempted as her. If they were, nobody gave it away.

"Do we still get the money?" All eyes spun to her.

"Oh, come on," she said, "you all want to know." She couldn't resist smiling when everybody then turned to their host once more, silently proving her point.

"No dear," Joyce replied calmly. "That *isn't* part of the agreement, is it?"

Hazel felt her hatred building once more. What was it about that woman she despised so much? "Not even half?" She was unable to control her compulsion to ridicule her host. "After all, we are into our second week," she added derisively.

Joyce continued to stare at Hazel. She didn't flinch, her expression constant, in control and totally emotionless. And the longer she glared, the more the tension rose between them. Finally, Ollie spoke up.

"What about Tony's share?" Hazel and Joyce both turned their attention to him, but not before one final moment stand-off. Ollie stepped from one foot to the other. "Well, we've taken on his part of the work, haven't we?" He sought support from Hazel, but she conveyed her disapproval by lowering her gaze to the ground, signalling for him to stay silent.

"I'm afraid not, Oliver," Joyce continued in her condescending manner. "I'll have to use more than what I would have paid him to get his damn body back to Britain." She stalled. "Unless any of you would like to chip in, of course?"

Silence ensued, and Hazel felt eyes flicker from her to the next person. The atmosphere was suffocating, nobody knew what to say. Inevitably, Joyce spoke again.

"It's all very sad, I know," she began. Hazel considered her subdued manner entirely insincere. "But I can tell you all, Tony wasn't a happy man," she took a deep breath. "Ever since our divorce," she continued, her eyes moving from person to person without dwelling on anybody in particular. "Well, long before then, Tony became depressed. He'd been on a cocktail of pills for years. Uppers, downers, goodness knows what."

Hazel studied Joyce intently, searching for any tell-tale sign of genuine bereavement. Even in the brief space of time they had been at the château, it was obvious to all that they didn't get on, to the point of despising one another. Hazel recalled the conversation in the dining room when Joyce commented on why Tony had been invited along. She said he had exceptional DIY skills, but what else did she say? *"It's the main reason you're here."* The *main* reason? What other reason could there be? Reconciliation? Well, that seemed pretty unlikely. You could cut the atmosphere with a knife when they were in the same room. So what did Joyce actually mean? She soon came to her own inevitable conclusion.

Joyce eventually informed everyone they were to do as they pleased for the remainder of the day. "Just stay on the island, as the police instructed," she added with a sarcastic smile towards Hazel.

"What will you do, Joyce?" Hazel asked as politely as she could muster. She didn't give a shit if truth be told, but it didn't harm to keep up the pretence. Joyce deliberated her question, as if trying to read her intentions. "I mean, are you going to be okay? It must be tremendously upsetting losing your husband, ex or not. And you do seem to be coping particularly well." Hazel could swear she heard a collective gasp within the room.

"I'm going to keep myself busy by helping Adrienne in the kitchen." She smiled derisively at Hazel. "But likewise, you appear to have overcome the shock of seeing a dead body for the first time remarkably quickly."

Joyce turned and walked away with Adrienne. Hazel noticed Ollie looking at her, but she ignored him and tried to hold herself together as she returned to her room. She was boiling with rage and knew she couldn't last another two or three weeks in the company of Joyce Young.

Something had to give.

———

24

THE FOLLOWING MORNING, Mel was happy to resume her tasks. She'd spent the previous day mooching around her room or venturing outside, unable to settle doing either. She even attempted to read Ed's book, both fascinated and equally scared, but each time she began, she shut it with a bang. Deep down, Mel didn't want to know who it was about. It still pissed her off, Ed hadn't told her. He dismissed the note as fantasy, whoever wrote it. "It's not about anybody I know," he declared. "It's all made up, make-believe." But Mel doubted him, and she could tell how shaken up he was about the entire situation. More reason not to find out for herself.

However, Mel was still delighted when Joyce paired her up to work with Ed. She loved being in his company and realised that she craved his attention. Perhaps it was because she had never been with another man. She met Charlie at school and never knew, until a few days earlier, what it felt like to be close to somebody else. It was akin to an adventure, a dare, and Mel Green wanted more.

Their latest task was to prepare the numerous flower

beds for new plants. Mel thought it ideal to take their minds off Tony's floating body and all the paraphernalia of the police asking questions.

Once they began work, Mel secretly watched Ed from the corner of her eye as he dug weeds and effortlessly tossed them into the wheelbarrow sitting between them. It scared her how attractive she found him.

After a while, she stood and mopped her brow. Struggling to think of anything in particular to talk about, she decided it would be an ideal opportunity to tell Ed about Hazel and her visit to Joyce's room. She had sworn to secrecy, but she needed to offload on someone, and Ed was the only person she trusted. She also wanted his opinion about what Hazel did. Would he concur and believe it out of order to go snooping around other people's personal space? He listened intently as Mel relayed the story, but as soon as she finished, he just resumed digging the flowerbed. But, just as she presumed he wouldn't make any comment at all, Ed stopped and turned his head to face her.

"I'm not so sure about Hazel," he said slowly, as if choosing every word on its own merit. "The way her work suddenly dried up. Joyce kind of made fun of her struggling and Hazel has detested her ever since. It's like a vendetta."

But his reply didn't convince Mel, and she didn't particularly believe Joyce had singled Hazel out.

"Joyce knows about all of our jobs," she replied, leaning on a fork protruding from the earth. "It's why I think Hazel may be right about her. I never saw her with a mobile phone back on the mainland and she doesn't give me the impression of being computer savvy, so how could she have followed us all on social media?"

Ed returned to his task once more, but instead of

being annoyed, Mel noticed the ease she was experiencing whenever in his company. He was the only person she could totally relax around, and their conversations felt natural. She was struggling to get on with any of the others, at continual pain to find any common ground, but Ed was different.

Deciding to change tack, she too bent down and dug her own section. The wheelbarrow sat between them and she wished she could move it without making it look obvious. She steered the discussion onto Ed's private life, something she knew very little about, and asked how he ended up in Ireland. Again, the conversation flowed easily, but as he explained what happened to his mum, Mel detected his voice beginning to break. He told her of his dad leaving home before he was even born. At first, she thought he was upset with his mum, but as he recounted the story of her latter days, her subsequent illness, and eventual passing, he found it difficult to keep his emotions in check. He was only fourteen years old, for goodness' sake. Mel stopped what she was doing and stepped behind the barrow to be by his side. He didn't appear to notice when she placed her arm around his shoulders.

"I'm so sorry, Ed. It must have been so tough to be on your own, and at such a young age."

"I'd had good practice to be fair," he replied, turning his head slightly. "Two years looking after Mum during her illness made me grow up fast."

"What did you do, you know, after she died?"

"That's when I moved to Lincolnshire and started at Ridgeview Grammar."

Mel detected he didn't want to particularly talk about school and that suited her fine. "And when did you go to Ireland?" she asked, pleased to keep him talking and desperate to find out as much about him as she could. He'd had a tough life, and Mel was becoming a little over-whelmed with sympathy.

"When I was twenty-one. I'd visited a few times after a friend recommended it. I guess I fell in love with the remoteness. It's an ideal place to write. However, the weather is unpredictable," he added, attempting to lift his mood. "When the sea mist rolls in, you can't see more than a foot in front of you."

"You've been there for over ten years then? It sounds wonderful. I'd love to visit."

Finally, Ed stopped what he was doing altogether and faced her. Mel realised what she'd just said. Their faces were inches apart and Mel fought every single desire within not to lean forward and kiss him.

Instead, she stood, stepped back around the barrow and picked up the garden fork.

"So?" Ed asked, changing the subject but looking equally flustered. He floundered for words, which somehow tickled her. "How are you and Charlie getting on now? Any better?"

It pleased Mel he asked her that. It allowed her the perfect opportunity to confirm what she'd already told him.

"Nothing has changed, Ed." She remained silent until he stopped bloody digging weeds and finally gave her his full attention. "I can't wait to leave him. I've honestly had enough. Being over here has brought everything to a head and made me realise what an idiot I've been these past few years."

"It might be okay once you get—"

"Ed." Mel dug the fork into the hard soil, her anger growing. "I'm leaving him. That's it. Final. And what's more? I told him this morning before breakfast. So," she paused, looking Ed in the eye. "Charlie knows and now you do, too."

To his annoyance, Ed was delighted when Joyce paired him up with Mel. He feared things may spiral between them and was worried about how much Charlie might know. Although he wanted to work with her more than anybody else, he realised the more time they spent together, the closer they were becoming. As he pushed the wheelbarrow from the barn, carrying an array of gardening implements, he noticed Joyce standing underneath the terrace. He followed her eyes as they moved from him to Mel and then back again. She smiled broadly. *Is this some kind of setup?* he thought. *Is she testing me?*

Pushing such paranoid notions to the rear of his mind, he purposefully placed the wheelbarrow in the centre of the first flower bed and set to work on one side.

Once he began the job at hand, he was thankful when Mel broke the silence and he soon became intrigued with Hazel's foray into Joyce's bedroom. Ed considered it both daring and downright crazy, but not once did he consider it intrusive. He was much more interested in what she found, and when Mel explained about the notebook with their names written inside, his attentiveness peaked. He wanted to know whose name was crossed out, but didn't want to show Mel how desperate he was. And when Mel suggested Joyce showed no interest in social media, he became equally curious about that subject, too. He hadn't given it much thought before, but now Mel mentioned it, Joyce certainly hadn't come across as someone who would be savvy at such things. He recalled her pathetic attempt at using buzzwords in the original invitation. *'The decency to* 'friend' *me?'*

Lost in thought, Mel changed the topic and asked about his past. He didn't like to talk about it, but with Mel it felt different. He even allowed his emotions to get the better of him and was so grateful when she stepped around to hold him. It took all of Ed's inner strength not to turn his head and kiss her. He knew she felt the same.

And then she confirmed she was leaving Charlie, and she made it quite obvious she wanted him to know above anybody else.

Hazel could have killed Ollie when Joyce informed them they would work together for the next two days. The kitchen needed a thorough clean. "Not just a dusting and a bit of polish," Joyce said, "but completely gutting and cleaned from top to toe." It sounded arduous, and Hazel knew it was a punishment following their stand-off at breakfast the previous day. It confirmed her suspicions when Joyce handed out duties to the others, including gardening or further decorating. But Ollie felt otherwise, and his face lit up. He even allowed a little yelp to escape his mouth. "Alright, calm down, dear," Joyce quipped, but Ollie appeared oblivious to everybody laughing at him. Until Hazel shot him a look, at least.

"Can you stop fucking whistling?" she said after closing the kitchen door to the outside world. Joyce informed everybody Adrienne would cook a barbecue the next two evenings, so Hazel and Ollie had the room to themselves for forty-eight hours.

"Sorry," Ollie replied, watching her like a child whilst awaiting his first instructions. Hazel was already beginning to regret selecting Ollie as her confidant.

"It's okay, but please, calm yourself down. You'll give us away if you carry on acting like a juvenile." She couldn't help but smile to herself when his little face lost all its energy and his mouth turned downwards. His cheeks appeared to sag in unison. Hazel stepped closer, lowered her voice and spoke in a condescending tone, even though she knew Ollie wouldn't pick up on it. "How are you at sneaking around? I'll need you to be as quiet as a church mouse."

Ollie didn't like being told off like a child, even by his new best friend. *He didn't want her to mistake him for a servant*, but her question about sneaking around soon rekindled his enthusiasm.

However, as she explained what he needed to do, he couldn't take his eyes off her hair. Several times she asked if he was listening and each time he nodded, even though it was far from the truth. Ollie's mind easily drifted. It always had.

Perhaps it wasn't just the alcohol in my system that caused the accident that day, he thought to himself, as Hazel continued with her set of complex instructions.

25

CHARLIE COULDN'T SLEEP. Mel had informed him in no uncertain terms she would leave him as soon as they returned home from the trip. He argued, refuted any claims he was having an affair and told her he had genuinely been canvassing for new business. "And you need to stay in posh hotels for that, do you?" After a while, Charlie found it impossible to argue, but he'd been in these positions before, and once they were back in England, with twenty thousand pounds in their bank account, he hoped he could dig himself out of yet another deep hole. But Mel appeared different this time, resolute, as if she didn't need him anymore.

As he lay on his back staring at the ceiling, he heard a door creak, somewhere out on the landing but very close by. He glanced at his wife. She had her back to him, curled in the foetal position, her breathing steady. Charlie felt a pang of guilt at the way he'd treated her over the years. It was one of his *middle-of-the night feelings* when every tiny concern was multiplied tenfold.

Slowly, he climbed out of bed. It wasn't the noise

which prompted him, more that he needed a drink and felt claustrophobic underneath the sheets, trapped inside his overactive mind. Another faint creak of a floorboard on the landing halted him abruptly, statue-like, with one foot positioned in front of the other. He listened intently, but everything remained eerily quiet, just the sound of vibrating cicada wings outside.

As a sudden chill washed over him, he made his way to the large wardrobe to grab a sweatshirt. He listened for Mel's rhythmic breathing before continuing to shuffle across the bare wooden floor.

When he finally reached the wardrobe, Charlie thought he heard someone on the staircase. It was certainly close by, but his attention to detail was now piqued, like an animal listening for prey. Putting it down to somebody returning to their own room after fetching a drink or getting some air, Charlie steadily opened the wardrobe door, and every other thought instantly left his head, as if someone had stuck a vacuum in his ear and sucked them all away.

Even though it took what seemed like an eternity to discern what hung within, he inhaled sharply before eventually slamming the wardrobe door shut with a loud bang.

That School Sports Day would live with him forever. He was fourteen years old, a bright sunny afternoon towards the end of term, and he'd been selected to run the bloody hurdles. Him, Charlie Green, run? And not just running; jumping fucking black-and-white striped painted wooden obstacles along the way as well. Not only that. It looked like every damn pupil and teacher from the school was lining the track, alongside every bloody parent in Lincolnshire.

He remembered standing behind the starting line, awaiting their turn to run, as the two or three other groups sprinted off before them. The hurdles appeared massive, as if they had heightened them since his last practice run. Charlie could barely get over them then, and he was such a slow runner too. Why the hell did Mr Peston, their PE teacher, select him to represent their team?

Pulling his shorts down as far as he dare – his thighs were so thin and the stupid PE kit was so damn small – he desperately tried not to show his yellow pants underneath. Why did I choose yellow fucking underwear this morning? *Charlie blamed his mum for putting them out next to his uniform. The PE top was inadequate too, just about reaching the top of his shorts. Finding a happy medium was difficult, and there was always far too much flesh on display. He had a reputation to uphold at school, even at that age, so why did he have to wear such an ill-fitting outfit? All the other kids seemed to fit fine, only accentuating how bloody ridiculous he felt and looked.*

Charlie spotted Mel in the crowd, and in return, her eyes were fixated on him. They'd been together for a few months and he knew all the other boys were envious. She was the prize catch. But now look at me. Will she even want to be with me after this?

Pulling his shorts down a little further, he picked up laughter from behind. It was the ultimate group to run the hurdles from the year above. And he recognised one of them straight away. Will bloody Parry, the guy everybody avoided. The one person who could make your life hell if you got on the wrong side of him. Charlie had heard rumours of him waiting outside school and demanding protection money from some of the more vulnerable kids. He'd always left Charlie alone though, maybe because he spent all his time with Mel, but he was still extremely wary of him. He looked menacing, not in a child-to-child way, but more like an adult who everybody had been warned to stay clear of. Although he had never heard him speak, Charlie always imagined he would sound like Al Capone in some Italian-style mafia movie.

The noise of the starter pistol for the runners in front sounded, and Mr Peston called their group forward to the starting line. Charlie's legs were trembling, and he was sure his teacher smirked when he saw him. Light blue top, dark blue shorts, little white socks which barely covered his ankles. So much flesh, Charlie, so much flesh.

The race ahead, finished, a fat kid bringing up the rear to taunts from the children, coupled by glaring looks from teachers at the far end. That's going to be me very shortly, *he thought.*

"Get ready boys," Mr Peston shouted. "Do your best."

One or two looked up at him and nodded, grateful for the pep talk. They were taking it seriously and Charlie had noticed them limbering up as they waited to be called forward. Should I have limbered up too? Why do you even do that? Does it make you run any fucking quicker? *Too late now. He glanced over at Mel. She had her arms raised, thumbs up, giving him the big build-up.* "Put your fucking arms down," *he said to himself, the extra attention only adding to his nerves. Charlie felt physically sick.*

"Right, in your starting positions."

Mr Peston raised the pistol above his head. The two boys who had been limbering up bent forward, ready to pounce along the hundred and ten metres before them. The hurdles looked like endless lines of six-foot fences now. How the hell am I going to get over them?

"On your marks…" Fuck, *"… get set …"* This is it, *Bang!*

What happened next was a blur, a hazy memory, but he'll never forget the laughter. It sounded ten times louder than the pistol and it lasted a million times longer.

The other seven boys ran off, already well on their way to the first jump, but Charlie stood still, his shorts and pants around his ankles. He frantically tried to hide his modesty from what felt like an audience of a thousand onlookers. Looking behind, he saw Will Parry doubled up in laughter, the other boys from his year group beyond him, holding onto each other's shoulders as they fell into hysterics. Parry had pulled his shorts and pants down at the exact moment the starting pistol sounded.

Charlie looked at Mr Peston, but he, too, could not control himself any longer. And then he glanced at Mel, but she wasn't looking at him. Instead, her head was turned, and she was with somebody. Is her head buried in his chest? *The distance between them made it difficult to tell, but Mel was definitely confiding in someone, and her body appeared to be convulsing with laughter; or was she crying?*

Turning, Charlie glared at Will Parry. And right then, he vowed one day, somehow, he would get his revenge.

———

"What the hell are you doing?" Mel complained, groggily sitting up in bed and straining her eyes. She saw her husband stood in his boxer shorts, apparently staring at a closed wardrobe door. His hand repeatedly ran through his hair, only accentuating the mess. "I said, what are you doing? You'll wake the entire house." Mel spoke through gritted teeth, desperate to keep her voice as low as possible whilst attempting to show her disdain towards Charlie. Eventually, he turned and as soon as he saw her, something seemed to click inside his head.

"Did you put that in there?" he asked forthrightly, making no attempt to lower his voice.

Mel leant to her right and felt for the switch on the bedside lamp. She blinked hard against the sudden beam and turned her head away from the glare to focus on her husband once more. He appeared oblivious to the bright light. "Put what in where? What the hell are you talking about?"

Charlie took a sideways step from the wardrobe. Suddenly, Mel felt quite afraid of what he could actually mean. What on earth could be inside a wardrobe? She pulled the duvet over her chest and tight to her chin in preparation. After what felt like an age, Charlie leaned forward and opened both doors simultaneously before standing back again. Most probably relieved it wasn't a dead body or a horse's head, it took Mel a few moments to focus on what all the fuss was about.

"Well?" he asked.

Mel slowly climbed out of bed and stepped towards the wardrobe, her eyes not leaving it once. She observed precisely what had startled her husband, and as she turned her gaze back to him, she immediately grasped the connection. *That school. That boy.*

Charlie never liked PE, and he'd never forgotten that sports day, ridiculed in front of so many people. Students, teachers, parents alike.

But what could an old PE kit have to do with where they were? They were at a reunion organised by their ex-history teacher. Joyce Young had never taken them for PE and Mel couldn't recall her being there on that day.

"Did you put it there, Mel?" Charlie repeated.

Her eyes flicked between her husband and the wardrobe, her head shaking gently. "Of course I didn't," she eventually replied. "How would I even get hold of one and what point would it prove, me hanging it in our bedroom?"

She watched as he slowly trudged to the bed before sitting on the edge, looking at the open wardrobe once more. "I'm going to find out who did this," he said, standing once more before storming past Mel and slamming the doors shut for a second time.

26

It pissed Ollie off when Hazel ignored him and all he could do was watch on helplessly as she scooted off upstairs following breakfast. They were outside on the terrace and Ollie expected her to approach him to talk more about her plan. He felt a little nervous too, because the previous day, he hadn't really paid attention to the detail and he had a mountain of questions to ask her. But instead, she kept herself to herself, most of her time engrossed in Joyce.

Desperate to follow her indoors, he decided it would make things too obvious, and Ollie waited for the rest of the group to disappear. Ed carried another cup of coffee onto the lawn, where he sat forlornly in a deck chair looking out to sea, whilst Louis headed nonchalantly towards the barn. Mel and Charlie slowly made their way inside, heading to their room to change before work. Ollie noticed they had barely spoken and could detect a tension between them. Finally, Joyce helped Adrienne clear away before disappearing into the kitchen.

Once everybody was out of sight, Ollie apathetically

trudged upstairs, feeling as downbeat as everyone looked. He thought Hazel might be using him, coaxed him into being her little helper when she had no intention of actually doing so. As he approached the top step, he heard Mel and Charlie arguing again, and paused outside their room, their door slightly ajar. But Charlie caught him and took the few steps over before slamming the door in his face. Ollie felt sorry for Mel. Charlie was such a prick and he should never treat a lady the way he did. Ollie would never have treated his wife like that. No, Charlie needed fetching down from his high horse.

He trudged along the landing, lost in his own thoughts. When Hazel's door suddenly swung open, he physically jumped sideways, and she signalled him to quickly step inside. She spoke quietly, but with authority. Ollie preferred Hazel like that.

"First things first, Ollie. Stop fucking looking at me every ten seconds when we're with everybody else. If I can notice it, don't you think everybody else can?"

Ollie felt himself flush, and he looked at the floorboards. His left foot bobbed up and down, despite urging himself to stop. "Sorry," he said rather pathetically.

"Listen." Hazel remained silent until he faced her. He noticed some strands of hair had escaped from her pink headband, and Ollie couldn't recall her allowing that to happen before. "I don't believe Tony topped himself. Do you?"

A rush of adrenaline engulfed him, immediately replacing his embarrassment and self-doubt. Hazel was angry, even though she tried to control it. Ollie congratulated himself again on his observational skills. He was getting good at this. "I'm not sure. The police seem to think—"

"Bollocks to the police. It looks like an accident or

suicide. It fits the narrative perfectly. Poor little Miss Young and her abusive ex-husband. Shit, I'd struggle not to punch her if I lived under the same roof."

Ollie gawked at Hazel, gobsmacked. Was she really saying those things? *She literally hates Joyce.* "So you think somebody killed him?" he finally asked. Hazel appeared exasperated at his question.

"I don't know, Ollie. I just don't know. But it all feels strange to me."

"Why don't you leave then? Joyce has given us all the opportunity."

Hazel looked at him as if he'd just asked her to cut her right arm off.

"Same reason as you. Same as everybody else. You heard what she said. We won't get a penny."

He realised it was a ridiculous thing to ask. "Yeah, yeah, I'm sorry." But Hazel wasn't quite finished.

"We all need the money. So much so, Joyce knew well before we arrived that we all need the money."

"Yes. She told us that."

"Hmm, but don't you think it strange she appears to recognise the reasons we're all so bloody desperate for it?"

Ollie recalled the day somebody stifled a laugh when he said he didn't drink. The entire reason he was there was because he had drunk alcohol in the past. Did Joyce know that? How?

After a few moment's silence, Hazel told Ollie to sit on the end of her bed and he listened to the best of his ability as she reiterated the plan. "What, now?" he asked when she finished, not quite so confident as to how much a part of it he wanted to play.

"Are you capable of following what I said?"

Ollie knew he couldn't let his partner down, not after she was putting considerable faith in him. But now Hazel didn't believe Tony's death was an accident, and she believed the entire reunion was some kind of sinister set-up. His previous enthusiasm was dwindling by the minute. "Of course I'm up for it," he forced himself to reply.

"Okay. I'll wait around in the hallway whilst you look," Hazel reiterated, as if knowing he still didn't get the plan. "If Joyce turns up, I'll stall her. Keep her away from her room, and if I can't, I'll make loads of noise." Ollie gulped. "You can remember that, can't you?"

Following his shock wardrobe discovery, Charlie persuaded Mel not to say anything to anybody about it.

"I'm sure everybody heard you banging the doors a hundred times," she replied. "What do we say you've been doing?"

"I want to find out who did it for myself, if I can," Charlie retorted, deep in thought. "Nobody believed you about the mirror, so why——"

"*You* didn't believe me about the mirror," Mel interrupted, her anger rising. "Perhaps it was you all along?"

They didn't speak for the remainder of that night and they barely spoke at breakfast, either. Charlie particularly avoided mentioning Will Parry to Mel again. *Was he the connection to all this?* Charlie wracked his brain, desperate to find some common ground between the old school bully and the reunion.

The following morning, nobody asked about banging wardrobe doors or raised voices in the middle of the night. *Perhaps they're becoming used to it?* Charlie mused. However, they did argue again once they were back in their room. At one point, Mel shot him another derogatory remark, and Charlie opened his mouth to respond when he heard footsteps outside on the landing. He turned and saw Ollie gawping inside their open doorway, so he stepped forward before slamming it shut in his face.

———

That afternoon, following a full morning's work, Charlie watched intently from underneath the shade of the terrace. He was already on his fifth beer. Ed and Mel had spent all morning working in the garden again, and now they were sitting in deckchairs on the lawn, chatting and laughing. *What the fuck are they talking about all the time?*

Charlie wondered if she'd told him about the PE kit, despite him pleading with her not to. Would she betray him? Surely not. What can of worms would it open, and besides, he'd mentioned he wanted to carry out his own investigations. One blab to that idiot and it could be all around the group before he knew it. Not only that, if she told Ed about the wardrobe discovery, she would have to relay the story of what it actually meant. Then again, Charlie presumed, as the alcohol played tricks on his mind, maybe it would be good if people were made aware so he could gauge their reaction. Would the culprit come forward?

Mel jumped when Charlie tapped her on the shoulder. He'd crept around the periphery, realising she wouldn't notice, so deeply ingrained in conversation with Ed as she was.

"Shit, Charlie. Don't do that," she said, smiling, looking at Ed and holding her chest.

Ed immediately stood to leave. "No," Charlie said. "Don't leave on my behalf. I need to ask my wife something, but it will only take a second." Ed remained standing.

"What is it?" Mel asked, clearly agitated, whilst gesticulating with her arm for Ed to sit back down.

"It's just your earring." Charlie watched as her hand involuntarily reached for her lobe. He then looked to Ed as he finished his question. "Did you ever find it?"

He couldn't help but smile as they both floundered before him.

"Not yet," Mel replied, her eyes darting between the pair of them.

"Oh, okay," Charlie said. "I just wondered if you've been back down to the clearing recently."

"What's your fucking problem?" Mel shouted as she found Charlie in their room. She and Ed had watched as he sauntered towards the terrace and inside the house. Although he was drunk, it secretly scared her how much he might know.

Mel had been enjoying her time with Ed during the morning at work and again sat outside in the deckchairs. The conversation flowed easily, and they had considerably more in common than she originally thought.

"My problem? *My* problem?" Charlie retorted; his voice just as animated. "Why don't you run off to lover boy and ask what *his* problem is?"

Mel glared at her husband, laying festooned on the bed, an empty bottle of beer on the bedside table. She removed her small green cardigan and threw it down before looking him up and down, as if meeting him for the first time. "What the fuck did I ever see in you?" she finally asked.

Charlie laughed, which pissed her off even more. She had to restrain herself from leaning over and punching him.

"You don't deserve me, Mel. You never did. I could have had the pick of—"

"Oh, don't you ever think I wished you *had* chosen someone else? I'd have given my right arm for it."

She felt his eyes bore into her back as she stepped over to the wardrobe. She removed her top and pulled a fresh white polo shirt from a hanger. After she put it on, she released her hair from the collar before putting her hand back inside the cupboard to retrieve something else. She turned around, holding the PE kit aloft, stepped over and pushed it down into Charlie's chest until he was forced to take it from her. He looked powerless as she leant forward and whispered directly into his ear, her voice full of venom.

"And I do remember that sports day. The day when Will Parry pulled your shorts down and the entire school laughed. And do you know why they laughed?" Charlie shook his head. "It was because of your tiny, little dick."

27

IF HAZEL PLACED such tremendous trust in me, why is she currently inspecting Joyce's room?

Yet again, Ollie fumed with his so-called partner. She said she'd had a change of heart at the last minute, just because she knew the bedroom layout better and she would therefore be much quicker. But Ollie didn't believe her. He realised it was because she didn't trust him.

Despite his reservations, Ollie had since considered the plan. How bloody difficult could it be? Sneak into Joyce's room, find a little book and check the names inside it. Perhaps Hazel didn't believe he would remember the contents though, and perhaps she was right, so when he suggested he took a photograph with his phone, he thought he'd come up with the best idea ever. However, Hazel believed it too risky, carrying evidence around on mobile devices. But Ollie deliberated she was belittling his brilliant suggestion, just because she hadn't figured it out herself.

Nonetheless, he was still a partner, and they were still a team. If Hazel found anything interesting, Ollie could say he was part of the process. Reluctantly, he took his hiding place in the hallway whilst Hazel sneaked along the corridor. But, a few minutes later, when the kitchen door opened and Joyce appeared, Ollie had his own change of heart. Maybe it was time to teach Hazel a little lesson of her own?

So, Ollie remained in the shadows, out of sight, and watched as Joyce stepped across the great hallway towards the door leading to the passageway. He grinned mischievously to himself before calmly returning to his room.

"Why the hell didn't you stop her?" Hazel fumed, standing in Ollie's open doorway. He deliberately left it ajar, knowing she would be paying him a visit as soon as Joyce allowed her to leave. That was around twenty minutes earlier.

"I didn't see her," he lied, propping himself up against the pillows at the end of his bed. A magazine lay unopened by his side, a prop to give the impression he was calm and in control. Inside, his stomach was doing somersaults though, as he wasn't sure exactly how angry Hazel would be and what she might do. "And I got bored waiting." But, as usual, Ollie had miscalculated the consequences of his actions.

Hazel stepped inside and closed the door behind her. "I thought we were a team?" she asked, her face flustered, but he didn't know if it resulted from him letting her down or Joyce interrogating her. "Why didn't you stop her, Ollie?"

He shuffled to the end of the bed and walked over to the window. Ollie was tired, swamped by all the planning and secrets and being trapped on the island. He couldn't shake what happened to his wife either and how he met her. And then the footsteps on the gravel in the middle of night. While waiting for Hazel, he considered telling Joyce he didn't care about the money anymore and he wanted to leave.

"Because I was pissed off with you." He spoke much louder than intended. "I'm pissed off with everybody. You all treat me like I'm an idiot." He pointed in her face, his anger not surprising him. "Especially you." Ollie was struggling to cope. He held a dislike for everyone in the house and felt no connection to any of them. Now Hazel had rendered him pathetic too. What was the point?

But Hazel was angry too, and she stood her ground as Ollie raised his finger. He wasn't sure what he would do if she came for him, but could sense his hands clenching in and out of fists.

"I didn't treat you like a fool," she shouted back. "But now I realise why everybody else thinks you are a cretin. You can't be trusted. You may have even killed Tony for all we know." Ollie took another step closer and Hazel raised her voice louder still. "You'll never be my partner. You're just a fucking useless imbecile."

Hazel turned to leave, and something triggered inside Ollie's head. She had him pushed too far.

Flying across the room, he slammed his back against the door, preventing Hazel from going anywhere. He noticed her expression change from control to something closer to terror. She looked around the room. *Something to hit me with?* But even if she spotted anything, she couldn't match his speed. Ollie sprang forward and gripped his hand around her throat. Hazel kicked his shins so hard; he immediately released his grip.

"Fuck you, bitch," he yelled, and propelled himself

forward once more. She dodged his advance and ran for the door, but before she reached the handle, it swung open and Louis stood on the landing. Moments later, Joyce appeared behind him, completely out of breath.

Twenty minutes earlier, and with a last glance along the corridor, Hazel lightly tapped on Joyce's bedroom door. Although her heart pounded, the thrill of what she was actually doing outweighed the fear. She knocked again, a little louder, and pressed her ear to the frame. All remained perfectly silent. Even those stupid insects outside appeared to have taken the afternoon off.

The door handle felt cool, and it turned and clicked effortlessly into place. Hazel pushed it open and called Joyce's name. Still no reply, and with no sound from Ollie in the hallway, she found herself inside.

Joyce's room was freshly cleaned. The pillows were plump and the duvet neatly tucked in on three sides. Two clean towels were folded and placed at right angles to one another at the end of the bed. *Like a posh hotel*, Hazel considered, a little envious that hers was never made up the same. It reminded her of travelling the world and exploring unknown places. Her heart yearned for such experiences, her dream job ending so abruptly. It reinforced the reason she was in her host's room and Hazel began the search for anything incriminating.

The first thing she noticed was the lack of the little black notepad which was previously on Joyce's bedside table. Quickly, she pulled the drawers open one by one, the initial two containing only an array of pens, a torch and a couple of cheap-looking bracelets.

Shit, Hazel thought. *She must have taken it with her.*

But the third one grabbed her attention. An envelope

with Joyce's name and address printed on the front. However, that wasn't what Hazel came for, so instead, she folded it in two and shoved it into her back pocket. That could wait for later.

Stepping over to the wardrobe, very similar to the one in her own room – large, shiny, mahogany with brass handles – it opened with a loud click, and Hazel held onto the door to stop it from swinging open and crashing in on itself. With her spare hand, she flicked through the hanging clothes, and rifled through a couple of pockets, but again, found nothing of interest. *Bollocks. There has to be something.*

Next, Hazel went to the bathroom, knowing it was unlikely that she would find anything incriminating in there. With a quick check in the small cupboard over the sink, she turned to re-enter the main room, frustrated and bitter.

"Looking for something in particular, dear?"

Hazel stopped dead in her tracks, her hand fixed on the door handle. She placed her other hand to her heart and watched in horror as Joyce stood in the open doorway.

"I came looking for you," she stammered. "Sorry, I thought you were in here, so I let myself in. I knocked, but I presumed you hadn't heard me." The more she spoke, the more pathetic she sounded. Hazel forced herself to shut up.

Joyce closed the door and stepped slowly across the room, away from Hazel and to the far side of her bed. Eventually, she turned. "Isn't it about time you spoke the truth, my dear?"

Hazel wondered why Ollie hadn't stopped her, or at least called out. There was only one way to the corridor, and she told him exactly where to hide so he could see everything and everybody. He seemed keen to help and now she wished she'd let him do the sneaking around, just as the original plan. But it was her own stupid fault. Why had she relied on such a useless fucking cretin in the first place?

"What truth?" Hazel glanced at the still-open wardrobe. Joyce's eyes followed. Realising her words were escaping like a pack of lies, Hazel came clean, well, kind of. "Okay. You never really offered me a satisfactory reply when I asked if anybody lived on the island." She studied Joyce before continuing, but her host gave nothing away. "So, when you didn't answer me knocking on your door, I thought I would see if anybody else stayed in here, you know, with you."

Joyce smiled. "Really? Like whom?"

"I don't know. It's just that nightmare I had. It seemed so real. I just thought—"

"You thought you'd break into my private accommodation and sneak around and try to pin something on me?" Joyce replied, before taking a step to her right, towards the door. Hazel's eyes flicked from Joyce to the exit, still believing she could easily make it first. "Do you think I killed Tony, Hazel?" She took another step. "Is that why you're *really* here?"

Matching her, Hazel took a pace to the left, surprised at the question. "No. No, not at all. Why would I think that?"

"I think it's time you left now. Don't you agree, my dear?"

Hazel nodded, but as she opened the door to leave, she offered Joyce a sardonic smile of her own.

You're hiding something, Joyce Young, and we both know it.

Back inside the sanctuary of her own room, after her altercation with Ollie and subsequent intrusion from Louis and Joyce, Hazel sat on the end of her bed, finally allowing her breathing to return to something near normal. She was well aware Joyce would never forgive her for creeping around like that. There was no excuse, but Hazel still knew Joyce couldn't pin anything on her either.

The envelope.

Shit. She'd forgotten she'd stuffed it into her pocket.

Quickly, Hazel opened the letter and removed a couple of sheets of folded A4. The letterhead on the paper showed it was from Joyce's bank, containing her monthly statement, and Hazel instantly experienced a twinge of remorse for taking such a private item.

Hold on.

She still couldn't help herself from prying, and what she saw made no sense. Quickly, Hazel checked the date at the top. Last month. The most up-to-date statement she would have.

She turned the papers over, back and forth. Surely there must be a mistake?

"… I'm giving you all ten thousand pounds…"

"Ten grand," Hazel repeated.

"… the thing is, I've come into a considerable inheritance…"

Hazel confirmed the ultimate figure one more time.

"… and I wanted to help you guys out…"

But Joyce Young was skint. No, not skint, destitute. According to her bank statement, she was thousands and thousands of pounds in arrears. So much so, it made Hazel look like a millionaire.

Quickly deducing that Joyce could easily have other accounts, she still couldn't understand why she would leave that one in such debt. Surely you would balance them out?

Hazel checked the statement further and the amount of interest Joyce was being charged only cemented her initial thoughts.

So, if Joyce Young had no money, how the hell was she going to pay any of them the promised reward?

28

THAT NIGHT, Ed lay in bed, his thoughts running wild. Earlier that afternoon, he followed Mel inside, scared for her safety, given how drunk Charlie was. And what did he mean about going back to the clearing? Could he know what really happened? Ed left his door slightly ajar, ready to pounce if things got out of hand in the room next door. He listened intently as their voices became louder and more vile towards one another. The arguing eventually abated, but would resume later in the night.

To add to the mounting nervousness between the group, the palpable tension at dinner that evening was the worst to date. Neither Ollie nor Hazel spoke and Ed noticed Joyce and Louis continually glancing in their direction, as if watching two naughty children who needed to be kept apart.

After they ate and the group reluctantly sauntered onto the terrace for drinks, Ed wandered over to Hazel and discreetly asked what was going on. Her abrupt reply took him aback. "Ollie tried to fucking kill me, that's what."

She burst indoors, and all eyes were fixed in astonishment as she marched heavily up the grand staircase, vanishing along the corridor and out of view.

"I'll see to her," Joyce said, one foot already in the hallway.

"What the hell is going on?" Charlie asked, accompanied by an annoying laugh.

"Why don't you go fuck yourself," Ollie replied, barging his shoulder into Charlie, causing him to spill most of his fresh glass of red wine. Charlie stretched out his drinking arm whilst pulling his wet T-shirt from his stomach with his spare hand. Ollie broke into a run as he made his way along the footpath, through the small gate before heading into the woods beyond.

"Oi!" Charlie shouted after him. "This is my favourite shirt."

"You dickhead," Mel said, before she too went inside.

It left Ed on the terrace with Charlie and Louis, and he couldn't think of a place he'd sooner not be.

"I'm calling it a night too," he said.

Ed lay on his back, the breeze from the open window refreshing against his bare skin. The weather was still warm, although Joyce said it would break soon and thunderstorms were approaching. She informed the group they needed to get as many jobs as possible completed in the garden before the end of the weekend, four days away.

The light knocking sound made him jolt, and Ed sat bolt upright. At first, he thought the banging was on his door, but when he heard the same noise again, he realised it was somewhere along the landing; Mel and Charlie's room? The sound of creaking floorboards on the other side of his wall soon affirmed his suspicions. Crawling slowly out of bed, Ed tiptoed across the room and pressed his ear against his door.

"Oh, good evening, Joyce. Something wrong?"

Charlie sounded strange, exaggerating a posh accent.

"I've had a complaint about the noise, Charlie. And not for the first time."

Charlie immediately dropped his mock voice and took on a substantially more aggressive tone. "Maybe they should mind their own fuck—"

"No!" Joyce interrupted, so loud that anybody who had been sleeping would now be wide awake. She continued unabated. "No, I'm not having that. This is my house and you will abide by my rules. If you and Mel are having, well, having problems, that's your business, but I won't have my other guests having to endure your constant arguing."

The sound of Mel's voice surprised Ed. He hadn't heard her walk across the room.

"Sorry, Joyce. It won't happen again. Charlie's had too much to drink. I'll make sure he sleeps now."

"Make sure it doesn't happen again."

Ed believed the show was over when he heard Joyce angrily stomping down the stairs, prompting him to turn and head back to bed. But Mel spoke again. She must have lingered outside, and Ed wondered who she was talking to. "Don't worry. It won't be for much longer."

Crawling into bed, Ed knew sleep would evade him for the rest of the night. Trying to take everything in, he lay still, staring at the ceiling once more. The argument from next door stopped, and although he heard muffled voices through the wall, Ed finally drifted off, exhaustion eventually catching up on him.

At first, he thought he must be dreaming. The sound of soft scratching was somewhere outside; the noise of nightmares. Rolling over, he fought against waking, until the scratching grew louder, more profound.

Groggily, Ed reached for his watch on the bedside table. Three-thirty. Laying as still as possible, the house fell eerily quiet, and he prayed he had somehow dreamt it.

With his heart pounding, he listened intently. Nothing. But then, without warning, the scraping resumed. It was definitely on his bedroom door.

All kinds of images flashed through his mind. He imagined a ghost-like figure outside, hovering above the ground, long bony fingers protruding.

"Ed," a voice hissed.

What the..?

"Ed, it's me. Mel."

Without thinking, Ed clambered out of bed, oblivious to the fact he was only wearing boxer shorts, and scrambled to the door. Opening it wide enough to peer out, still hoping it was some kind of silly prank, Mel stood there, shaking, in her pyjamas.

"What is it?" Ed whispered.

"Can I come in?" Without waiting for a response, she pushed the door open far enough to squeeze through and made her way to the centre of his room. Closing the door as quietly as he could, Ed turned to face her. He became aware he was almost naked and his hands involuntarily moved to cover his modesty. Moonlight seeped through the half-opened shutters, giving Mel a silhouette-like appearance.

"What's wrong, Mel?" he whispered again, this time barely audible.

"I can't stand him, Ed. I can't even be in the same room…"

Her shaking became more exaggerated and instinct caused Ed to move closer. Although fully conscious of how inappropriate it was, he held her, and Mel reciprocated. Burying her head into his bare chest, her hands gripped his back tightly, as if holding on for dear life. She must have been aware of his heart thudding heavily against her, but she made no attempt to step away. They remained locked together for several moments. Ed knew he had to do something.

"What are you going to do?" he asked, holding her at arm's length.

"I don't know. Seriously, I just don't know. I want to kill him. I genuinely want to kill him."

She shook again, so Ed comforted her once more. "Mel?" he asked. "Is Charlie asleep? I mean, he doesn't know you're …"

Mel removed her head from his chest and managed a smile. "No. Don't worry. He's out of it. Far too much wine again. He went downstairs and helped himself to another bottle. It's why we argued…" she paused mid-sentence, "…shit, did you hear us?"

Ed nodded. "And I heard Joyce come and tell you off."

Mel smiled again, this time a little more naturally. "Have you been telling teacher about us?"

Ed laughed nervously. He could feel her relax. But she was in his bedroom, at three-thirty in the morning, wearing pyjamas, and him in boxer shorts. Attempting to keep control, he consciously stepped away.

"You need to sort it out, Mel. I think he might

know—"

She stepped closer, following him. "I know I need to sort it out. It's only for a couple more weeks, but I don't know if I can cope that long." Ed watched her helplessly. "I'm scared. Scared what we might do to each other."

Unsure how to react or what to say, he allowed her to hold him again. She looked so frightened, fragile. Mel rested her head on his shoulder and he felt her breath against his neck.

Fucking hell. This is getting out of hand.

Her hands ran the length of his back, her fingernails tickling as they made contact. Despite the internal screams, to get the fuck away, his pathetic willpower did nothing to prevent her.

Finally, her fingers made their way into his hair and she rested her palms on his cheeks, holding his face only inches from her own. And then she kissed him.

It didn't take long to remove the last items of clothing they were wearing before they fell onto his bed, laughing, kissing.

Afterwards, Mel cried. Soft sobs. Ed held her, willing her to make a move, apologise to him, take full responsibility and return to her own room. But she made no such attempt, and Ed knew he was only kidding himself.

He allowed her to drift off, but sleep evaded Ed. At first, he listened to Mel's shallow breathing and the sound of the insects outside the open window. Every now and then, something else caught his attention. The noise of very quiet footsteps. Along the landing and up and down the staircase, like somebody on night patrol, ensuring everybody remained exactly where they were supposed to be. *Little do they know*, he thought.

Eventually, Ed fell asleep too. Only a wall's width away from Mel's sleeping husband.

29

JOYCE PACED UP AND DOWN, as much as her bedroom would allow. For twenty-four hours, since she caught Hazel in her room, and the subsequent aggressive argument between her and Ollie, she had been deliberating what to do next. Had Hazel found anything in her room? Had she said anything to Ollie? Joyce doubted it, as Ollie could never keep his mouth shut. But she knew Hazel was at breaking point and would surely have mentioned it if she had discovered something; wouldn't she?

Things were getting out of control. Not only were Joyce and Hazel at loggerheads, but Ollie had lost it with Hazel, too. And Mel and Charlie had reached the stage where Joyce didn't know how much longer they could put up with each other, either. It was as if the island was somehow tearing them all apart.

But Joyce wasn't stupid. Long before their arrival, she understood she would be bringing diverse personalities together, confined in a relatively compact space with no escape from each other. But it was only for four weeks, for goodness' sake. Couldn't they just be civilised? *Think of the bloody money, you fools. I know I am.*

So, she spent the night before on patrol, like a warden in a prison. She paced the landing, spent time on the terrace, and sat alone in the grand hallway. And all the time, her ears and eyes were primed for every movement, every little sound. Joyce needed to know what was going on, especially if Hazel decided to leave her room. Even so, she was caught completely unawares when Mel sneaked into Ed's room at three-thirty in the morning.

The sound of the bell ringing made Mel jump from her skin. She sat bolt upright, instinctively covering as much of herself as she could.

"Fuck, fuck, fuck, Ed," she said, staring down at him. "That's Adrienne. It must be breakfast. What time is it?"

She watched as Ed jumped out of bed, frantically searching for his boxers. Mel followed his lead, scooping up her pyjamas and awkwardly redressing through flailing arms and legs.

"Eight o'clock. Shit," Ed replied, gawking at her, "why didn't I set an alarm?"

"Bollocks to that. What are we going to do?" she asked, hoping Ed would have some master plan.

"How do I fucking know?"

Although frantic with despair, Mel couldn't help but watch Ed dress. What happened hours earlier hadn't been on her agenda, but she could no longer control herself. Jeez. She started to fall for him, walking from the airport terminal to the minibus. Why else had she held back so they could be together?

Quickly coming to her senses, she fastened the final button on her top and heard a door opening. It sounded extremely close. Then another, this time further along the landing.

"Morning, Ollie."

Fuck, it's Charlie.

Mel glared at Ed, open-mouthed.

"Oh, morning." Ollie's reply sounded forced, as if Charlie was the last person he wanted to converse with.

Silence. Mel and Ed stood perfectly still, neither daring to move a single muscle.

"Have you seen my wife?"

Charlie asked the question so nonchalantly; Mel considered it might be something he'd ask every day of the week. She continued to glare at Ed. He had gone white.

"Nah. Have you lost her?" Ollie retorted. "She's probably down at breakfast already. Then again, I wouldn't blame her if she had done a runner."

Mel and Ed listened intently as Charlie made his way downstairs, his voice drifting as he continued to probe Ollie.

"Listen, Mel," Ed whispered. "Go to your room and get dressed. I'll go down to breakfast. You go out the front door, walk around the house and approach the terrace from the footpath in the woods. Our only chance is that you've been for an early stroll. Say you couldn't sleep or something."

Although Mel didn't appear convinced with the plan, she knew she had nothing better. She nodded her approval. But as she moved to leave, she grabbed Ed's arm and pulled him towards her before kissing him passionately.

"Thank you, Ed."

"What for?" he replied.

"For everything. You're the only person holding me

together. I hate Charlie and I hate it here." She looked around the room before returning her attention to Ed. "I'm frightened by what happened all those years ago and if this is all connected."

Ed's plan turned out to have one major flaw. Not everybody showed up for breakfast. Doing a quick head-count, he soon realised one was missing.

"Anybody seen, Louis?" he enquired, as composed as his pathetic acting would allow.

"Louis?" replied Charlie with a snort. "Forget Louis. Has anyone seen my wife?"

Freezing to the spot, Ed expected all attention to fall on him. His cunning scheme foiled before it even began. Fortunately, nobody appeared interested in him, instead focussing their attention upon Charlie.

"Still not found her? I tell you; she's bloody left you," Ollie replied. Ed noticed a distinct glint of scorn in his eyes.

As Charlie responded, sounding very calm given the fact that his wife wasn't in his room when he woke up, as well as ignoring Ollie's snide remarks, Ed instead focused his attention on the end of the garden.

"Why would you be looking for Louis, Edward?"

Joyce made him jump. Her annoying habit of popping up from thin air was pissing him off. Ed floundered his reply. "I wondered if I could borrow one of the long hoses, and maybe a sprinkler for the flower beds. That's all."

His quick thinking amazed him, but Joyce still offered a sarcastic smirk in response.

"He's gone to the vegetable garden to pick fresh

food," she said. "I'm sure he'll help you out once he gets back. Louis is a very helpful guy, you know."

What does that even mean?

Joyce's calm temperament was grating on him. She always kept her tone so remarkably steady, forever in control. Nothing appeared to unnerve her. He nodded his approval before spotting Mel. She was walking towards the house, across the lawn. "There's your wife, Charlie," he announced, feeling quite pleased that his plan may have come to fruition after all.

"Aha, you're right." But instead of following everyone's lead and looking to Mel, Charlie glared at Ed. "I wonder where she's been?"

As Ed stumbled for a reply, Hazel spoke on his behalf. "For a morning stroll, I'd say."

Had she noticed him struggling? But that threw more doubts into his head. Did she know the truth and was covering for him? And did Charlie know more than he was letting on? And right on cue, to mock him further, Ed caught Joyce smiling, too.

"Morning, darling. Didn't hear you get up."

Ed could have killed Mel as she glanced nervously towards him before replying to her husband.

"You wouldn't have heard a thing. You were out for the count all night. Snoring like a trooper." She laughed, but it came out so unnaturally, she instantly blushed.

All focus was now on Mel, including Adrienne, who had returned from the kitchen. As Mel stepped over to the coffee percolator and poured herself a drink, Ed's heart pounded. He desperately needed to keep his emotions under control. The whole situation felt so surreal. Joyce eventually broke the silence.

"I hope you all had a good night's sleep, and not just Charlie," she quipped. Everybody suppressed a false laugh. "Anyway, now you're all here, I wanted to give you all a little surprise. Something to give you all a break from your hard work."

Everyone glanced at one another, as if dreading what might come next.

"So, what is it?" Ollie asked impatiently.

Joyce looked at him before addressing the group once more. "I have arranged for you all to go canoeing. There are boats, or whatever they're called, and life jackets in the barn."

"Yes!" exclaimed Ollie, far too enthusiastically. "It's, I mean, it's supposed to be brilliant."

Joyce arched an eyebrow, her eyes narrowing as she gave Ollie a quizzical look. "Calm yourself down, dear," she teased. "It's just an idea to raise spirits. I can tell the amount of work is having an effect."

Ed almost laughed. *The amount of work?* The *work* was the easy bit. It was the company and the surreal circumstances which were causing the rising angst.

"Do you mind if I skip it?" Hazel spoke softly. "I've a dreadful headache and I'm not really one for water sports."

Joyce looked at Hazel, as if contemplating how truthful she was being. However, following a moment's contemplation, she broke into a smile. "Of course, dear. You should rest in your room. I'll arrange for Adrienne to bring up some paracetamol."

If Ed didn't know better, Joyce's words dripped with sarcasm. He noticed Ollie glare at Hazel, too. If any of the tension had dissipated, it swiftly returned.

"Thank you," Hazel replied nonchalantly. "I'd like to rest today, if that's okay?"

"Must be all that thinking you've been doing, dear," Joyce quipped before turning to face the others again.

"But yes, I agree. I need you all fit and well to carry on with tomorrow's duties. The weather is going to break any day, so we must finish the gardening and outdoor work as a priority."

The sound of footsteps came as a blessing. "Aha, here's Louis," Joyce announced, and all eyes fell on the guy with the scars, carrying a wooden box of fresh vegetables. Ed realised how little interaction he'd played with the group. *Who is he exactly?* "You're missing all the fun, Louis," Joyce continued. "Ollie is so excited about canoeing that we may need to tranquillise him." Louis looked from Joyce to Ollie. "And guess what else has happened? Hazel's got such a terrible headache she needs to lie down, and you won't believe this. Charlie somehow misplaced his wife this morning."

Louis stared from one person to the next, his expression not once changing.

"I, I just went for a walk," Mel stuttered. "Just down to the shore and back."

"What time was that?"

Louis was a man of very few words, so Ed couldn't believe he chose that moment to speak. Mel blushed again.

"Not sure, really. Between seven and seven-thirty."

"I was in the barn. I didn't see you."

The scars on Louis' face and neck caught the low sunlight. He appeared frozen to the spot, somehow mesmerised by Mel's story. The rising panic in her voice only accentuated the issue. Thankfully, not for the first time, Joyce came to the rescue.

"Get the canoes ready, Louis," she said, not appearing particularly pleased at his questioning of Mel either. But just as Louis turned to leave, Ollie called after him.

"Oh, Louis." He stopped. "Ed wants to ask you something."

Do I?

Ed didn't know what Ollie could mean. All eyes fell on him and he faltered, too.

"Ed wants to hold your hose, Louis!" Ollie laughed out loud at his own little joke.

As everybody joined in, Ed could feel his cheeks burn. And out of the corner of his eye, he noticed Joyce. She smiled, and the way she looked at him and then at Mel, Ed realised she knew exactly what happened in the middle of the night.

30

LOUIS HANDED out life jackets before giving a brief demonstration on how to make them as comfortable as possible. Charlie didn't like the feel of his. It felt restrictive, like being on a roller coaster when the automatic safety harness locks you into position.

He noticed Ed looking at him and wondered what his problem was. Ed averted his gaze and instead looked at Mel. Charlie was on the brink of saying something when Louis signalled for the four of them to help carry the canoes.

Nobody spoke as they trudged through the woods, along the well-trodden footpath and towards the clearing beyond the bench. Charlie considered the tension tangible, not just between himself and his wife, but also between the others. He noticed how eyes darted from one person to the next and realised he hadn't heard Ed and Ollie speak recently and he was barely speaking to Ollie himself. Hazel also appeared to have an issue with him.

The PE kit in his wardrobe still played on his mind. Who would have taken such a thing to France? And whoever hung it there, how did they get into his bedroom without him or Mel noticing? But then Mel ridiculed him, shoving the kit in his face and telling him exactly why everybody laughed that day. He hadn't seen her pack before the trip and again, they unpacked separately when they arrived. Could she have brought it? And then there was her missing earring; had she *really* lost it? And could her so-called message in the mirror be a smokescreen, whilst she had her fun and games, constantly mocking him?

However, the thing which played on Charlie's mind the most was where on earth had Mel spent the night before?

Once they arrived at the spot to launch the canoes, Ollie took in his surroundings. Louis told them all to remain where they were whilst he fetched the paddles and the final vessel. After what seemed like an age, they stepped to the water's edge and were given further instructions.

"We're only going fucking canoeing," Charlie said. Ollie thought it totally unnecessary and glared at him. The first few days, Ollie respected Charlie, almost looked up to him, but by then, he felt nothing but hatred towards the guy. Judging by the reaction on everybody else's face, they'd had enough of him, too. Charlie's pathetic smile pushed Ollie over the edge.

"Shut your fucking mouth." He raised his hand above his head. "We've had it up to here with you."

Louis outstretched his arms to separate the pair. Not that either of them were up for any physical confrontation. The voice of a girl from behind took Ollie by surprise.

"Let's all calm down. This is supposed to be a fun trip."

Ollie hadn't even noticed Adrienne was there. She carried a wicker picnic basket, no doubt full of refreshments.

"She's right," Ed spoke next. "Can't we all get along?" Ollie watched as he turned to face Charlie. "Any chance you can keep your thoughts to yourself for a while?"

"Any chance you can shut the fuck up?" Charlie responded, his face flushed.

Ollie took a step closer to Charlie, although they were still too far apart to come to blows. "Leave it, Charlie," he said. "You're pissing everyone off."

"Or what? You going to run along to Hazel to ask what to do next?"

Shit. How does he know about that?

Ollie stepped closer still. "Just bugger off. Everybody hates you. Even your wife."

Anticipating the inevitable, Louis stepped between them, again stretching his arms to form a makeshift barrier. Nobody spoke, although Mel chuckled to herself in the background. Charlie mumbled something under his breath, but it was barely audible.

Louis said something in French to Adrienne and she placed the picnic basket on the ground before putting on her own life jacket. Ollie smiled again, somehow invigorated by the idea she was coming along too.

Once the four of them were given a gentle nudge off the bank by Louis, the canoes took care of themselves. Although Ed wouldn't give him the satisfaction, Charlie was correct in his assumption that the directives from Louis had been over the top. The calm water literally moved them along, albeit at a snail's pace, and he barely had to paddle.

After they negotiated their way to an orange buoy floating serenely, roughly fifty metres out to sea, Ollie attempted to bump his canoe into everybody. He giggled enthusiastically as he made contact.

Wishing he would just bloody stop, Ed forced himself to smile, desperate for no more arguing. The emotional strain was becoming unbearable.

Fortunately, Ollie soon got bored, and went off on his own. Louis paddled after him and Ed heard them laughing as they raced to some predetermined finish line. He'd never witnessed Louis so animated before.

As he became lost in his own thoughts, Ed must have missed Charlie and Mel paddling off to his right. They were talking, but it definitely wasn't a convivial conversation. Secretly, he desired to be alone with Mel. The thought of spending the day messing around on the water, followed by a picnic on the river bank, captivated him. But he knew he had to keep a distance. The big problem was, could he?

Charlie couldn't keep it to himself any longer. He purposefully manoeuvred to the right, away from everybody after asking Mel to keep in tow. She was being sheepish, and Charlie hoped she would open up once they were alone. Once he'd put sufficient distance between them and the others, he dragged his paddle into the water so his canoe spun back on itself, facing his wife.

"So, where were you all night?"

His question had the desired effect. Mel immediately became flustered, her canoe wobbled, and she splashed her paddle into the sea to regain her balance.

"I told you. You were fast asleep. Snoring all night long. And I got no sleep at all lying next to you. It's why I got up early and went for a walk."

Charlie smiled. The kind of smarmy grin which he knew Mel detested. "Then why didn't I see you when I had a piss at four o'clock?"

"Rubbish. You barely moved."

He pushed his paddle gently into the water until his canoe bobbed alongside Mel's. Their boats knocked against one another and Charlie gripped hard on the paddle in Mel's hand. "I'm being serious," he continued, his voice lower and his anger rising. "Somebody was walking around on the landing. Up and down. Up and down. Whoever it was woke me, so I checked my phone and it was just after four. I went to the bathroom, Mel, and I swear on my life, you weren't in our room."

"They quarrel so much."

The sound of Adrienne's voice startled Ed. He hadn't heard her approach; such was his focus on Mel and Charlie out at sea.

"Oh sorry, Adrienne," he said, manoeuvring his canoe to join her. "What did you say?"

"Charlie and Melanie. They argue all the time. Why are they even married?" She added an exaggerated flick of her head, repeating it a few seconds later.

"Yes, they don't appear to be very happy, do they?"

She grinned. *Is that sarcasm?* "And you, Edward? Are you happy?"

Adrienne's abruptness took him by surprise. They had barely spoken since they arrived, yet here she was, asking him a personal question. Ed also couldn't understand why she was actually there. She had previously kept herself well away from the group. "What brings you along today?" he asked, changing the subject. "You don't normally socialise with us."

Adrienne shrugged her shoulders. "Joyce told me to. It surprised me too. But after asking me where the parac-etamol is kept, she suggested I come out and enjoy myself. Between us two, I didn't particularly want to."

Ed considered her response before she revisited her previous point. "So, are you happy? You are often, how do you English say it, in a world of your own?"

He couldn't help but smile at Adrienne's acute aware-ness. "I'm okay. Just a few things on my mind. And you? How are you?"

Although she initially clammed up, she soon recov-ered, smiled and replied. "I am okay. I am finding this whole situation really strange, though. Joyce flying people to France to renovate a château. Who does that?"

Despite balancing a stationary canoe on the ocean's waves, Adrienne remained steadfast, her eyes not leaving Ed's. He could tell she was serious and had given the subject some thought. "Well, when you put it like that, I don't really know."

Adrienne didn't hold back.

"Well, how else would you put it? That is exactly what she did. And I've heard how much she is paying you all. It's absurd. I know of decorators and builders in Pont-Aven who would do the work for much less. And no disrespect, they would do a better job. They are profes-sionals."

Aware that her outburst could easily be lost in transla-tion, Ed couldn't decipher how angry she really was, despite her aggressive tone. "I, I don't—"

"It's crazy. This entire charade is crazy." She swept her arm in a circular motion. "Look at the way everybody argues. None of you even like each other. Something isn't right."

The more she spoke, the more animated she became. Ed thought she would lose her balance; such was her theatrical display. "And what exactly do you think is going on?" he asked.

She studied him, as if weighing up if he had any ulterior motive. "I'm guessing the same as you. You are not stupid."

What the hell does she mean by that?

"I don't know what you mean. Joyce just—"

"Ha! Joyce. An old spinster. Then her crazy ex-husband, Tony. He was mad, always angry, always wanting a fight. I'm pleased somebody taught him a lesson."

Somebody taught him a lesson? "What? You don't believe it was an acci—"

Adrienne interrupted him.

"And then there's Ollie and Hazel. Sneaking around together. All crazy people. Nobody should be here." Although she didn't hold back, Adrienne only said what Ed thought himself. He was just grateful she hadn't mentioned him and Mel. However, she wasn't quite finished and Ed braced himself. "You need to be careful, Edward," she concluded, thankfully a little calmer.

"Careful? Why do you say that?"

"Because something isn't right. I don't believe why you are all here."

"That's for us to dec—"

"And I don't think everybody will stay until the end. I have a feeling." Despite her protestations, she finally steadied herself. But Ed was still deciphering what she could mean. *Not everybody will stay until the end?* "Watch your back, Edward. Do the jobs that Joyce wants you to do, take your money, if it even exists, and go home. That is my advice."

A scream from elsewhere caught the reply in his throat. They both spun in unison and in the distance, Ed could see someone flailing around. At first, he thought it was somebody having fun, messing about. But the splashing became more severe, out of control.

It wasn't until they heard the distinctive voice of Charlie shouting for help that he realised it was Mel in the water. And she was in trouble.

31

ATTEMPTING to turn his bloody canoe, Ed quickly became frustrated. The damn thing wouldn't face the way he wanted it to, and the more he dug his paddle in, the more it seemed to want to go in the opposite direction. At one point, he considered jumping in the water and swimming after Mel. *My infatuation is getting out of control.*

With the help of Adrienne, they both lined up each other's canoes and paddled towards the commotion. Thankfully, by the time they arrived, Mel had stopped flailing around and instead clung to her upturned canoe. Unbelievably, Charlie wore a smirk across his face.

"What the fuck are you grinning at?" Ed shouted at him.

"Oh, here he is," Charlie retorted. "Don't worry, darling. Your lover has come to the rescue."

Not knowing where to look, Ed turned his head sideways, directly towards Adrienne. She had good enough manners to shrug her shoulders before nodding at Mel and reminding Ed why they were actually there.

"We need to help her out," she said.

"Not my fault she fell in," Charlie remarked. "Silly girl just—"

"Just what?" Mel shouted, blowing seawater from her mouth as she spoke. "You pushed me over, you bastard!"

Ed looked around for the others, but Ollie and Louis were nowhere to be seen.

"Don't believe her," Charlie shouted aloud to nobody in particular, paddling in circles. "She just tipped over. Quite funny, it was actually."

"Hold that end of it," Ed instructed, and Adrienne held as firmly as she could. With a heave, Ed hoisted Mel far enough out of the water so she could slide herself up onto the canoe. After a bit of wriggling, she turned and dropped her backside into the seat. She lifted her knees to her chin and wrapped her arms tightly around her legs. Instructing her to remain as steady as she could, Ed paddled awkwardly to shore whilst dragging her canoe beside him. And all the while, he wondered if Charlie did indeed know about them.

Once they reached dry land, Ed clambered out of his canoe and waded through the water to push Mel up onto the bank. He lifted her out and supported her to the now familiar bench. Charlie and Adrienne had caught up, and it pleased Ed when Adrienne took over and offered Mel a drink from the picnic basket. Charlie looked at him out of the corner of his eye, and with a wry smile, helped himself to a cold beer.

Ollie soon got bored. He raced Louis a couple of times, but lost them both by quite some distance. Louis smiled and made some gesture with his hands, but Ollie didn't understand what he meant.

Allowing his canoe to drift, he watched Louis as he

ploughed his way through the waves and towards the shore. It wasn't where they set off from, though, a considerable distance away. Louis climbed out of his canoe, elevated it above his shoulders in one movement, collected the paddle, before disappearing into the dense trees. Ollie couldn't understand why he would leave the others out at sea and thought he looked as though he was in a hurry.

The rest of the group were out of sight. They must have raced around the shoreline further than he expected. And then he got cold. His flimsy T-shirt was wet from his excessive exuberance and the wind picked up slightly too. Ollie slowly began paddling towards the spot where he had seen Louis go ashore. He was too tired to return to the others, not that he had time for any of them, anyway.

As he drifted, he thought of his argument with Hazel the day before and how Joyce had remonstrated with them. She gave them strict instructions never to repeat such behaviour and stated that she would seriously reconsider their payment if they continued to disrupt the group. But Ollie doubted she meant it.

However, he did feel guilty for not stopping Joyce or informing Hazel that their host was on her way to her room. It was a selfish thing to do and could have landed Hazel in big trouble. Maybe it already had because, after Joyce lectured them, she asked Ollie and Louis to leave so she could speak to her in private.

Bollocks, Ollie thought, paddling as fast as he could, despite his aching scrawny arms. *Have I left Hazel in deep shit?*

Finally, he reached the shoreline, where he presumed Louis had gone ashore a good thirty minutes before. He jumped into the sea and dragged his canoe out of the water. Ollie was agitated, panicking, and couldn't understand why Hazel had decided not to join them for the day. What did she say, a nasty headache? Ollie didn't believe her. Did she really want to be left alone? And Joyce had subsequently sent Louis and Adrienne out canoeing, too. They hadn't socialised with the group since they arrived, so why now?

Shit, shit, shit.

As he pulled his canoe up the bank, the pathway through the trees was barely passable, so he decided he'd come back and collect it later. Peeling off his life jacket, he broke into a jog, running up the narrow path, over-grown thistles catching his wet ankles and calves. The château was at the top of the hill, all tracks led there, so he knew he just had to follow his nose.

Eventually, he reached the welcoming green grass. The familiarity somehow had a calming effect on him, and he allowed himself to slow down, walk at a more realistic pace as he approached the terrace from the rear.

"Aha, here he is," Joyce quipped as Ollie walked across the lawn to join the others underneath the canopy. She watched as he took in the rest of the group, as if bewildered by how they had beaten him back. Next, he glanced up at the upstairs windows of the château and Joyce wondered if he'd heard the same door slamming, which she did a few moments earlier.

She waited patiently until he sat down. Adrienne offered him a bottle of cold water, which he readily accepted, but Ollie looked in a world of his own, preoccupied, perturbed. Joyce didn't like the way he was acting. Nonetheless, she painted on her best smile before standing in front of the group and addressing them directly.

"A couple of things you all need to know," she began, instantaneously gaining everybody's interest. She studied their faces, not a hundred percent sure what she was actually looking for. "The police called earlier, whilst you were all out enjoying yourselves." Joyce couldn't help but smile at the glazed expressions which greeted her statement.

"I didn't see them," Ollie retorted, hoping his fellow guests would support him whilst taking a sip of his water every other second.

"It's quite a large expanse of water, Oliver," Joyce replied, half-expecting somebody to question her. "You would need eyes in the back of your head to follow every single vessel going back and forth to the mainland."

Ollie didn't appear over-convinced, but the lack of advocacy ensured he kept his mouth shut. Joyce continued unabated. "The post-mortem is complete and I'm pleased to set your minds at rest that Tony's death was indeed an accident." Nobody moved, their focus on Joyce never waning. "They say he either fell into the sea, or…" Joyce paused and exchanged a glance with Louis. He nodded, as if giving permission for her to continue. "… or, he jumped."

Over to her right, Adrienne gasped, compelling Joyce to flinch in return.

"Which one do they think?" Ollie spoke again. Joyce struggled to hide her contempt but still responded in a diplomatic tone.

"I'm not sure, Oliver. Could be either. And to be honest, I could believe whichever one turned out to be the truth." Joyce contemplated her own reply, giving each version its own merit, but she knew she had to remain upbeat. "Anyway, however sad, and however upsetting, especially for Hazel finding him, the show can now go on.

I'm sure Tony would have wanted the château to be finished."

I doubt he gave a shit, was the collective response she read on everybody's face. Joyce almost laughed.

She went on to explain the police would deal with the coroner and get in touch with Tony's brother back in England to arrange what to do with the body. He was his only living relative, although they hadn't spoken for several years. Joyce said a local funeral could take place if necessary, but there would be a lot of bureaucracy and something she wanted to avoid.

As long as you gullible fools believe me, that's all that matters, she concluded under her breath before exchanging a further look with Louis.

32

MEL LISTENED INTENTLY, her eyes not once leaving their host. Joyce appeared genuine, but then again, she'd come across as authentic since the very first email inviting them all to France. But once she finished, Mel found the smile on her face somewhat disturbing, as if removing the very last remnants of her ex-husband was quite therapeutic.

However, Joyce's next topic of conversation ensured Mel remained upright, her back stiff and her eyes wide. From that evening onwards, she instructed Charlie to sleep in Tony's old room. Adrienne had stripped the bed, cleaned the ensuite, and given the place a thorough makeover.

"I think it's for the best if you two give each other some space, don't you? Louis told me about the *incident* whilst canoeing," Joyce air quoted. "He came back early to tell me."

She spoke to Charlie and Mel as if she'd broken up their fight in the playground.

"It will give us all some space, if you ask me."

Mel glared at Ollie.

"Well, nobody did ask you, did they?" Charlie said, a vein in his temple protruding.

"Now, now," Joyce attempted to act as peacemaker. Mel thought she looked quite exasperated. Was she losing control?

"What about Hazel?" Ollie asked next, bored with the ongoing Mel and Charlie saga. Mel was pleased with the change of subject and she was also secretly ecstatic she didn't have to share a room with her husband. She caught herself glancing towards Ed. He was already looking at her.

Joyce informed everybody Hazel still had a migraine and wouldn't be joining them that evening. Mel didn't like the sound of it. Just how bad was this headache?

"Has she been out of her room at all today?" she enquired, desperately attempting to compose herself.

"Yes, she has," Joyce replied, very matter-of-factly. Her change of tone surprised Mel. Joyce's lack of sympathy for anybody's situation was quite sobering. The woman had a heart of stone.

"And did she have her headache then?" Mel ignored Joyce's initial response, keen to probe further. She noticed Joyce sigh, obviously irked with the ongoing questions.

"She had one this morning when you went canoeing. But then I found her later in the garden and she said it was better. But about half an hour before you returned, she found me in the kitchen and said it had come back. I gave her some stronger painkillers to help her sleep."

"So, is it a migraine? A normal headache?"

"Wow, so many questions, Melanie. I'd have thought you have enough of your own problems to resolve rather than try to fix everybody else's."

With that bombshell, Joyce excused herself and asked Adrienne to bring dinner to her room that evening.

Louis followed her inside, leaving the four remaining guests and Adrienne on the terrace. Nobody appeared to know what to say. It pleased Mel when Charlie finally said he would go upstairs and sort his stuff out if he was going to be using Tony's room. Mel didn't believe he looked as contented as her at the news. "Are you coming to help?" he asked, turning in the doorway. Mel shook her head, not even wanting to talk to him. How could she forgive him after he tipped her out of her canoe and laughed in her face? He mumbled something under his breath before asking Adrienne if she could take him some food later, too. "And two bottles of red," he added, laughing out loud.

As soon as Charlie disappeared, Ed spoke up. "That sounds like a plan, Adrienne," he said, winking at Mel. "Any chance of a bottle out on the terrace?" Ed then turned to Ollie. "Oh, and two glasses, please."

Ollie watched Ed disparagingly. The way he looked at him when he said *'oh, and two glasses please'*. Who did he think he was, some big shot writer and Ollie wasn't worthy of his company? And Mel smiling, happy that Ed was thinking of her. She should have followed her husband upstairs, attempted to sort out her marriage, not go drinking with some stranger she'd only just met. Ollie felt yet another pang for his wife and what he'd give for one more conversation with her. Perhaps Ollie was jealous of Charlie and now he was becoming envious of Ed? It would certainly explain why he didn't like either of them.

He glared towards Ed and Mel, who had repositioned two chairs to overlook the gardens. A small table sat afore them, holding a bottle of wine in a cooler and two glasses. Ollie noisily dragged his wooden seat back and stomped off into the house. He didn't look behind but felt assured they would look at him over their shoulder and feel nothing but guilt for leaving him out of their little tête-à-tête. Ollie smiled as he took the grand staircase two at a time, a renewed spring in his step.

Once in his room, he paced for a while. To the window and back to the bed before repeating the same action over and over. He remembered the footsteps outside on the gravel and then a door banging from somewhere inside when he returned from canoeing. *Shit, Hazel.* Cursing himself for having a mind like a sieve, Ollie recalled his original plan to check on his accomplice.

Hearing voices along the landing, he soon determined it was Joyce and Charlie. Wasn't he supposed to be in Tony's old room? Impatiently, he waited for them to stop talking, but the conversation laboured, leaving Ollie with no option but to bide his time. He lay on his bed, reached for the remote control and flicked through endless films and TV programmes on Netflix. It was the only thing he'd been able to find in English since they arrived. But Ollie couldn't see anything worthy of his attention, so he switched the set off and rested his head onto the large soft pillows. They felt cool against his neck, soothing, and he allowed his eyes to close, counting down the days until they left the island.

An hour later, Ollie had barely moved, totally immersed in thought. He considered how he'd become so desperate for money back home in London. The accident which cost him his driving licence. But how could he have failed the breath test? Ollie didn't drink, and he remembered hearing somebody laugh when he announced he never touched the stuff.

The pub was his last drop-off that day. A parcel for the landlord. The same landlord who asked him if he would like a drink on the house. "Why not?" Ollie replied, pleased at the generous offer.

He stayed for two. Two fresh orange juices. Ollie found alcohol made his OCD ten times worse. Even the doctor told him to avoid it. So how did two normal orange juices contain enough alcohol to push him twice over the drink driving limit? Simple. His drinks were spiked.

For six months, Ollie deliberated who could have done it. Of course, the police weren't interested. They were far too busy to listen to such complaints and follow it up. They did tell Ollie they'd spoken to the landlord, but he had seen nothing because Ollie took his drinks outside underneath the canopy. The outdoor heaters were on, and Ollie told the landlord he wanted some fresh air after being stuck in his van all day.

The pub garden was deserted. It was a Wednesday afternoon at four o'clock and people were still at work. He left his drink twice; once to go inside and visit the restroom and on the second occasion to fetch his phone from the van in the car park. And it was when he was in the car park Ollie spotted someone in a car. He was talking on his mobile, wearing a baseball cap, tipped low and covering his face. A blue Ford car. Ever since, it's the only person Ollie could believe had spiked his drink.

After leaving the pub, he drove into a parked car. Nobody was in it, and Ollie wasn't injured. However, there were witnesses. It was on the outskirts of London in rush hour. The police arrived within minutes, took statements, and made Ollie take the dreaded breath test. He'd been cocky. Told them he hadn't touched a drop for years, but the officers regarded him sceptically, as if they'd heard it all before. "Just blow into the plastic mouthpiece, sir," one of them instructed.

Ollie couldn't believe it as the test turned positive. He protested his innocence, but it fell on deaf ears. A further urine and blood test back at the station confirmed he was over the limit and, as a result, Ollie lost his licence for twelve months. Already on the poverty line, the lack of income threatened to push him over the edge. *Until the email from Joyce.*

This isn't a coincidence, he concluded, standing and pacing his room to the large window once more. *Could whoever drove that blue Ford Escort know he would end up in France?* That's ridiculous. It's six months later. How could they know?

But Ollie was no longer sure. He'd never put two and two together before, but he now doubted everything and everybody. Returning to his bed, he contemplated the other thing he always tried to push to the back of his mind: how he met his wife.

It was a good few years after he left school. Ollie was twenty-six and was spending a week in Lincolnshire, catching up with old friends and family. He didn't recognise her, but as soon as he set eyes upon Chloe Jones, his heart did somersaults.

They were in the village pub, the only place for anybody to convene, given the rural location. As usual, it was busy on a Friday evening and all the tables were taken, leaving standing room only around the bar. Ollie bought his friend a pint of ale and himself a Diet Coke. Whilst propped up against the mantlepiece over a huge inglenook fireplace, they settled for a chat. And that's when he spotted Chloe, and she spotted him.

For the next fifteen minutes, Ollie's friend continually nudged his arm to get him to pay attention. "Yeah, yeah," Ollie replied, without listening to a word he said. Chloe was with a friend. Her boyfriend, Ollie discovered later. He looked like a geek: tall, scrawny, and unkempt. Ollie realised he was no substitute for Brad Pitt, but compared to that loser, he wondered what the hell Chloe saw in him.

But the geek soon noticed Chloe watching Ollie too, and in return, Chloe watching him. He said something to her, and they began to argue, but the packed pub drowned out anything they might be saying. After a few more moments of silence, Chloe stood and stormed out the rear door, and Ollie took it as his cue.

He found her in the garden, pacing up and down. He couldn't help but admire her, despite her mood. She had long brown hair and wore a flowing dress. Ollie knew she wasn't fashionable or obsessed with her appearance. Perhaps that was the appeal? Chloe was different. He subsequently discovered she was an artist, talented at that. He'd landed on his feet.

Her boyfriend found them kissing in the beer garden. He took a swing at Ollie but missed miserably despite several attempts. The landlord eventually split them up and asked the guy to leave. He went wild, cursing and threatening retribution, much to the amusement of everybody in the crowd which had grown during the confrontation.

For the following month, Chloe's former boyfriend engaged in intimidating phone calls and sending numerous sinister texts. However, soon after, she moved into Ollie's flat in London and changed her number. It was the last time Chloe heard from her ex.

It was a whirlwind romance, and Ollie was head-over-heels. They both were. They'd met their soulmate. Within a year, they were wed, and despite Ollie having no interest in art, he loved the fact that he was married to somebody so talented.

They spent nine blissful years together. They had little money and lived in a rundown flat in north London. But wealth didn't bother Ollie, as long as they had enough to survive. They were the best nine years of his life. Until that fateful night, almost a year ago, as Chloe walked to her car following an art exhibition.

Ollie stood again and paced to the window. *Is this all connected?* He recalled those threatening text messages; the way Chloe's ex-boyfriend cursed them as he was dragged from the pub kicking and screaming. But the thing that played on his mind the most was when Chloe explained where she met that boy. It was whilst they worked at the same travel firm, but she'd first known him at Ridgeview Grammar School. When Ollie asked why they didn't get together earlier, she said they had expelled him before she had the chance.

Without an accomplice, Ollie knew he could never prove if the trip to France was connected. *That school.* He realised his own inadequacies. He wasn't too bright, and he needed somebody to help him think. And until they fell out, he had a collaborator, and she was asleep in the room just along the corridor.

Yes, he remembered, *I need to talk to Hazel. And this time I'll tell her my full story. Every last detail.*

Even though she called him a cretin, told him he was an imbecile, Hazel was all he had.

Splashing his face with cold water, Ollie looked at his gaunt reflection in the mirror and set off to knock on his partner's door.

33

Ed watched Ollie as he stomped to the house. The way he dragged his chair back and tutted his disapproval so loudly almost made him laugh. He had no time for him though. His inadequacy of holding a decent conversation wore Ed down. Not long before, he would have been upset with himself for having such inconsiderate thoughts towards someone, but the trip was changing Ed. His patience was wearing incredibly thin. He even noticed how little compassion he felt for Tony when Joyce told them of the police findings. *It's a dead human, for crying out loud.* But he didn't care, and his lack of sympathy frightened him.

"How you feeling?" he asked, taking the bottle of wine from the cooler before filling Mel's glass.

"I'm okay now. Thanks for helping today."

After pouring his own, Ed sat back and took a long sip of the ice-cold drink. He felt it run along his throat and continue its journey to the pit of his stomach. It was a pleasant feeling. Reassuring, calming. "And what about Joyce's suggestion that you and Charlie sleep separately?"

Mel nodded without speaking. Instead, she looked into her glass, deep in thought. After realising she wasn't going to offer a reply, Ed became lost in his own world, too.

"Ed?"

Although enjoying the silence, he noticed Mel's concerned expression. "Yeah?"

"Don't you think Joyce acted a little strange earlier? She hasn't once shown any remorse towards Tony, and she described the police findings so matter-of-factly, you would have thought she could have been talking about him committing a speeding offence or something."

Ed tried to lighten the mood. He'd already given Tony as much of his time as he'd wanted.

"To tell you the truth, I'm finding everybody a little strange." He nodded at Mel, smiling.

"Hey, thanks." She punched his arm, but within seconds, her apprehensive expression returned. "I'm being serious. Have you noticed she has no sympathy for Hazel, either? Poor girl, those headaches, and she was the one who discovered Tony in the sea."

Ed took another sip of his wine. He recalled Hazel sneaking into Joyce's room. Had she found something or subsequently discovered something else? And that dream. Hazel was convinced somebody stood at the end of her bed. *Not just somebody, Ed. She told you his name.* He opened his mouth to reply, but Mel hadn't quite finished.

"And not only today. She's *never* had time for Hazel. She's always despised her. I haven't heard her say a good word to—"

"Mel," Ed interrupted. Mel stopped and stared at him. He couldn't help but admire how beautiful she was. "If you think about it, Joyce doesn't have time for anybody. I get the impression she's using all of us for her own benefit. And all that bullshit about us being the group she remembers the most from school, or we're foremost in her mind. I don't believe a word——"

"I'm not so sure." It was Mel's turn to interrupt. "In fact, I'm beginning to think we might be at the very centre of her thoughts. We always have been."

Ed's mind wandered back to his conversation whilst out canoeing earlier. "Adrienne thinks there's something odd about it all, too. She told me we had to be careful." He lied about the 'we' part, but he had genuinely thought of Mel when Adrienne only addressed himself. He went on to explain Adrienne couldn't understand how much Joyce was paying them, or how crazy people like Ollie and Hazel were and how angry Tony was all the time.

"Maybe she's right," Mel replied, "but Joyce has explained all of this. She knew we all needed the money, and she has cash to burn."

"And do you believe her?"

Mel looked at Ed before switching her focus on to the woods at the end of the garden. She never answered, but Ed knew exactly what she thought.

Charlie placed his bag on the bed and stuffed it with his clothes from the wardrobe. He knew he should keep them on their coat hangers and instead carry them to his new room, but Charlie was far too angry to waste time and countless excursions up and down the landing. He surprised himself that he was allowing his appearance to drop. Not once during his life had Charlie Green not prided himself on how he looked. Pristine clothes, highlighted hair, always held in position with wax or gel, and personal hygiene fit for a king. But he was losing interest in what people thought of him. "What the fuck is happening to me?" he asked himself aloud in between trips to his wardrobe.

After shoving his toothbrush and other toiletries into the top of the holdall, Charlie sat on the edge of the bed. He looked at the pillows propped up behind him; his and Mel's. Then he turned to the wardrobe, half empty, only her pretty items left, hanging neatly to one side. *The PE kit!*

It was gone. He emptied his bag onto the bed, checked every item as he bundled them all back inside before sitting down again. It was definitely missing.

"What is this?" Again, he asked out loud, as if somebody was standing on the far side of the room. "Why the hell are we here?"

Charlie stood and stepped over to the wardrobe. He pushed both doors shut simultaneously with a clatter. The mahogany cupboard shook and the empty coat hangers bounced against the interior walls. He opened it again, with just as much force, and threw Mel's clothes onto the floor. Once he emptied it, he stepped over to the chest of drawers and did exactly the same with her underwear and other small garments. He looked behind him; the floorboards strewn with all her belongings.

"Ha!" he said to his imaginary friend. "Melanie Green is my wife, and she belongs to me. If I can't have her, then nobody can."

Charlie kicked her clothes into a pile in the middle of the room. He eventually stopped with a gasp when he saw a figure standing in his doorway.

"I think you need to tidy this up before you go to your own room," Joyce said calmly. "Don't you, Charlie?"

. . .

Ollie opened his bedroom door a fraction, enough to pacify himself the coast was finally clear. He hoped Charlie would now be in his new bedroom, out of the way, before smiling to himself as he remembered what happened to the last occupant of that room; *washed up in the sea with the fish nibbling his dead skin.*

Creeping along the landing, he soon found himself outside Hazel's door. He had second thoughts. What if she yelled at him again? It would alert everyone, and then the inevitable questions would begin. *Why are you sneaking into Hazel's room? Where else have you been?* But Ollie had come this far, and he knew Hazel was the only person he could trust. With a glance over the balustrade, he tapped lightly on the sturdy wooden door. Silence. He tapped again. Nothing. With a shrug of his shoulders, Ollie turned the door handle, oh so slowly, until it clicked into place.

He opened it just wide enough to peek inside and saw Hazel laying on her bed. From his position, she looked comatose. After one last glance behind, Ollie entered the room and tiptoed over to her side, fully conscious she might awaken and scream the roof down.

"Hazel," he whispered, "Hazel."

She stirred. "Hmmm?"

"Hazel, it's me. Ollie."

She slowly opened her eyes, enough to squint through and see Ollie leaning over her. Quickly, he lifted his head, aware of how close he was and put his finger to his lips. "Shh. It's only me. I'm on my own."

He watched as her eyes opened a little wider. She looked to her bedroom door, as if checking Ollie was telling the truth.

"Ollie?" she asked. Her voice was groggy, and Ollie couldn't believe how pale she was since he'd last seen her.

"I'm here to check if you're okay. I was worried about you."

Hazel attempted to lift herself onto her elbows, but she was too shaky. Ollie quickly grabbed a spare pillow from her side and placed it behind her head. She smiled weakly as she allowed herself to lie back down.

"Ollie?" she whispered. Her eyes closed, and he thought she was drifting back off.

"Yes. What is it?"

Her eyes opened again, ever so slightly. She looked eager to keep them open, but they fought desperately against her. "I think…"

"Yes, yes. You think what?" Ollie was impatient. He could feel his right leg twitching, and he placed his hand on it to quell the movement.

"I think she's drugged me."

Ollie glanced at the bedroom door over his shoulder, his interest piqued and adrenaline gushing around his body. He raised his voice just above a whisper. "Who, Joyce?"

Hazel nodded. Once. Twice. The slightest of movements.

"How do you know?"

"I'm too sleepy." Her eyes closed, as if to emphasise her point. "I've never felt so tired…"

Hazel's head dropped to one side. Ollie wanted to slap her cheek, like in the movies. Fortunately, he spotted a glass of water on her bedside table. "Have a drink of this."

Her eyes opened faintly as she took one or two sips.

"But why would she be drugging you? It makes no sense."

"She found me… in her room…"

"When? When?" He knew exactly when, but Ollie's

excitement threatened to boil over. Both legs jerked, and he kept scratching at an imaginary itch on the back of his neck.

"The other day, when you…"

Yeah, yeah. When I let you down.

"What happened, Hazel?"

"I found something."

"Found what? What the hell are you talking about?"

"Ollie. You must get away. She doesn't have any—"

The door opening made Ollie spring to his feet. He spilt water from the tumbler. Joyce stood in the doorway.

"What on earth are you doing in here, Oliver?" she asked, quickly striding across the room.

"I came to see Hazel," he replied, looking back at the bed. Hazel had already drifted off to sleep. He looked at the glass. "I just gave her a drink. I hope that's okay."

Joyce grabbed the tumbler. Ollie didn't know if she believed him.

"Did she have a drink?"

"Yes, just a little sip. But she didn't say anything."

They both looked at Hazel, her eyes shut and her breathing steady.

Joyce walked to the door and opened it for Ollie to leave. As he reached her, she took the smallest of steps forward, not enough to stop him from exiting, but enough to inform him she hadn't quite finished.

"You lied to me, didn't you, Oliver Ramsey?" His eyes opened wide and he couldn't think of a single thing to say. "I heard you *both* talking," she continued quietly. "And I've never liked liars."

34

HAZEL WOKE WITH A START, her heart racing and the back of her neck cold with sweat. *Another nightmare?* Checking her watch, she realised she'd slept all afternoon and now missed dinner. It was eight-thirty. Her stomach complained, and she considered finding Adrienne to ask if she could fix her a sandwich or something light to eat. *Adrienne?* Hadn't she provided her with paracetamol earlier? Yes, and later she found Joyce in the kitchen, informed her the migraine had returned and Joyce said she would bring something stronger. *Something to help you sleep.*

But that was hours ago. What the hell had she given her?

Ollie? Did Ollie visit her too? *You must get away…*

Standing groggily, Hazel stepped over to her mini fridge and helped herself to a bottle of ice-cold Coke. It hit the spot perfectly. Realising how rough she must look, she decided to shower, turned it to a cool setting and undressed. Instantly, the water felt invigorating, and she tilted her head to let the rushing stream flow over her face and body. She wanted to stand there forever, the effect washing away all the negative feelings. But despite her efforts, the dream, the notebook, the bank statement, all flashed in and out of her mind, like somebody shouting each one in turn.

Hazel forced herself to count down the days until the entire charade was over. *Maybe fifteen more*, she calculated. *Thirteen or fourteen if we get the work done on time. Take the money and run and never reply to another message from Joyce Young for the rest of your life.*

The knocking on her door abruptly jolted her from her trance-like state.

"Who is it?" she shouted, annoyed that she couldn't be left alone.

Nothing.

Tutting, she turned the shower off and dragged back the curtain. "Who is it?" she called for a second time, her head peeping out. Again, nothing. Cursing some more, Hazel stepped onto the bath mat and grabbed a pristine white towel from the rail. Quickly, she soaked up most of the water from her hair before drying her body as efficiently as she could. Wrapping the towel around herself, she reluctantly tiptoed into her room and made her way towards the door.

But the silence scared her. Had they left? But it didn't feel that way. Hazel had an overwhelming sensation that whoever knocked was still stood on the other side.

"Hello?" she said, her voice only a murmur. She stepped closer, her hand poised next to the handle, but not daring to actually grab hold of it. "Is somebody there?" Her heart thumped, and she grabbed the top of the towel. "I'm not opening the door unless you speak," she said, feeling a little more hopeful that whoever it was had left. Her hand dropped away from the handle and she turned to make her way back to the bathroom.

But as soon as Hazel peered in the mirror to inspect herself, she heard the bedroom door open. Almost jumping from her skin, she caught her knuckles on the base of the sink. It stung like hell and she immediately knew it would bruise.

"Is that you, Adrienne?" The bathroom door was closed, a thin wedge of wood between her and whoever had let themselves in. "Joyce?" Again, no answer. "Look, whoever is there, stop playing bloody games. It isn't funny."

Her heart pumped harder. Quickly, she scurried to the door and pushed it shut with a click, angry there was no lock. Frantically, she looked around the room, searching for something to defend herself with, but there was nothing. A loo brush and a can of deodorant were the only two things of substance she could see.

A footstep creaked on the wooden floor directly outside the door. Whoever it was, they were only inches away. Hazel backed off, gripping firmly onto the top of her towel.

She made it to the far side of the ensuite and squatted on her haunches. Although ridiculous, she couldn't think of anything else to do but to somehow make herself as small as possible. The handle turned and she watched as it clicked into position before the door rattled on itself, once, twice, until it eventually opened.

Hazel remained crouched, her entire body shaking, as the silhouette appeared before her.

And she knew exactly who it was, and this time it definitely wasn't a dream.

. . .

The following morning, Mel showered, desperate to invigorate herself after a dreadful night's sleep. It felt strange not having Charlie next to her, despite the sense of relief there would be no arguing and not wanting to beat the living daylights out of him.

But that wasn't all. She craved the attention of Ed. Not only did she want him, but she considered him the only person on the island who appeared to be coping with the growing unrest. By now, she detested her husband, but that was domestic and nothing to do with where they were. *Wasn't it?* It made Mel think. How were they getting on at home before they left? Not good. Not good at all. But was it just a bad patch? A period every marriage goes through? Mel had deliberated whether Charlie was having an affair in England, but she hadn't really contemplated actually leaving him. Then she overheard his phone call. All the "can't wait to see you" and "I won't be gone for long" to whoever was on the line. But even though Mel threatened to leave him, would she truly go through with it?

But as the days passed by, she'd turned against him more and more. An entirely separate feeling to anything she'd discerned before. Something deep inside, embedded, as if dormant for years and something had finally disturbed it, waking it from its slumber. And now, however much Mel tried, she simply could not put it back to rest.

The others were turning on each other, too. She recollected Ollie and Tony chatting. Hadn't they walked together at the airport? But it wasn't just Ollie. Nobody liked Tony by the time he left. And recently, Ollie detested Charlie, and Ed too. Charlie couldn't abide anybody, but it hadn't always been that way. He had beers with anyone who would listen to his stories, been chipper with Ollie and even asked Ed to go looking for her bloody earring. It may have been to get him alone, but Ed had mentioned nothing untoward happened, more of a general question of Ed's whereabouts when she lost it. Mel knew if Charlie really wanted to accuse Ed, he would have challenged him there and then. Her husband took no prisoners. But now, Ed and Charlie despised each other, too. Was it because of her or for some other reason altogether? Joyce and Hazel were constantly at each other's throats, and Ollie no longer had time for anybody, even ending up alone whilst out canoeing. It was as though the island was turning everybody against one another. The thought made Mel shiver.

Exhausted, she eventually fell asleep, but it was a painful nap, full of nightmares and sounds repeatedly waking her. She contemplated sneaking into Ed's room, but the sound of continual creaking floorboards outside on the landing meant somebody was sleeping even less than her.

Charlie eyed his wife sceptically when she came downstairs for breakfast. She looked tired, as exhausted as he felt. He had done as Joyce instructed and hung her clothes back in the wardrobe and replaced the other stuff in the chest of drawers.

But Tony's room gave him the creeps. He couldn't shake the sensation of a dead body once laying there, even though he knew it wasn't where Tony actually died. Charlie didn't even want to get into bed, especially naked, as he wasn't certain Adrienne had changed the bedding. The idea of his skin laying where Tony's once had made him feel nauseous. So he lay on top of the duvet all night and he put a towel on the pillow to rest his head. And he barely slept. The groaning floorboards on the landing saw to that.

Mel glanced at him after pouring herself a coffee, but showed no inclination to sit near him. Instead, she carried her breakfast to the table as far away as possible. The same table where Ed Lawson sat.

The last person to arrive was Ollie. Now he really did look like shit. So much so, it made Charlie feel a little better about himself.

There were three tables on the terrace. Ollie grabbed himself a coffee and eyed them individually. Ed and Mel sat at one. *Well, I'm not going anywhere near them*, he thought. Charlie occupied another by himself. *And that twat can sit by himself.* The final table was taken by Joyce and Louis. *She caught me in Hazel's room and I certainly can't be doing with any further questions this morning.*

So Ollie remained standing, his back propped against the wall. He half chewed on a warm croissant, but he had no appetite. However, the coffee was excellent. He finished one and quickly poured another.

"What work are we doing today, Joyce?" Charlie asked, breaking the silence like an ice-pick penetrating a frozen lake. Everybody turned to face him before focusing their attention on their host. Ollie noticed how pale everyone appeared, dark patches beneath their eyes and they all cradled coffees as if their lives depended on it. Joyce pushed her chair back and stood, facing the group the best she could, given their proximity.

"Melanie and Edward will continue with the flower

beds." She spoke confidently, her authority not once diminishing. The ideological school teacher. "Charlie will cut the hedges, and you, Oliver, will finish pruning and weeding. The gardening needs to be finished today, as the weather is definitely breaking."

Ollie couldn't believe Joyce was carrying on as normal. Her ex-husband had just died. She had a member of the party in bed with dreadful migraines and a married couple threatening to cut each other's throats. Nobody was getting on. The atmosphere dripped with tension and now Hazel had told him to get away from the island.

"What about Hazel?" he enquired. Ollie expected the look Joyce gave him. Her eyes narrowed and mouth pursed in a straight line. However, she soon recomposed herself and addressed the group rather than him individually.

"I think I'll take Hazel to the mainland. It's probably best they check her over as her headaches appear to be getting worse." She then turned to Ollie. "As you well know, Oliver."

"Do you mean take her to see a doctor?"

Everybody turned to Mel.

"Yes," Joyce replied derisively. "Of course, a doctor. Where else would I be taking her? To an art gallery?"

Louis chuckled, but for the first time since they arrived, nobody else joined in with Joyce's derogatory remark.

"I'd like to come, too," Mel said, standing and with a defiance in her voice. But Joyce laughed mockingly.

"No, no, dear. The gardens need finishing. We're already one man down, and now, with Hazel feeling unwell, I can't afford anybody else dropping out. The jobs are stacking up and they—"

"What jobs?" Ollie stepped forward from the wall, holding a coffee which trembled slightly in his hand. Joyce spun to face him. "We're mowing the lawn, picking some weeds. It's nothing a qualified gardener couldn't handle himself in one afternoon. And then what, repaint all the rooms again? This is all bullshit—"

Joyce stood abruptly and took a step towards him. The smile had left her face, replaced by something much sterner, as if she was addressing a badly behaved schoolboy in one of her classes. "I told you last night, Oliver Ramsey. You need to do as you're told, do the jobs you're assigned to do, and keep that big mouth of yours shut." She took yet another step closer and Ollie found himself stiff against the wall. "Unless you want to come to the mainland, too?" He shook his head slowly. "But bring your belongings and your passport, because you won't be welcome at my château for one minute more. Do I make myself clear?"

Ollie's eyes darted over Joyce's shoulder. What was he looking for? Camaraderie? A little solidarity from his fellow workers? Well, if he was, he soon realised none was coming his way. That particular horse had long bolted. Charlie, Ed, Mel and Louis all glared at him. Were they daring him to stand up to Joyce? Willing him on, even? See how far she really would take things? He felt like their sacrificial fucking lamb.

But then something struck. If Joyce was taking Hazel to the mainland, she would be gone for at least two hours. The group had been given menial tasks, jobs she wouldn't possibly know they'd actually completed. If he did the minimal amount, he could easily slip inside and sneak into her room. Yes, he would even be doing Hazel a service, keeping the team together.

Ollie smiled at Joyce, which only appeared to irritate

her further. But he no longer cared. Joyce was just another name on his list of people he despised. He had far more important issues on his mind and he couldn't wait to find out exactly what Hazel was talking about the previous day.

35

WITH A PETROL-DRIVEN hedge trimmer gripped in his hands, Charlie hovered his finger over the stop-start button. It was only when the bell rang that he snapped out of his trance, realising he'd been gazing out at sea for several minutes. Shifting his attention to the house, he spotted Adrienne in the distance, carrying a tray, and Ollie leisurely making his way across the lawn towards her. Meanwhile, Louis emerged from the barn. Lifting the heavy machinery straps over his head, he lay the trimmer on the floor before casually strolling over to the terrace too. With one last look out to sea, he wondered if Hazel and Joyce had made it safely to the mainland and how many more bloody days he would be stuck on the island.

"Thanks, Adrienne," Ed said politely as he took a bottle of ice-cold water from the tray. Charlie wanted to punch his posh lights out. "Yes, thank you, Adrienne," his wife repeated, taking her own. *They're like a married fucking couple*, Charlie thought. *Look at them, chatting and working together, as if they're the bloody dream team.* He looked away when Ed glanced in his direction, not wanting to give him the satisfaction that their newfound friendship bothered him. Underneath the surface, however, Charlie fumed.

"Don't any of you think it's strange Will Parry was murdered just a few weeks before we all came here?"

Ollie's question stunned everyone. The terrace fell silent in a heartbeat. Ed almost spat the drink from his mouth, whilst Mel stared wide-eyed at Ollie. Even Louis stopped whatever he was doing and instead glared at Ollie. The only person who the question didn't appear to affect was Adrienne. She continued to busy herself laying out a plate of pastries on the far table, her back to the group.

"I didn't know you knew him?" Ed eventually broke the silence. Charlie couldn't help but notice how shaky his voice was.

"Who said I did?" Ollie replied, far too quickly and so riddled with guilt, Charlie almost laughed.

"So why mention him?" Ed asked, a little calmer, no doubt encouraged by Ollie's obvious lie.

"Just something Hazel mentioned to me. She said she saw it in the local—"

"Aha, the famous detective duo," Louis laughed, his attention already diminishing.

Ollie blushed, and Charlie noticed his right leg jigging up and down at the knee.

"Fuck off, Louis," Ollie said out of nowhere. Louis stood; his eyes boring into Ollie's. Adrienne darted in front of him and began talking quickly in French. Louis glanced between her and Ollie. She placed her hand on his shoulder, and he sat back down, his gaze not shifting from the guy who dared to confront him.

"As I was saying," Ollie continued. He was visibly shaking, but somehow determined to say what he had to say. Charlie admired his tenacity, at least. "Surely it can't be a coincidence?"

"What do you mean?" Mel looked scared, and Charlie wished he could walk over and put his arm around her.

"Well, come on, Mel," Ollie replied. "We're all ex-pupils from Ridgeview Grammar School. Invited by an old history teacher. And during our time at that school, there was a bully who was subsequently expelled, and then he gets himself mysteriously murdered only a few weeks before we arrive here."

A moment's silence fell between the group.

"It has to be coincidence," Ed finally suggested. "None of us have seen him since he left." He paused, scanning the others. "Have we?" Everybody looked at one another, but nobody committed to answer the question either way. Ed took the silence as an affirmative. "There you go, Ollie. It's pure coincidence."

Charlie looked from Ed back to Ollie and noticed Ollie didn't appear at all convinced.

Will Parry glared at his computer. It was old, slow and needed replacing. But Will only used it for social media and email, and he got so few of those, apart from junk, so he considered buying a new one a complete waste of money. Not that he could afford it, anyway. Jeez, he was struggling to put food on the table, let alone purchase new electronic equipment.

Seven months before, he celebrated sixteen years working as a postman, a job he didn't mind doing given the easy lifestyle and perks of the role. But it all came crashing to a sudden halt after he literally got caught in the act.

Will had befriended a woman ten years his senior, a year or so before. Her address was part of his regular morning round, and it all began when she needed to sign for one particular letter. She answered the door wearing only her dressing gown and Will couldn't help but notice she hadn't quite tied the belt tight enough. She immediately followed his eyeline and smiled broadly in response.

It transpired her husband regularly worked away, weeks or months at a time, and she was lonely, missing male company. Will had recently split with his own long-term girlfriend, so the timing couldn't be better where he was concerned. Their meetings became a regular occurrence. So much so, his boss quizzed him a month later about why his round was taking an hour longer than normal. So, he would go around after work rather than during and they would spend most afternoons in bed, like teenagers discovering sex for the first time.

However, just after his sixteen-year anniversary with the postal service, her husband returned home unexpectedly. He caught them in bed and tried to fight Will Parry, a desperate show of masculinity in front of his wife. But Will never lost the ability to defend himself, and despite being naked, he punched the married guy until he lay unconscious on the floor.

Following prosecution, they handed Will a large fine and sixty hours of community service. He was dismissed from his job, after they proved he began the affair during work, and hadn't been able to land another position of employment since. Not that he bothered too much.

Intensifying his misery, Will's fling told him she didn't want to see him again and wanted to give her marriage one more chance. However, the one thing neither Will nor she could ever believe was why her husband turned up that day. He wasn't due home for at least another fortnight. She asked him and texted Will soon after to inform him someone had tipped him off she was having an affair. Neither of them ever found out who blew the whistle.

. . .

But Will Parry refused the invitation from Joyce Young. He ignored the caveat, and he deleted the email. The money sounded unbeliev-able, but so did the request. Ten grand to clean a château? They must think I'm fucking mad.

One week later, he was dead. Murdered in cold blood in his own home. The day they turned up on his doorstep, he realised he should never have let that person in, but hindsight is a wonderful thing. Besides, what did he have to worry about with him, of all people?

The last thing Will Parry could remember was the steel blade as it sliced into his throat and the distinct sound of laughter from behind.

36

BORING BLOODY WEEDING. *What kind of task is this?* Ollie dug the hoe into the ground for the umpteenth time and dragged it back across the rock-hard soil. The sharp blade caught some of the greenery as it reluctantly gave way and lay forlornly on the surface. He thought they were weeds, but how should he know? Nobody showed him which were the real plants. It's how Ollie recognised the tasks Joyce was setting them were just a ploy, and why he told her it was all bullshit. Of course, she flew off the handle. She had to cover her tracks. But he knew the entire charade was just that. A farce. But there still had to be a reason, and he still needed the cash.

Now and then, he looked back to the château, awaiting his opportunity, but Adrienne sat on the bloody terrace reading a book. Was it Ed's book? Ollie had forgotten all about that. Perhaps he should read his own copy, see what that clever idiot had written about. *I bet it's all big words, though*; he considered. *Something I wouldn't understand.* He wondered if Mel had read it. Yes, she would be just the type of person to creep around her new author friend. *Get in his good books*. Ollie chuckled at his own little play on words.

Out of the corner of his eye, he saw Adrienne stand and stretch. She put her book on the table and slowly stepped inside. He checked his watch. Two-thirty. She would be ringing the bell soon, alert everyone it's time for afternoon drinks. He calculated he had about twenty minutes to get into the house, find Joyce's room, have a quick scout around before getting back outside and picking up his pathetic hoe once more.

Giving Adrienne a good couple of moments to disappear into the kitchen, Ollie lay the garden implement down and ran to the back of the house. Creeping along the wall, he felt like one of those detectives from a poor cop show on TV. *If only I had a gun*, he thought, and held his right hand by the wrist before making a shaft and trigger from his index fingers and thumb. Ollie couldn't help but smile at his own immaturity.

Once on the terrace, he stood motionless and listened, but all he heard was a radio playing from inside the barn. Convincing himself it must be Louis, Ollie scooted indoors, stopped in the giant hallway before checking himself. He then walked casually towards the door, which led to the corridor Hazel told him all about.

Clicking the outside world shut behind him, he slowly stepped past half a dozen rooms. Which one did she say was Joyce's? Second from last. He remembered.

With a final look behind, he tested the door, and as soon as he opened it, a rush of excitement surged through him akin to a speeding locomotive. Not much happened in Ollie's mundane world, so this was an entirely new entity. He stifled a laugh, such was the adrenaline hit, so he leant his back against the closed door, desperately trying to regulate his breathing.

Thinking hard, he recalled what Hazel said. *"You must get away. She doesn't have any…"*.

"Any what?" He looked around. "Any bloody what?"

Shushing himself, Ollie began searching for whatever clue he could discover. First, he noticed a pile of books on Joyce's bedside table, but as he read their spines, he soon recognised they were all about history. Ollie considered that particular subject a complete waste of time. *It's the future we should be concerned about.*

So he tried the set of drawers. There were three of them, and in the very first one, he spotted something laying on top.

He retrieved a little black book and shut the drawer behind. It had '*Notes*' printed with gold embossed across the front. He thought it looked tatty, the spine badly creased and the lettering peeling away. Sitting on the edge of the bed, he skimmed through it, but soon became bored with the meaningless dribble Joyce had written inside.

There were dates of what Ollie assumed were moments in history. All boring stuff, which made little sense to him. Becoming impatient, he grabbed all the pages with his thumb and flicked through from the back. And soon, he found something of much greater interest. He flicked back and forth, licking his finger with his tongue to grip the sheets. There! He saw Tony's name. Then Hazel; Mel and Charlie immediately after. Next his own name, then Ed's. Every one of them had a tick adjacent to them. But it was the red ink which made Ollie's blood curdle.

An uneven line was scrawled right across Tony, with notes scribbled alongside. But Ollie couldn't decipher Joyce's terrible handwriting. *Call yourself a teacher?* They were illegible, but soon he didn't care, because when he turned back another page, he saw another name and another red line crudely scratched through it. Will Parry.

Fuck.

Ollie dropped the book, cursed himself, retrieved it, and quickly tried to find where he was. After what felt like an eternity, he landed on the same page.

Something different against Will's name. Ollie snapped the page forward and then back again. Forward and back. Shit. Everybody on the second page had a tick against them, but when he flicked back to Will Parry, there was a blue cross. *Of course*, Ollie thought. *He isn't here*. Did that mean Joyce knew he wasn't coming?

Although it didn't actually prove anything, it pleased Ollie he'd worked out the meaning of the crosses by himself, and crouched to put the book back into the drawer. *Which bloody drawer?* He heard a sound from somewhere outside. A lawn mower or some other garden machinery. He opened the top drawer and placed the notebook inside. He couldn't remember if it was the right way up or even the correct place, but he had no time to contemplate such things.

Standing, he glanced around the room again. What else is there? On the far side, on top of a large chest of drawers – Ollie had the identical furniture in his room – were perched some photographs. Walking around the bed, he picked them up, one at a time, to take a closer look. There was one of Joyce and Tony, no doubt taken during happier times. Ollie thought it strange she would have such a memento of the guy she obviously detested. Next, a picture of a dog. *What the fuck?* He thought. *Who brings a photograph of a bloody dog with them?* But the third photo hit him like a hammer blow. Joyce and a young man, not much older than a boy. He looked as though he was in his late teens, and Joyce in her forties, maybe? Ollie wasn't good at ageing people, but she definitely looked fifteen or twenty years younger than now.

And Ollie instantly recognised the boy. He should do. A few years after the picture was taken, Ollie spotted the same boy and his girlfriend in a pub and subsequently started dating her that same evening. Within a year, they were married.

Right on cue, at three o'clock, Adrienne rang the bell. Charlie lifted the trimmer off his shoulders and placed it on the lawn, just as he did at morning break and again at lunchtime. He was bored, cutting hedges which didn't need cutting. Again, he pondered the tasks they were assigned, ever since Ollie raised the subject at breakfast. Charlie hadn't considered it before, but he too thought she was handing out mundane jobs for the sake of it. *We've got two more weeks of this. What on earth will she find us to do?*

Grabbing himself a cold beer, he studied Mel as she approached from the side of the house. During the morning, he'd contemplated checking how her gardening was going, ask her if she thought there would be enough jobs to last another fortnight. But he knew she wouldn't speak to him. He had lost her and there was no return. Although he would never admit to it, Charlie felt incredibly hurt, betrayed even.

Ollie looked flustered when he joined the others in the shade. His eyes darted everywhere, and he continually scratched at the back of his neck and again underneath his T-shirt. Charlie wanted to tell him to sit the fuck down and stop fidgeting.

Ed, too, appeared agitated. Charlie didn't see what direction he came from, such was his distraction watching nervous Ollie going through his restless routine. Ed looked across at Charlie before taking a beer for himself.

They all sat separately, a table to themselves. Louis stood in the shade at the back and Adrienne kept herself busy wiping tables that didn't need wiping. *What a fucking ensemble*, Charlie thought.

Joyce stepped onto the terrace from indoors. She smiled to herself after she coughed to announce her arrival, and the entire group jumped in unison. Once she had everyone's attention, she took another step forward before nodding her appreciation to Adrienne. She passed her a tiny cup containing her favourite tipple, an extra-strong espresso. But it wasn't nearly hot enough, so she knocked it back in one swig, hoping the caffeine would make an instant hit.

Before saying what she had to say, she looked around the group, trying to catch if any of them were evading eye contact with her. And as she suspected, Oliver Ramsey's pupils were set firmly onto the ground beneath him. His knee jigged vigorously, and he picked nervously at his fingernails and that imaginary itch on his bloody neck.

Joyce smiled. She knew somebody had been in her room, and there was the culprit, directly in front of her.

37

————

"Hazel has decided to leave us," Joyce announced to her ever-admiring onlookers. She still enjoyed her role of authority, the importance they hung on to her every word. Her latest declaration caused a collective intake of breath, which did not surprise Joyce. However, she only had eyes for Ollie. Finally, he succumbed and lifted his head to meet her gaze full on. If he appeared on edge before, he now looked startled, like a baby bird in its nest with a bloody great sparrow hawk gawping directly at him. *His little sidekick has left him all alone*, she thought. *What* will *he do now?*

"Leave us?" Ed asked on everybody's behalf. Joyce was half-expecting it to be him who initiated the response. He was becoming the group's spokesperson, something she didn't take kindly to, but at least he had a brain and didn't spurt out crap without thinking first.

"Yes, Edward, leave us. I've just returned from the mainland. On the way over in the boat, we spoke at length. She told me how unhappy she was here and thought her headaches were getting worse. She said she wanted to get to the airport and put all this behind her. Of course, I tried to make her see sense. I told her we are halfway through, maybe even more, and if she could just hold on a little longer, then the money would be all hers."

"Why didn't she come around then?" Mel asked. Joyce couldn't help but notice the way she scratched her arm, all four fingers raking up and down, up and down. *They're becoming nervous wrecks. I need to calm them down.*

"I don't know, dear. I just couldn't persuade her. Silly girl. As I'm sure you have all worked out, the jobs aren't taking as long as I originally presumed. I think another week at most and you'll all be free to go."

The statement had the desired effect. Mel immediately ceased scratching, a smile broke out across Charlie's face and Ollie's bloody leg finally stopped jigging up and down. Ed looked at Joyce wide-eyed. Didn't he believe her?

"But what about the flights home?" Charlie asked, unable to contain his excitement. "They're not for two more weeks."

"Well," Joyce continued, satisfied she had regained control and the moment of panic dissipated. *They've forgotten about Hazel already*, she thought. *They're all in it for themselves. Just as well really...* "You can either stay here..." She allowed her words to sink in and enjoyed the look of despair on everyone's face. "... thought not," she quipped. Everybody laughed nervously. "Or you can return to the mainland. Spend some time in Pont-Aven. It really is the most delightful town and there are one or two cheaper hotels, too. Otherwise, you can use some of your money and take an earlier flight home. It really is your choice."

A few moments of silence ensued. Joyce watched as they individually digested her news. An early escape, hands on the money sooner than expected, and all for such little work. But then Joyce's latest nemesis threatened to ruin the mood once more.

"I can't believe Hazel wouldn't have stayed if there is only one week to go," Ollie said, immediately reigniting the tension. Joyce glared at him.

Why can't you keep your bloody mouth shut, Oliver Ramsey?

Ollie watched the group return to the garden to continue with their original tasks. Charlie hadn't stopped smiling since Joyce's announcement, and he said something to Mel as they separated at the far end of the lawn. Charlie attempted to put his arm around her, but Mel replied and flung her own arm in defiance, although Ollie couldn't discern what she said. It looked as though Charlie was remonstrating with her, trying to grab her arm, but she flailed back, not allowing him to take hold. Their voices became raised and the next thing Ollie noticed was Louis sprinting across the grass. He pushed the couple apart and gestured for Charlie to go one way and Mel to return to the front of the house. Charlie walked backwards, mouthing something to his wife, pointing at her. Mel flicked her head back now and then, as though making obscene comments, whilst gesticulating wildly with her arms. *They'll end up killing one another*, Ollie thought.

The sound of footsteps from behind caught him off-guard. Ed stepped out onto the terrace.

"Good news eh, Ollie?" He remarked, looking him up and down as if to ascertain why he was still sitting doing nothing when there was work to be done.

"Do you believe her?" Ollie stood, scraping his chair back, his eyes darting and his head turning from side to side to check whether anybody was in earshot.

"Eh? Who?"

Ollie considered Ed was being deliberately obtuse. He didn't really want to speak to him anyway, but who else was there? Charlie and Mel were more engrossed in throttling each other, Louis made no sense at the best of times and Adrienne was just a local girl who spoke such little English. He would be hard-pressed to get a conversation from any of them. That left Joyce and Ed. Well, Joyce hated him, the feeling quite mutual since he sneaked into Hazel's room. Joyce called him a liar, but Ollie wasn't convinced she heard them talking. Surely she would have spoken to him privately if that were the case? Either way, Joyce wasn't on his radar for someone to converse with. So that left Ed. Clever little shit, Ed and his books and his writing and his all-round superior intelligence.

"Joyce, of course," Ollie replied. Ed's eyes inadvertently dropped to Ollie's mouth. Immediately feeling self-conscious, he licked his lips and tasted blood. He licked again before dabbing his mouth with the back of his hand. He must have bitten too hard and cut his lip. He'd done that before. The day in court sprang to mind when he awaited his fate after the accident. It was whenever nerves completely got the better of him. He pushed his hand firmly against his mouth and sucked at the cut, desperate to stop it from bleeding. "Just then, when she said she tried to persuade Hazel to stay." Ed appeared mesmerised by his bleeding mouth. "Did you hear what I just said?"

Ed looked him in the eye once more. "Yes, Ollie. Of course I heard what you said. And to answer your question, I can understand Hazel wanting to get away. She's had enough. However, I find it strange she couldn't hold on for just one more week."

Ollie watched Ed as he walked away. He deliberated

calling after him and telling him what he'd found in Joyce's room, but he couldn't be certain how Ed would react. He was so matter-of-fact, just get the jobs done, count down the days and grab the money. He didn't want conflict. He'd avoided all the debates, all the cross words as far as Ollie could recall, and he knew he'd be wasting his time trying to convince him to listen.

Besides, did Ollie want Ed knowing what was written in the notebook? And far more importantly, if he told him about the photograph, he would also have to explain why it was so damn personal. He soon decided he needed to keep it very quiet and cursed himself for ever going into Joyce's room at all.

Following her altercation on the lawn with Charlie, Mel was pleased to be working alone. She and Ed had moved onto separate tasks, and although she originally missed him, after Joyce's big announcement, she craved her own company. Besides, her blood was boiling and only Louis' intervening stopped her from hitting her husband. She wanted Charlie dead, and she was so fearful she might actually do it herself. And it wasn't just wanting him out of her life forever. Mel didn't want him to get his share of the money, either. If he didn't make it home, would Joyce give her the entire quota instead? After all, she admitted the work was almost complete, so surely she would have to keep to her side of the bargain and pay up in full?

But that wasn't all that played on her mind. She remained sceptical about Hazel suddenly departing. Yes, she'd shrunk into her shell after the first few days, but, even so, they were virtually there. Joyce admitted she'd told her as much. *Hadn't she?*

Mel sat upright, her knees aching from kneeling and

planting stupid bloody flowers. She placed both hands on the arch of her back and pushed her stomach forward. It felt good, her muscles and bones returning to their rightful place. And as she stretched, she considered her own question. Was Joyce paying lip service to the group? She would have to say she tried to convince Hazel to stop, but what if it was the exact opposite? Hazel wanted to stay but Joyce told her it was best if she left?

She recalled the day when Joyce informed them all that Tony had been to see her and was thinking of leaving. What had Hazel said? *"It's a surprise he would give up on that amount of money. We're already a week into it. Couldn't he just stick at it?"* If Hazel thought that after just one week, then surely she could handle another seven days or so?

Mel stood, her hands still in the middle of her back, the stretching therapeutic.

And what about the time Hazel told her about sneaking into Joyce's room and finding the notebook? The name crossed out who Hazel said she didn't know, but Mel knew she was lying. Hazel said she would return and find out more. Had she? Was that why she was no longer there, because she found something she shouldn't have done?

Shit. Mel looked around her, convinced somebody was watching. Her eyes darted into the dense trees, across the vast garden and up to the windows in the château. But nobody was there. The only sounds were from the insects occupying the long grass surrounding her or the occasional bird chirping from somewhere high in the branches.

She knelt back down and dug another small hole for the next plant to set up residence, and all the time, Mel realised she would have to go into Hazel's room herself to see if she could find any kind of clue why she'd left.

38

THE SOUND of something clanking outside awoke Ollie in the small hours. At first, he thought he was dreaming. He'd had nightmares ever since hearing footsteps, so as he woke, he allowed himself time to listen, convinced it was yet another terrible night which accompanied his awful trip abroad.

Just as he surmised he was right, a clattering sound jolted him, prompting him to pull the duvet higher. It sounded like metal against metal. The curtains blew inwards. Perhaps the storm had arrived? He cursed himself for leaving the window open, but he'd never wanted to give Charlie the satisfaction of being correct. What had he said? *"It only allows more warm air inside."* So, defiantly, Ollie left it ajar every night, sometimes as wide as it would go, just to defy the fair-haired idiot. Not that Charlie ever knew he'd done it, and suddenly Ollie felt rather foolish.

A rumble of thunder echoed somewhere in the distance, quickly followed by a flash. *Lightning?* he considered. But then an unwavering beam illuminated his room. *That's not fucking lightning. It's that torch again.*

Clambering out of bed, furthest from the window, Ollie kept himself low, half crawling around his room looking for some kind of weapon.

"Ollie."

He instantly laid himself as flat as he could, his ribs digging into the wooden floor, and he pushed both hands hard against his ears. Although he didn't recognise the voice, he certainly didn't want to hear it again.

But whatever he tried; he couldn't block out the sounds. More clanking of metal against metal followed by footsteps on gravel. Allowing his hands to leave his ears, he lifted his head until his chin rested on the hard floor. He was so damn uncomfortable but also too bloody scared to move.

Ollie couldn't be sure how long he lay there, but a crack of thunder eventually stirred him into action. *Surely that's woken everybody? I'm safe now.*

Gingerly, he stood, unsure whether his bones or the floorboards objected the most, and he crept towards the vast window. Slowly, he pulled the curtains apart and stepped into the void between them and the open space before him. Ollie immediately felt the warm breeze encircle his bare legs.

The sky lit up as a streak of lightning zigzagged above. It made him gasp, but not in a frightened way, more in relief. Perhaps he'd imagined the sounds all along. The storm had arrived, and as the thunder clap followed, he knew it was very close by. And then he spotted something.

Ollie squinted and blinked hard. There was something on the outside windowsill. Mesmerised, he leant forward, his hand searching the wooden frame for whatever he thought he'd seen. Another flash of lightning illuminated the garden, allowing Ollie to reach forward and grab the object.

It was a car, a toy car. He collected them as a kid. Ollie had always been interested in cars and lorries and buses. Any form of transport, apart from aeroplanes. He didn't believe them to be safe, hence his flight to France was the first time he'd set foot on one. *The things we do for money*, he'd said to himself a thousand times, ever since accepting Joyce's invitation. But Ollie hadn't told anybody he'd never flown before. He had to save face.

Waiting for the next lightning strike, he lifted the model car, and when Mother Nature duly obliged, Ollie gasped and dropped the toy to the ground below. He heard it hit the gravel and held his breath as he tried to take in what he'd actually just seen.

It was definitely a toy car. A blue toy car. A blue fucking Ford Escort. The same make as the vehicle in the car park on the day his drinks were spiked. *What the actual...?*

A flapping sound diverted his attention, and he saw a sheet of paper hanging from the windowsill. Quickly, Ollie tried to retrieve it, his mind no longer functioning at normal levels, not that Ollie's *normal levels* were particularly well balanced, anyway. The paper wouldn't move but, as if on cue, the clouds rushed overhead, leaving a moment's respite, and the moon peered through. The sheet was stapled several times into the wooden sill. And it was laminated too. Ollie realised it would be easier to read the contents from where he was. Squinting his eyes, he leant out a little further.

And as he read, he never did hear his bedroom door open. Nor did he hear the footsteps on the floorboards behind him. The first time Ollie knew somebody had crept into his room was when a pair of icy hands shoved him sharply in the centre of his bare back and sent him flailing head first through the wide open sash window.

The scream made Mel jump from her skin. Crouching at Hazel's bedside chest of drawers, she clutched her fellow traveller's passport in her hand, still in shock that she could be holding it at all. Without thinking, Mel stuffed it into her dressing gown pocket and quietly tiptoed across the room to the door.

Earlier, she had bided her time, sitting in silence and waiting for the inevitable footsteps on the landing. But she didn't hear any that night. Perhaps it had been Hazel sneaking around after all? That would make sense. Hazel said she was determined to find out more about Joyce and the circumstances why they were there. Was that her mission, creeping around, watching, listening in the depths of the night? And not only that. Was it the real reason she was no longer on the island? Mel wondered if Hazel had found out *too* much?

So, Mel left her own room at just after two o'clock. She had heard thunder, the deep, resonating sound growing louder with each occurrence, promptly followed by lightning, inadvertently illuminating the château. In comparison, the landing was eerily quiet and long, elongated shadows hung from the rafters above. Dark corners and hidden crevices only adding to the far too creepy ambience. Quickly, Mel strode towards Hazel's room, keeping her feet as light as she could.

As soon as she entered, she switched on her torch, happy to have some light and finally see objects in their true form.

What's that?

Mel crouched down for a closer look and saw a suit-case protruding from underneath the bed. She recognised it from the day they met at the airport. A designer label and a chic design. It stood out against the other drab and well-used travel bags. *Why would she leave that behind?*

Dragging it out from its poor hiding place, it scraped annoyingly against the bare floorboards. Once on the bed, Mel sprang the two clips open and lifted the lid. Empty. Leaving the suitcase where it was, she stepped over to the wardrobe and carefully turned the small metal keys until the doors fell free in her hands. Again, empty. It really did look as though Hazel had taken her clothes, so why the empty suitcase? How else could she have carried all her gear?

Mel shone the torch around the room. She didn't know what she might be looking for, but she knew something wasn't right.

The small bedside chest of drawers caught her attention, prompting her to hurry over and kneel in front. They all appeared empty, but Mel wasn't leaving without finding something. Her hands scrambled frantically inside, feeling for any kind of clue hidden in the depths. There! Using her fingertips, she dragged what felt like a thin wallet and immediately recognised it was a passport. Using the torchlight, Mel quickly found the page containing the most vital piece of information; the photograph. She only had to see the wild hair to recognise it was Hazel's. Mel's heart pounded deep in her chest.

As she contemplated what the hell was going on, the scream made her jolt and she dropped the passport. It sounded so close, so shrill. *Shit, shit, shit.*

Standing slowly, Mel scooped up the document and considered looking through the curtains to determine where the commotion was emanating from. But common sense kicked in. Not only did she not want to see what or who had caused the high-pitched yell, but what if they looked up and spotted her in the wrong room?

Once she made it to Hazel's bedroom door, she halted and listened for sounds on the landing. She heard a door close, not loudly, but quietly click into place. Mel thought it strange somebody would be so meticulous about closing their door when a scream would have woken the entire house, anyway.

Another door opened and closed. "What the hell was that?" she heard her husband shout, before his heavy footsteps pounded along the landing and down the stairs. "I'm coming," Louis called after him. "It's Adrienne." Then it all went quiet. Where were the others? Ollie, Joyce, and Ed?

A few minutes after the scream, Ed leant out of his bedroom window. On the gravel below, he could make out the distinctive shape of a body laying at an odd angle. He felt sweaty, as if waking from one of his recurring nightmares. Straining his eyes, he saw Adrienne holding a hand over her mouth whilst her other shone a torch directly onto the near naked person beneath her. Seconds later, he heard footsteps sprinting on the loose stones, and Charlie and Louis arrived in tandem. A rumble of thunder momentarily averted his attention.

"What the hell is going on?" Ed called out from above, and the two of them instantaneously looked up. Adrienne's head didn't move, though. She was transfixed on Ollie.

"It looks like he's fallen," Charlie shouted, looking up the building just along from Ed's bedroom. "His window is wide open."

Louis grabbed Adrienne, and she yelped in dismay. He spun her until her head buried into his chest. She didn't protest, but flung her arms around him and gripped tight onto his back. Under the moonlight, Ed could see her hands clutching Louis's T-shirt, making clenched fist-like actions. *Are they an item?* he thought, and wondered what made him think of such a thing in those circumstances.

Ed then considered where the other two were. He wasn't so bothered about Joyce, but where the hell was Mel?

On cue, Joyce stepped from the shadows and joined the small gathering below. Her level of concern seemed far less pronounced than that of the others upon seeing Ollie's lifeless form.

Quickly, he pulled on a sweatshirt, a pair of shorts, and slid his feet into his flip-flops. They clicked loudly against the wooden floor as he made his way to the door, and as soon as he opened it, he got the fright of his life.

Mel stood motionless, facing him. She didn't appear as though she was going to knock. Instead, she was as still as a statue. *How long has she been there?*

"What's wrong?" he asked, grabbing her by the shoulders. "Did you hear the scream?"

Mel nodded before lifting her arm and pressing something cold against his hand.

"What's that?"

Finally, Mel spoke.

"It's Hazel's passport." Her voice sounded robotic. "Why would Hazel leave without her passport?"

39

CHARLIE NECKED his brandy in one quick swig before helping himself to the bottle and swiftly pouring himself another. He turned to face what remained of the group, convened in the dining room and sat around in a circle; ashen-faced, either staring at the ground or blankly into thin air.

"We can't just leave him out there," he suggested, not aimed at anybody in particular. "Aren't there wild animals on this island? I don't know, foxes?" He paused. "Or something else?" he added, unable to think of another.

Joyce looked at him and then at Louis. Charlie's question caught her off-guard. Until then, she hadn't shown an ounce of pity, something Charlie considered inhumane.

"Is he right, Louis?" she suggested. "Should we put him in the barn until morning?"

"Why can't the police come now?" Mel asked. Charlie noticed his wife visibly shaking, her arms wrapped around her shoulders like some kind of straight jacket. She rocked back and forth, only adding to the illusion.

"They're coming at first light, dear. Although the eye of the storm is due to hit by then. I do hope they can make it."

Charlie studied Joyce. She didn't look as though she gave a shit whether the police made it or not. He glanced at Louis, who too didn't appear concerned. *There's a bloody dead body outside on the gravel and nobody cares.*

He necked the stiff drink, swallowing hard as the warm liquid burnt his throat before pouring another.

"Go easy with that," Mel said. He turned to face her, hoping for some kind of reconciliation, but instead, he was met with a fierce glare. "You don't want to say something stupid when the police finally arrive, do you?" Charlie necked his drink and poured an even larger shot. He grinned at her sarcastically as he replaced the bottle and found a seat on the far side of the room.

It was four o'clock in the morning when Joyce eventually allowed them to return to their respective rooms. Ed was exhausted, and despite Ollie being dead, he secretly prayed their host would allow them to sleep sometime soon. He and Charlie helped Louis carry Ollie to the barn after Charlie pointed out he might get eaten by a pack of hungry wolves or such like. Ed knew they shouldn't move the body until the police arrived. They would want to rule everything out, including foul play. But it looked like a fall, or even a jump. *The same as Tony.* Ollie had been immensely distressed, tipped over the edge when his comrade Hazel suddenly upped and left. Maybe he sleepwalked, someone suggested, although Ed couldn't recall who. Either way, he fell head-first from a sufficient height, and possibly cracked his skull in a multitude of places. Charlie suggested the latter, albeit with a laugh and after far too much brandy.

The knock on Ed's door didn't surprise him. He'd been expecting it. It was only ten minutes after Joyce allowed them to retire for the evening. Ever since Mel stood in his doorway clutching Hazel's passport, he knew she would want to discuss it further. Earlier, she kept glancing nervously towards him across the dining room, not unnoticed by Joyce. He wanted Mel to calm down, but how could he convey such a message in a room so full of tension?

"It's open," he called quietly, too drained to move from his bed.

Mel stepped gingerly into his room, peeping back through the door until it was fully closed. After what felt like an age, she turned to face him, her expression now marked by uncertainty. Ed sat upright despite his body screaming at him to sleep.

"If you've come to ask about the passport, Mel, I honestly don't have the energy."

Her shoulders dropped imperceptibly as a flicker of disappointment crossed her features. He knew it was exactly what she wanted to talk about, but Ed just couldn't summon the verve to do so. How should he know why Hazel left it behind? He could speculate, but what good would that do?

A flash of lightning attempted to illuminate the room. The thick curtains were drawn, only allowing a sliver of light to creep inside. A rumble of thunder followed seconds later.

"The storm is getting close," Mel said, her eyes fixed on the curtains. She looked back to Ed. "Do you think the police will make it?"

Finally, he shuffled himself off the bed. He couldn't

help but notice the disappointment on Mel's face as he stepped to the window instead of to her. But he needed to keep his stupid desire under control although his willpower was being pushed to the limit.

Pulling back the curtains, the entire room was immediately shrouded in a bright white radiance. Mel gasped as an even louder crack of thunder appeared to shake the very island itself. She could no longer cope and ran across the room and grabbed Ed around his midriff. She made space for him to pivot, and he embraced her in return. Everything he promised not to do, ever since that one night they spent together, but deep down, Ed knew it was futile. Powerful emotions stirred within him, and he knew that could only mean one thing; trouble.

Mel woke with Ed's face only inches from her own. His eyes were closed, immersed in sleep, with his arm trapped underneath her body. She craved to kiss him, relive what happened only hours before, but she doubted how much Ed would want to reciprocate.

When she arrived in his room, she quickly became dismayed at how little attention he bestowed upon her. Just sitting on his bed, looking nonchalantly around the room at nothing in particular. She desperately needed to discuss Hazel's passport, Ollie's fall — if that's what it was — and Joyce's unmoving temperament. How could she show such disdain towards a dead body laying festooned on the gravel? She had also dismissed her husband's death as a sad consequence of his own incapability. And Hazel leaving with only days to go. Mel didn't believe a word of it and now she feared the worst.

When the second thunderclap hit, the entire house appeared to shake, and Mel took it as her cue to insist upon Ed's attention. She ran across the room, grabbed him, forced him to turn to face her, and she kissed him hard. Ultimately, he yielded. She knew how much he liked her, so why was he being so bloody difficult?

Ed stirred, his eyes reluctantly parting, blinking as he tried to focus.

"Morning, sleepy," she urged herself to be upbeat, leaning forward and kissing his forehead. Mel again felt a pang of despair as he appeared disappointed she was there. A split second of hesitancy was all it took. She couldn't understand why he was acting that way.

"Hey," he said, impelling himself to smile. He pulled his arm from underneath and slowly sat upright, his back to her as he perched on the edge of the bed. She could hear the rain drumming against the window and just wanted Ed to rejoin her so they could lie and listen. But more importantly, talk. To her growing displeasure, he instead stood and stepped to the window before pulling the curtains far enough apart until she could see outside too.

The skies were so dark, as if it was still night-time. Mel checked her watch. Just past seven. They had an hour before breakfast.

"Come back to bed," she said, putting on her best sultry voice. She pulled the duvet back on Ed's side, sufficient to tempt him. He turned and looked at her. He smiled, and for a moment, she thought he would join her. However, he stepped towards the bathroom instead.

"We can't do this, Mel." He propped his arm against the doorframe and rubbed his hand through his hair.

"Why not?" she replied, sitting up whilst making no effort to cover herself. "We want each other. My marriage is over. We just need to get off this damn island, take the money, and see where we are once we arrive back home."

Mel paused, desperate for a reaction, but he gave nothing away. "Once this is all over, I thought I could come to Ireland, see where you live," she paused again. "See where you write. You know, Ed. Those books."

The last two words finally had the desired effect. Ed let go of the doorframe, straightened himself, and stared at Mel.

"What do you mean by that?" he asked.

Mel pulled the duvet up to her chin. She had his attention, but not for the reasons she originally intended. However, if he was going to be distant with her, then he needed to know it wouldn't all be on his terms. She'd lived a life of that and she was already feeling that all men might actually be the same.

"I finished your book a couple of days ago."

Ed flinched, a definite sign of irritation in his eyes.

"And?" he snapped.

"And don't forget, I went to the same school as you." She pushed herself upright, her back square against the headboard. "And I know who the boy is."

Ed waved his arm nonchalantly at her. "Pfft. You don't know anything, Mel. The character in that story is make-believe, all in my head." He tapped his temple to emphasise his point before turning back to the bathroom.

"I think you should come back to bed," she called after him. He turned again. Mel was smiling. The duvet now pulled to one side again as she slowly patted the space next to her.

"What? What do you mean?" Ed appeared genuinely dumbstruck by whatever she was proposing.

"Well, unless you want my Charlie to know about the book, too?"

Ed shook his head. "Even if your crazy notion is correct, Charlie wouldn't have a clue who that person——"

"Oh, he does, Ed. Both Charlie and I know him very well." The colour drained from his face right before her. Mel had him on the ropes and so she went for the jugular. "And I believe you realised from the moment Joyce handed out copies of your novel that we would recognise him." His legs appeared to wobble slightly, and he clutched the doorframe for support. But still, she wasn't finished. Mel had asked him who the book was about days ago. The time Ed told her about the scribbled post-it note. But he never gave her a satisfactory reply, so she read a copy for herself. "And Hazel told you about the person at the end of her bed, didn't she?" Still, he didn't move. "I thought so," Mel half-smiled. "She told me about it, too. The day she told me about going into Joyce's room."

She looked at Ed, waiting for any kind of response. He was ready to respond, but Mel cut him off before he could say anything.

"And I'm beginning to believe he's the reason we're all here."

40

————

CHARLIE'S SKULL throbbed as the sound of the breakfast bell woke him from his comatose slumber. As he painstakingly lifted his head from the pillow, the first thing he heard was the rain lashing against his window. The weather had finally cracked. Yearning to hide away under the covers, a sudden clap of thunder jolted him awake, forcing him to face reality yet again. Groggily, he crawled out of bed and stepped across the room. Parting the curtains, he couldn't believe the transformation. Dark greys and a leaden atmosphere had replaced the deep blue and cloudless skies. The rain pelted against the glass, streaming down as though somebody was pouring buckets of water from above. And the wind. The tops of the trees bent at right angles, all pointing towards the mainland, mocking him. *Shit*, he thought, suddenly remembering Ollie's corpse in the barn and the prospect of facing everyone downstairs once more.

· · ·

"I really am going to shower this time," Ed forced himself to smile. He kissed Mel against his better judgement. "And you need to get back to your room so nobody knows you've been here." He kissed her again. "Okay?"

Mel smiled back, and Ed tried to decipher what she was thinking. It certainly wasn't a seductive smile; the type he'd associated with her every time they'd been alone together before. It was more of a *'can I trust you?'* kind of smile.

Ed needed space to think. He'd given into Mel's demands thirty minutes earlier. She was in his room, in his bed, and she'd figured out who the protagonist was in his book. But she didn't know any more than that. She couldn't. Nonetheless, she was onto something. *"I'm beginning to believe he's the reason we're all here…"*

He had no response because he had long reached the same conclusion himself. Thankfully, he'd had the hindsight to remove the note from Ollie's windowsill. If Mel, or any of the others, knew what that said too, then Joyce could have a mutiny on her hands. During the night, after Mel confronted him with Hazel's passport, Ed sent her downstairs to the others, stalling for time, telling her he needed to dress. She said she'd wait, but he said it was too risky and Charlie would soon put two and two together. As she reluctantly disappeared, he darted into Ollie's room and ran to his open window. Nobody looked up as he carefully tore the laminated sheet from the staples.

However, Ed's anger was shifting onto Joyce. Why the hell did she hand a copy of his book to everyone? Did she know somebody may deduce who it was about? Was that her intention all along? She'd certainly never discussed it with him. But now Mel had worked it out and Hazel had described the same intruder, too. And if Ollie had read the note on his windowsill, he would have realised moments before his death. Ed realised Tony would have suffered a similar fate. And Charlie had quizzed him about Will Parry, so was he also coming to a likewise deduction? The one common denominator was that boy from their school.

He is here.

"The police aren't coming," Joyce announced, as Mel eventually joined the rest of the group for breakfast. Joyce looked at her disapprovingly before speaking, but not before she'd glanced towards Ed, too. The way he regarded her in return caught her off-guard. Pure hostility.

"So, what do we do with a dead body in the barn?" Charlie asked, nursing his second espresso in as many minutes.

"We will need to cover it," she replied, again peeking at Ed out of the corner of her eye. Why was he glaring at her like that? Joyce attempted to compose herself, re-establish her authority. But she was floundering, her voice weak as she picked at the handle of her cup with her thumbnail.

Mel was glaring at her too, before her eyes followed Joyce to Ed. She flicked between the two of them, as if trying to determine the strange chemistry in the room.

"There's some tarpaulin in the shed," Charlie piped up, failing to gauge the atmosphere. The caffeine appeared to be having the desired effect though, metamorphosing him back into the irritating little twerp Joyce knew he was. "I saw it when I fetched some petrol for the hedge trimmer."

"Yes," Joyce replied, her words caught in her throat. She attempted to clear it before continuing. "Good idea,

Charlie. Make sure it's weighed down with something. You and Louis can do that after—"

"We need to move him from the barn," Ed interrupted, still looking Joyce in the eye. "There will be rats before we know it."

Joyce noticed Mel shiver beside him. Adrienne gasped from the back of the room. "Very well. You and Charlie sort it out after breakfast. Probably best to transfer him to the boathouse. That way, when the police do arrive, they can go directly there."

Ed nodded condescendingly, as if she'd done well. Joyce decided she needed to talk to him later to find out what he may know. "Don't forget who I am, young man," she whispered to herself as she left the room in a hurry.

"We should wrap him in tarpaulin first," Ed suggested as he and Charlie put on waterproofs underneath the terrace. The rain had subsided, but it was steady and the skies were still extremely dark. The wind was the biggest threat though, and Charlie wondered whether the police would get there soon.

"There's string in the barn too," he replied, kicking himself as he sounded as though he was actually enjoying himself. However, he couldn't stop himself. His nerves were on edge and he realised he was struggling to stay in control. Charlie had never felt such a sensation before. "We can tie him and then use the ride-on mower and trailer to get him to the boathouse."

"You sound as though you've thought it through, Charlie? You haven't done anything like this before, have you?"

Charlie grinned sarcastically. "Shall we just get on with it?" he suggested.

They worked in silence, enveloping Ollie's corpse in the plastic sheet and then carefully rolling him onto the pre-arranged lengths of string on the floor. Pulling them tight, they each tied three pieces before Charlie stood and inspected the mummified body below.

After dragging Ollie to the trailer, Charlie sat next to him whilst Ed started the engine and slowly drove outside into the driving rain. He followed Ed's steer and pulled his hood over his head, one hand gripping the collar together whilst the other held tight underneath a length of string. It felt so bloody surreal as the trailer bobbed up and down along the track through the woods on their descent towards the boathouse.

Charlie wasn't the brightest of people, and he'd got through life on the premise of charm. Whether it be a girl he found attractive or a prospective client for his printing firm. Somebody once told him he could sell hay to a farmer, and he believed that was the finest compliment anyone could ever bestow upon him. But even though he wasn't particularly astute, he wasn't stupid. He thought something was wrong days before. The murder of Will Parry and Tony's body washing up on the shore first alerted him. But now Hazel had gone, and Ollie's corpse lay beneath him.

But nothing appeared contrived. The police had already dismissed Tony's death as an accident or suicide and Will Parry was killed back in England, a month before they left. Ollie was stupid, and could easily have fallen and Hazel fled of her own free will. But what about the PE kit hanging in his wardrobe? Mel's mystery notice? Hazel seeing someone in her bedroom? Were they just pranks, somebody winding them up? No harm came to anyone, so it could be harmless fun. But what about the patterns he deduced in the first few chapters of Ed's book? That boy. Ed's bloody book.

Charlie could no longer allow his feelings to remain bottled up. Once under the semi-shade of the trees, he pushed his hood back from his head and smoothed his hair the best he could with his free hand. He looked up at Ed, his back to him, and Charlie knew he was the one person he loathed the most.

Ed was pleased it was just the two of them, and he was equally happy they were going far from the château, especially to the boathouse. He knew Joyce would suggest there, and even though he despised her for what she'd done, he realised she was still trying to help.

He pulled up alongside the wooden structure he had spotted during his long walk. He didn't think he'd be back here until it was time to go, but he knew this was the best place to put Ollie's body. Cutting the engine, he climbed off the mower and turned to face Charlie. He immediately jolted as Charlie stared through wide eyes and what looked like spittle forming in the corners of his mouth.

"You ready?" Ed asked, as casually as he could, freaked out by Charlie's sudden change. Although he nodded, Ed knew something was very wrong, and he needed to get the task over and done with.

They dragged Ollie into the boathouse, a shed-type of structure built of wood on three sides with a slate roof and exposed beams above. He watched Charlie as he straightened himself and took in their surroundings. The waves lapped against the open end, causing the small green dinghy to sway lively, almost as if it were attempting to break free from the firmly fastened ropes connecting it to two posts. Charlie was lost in his thoughts, something

Ed had never caught him doing before. Normally happy-go-lucky, feckless and immature, this was an entirely different Charlie Green, and Ed didn't like it.

"We should put him in the boat and loosen the ropes. Let it drift out to sea a little to stop any scavengers getting near him."

Charlie continued to look at the boat, as if hypnotised by the constant bobbing up and down. "Did you hear me?" Ed shouted; his tone harsher as his annoyance grew. Slowly, Charlie turned to face him. Ed noticed a vein in his temple protruding, as he tilted his head slightly downwards and glared at Ed from the top of his eye sockets.

"Have you been fucking my wife?" he asked, his voice deep, throaty and altogether scary.

41

Louis addressed Adrienne in their native language, something which was grating on Mel. She didn't like not understanding a word they said, especially when they paused and looked around the room. *They're talking about me*, she would instinctively presume, and grin nervously, whilst deep down, wanting to tell them to speak bloody English.

On this occasion, Adrienne just nodded her head in response to whatever Louis was saying. They both stood, half-smiled towards Joyce, and left the room. Since Ed and Charlie departed to put the body in the boathouse, the conversation between the remaining four was, at best, stifled. Joyce and Mel made small talk whilst Louis and Adrienne did the same. It became suffocating, strained and, in Mel's opinion, downright depressing. The weather only added to the misery. Relentless rain and a wind which appeared to whip the very foundations of the château.

Joyce smiled awkwardly at her once they were left alone. They were gathered in the drawing room; a place

Mel hadn't visited before. Joyce said Ollie decorated it, and dismissed his efforts as *shoddy*, pointing out the splashes of paint around the edges. Mel considered it a callous thing to say, given that two of the group were currently carrying his corpse on a trailer through the woods. But Mel was beyond reproach where Joyce was concerned and she believed her to be a rude, self-obsessed individual who only had her own interests at heart.

"Joyce?" she enquired, matter-of-factly, not wanting to alarm her. Joyce looked up from her high-backed chair, her face giving nothing away.

"Yes, dear?"

Stop calling me fucking dear for a start.

"Do you know why Hazel would leave without her passport?"

In amongst his burning rage, Charlie couldn't believe he found time to be disappointed in Ed's reaction. He'd just accused him of shagging his wife, but he showed absolutely no remorse in return.

"What are you talking about?" he responded, so casually it actually annoyed Charlie more than if he'd admitted to it outright.

"Don't fuck with me," he exclaimed. He was losing control, but did nothing to quell it. "I know it was you with her in the clearing that day. The day she lost an earring. What were you doing with *my* wife, you bastard?"

Still, Ed remained on his haunches, as if waiting impatiently for Charlie to help shift a bloody dead body into a boat. Was Charlie not wording his questions correctly, or was Ed being deliberately crass?

"I went for a walk with her that day, yes. I walked with Hazel too, actually." *Stop bloody patronising me!* "But I don't know anything about missing earrings." Finally, he stood. "Is this to do with you and Mel not getting on?" He turned his back and attempted to lift Ollie's body by himself. Charlie thought he caught Ed smirking, but Charlie's rage was so out of control, he could easily have imagined it.

He wiped his mouth with the back of his hand, surprised at the amount of saliva it held. Charlie couldn't recall feeling such hatred inside ever before. A gradual build-up and a realisation he was losing his wife forever. She'd made it clear, told him outright, and Charlie needed to blame someone. He could hear his father. *It's not your fault, son. They only leave you if somebody else is involved, someone trying to prise them away.* His face contorted, and he slowly stepped forward to deal with his nemesis once and for all. He'd tell the others Ed fell into the sea. Banged his head on the wall of the boathouse. Of course, he tried to save him, but with the storm so violent, it was all in vain.

"What are you talking about, dear? What passport?"

Joyce felt her heart plunge. Why hadn't she checked for such an obvious thing? She remained seated, although her body cried out to stand and move.

"I just said," Joyce immediately picked up on Mel's sarcastic tone. "Hazel's passport. I found it in her room. You told us she asked to return to the mainland to get back to the airport."

"That's right. She did say that."

"Then why would such a seasoned traveller not take her passport? After jetting around the world for so long, I'd have thought it would be the first thing she ever packed."

Joyce watched as Mel stepped across the room,

reached into her back pocket before placing the burgundy document on the arm of her chair. She waited a few moments, no doubt desperate for Joyce to open it and have to confirm who it belonged to. However, when she made it clear she would do no such thing, Mel retrieved it once more, flipped through the pages until she found the photograph section and firmly set it back on the arm. Joyce glanced at it as Mel continually tapped the picture.

"Silly girl," she eventually said, giving into her body's demands and finally standing. She stepped across the room, to the unlit fire, as if she intended to warm herself in front of it. Slowly, gaining some confidence, she turned to face Mel. "But of course, our phones don't work. She wouldn't be able to call us, would she?" Joyce could see the look of one-upmanship disappear from Mel's face. "I bet she's in a hotel in Pont-Aven, waiting for the rest of us to go over." Mel opened her mouth to speak, but Joyce still wasn't finished. "When the police eventually arrive, I'll give them the passport and get them to pass it on to wherever she's staying in town." She gave it a few more seconds. "That okay with you, dear?"

The blow to the centre of his back caught him completely unaware. Ed buckled forward and found himself hunched on top of Ollie's body. But Charlie had missed his opportunity. He should have hit him harder on the skull, finished him there and then, because although winded and shocked, Charlie had barely injured him at all. Before he could strike again, Ed spun onto his back and kicked Charlie hard in his midriff with the sole of his shoe. He immediately doubled up, dropped the length of wood, winced in pain, before placing his hands over his groin to prevent a further strike. But Ed wasn't finished. This time a blow to his unprotected face. He knew he'd hurt him, because he'd hurt himself. He shook his fist as he watched Charlie recoil, blood spurting from his nose.

"Your wife deserves so much better than you," he said through clenched teeth. He was only a step away from Charlie, who now held his hands to his face, both already covered in dark crimson liquid. "And yes, I am screwing her." Charlie's eyes widened further. "And yes, she is good."

Ed expected the retaliation for his mockery. He couldn't stand Charlie and he could now finally allow his emotions to spill out. Charlie swung, his fist catching the top of Ed's shoulder. But Ed punched back, fully focused on his target, and the blow to Charlie's cheekbone sent him hurtling backwards. But still he wasn't done. Charlie stood and flew forward once more, his arms flailing with no genuine conviction, and Ed quickly deciphered he wasn't a fighter. With easy pickings, he jabbed at Charlie's jaw, landed a further heavy blow to his guts before finally punching him directly in his mouth. That one hurt Ed the most and he immediately realised he must have dislodged at least one of Charlie's teeth. But that was the smallest of his concerns. He hit him so hard, Charlie's eyes rolled and his legs buckled beneath. Ed desperately tried to catch him, but was too slow, too late, and Charlie fell despairingly into the sea beside the bobbing boat. Just for good measure, his head clunked hideously against the side, jolting his neck in a sickening twist in the opposite direction to his torso. The splash completed the fall and an incoming wave instantly flipped him over.

Shit.

The drop was over four feet to the sea and despite lying flat on his stomach, Ed couldn't reach Charlie's body. All he could do was watch as a pool of blood dispersed around his head. Quickly, he jumped into the boat and found himself able to get his arms underneath Charlie and flip him over. Unbelievably, Charlie coughed, blood mixed with salt water. He opened his eyes and glared at Ed. *Do I kill him?*

A few minutes later, Charlie lay festooned on the deck of the small boat. His breathing was rapid, and he was bleeding heavily. Ed knelt over him. "If I get help, will you say you fell?"

Charlie nodded.

"And will you leave Mel once you get home to England?"

Again, he nodded.

Ed stood and jumped back onto the wall inside the boathouse. He took one last look at Charlie and knew he had to fetch Louis to help. Ollie's body still lay in the trailer and Ed remembered the police were supposedly on their way. He knew how bad it looked and he had to act fast.

But as he left the boathouse and began the climb up the hill to the house, he glimpsed something over to his left. Squinting his eyes against the now torrential rain, he couldn't be sure, but somebody appeared to be watching him deep in the trees.

It can't be him.

As he strained to see, the figure disappeared.

It's your imagination, Ed. It's this place, this island.

Ed pulled his hood over his head, dragged his collar in tight around his neck, and forced himself to concentrate on Charlie instead.

42

MEL KNEW JOYCE WAS LYING. Despite her quick thinking about the lack of a phone signal and Hazel being a *silly girl*, she stalled once too often. However, Mel couldn't understand what part she was playing in the whole charade. Was she just determined to keep the group together? But for what purpose? People had died, Tony and now Ollie. And it didn't appear Hazel had fled of her own free will either. She had left without her passport, as if forced to leave. But again, why? What did Joyce know they didn't? Mel had to ask, despite realising she was alone with her host. She wished Louis was still there. Adrienne, too. They wouldn't know what she was talking about, but at least Mel couldn't come to any harm.

"Erm, Joyce?" She had returned to the same chair, obviously satisfied she'd explained why Hazel hadn't been in contact regarding her passport. Mel watched as she placed it into her handbag, out of sight. But Mel noticed something different. Joyce was definitely agitated, her fingernails dragging along the suede arm of the seat, leaving furrowed lines in the material, before smoothing them out with the palm of her hand. Eventually, her eyes drifted to Mel.

"Yes," she replied with an exaggerated sigh. "What is it now, dear?"

"There was a boy at school. My age——"

"Yes, yes. So what?"

Joyce stood again and paced to the window. Her distress was palpable. Mel took a deep breath. She hadn't mentioned that boy's name since she left Ridgeview Grammar, and she had purposefully tried to dislodge him from her mind entirely from the moment she received the invitation. During the past two weeks, she had secretly pleaded with Charlie not to get drunk and spill out his name, convinced that there *could* be some connection. But the message in the mirror and after reading Ed's novel, she was adamant it was too coincidental not to be true. But the thing that nagged the most was where the others fitted in. Maybe Hazel had seen him standing at the foot of her bed, but Ollie, Ed, Tony too?

Mel stared at her host's silhouette in the window, waiting impatiently for her to continue. The look on Joyce's face told Mel she knew what was coming.

"I think you knew him, Joyce."

For the first time Mel could recall, Joyce didn't offer an instant reply. She had no quick repartee. No ready-made response. Instead, she allowed herself time and indicated at Mel to retake her seat. After finally making herself comfortable too, Joyce smiled, a warm smile. A smile of recognition that she could no longer hide from the truth.

"It was you and Charlie, wasn't it, dear?"

Mel nodded apologetically, without the need for Joyce to disclose what she was referring to. She continued anyway.

"It was you two who informed the authorities that this," she stalled, "this, erm, boy, had an affair with a teacher at Ridgeview?"

This time, Mel didn't nod. She didn't have to.

"But you never knew who the teacher was. Nobody knew. Well, apart from me and him, of course. Oh, and Tony, too." She laughed nervously, unbefitting to the content of her revelation. "I knew I'd hidden it from everybody, but as soon as someone told the authorities," she looked at Mel with a hint of haughtiness, "about the boy, well he told me he wanted it out in the open."

"And you didn't?" Despite the predicament, Mel actually felt a pang of guilt towards her host.

"Of course I didn't. So, I resigned, or was told to resign, and I told him I never wanted to see him again."

Mel was struggling to comprehend what she was hearing. "And have you, you know, seen him again?"

As before, Joyce could no longer remain seated. She retraced her steps and walked to the window where she continued to talk, her back to Mel. "Only once. He threatened…" Joyce turned to face her and she could see how scared she looked, as if by using the word *threatened* had struck a chord. "He threatened to kill me, Mel. Said he could never forgive me. Asked how I could live with myself by remaining with a wife-beating husband."

"He knew Tony hit you?"

Joyce nodded slowly. Mel could tell how painful it was, but also downright scary. "Yes, he knew. During our brief affair, he even asked if I wanted him to deal with Tony." She air quoted 'deal.' "I just presumed he was a young boy, scorned and let down. I thought nothing of it." And then, as if a lightbulb clicked inside her head. "You don't think this is why we're all here, do you?"

What the fuck? You don't know why we're here?

"The book, Joyce." Mel instantly noticed the bewildered look on Joyce's face. "The novel. Ed's novel. Have you read it?"

Joyce replied whilst shaking her head, as if unable to decipher where Mel was taking the conversation. "Yes. Yes, I've read it. What on earth has—"

"It's about the same boy, Joyce. It's him."

Continuing to shake her head from side to side, Joyce appeared to be revisiting the story inside her head. "It can't be. It doesn't make—"

"It makes complete sense. I think it's why we're here. Ed wrote a book about him. You had an affair with him, Charlie and I helped finish that affair, and he knew Tony hit you. We're all connected. And as you said, he threatened to kill you. Does he want to kill us all?"

Mel thought Joyce might collapse, and she ran over and helped her back to her seat.

"But what about Hazel? Ollie?" Joyce asked groggily, her arms gripping the end of each arm.

"I don't know about Ollie," Mel replied, exasperated she couldn't put all the pieces together, if indeed she was on the correct track. "But Hazel's dream. It wasn't a dream. There *was* someone in her room. It must have been—"

"Mel." Joyce's authoritative voice snapped her from her spiel.

"What? What is it?"

"Sit down, please," she begged, suddenly sounding altogether melancholy. Mel noticed the colour had drained from her face and she looked as though she had somehow aged ten years during the past twenty minutes. "I don't know what Hazel did, if indeed she is connected to him..." Mel almost laughed that neither of them could bring themselves to mention his name. However, Joyce's expression soon reaffirmed this was far from a laughing matter, "… but I've not been entirely truthful about Hazel Dunn."

Mel listened intently as Joyce explained she also received an email, completely out of the blue, approximately two months before the trip. And as she informed Mel of the content, she realised it was worded differently than the message she and Charlie accepted. However, the principle was identical.

Joyce was flat broke. Living on handouts from food banks and a house so cold, she stayed in bed twenty hours a day to keep warm. But it only went downhill months before. Somebody scammed her of her last three thousand pounds from an email which she perceived to be her electricity company. As Hazel had guessed, Joyce wasn't computer savvy. She barely used social media and only had an ancient laptop to accept emails or buy the occasional book from Amazon. She took the email as kosher, clicked on the link, and gave her personal banking details. Twenty-four hours later, her account was empty and there was nothing she could do to retrieve it.

"What about your pension?" Mel asked, barely able to listen to much more.

"Never had one. Tony was so desperate for money, too. I used to help him out each month, God knows why, but when I lost everything, he lost what very little he had too. It's why we both snapped whoever's hand off to come here."

She went onto explain that her *role* was to host a group of ex-students, all in return for twenty grand. Her email gave her guidance. Who was invited and why. Joyce knew their financial backgrounds, what jobs they did — or used to do — but only that. She just had to play the part.

"But didn't you see the email address who sent the invite?"

"It came from a name I didn't recognise. Someone who claimed they'd seen my story in the local Lincolnshire papers about being scammed of all my money. My knight in shining armour, he, or she, called themselves. Bloody hell, Melanie, I was desperate, out on my feet. I would have come here if Adolf Hitler sent the invite."

"So, what about Hazel?" Joyce appeared to clam up. "You said you haven't been entirely truthful about her."

Mel stepped across the room and knelt at Joyce's side. Joyce had said nothing that made little sense, not in the surreal situation they all found themselves in, at least. Mel reached out and held her hand. She couldn't believe how frail Joyce felt, her skin cold and loose against her bones.

"I didn't like her, Mel. I remembered her from school." She paused, looked at Mel, and smiled. "Genuinely, I remember all of you." Joyce took a deep breath. "And I never liked her then."

"I must admit, you didn't appear to get on well."

Joyce smiled again. "No. I couldn't stand her. I also thought she was giving me the most problems. All those questions. The sighting at the end of her bed." Joyce looked Mel directly in the eye. "She even sneaked into my bedroom, you know?"

"Yeah," Mel replied sheepishly. "She told me."

"Ha! You see," Joyce quipped. "I knew I couldn't trust her. I suppose she told you about the little book I carry too? Names of people who were supposed to be here. Will Parry was the only one who refused. It's why I crossed his name out."

The murder a month before we travelled.

Joyce's silence informed Mel she was thinking exactly the same thing.

"Parry bullied him at school, Mel," Joyce eventually said. "Made his life hell. You don't think he killed..."

Her words trailed off. They both knew the answer.

"Anyway. Hazel. She was causing too much trouble, and we were almost halfway through. I knew I couldn't keep finding jobs. You were getting through my list far too quickly. It's why I gave you all so much time off. So, with only a week or so to go, I begged her to keep her head down, just do as she was told. But she wouldn't listen. Question after question. Accusation after accusation. She was on the brink of ruining the entire trip, and I need the money more than I need Hazel Dunn. Eventually, her headache was a godsend." Joyce smiled again. "I tried again. Went to her room as she was showering, but she still wouldn't listen. So, I gave her enough paracetamol to knock out a horse. I got Louis to carry her to the boat, said I'd get her to a doctor, and halfway across, she *accidentally* fell out."

Mel gasped and held her hand to her mouth. "You killed her?"

"And you found her passport. I messed up there, didn't I, my dear?"

"And what about Ollie? Did you have anything to do with him, erm, falling?"

Joyce looked a little taken aback at the accusation, but how could she blame Mel for asking? "No, nothing. And neither Tony, however much I despised him."

Joyce turned her hand over so she could reciprocate and hold Mel's in return. Mel felt a lump in her throat. The lady before her had been to hell and back since leaving Ridgeview Grammar School, and Mel had played a huge part in her demise. "I just did it for the money, Mel. I'm absolutely desperate."

———————

They were both so wrapped up in their emotions, neither heard the front door clatter open, the subsequent footsteps across the grand hallway or the door to the drawing room smash open.

"Quick," Ed shouted, his hands smeared with blood and his clothes drenched to the skin.

Mel stood quickly, but not before Joyce's fingertips dragged along her palm. "What's happened?" she asked tentatively. "Is it Charlie?" Mel suddenly realised the mortal danger they were all in. Three of the group were dead, plus one back in England for refusing to come. That left her, Charlie, Ed, and Joyce, and Mel knew they were not alone on the island.

43

DESPITE THE PREDICAMENT he found himself in, Ed couldn't help but notice Mel crouching at Joyce's side. They were holding hands, deep in conversation. Joyce appeared despondent, as if all hope was drained from her body.

"Ed!" Mel screaming snapped him from his trance. He peeled his eyes from Joyce and rested them on Mel instead. *Is she crying?* Ed nodded his head slowly, remembering her question. "Yes," he said quietly, "it's Charlie. He's had a fall."

Mel looked back at Joyce. Ed thought the entire situation was so damn bizarre. The last time Mel had discussed Joyce, he thought she might kill her, such was Joyce's derision towards Hazel, towards everybody. But now, they were like two long-lost friends, reconciling at a reunion.

Joyce nodded to Mel and spoke so softly, Ed had to strain to hear. "You go, my dear. See to your husband." She accompanied the last word with a sardonic smile, which Mel reciprocated.

What have *they been talking about?*

"You sure you'll be okay?" Mel asked her, her face full of sympathy and concern. Joyce nodded. Ed glanced at Mel as she stepped by him, but couldn't help but stare at Joyce once more.

"Come on," Mel called out behind him. "We need to act fast."

Ed looked from Joyce to Mel and back to Joyce. Eventually, Joyce nodded towards him. A signal to leave.

"What the fuck's going on, Mel?" Ed shouted after her as she sprinted along the footpath in the direction of the small white gate leading to the woods. The rain was coming down sideways and Ed noticed Mel hadn't put a waterproof on, her T-shirt already stuck to her as if she'd just climbed out of a swimming pool.

"We're not on the island alone, Ed," she shouted against the storm as she held the gate open for him. Ed realised he needed to lead the way. "And Joyce is just as culpable as the rest of us."

Mel relayed her conversation as they quickly navigated through the trees. At least the canopy gave them some respite from the rain and allowed Ed to take in exactly what he was hearing. Now and then, he would stop and turn to face Mel, asking her to clarify what she had just said. But she became annoyed, and pushed him forward in a haste to get to her husband. Ed's irritation grew at Mel's renewed allegiance towards Charlie.

"So she did it for the money. The same as all of us?" Ed asked as they neared the boathouse.

"She's desperate, Ed. We all are."

"Do you believe her? You sure she's not lying to you? If she killed Hazel, she could be behind Tony and Ollie, too." The thought hit him like a steam train. Ed stopped suddenly again and Mel bumped straight into him. She cursed, but Ed held her shoulders at arm's length, unabated. "We've just left her alone, Mel. She could be planning our demise. She told us both to leave. Why would—"

"It's not Joyce, Ed," Mel said, her own hands reaching out to his shoulders in response. Her hair stuck to her forehead, raindrops ran down each cheek, around her neck, and dripped from her arms. "She just followed orders, and in return, we have followed her orders." Ed couldn't find any words. "It's him, Ed. The boy from your book. I can't vouch for Ollie or Hazel, but the rest of us knew him."

Ed nodded slowly. "Hazel knew him too." Mel stared at him, aghast. "She had him sacked from his job. His *dream* job. *His only hope*, I think she said."

"Fuck," was all Mel could say. She looked to the ground, deep in thought, before staring Ed in the eyes once more. "And Ollie?"

"Ollie stole his girlfriend. The love of his life," Ed air quoted, momentarily releasing his grip on Mel's shoulders. "There was a note on his windowsill. The night he jumped."

"But he didn't jump, did he?" Mel intervened. "*He* pushed him."

Mel fought back more tears as she let go of Ed.

"Let's get Charlie back to the house, back to Joyce." She noticed a flicker of disappointment on Ed's face. "He's still my husband and I have to damn well save him. Surely you can see that?" Ed nodded, but she knew he didn't give a shit if they spared her husband or not.

Grabbing his hand, she indicated for Ed to go first. She remembered the blood when he returned to the château and suddenly realised she didn't know how badly injured Charlie was. *He's had a fall.*

She gripped tightly and felt him reciprocate. He led them down the remainder of the hill, and Mel took in the wooden structure before them. She could see it was open at the far end and knew it could be their escape route, the only way out. But the storm was getting worse, and the waves were huge as they crashed against the shore. Mel remembered the day they arrived and what Joyce said. "… and I'll arrange for Louis to take you back to the mainland in the small dinghy which is kept in the boathouse…". Mel dismissed it, fearing just how inadequate this *dinghy* could be. But now, she knew, it was their only option.

"He's gone!"

Mel hadn't realised Ed had stepped ahead without her. He stood at the entrance to the boathouse.

Quickly, she scrambled down to join him.

"And Ollie's gone too."

Five minutes later, they begrudgingly made their way back to the house. They searched the water and the immediate surrounding areas. But there was no sign of Charlie or Ollie. But of course there wasn't, because the mower and trailer were missing too.

Mel broke down. The realisation of her husband's absence hitting her much harder than she expected. Ed held her, but not as tightly or as compassionately as she hoped. But at that moment, Mel Green had no time for Ed. Her grief was for her husband, and however poorly Charlie treated her over the years, she still loved him. Loved him deeply. *Childhood sweethearts.*

"What are we going to do, Ed?" she spoke for the first time since leaving the water's edge. They stepped through the wooden gate and along the footpath to the house. "The water is too rough to cross. There's no phone signal, no hope."

"I'm not sure," he replied, deep in thought. "But didn't Joyce say the police were on their way?"

A creaking sound from the barn to their right alerted them simultaneously. Mel flinched, making Ed jump beside her. She heard him curse, giving her a look she hadn't noticed before. He reached out and held her hand, and Mel recoiled at how hard he gripped.

Ed flicked his head towards the barn and led them towards it. "Are you mad?" she asked through gritted teeth, yet barely audible.

"We can't run forever, Mel," he replied, his voice surprisingly level given their assailant could be only metres away.

"But what if he's in there?"

Ed didn't answer. Instead, the creaking sound came again, rhythmic, like a ticking pendulum. He slowed his pace as they reached the front of the barn, only the door between them and whatever made that noise. Mel could feel her heart hammering and could have killed Ed when he released his grip from her hand. She shuffled directly behind him as he opened the barn door.

Ed gasped and almost banged the back of his head into her face. "Holy fuck," he said, taking a further step forward. It allowed Mel the opportunity to see what the hell he was talking about.

From one of the rafters, Joyce Young rocked back and forth, her neck at an acute angle where the rope dug in. Beneath her was a plastic chair, the same chair the group used on the terrace for pre-dinner drinks. It was toppled onto its side, Joyce's shoes dangling a few feet above. Mel followed the sound of the creaking and watched as the rope caught the wooden beam on each undulation.

The next thing she knew was Ed shaking her. "We have to get away, Mel." His eyes fixed on hers.

"What about Adrienne? Louis?" she replied, unsure where the recollection of their fellow guests came from. Ed shook his head, still gripping her tight. He was hurting her now.

"They'll be okay," he said. "Joyce was the last."

She suddenly snapped from her trance-like state. "We're the last, Ed. Us two and Adrienne and—"

"No," he interrupted. "Those two are safe. You said so yourself. They're nothing to do with Ridgeview Grammar. I know he'll leave them alone." He paused, and she realised he was waiting for her to respond. She nodded her head, totally devoid of words. "We need to take the boat, Mel."

"But the storm. It's too—"

"We can make it. I know we can. It's less than a mile and the storm isn't that bad." He stopped to think again. "Go get your passport. A change of clothes so we don't look so conspicuous when we get to the mainland."

Still, Mel struggled with how easily Ed considered the escape. "But we have no money. How do we afford flights? What do we say to the police?"

"We tell the police the truth. There's a fucking madman on the island. They'll find bodies. I'll leave the note he left for Ollie. They'll find Joyce's notebook, the emails to entice us here. We have nothing to worry about." He saved his biggest surprise until last. "And I've got money, Mel. Enough to get us home."

44

THREE WEEKS LATER

APART FROM CHARLIE'S, Mel found Joyce's funeral the most difficult to cope with. Those last thirty minutes together at the château affected Mel much more than she originally considered. Joyce Young was a long way down on the list of people she had regarded as a friend, especially as the days drifted by on the island, but the way she opened up in the drawing room would live with her forever.

Of course, it didn't help Mel's already frail conscience that it was her and Charlie who had begun Joyce's awful demise in life to begin with. If they hadn't told the authorities of the boy having an affair with a teacher, Joyce would never have had to resign, never fallen into destitution, and never had to play her part as hostess. But what did they know? The boy forced their hand and brought it upon himself.

At first, Mel had been grateful to him. She'd looked on in horror as Will Parry pulled Charlie's shorts down on that infamous sports day. Following the helpless fits of giggles as the unsuspecting Charlie attempted to cover his modesty, many faces slowly spun to gauge her reaction instead. After all, they were the *darling couple* of Ridgeview Grammar. And Mel Edmunds wanted to crawl underneath the seat until she turned and saw the boy's friendly face beside her.

She didn't even know he'd sat there; such was her fascination with Charlie awaiting his turn to run the damn hurdle race. He never did want to take part and Mel could barely take her eyes off him, fearing he may be sick or make a complete fool of himself by running in last. But when Parry carried out his deed and the entire school fell into simultaneous laughter, the boy offered her some solace. A comforting face and, as a result, she buried her head in his chest. Anywhere to hide. Anything to stop the prying eyes.

But he got the wrong idea. He began to follow Mel, would find her at break time, ask if he could walk her home or buy her sweets. All much to the annoyance of Charlie, who continually told him to 'fuck off'. Mel's newfound friendship soon evaporated, and she begged the boy to leave her alone. She called him a freak, much to Charlie's amusement, but still he wouldn't budge.

Until one day, when somebody informed them the boy was having an affair, secretly seeing a teacher after school. Nobody knew who the teacher was, but Mel and Charlie told the head teacher, anyway; anything to get him off their backs. The school carried out their own due diligence, and the next they heard, the boy had been expelled. Again, nothing was ever released regarding the identity of the teacher, and Joyce Young quietly slipped away during the summer, announcing her retirement.

"Fourteen years ago, almost to the day, was my final year at Ridgeview Grammar School," Joyce told the group when they arrived at the château.

"I didn't know you retired that year. That's when we left, wasn't it, darling?" Charlie asked Mel aloud.

"Yes, Charlie," Joyce continued, "I'd had enough, had enough of teaching, of my time at that school. Perhaps that's all you need to know." She had paused. "My reasons were, and shall remain, quite private."

Mel struggled to contain her emotions as Joyce's coffin slid effortlessly back into the hearse for one last journey to the local crematorium. There was a small gathering, but nowhere near as many as three days earlier, when Mel had to endure the heart-rendering task of burying her beloved husband and soulmate.

She was thankful her mum was in a wheelchair that day. It gave her something to hold on to as they watched Charlie's coffin being lowered into the ground; her legs like jelly and her sobbing out of control. He'd wanted a burial. "I don't want to be burned. What if I'm still alive and I wake up?" he once said to her, laughing.

In contrast to Joyce's modest affair, his congregation was huge. It was standing room only in the church, with many left outside to listen and reflect. Charlie was popular, despite his male chauvinistic ways, and he had a lot of friends from the town they grew up in. Ironically, the current head teacher and a couple of teachers from

Ridgeview Grammar showed their respects too, desperate to maintain dignity the school now craved. The news from France had gripped the town, gripped the nation for a few days even, and everybody appeared keen to do their bit. Mel wondered if that's why so many people turned up for the funeral, like some bloody circus in town, but immediately rebuked herself for not believing her Charlie could be loved, despite the charade of cameras and journalists.

Charlie's was the third funeral, and Mel promised herself to attend each one. Joyce's was three days later, and Tony's two days after that. Mel didn't want to go to his, but would do it for Joyce. She also believed there would be such a small turnout, even that lecherous twat deserved someone to see him off.

Ollie's and Hazel's had been the previous week, the latter's body eventually washing up on the mainland four days after Joyce toppled her out of the boat. Mel kept that bit to herself. Both she and Ed told the local police that Hazel had taken her own life, paddling a canoe out to sea before throwing herself overboard. Mel persuaded Ed that's what Joyce told her in the drawing room, although he didn't appear convinced. But Mel didn't want to leave Joyce's legacy tarnished and having to take the murder of a former pupil to her grave.

Charlie's corpse was discovered the day after she and Ed made it safely back to the mainland. Fortunately, the worst of the storm passed overnight, allowing the authorities to get to the island in numbers. Ironically, Charlie's body was in the same stretch of water where Hazel found Tony floating. Ollie was there too, still wrapped in tarpaulin like a mummy bobbing on the waves. The police also discovered tyre marks leading directly to the bench. They were from the ride-on mower, the one Ed and Charlie took Ollie down to the boathouse in. The mower was abandoned in the clearing and it satisfied the authorities that's how the killer moved the bodies. Mockingly, whilst scrupulously surveying the area surrounding the bench, the police found Mel's missing earring, too. Ed laughed at the irony, but she didn't find it particularly funny.

Mel and Ed escaped soon after discovering Joyce's hanging body. Despite her initial doubts, the boat coped admirably in the choppy seas. Whilst crossing the mile-long expanse of sea, memories resurfaced of the day they arrived, when she confided her fears to Joyce. But boats didn't bother Mel, and she was a good swimmer. She just didn't want to be on that damn island, and her hideous premonitions from the day they set foot on the harbour had turned out to be frighteningly accurate.

After reaching the mainland, they headed directly to the police station and spent the next two hours explaining all that had happened. True to his word, whilst she changed and collected her passport, Ed gathered all the evidence he could find in the house. His thinking proved very shrewd as the police nodded and continually agreed as they relayed the facts and produced documentation to back up their stories.

They were told to remain in Pont-Aven until the police carried out their own enquiries, but twenty-four hours later, they were free to leave. The authorities were completely satisfied with their version of events, especially when they discovered Louis and Adrienne in the château's basement, who also testified to everything they said. Mel hadn't wanted to leave them there alone, but Ed convinced her they would be safe, and sure enough, they were bunkered underground, locked away from the lunatic looking for his next prey.

Ed returned to Ireland and Mel went home to her mum, where she'd spent the past three weeks. She had little contact with Ed during those initial days, apart from one long, emotional phone call following an arrest on the island. Ed called her to forward the information he'd just received from the French police. Apparently, they found a suspect hiding in the woods and, ironically, near the clearing. They wouldn't give him details or a name, but said they would be in touch in due course. "They haven't even told the press yet," Ed explained, "but we can finally move on, Mel. It was him. It's all over."

Mel had so many questions, but Ed told her to concentrate with what she had to deal with instead. "You've got your husband's funeral," he said, although she detected a hint of jealousy down the line.

She still had feelings for Ed, but declined his offer to join him in Ireland once the final funeral was over, despite his protestations. Mel made excuses about needing to look after her mum as well as grieve for her loss. Again, she noticed an inkling of envy in Ed's voice. He repeated his plea for her to visit, and she declared she would, as soon as she'd regained the strength.

Twenty-four hours after Joyce's funeral, Mel returned to Charlie's grave to lay flowers. It was the fourth fresh bouquet in as many visits after Mel promised herself to visit him every day, despite her mum's misgivings. "You'll eat yourself up," she told her. "You need to give yourself space to mourn." But Mel was stubborn, and Mel would grieve in her own way.

After laying the flowers and talking to Charlie for at least twenty minutes, she slowly stood, dabbing her eyes and cheeks with a fresh tissue. How many packets of those damn disposable wipes had she got through in the last week? But as she reluctantly turned away from the freshly laid grave for another day, she caught sight of someone on the far side of the cemetery.

Fuck. It can't be.

Mel strained to see; her brain unable to comprehend if it was actually him.

Ed Lawson.

And he was laying his own flowers on another grave. Mel couldn't believe her own eyes, as if someone was having one last laugh at her expense. Why would Ed be in Lincolnshire, and why hadn't he told Mel he was over from Ireland? He'd been desperate for her to visit him. But she hadn't seen him at any of the funerals. He even told her he didn't plan to attend any. So why was he there?

His mum? Mel thought, remembering Ed's description of his own awful circumstances when his mother died. She recalled him struggling to contain himself as they dug into the flowerbeds in that mid-afternoon heat. He was only fourteen when it happened. Poor–.

But hold on, what had Mel asked him?

"What did you do, you know, after your mum died?"

"That's when I moved to Lincolnshire and started at Ridgeview Grammar."

So his mum can't be buried here. Can she?

Mel took a few steps to her left and crouched behind a tree. She had been to four funerals that last week, and only Charlie had been consigned to the grave, the others cremated. Nobody's ultimate resting place was in that cemetery. It couldn't be any of the ill-fated victims from the island reunion, and it couldn't be his mum.

So whose grave was Ed visiting?

45

ONE WEEK LATER

Not for the first time during the past two days, Mel glanced at Ed out of the corner of her eye. They were in his small cottage on the west coast of Ireland, just as she had once asked.

"You've been there for over ten years then? It sounds wonderful. I'd love to visit…"

But these were not the circumstances she had in mind, and as time dragged painfully by, Mel wondered if she had done the right thing. Her husband was barely cold, and she'd just been through the most traumatic few weeks of her life, yet here she was, sat in an isolated house with a guy she'd only properly met for the first time a month or so before. Yes. She had been captivated by Ed Lawson's charm and the stark contrast to how he treated her compared to Charlie. However, during their time on the island, she was unaware of what she now knew.

You're doing it for your husband, Mel…

She made sure Ed never spotted her looking at him,

though. She did it fast, when he was reading or busying himself with a chore. What was she hoping for? To catch him out? But doing what exactly? No, Mel had to speak to him, tell him what she knew, but how the hell did she pick the right moment and, even worse, how would he react?

But would it all be okay? He saved her damn life, for heaven's sake. Apart from Louis and Adrienne, no other guest got off that island alive and she knew, without Ed, she wouldn't have made it either.

Mel cursed for being so hard on herself. So much had happened in such a brief space of time. Barely two months ago, she was sitting in her Lincolnshire home with her husband, planning how the hell they could drum up enough business to keep their company afloat. At the same time, Charlie was most probably having an affair, although Mel had doubted her own theories on that subject too. The more the days passed by, and the realisation that her husband was actually gone, she wondered if he ever was unfaithful or if it was just a figment of her own vivid imagination. Sure, she'd overheard him on the phone several times, but Charlie flirted with every damn woman in the world. He never could interpret the difference between business and pleasure. But even if he was seeing another woman, Mel still loved him deeply and the inevitable guilt seeped into her every thought. And to add to her self-reproach, she knew she had caused the rift between Charlie and Ed in the first place. Did they fight in the boathouse? Is that what caused Charlie to fall and hit his head? Ed repeatedly told her there was no altercation, just the wind from the storm caused Charlie to lose his footing.

Why hadn't she insisted Louis help shift Ollie's body rather than Charlie? She'd noticed the apprehension on

her husband's face when Joyce instructed him to carry out
the hideous deed, so could she have stepped in, told Joyce
he didn't want to do it? But then she would laugh at the
image of Charlie's face if she'd done any such thing.

Since she arrived in Ireland, unbeknown to Ed, Mel
cried every time she found herself alone. Sobbed for her
husband, for the way he died, but the worst of all was
how they had argued to the very end. That would always
be her last memory of Charlie Green. Bitter, angry words,
when deep down, they truly loved one another.

Yes, she was there for him.

Ed noticed Mel glance towards him for the umpteenth
time since she'd arrived roughly forty-eight hours earlier.
This time, he offered a weak smile in return and asked
why she kept looking at him. It pleased him when a
momentary panic made her falter.

Her phone call surprised him. It was the day after
he'd flown to Lincolnshire to visit the grave. Ed had
purposefully chosen that day, a day when there was no
other funeral planned. One day after Joyce's and a day
before Tony's. He didn't want to be seen, for obvious
reasons.

So Mel's call caught him out. He'd phoned her a
couple of weeks prior, soon after they returned from
France, but she declined his invitation. Said she needed to
be with her mum and grieve for her Charlie. That made
Ed angry. Couldn't she see how that guy had treated her
all her life? Mel could do so much better, and now Charlie
was out of the way, surely it was time to move on?

But Ed only needed to remain patient. After all, she
did only last a few weeks until she called and asked if she
could visit him in his remote Irish cottage. He knew that

once she'd buried that idiot of a husband, she would come running to the man who could make her truly happy. The man who saved her life.

Earlier that day, Ed watched her from his bedroom window as she paced up and down his long front garden, to the edge of the cliff and back again. Up and down she went, maybe half a dozen times. When he asked her what she'd been doing, she looked at him doubtfully and said she'd been so lost in her own little world. She didn't even realise she'd been pacing.

As nightfall settled on Mel's second evening, the clouds descended and shrouded his small cottage into darkness. It was always the same when the weather drew in and the sea mist engulfed his modest home. There were no street lamps, only a neighbour's house a little set back from his own, yet offering no light. If the moon was hidden, it could be quite scary, but Ed was used to it and considered it more of a deterrent to intruders than any actual incentive.

"Want a drink?" Mel asked over her shoulder as she stepped into the kitchen.

She returned minutes later with two glasses of red wine. They clinked them forlornly, and she leant forward and kissed him delicately on the forehead. He smiled in return.

"Thank you," he said as she took a swig of her own. "I'm pleased you called and asked to visit."

Mel watched as Ed finished one glass and then a second. She'd barely touched hers, consciously keeping it by her side whilst taking the tiniest of sips to keep up the pretence. Once Ed polished off one bottle, she opened another.

Earlier, during the day, Ed had caught her walking up and down his long expanse of grass, down to the cliff's edge and back. She lost count of how many times she actually traced the steps. Six, maybe seven.

"Why were you pacing up and down the lawn?" he asked her when she returned inside. It caught her out. She hadn't even realised he'd been watching from his bedroom window, so lost in thought she'd been whilst counting.

"Eh?" she floundered. "Oh, that," she laughed rather pathetically. "I was miles away, thinking about everything that's happened. The ocean can be so therapeutic. You've got a lovely spot here, Ed."

As she poured his fourth or fifth glass – she'd lost count herself – Mel finally picked up the courage to ask what she'd come for. She recalled Ed telling her of how dark it was at his cottage when the sea mist rolled in and the moon wasn't able to penetrate the clouds. She so craved it to be that way on her first night, just to get it over and done with. The question on her lips had threatened to spill out ever since she arrived, but she knew she had to remain patient and wait until the time was right.

Before she stepped into the kitchen and asked Ed if he wanted a drink, she'd stood at the curtains overlooking the garden. And Ed was right. With no illumination, it indeed blanketed his cottage in pitch darkness.

You need to ask him now.

A week earlier, she waited patiently for Ed to leave the grave he was attending. Once satisfied he'd departed the cemetery, Mel stepped from behind the tree and scooted over to the same spot. She remained crouched and almost laughed at how stupid she must have looked, running across a graveyard, in and out of the headstones like a child at play.

But the smile didn't last. As soon as she found the fresh flowers, she knew she was at the right grave, but the headstone was small and contained no engraving. Mel rushed home and immediately booted up her laptop. It surprised her how easy it was to trace whose burial site it actually was. Several ancestry-type websites offering such information at ease. But it still didn't make her discovery any the easier to digest.

The boy she presumed stalked them on the island was buried in the same graveyard. Mel confirmed her findings by eventually finding the announcement in the obituary column of the local online newspaper. She had never read those listings before and considered it something old folk did to see if they recognised any of the names. However, she found the boy in amongst the list of dead people. But no longer a boy; he was a man of thirty-one years on the day he passed. Just over a year ago.

So what was Ed doing at his grave? And, more importantly, who was it on the island?

Mel and Ed never gave the police a name. They hadn't even disclosed it to one another. Mel presumed that neither could find the courage to actually say it out loud. They just told the police everything else they knew and a crazy person was still at large.

———

"Er, Ed?" she asked casually.

He looked at her, his eyes a little sunken, and when he spoke, she realised the alcohol was well into his system.

"Yes? What is it?" he replied, noncommittal.

No turning back now.

"I saw you last week." She paused, his face twisted slightly, but she couldn't determine his expression.

"What?" Ed eventually replied, as if he'd finally deciphered exactly what she'd just said to him.

"Last week. In the village."

Ed laughed. "What village? Why are you talking in riddles?" His words were definitely slurred.

"The village where I live. The village in Lincolnshire."

He stood, gripping the arm of his chair.

Is it shock or is he that drunk?

"Nonsense. I said I wouldn't go to any of the funerals and I—"

"No, Ed. You weren't at a funeral. But you were in the graveyard."

His face unquestionably contorted. Disbelief? Irritation? But Mel wouldn't allow him to speak until she'd asked what she came for.

"Why did you put flowers on that boy's headstone?"

Again, Ed opened his mouth to reply, but Mel was too quick.

"And why didn't you tell me he died just over a year ago?"

46

ED HAD COVERED ALL the tracks, given the police as much information and evidence as he had to hand. Even Adrienne and Louis backed him up. He rescued Mel from mortal danger. She wasn't supposed to come home from that island alive. So why, a month later, did she ask about *that* boy?

That boy? Ed raged inside his head, cursing himself for drinking so much, so quickly and equally livid that he'd been so stupid to be spotted in that graveyard.

Still, he thought, *that boy?*

He does have a real fucking name.

'That boy' does indeed have a name, but Melanie Green already knows that. And so did her ever-loving husband Charlie, and all the others, too. But they all avoided the subject, not one daring to mention his name, or much more importantly, how they knew him.

His name is, or was Martin Pell. I say 'was', because he died last year, not that anybody cared. His death made the small print in the local newspaper, the column nobody ever reads. Well, that's not entirely true. Joyce Young read it. She even attended his funeral. But I didn't speak to her then, I barely recognised her. However, it planted a seed, their little 'rendezvous' during his adolescent years. So, I did contact my old history teacher, several months later.

Leukaemia finally took him from this world, but not before he attempted to take his own life on two or three previous occasions. And how do I know all of this? Because Martin Pell was my brother, well, half-brother. Same mum, different dad. Then again, I can never really be sure of that either. It's not as though I'll ever ask for a fucking DNA test, is it?

My father was killed in a road traffic accident whilst Mum carried me in her belly, but Mum didn't mind. She was already shacked up with some guy from the village and within months of dad dying, she was expecting my brother. God knows how long she'd been seeing this person before my 'dad' died, so as I say, I can never be a hundred percent certain that Martin and I didn't share the same father, too. Brother, half-brother, what's the fucking difference, anyway? Well, quite a lot actually. It's all in a name, you see, and if we hadn't had different surnames, then everybody would have always known we were siblings.

Martin's dad, Harry Pell, pissed off soon after Martin was born, leaving mum to cope with two of us. And Mum struggled, especially with him. He was a problem child and grew more of an 'inconvenience' the elder he became. Eventually diagnosed with 'Attention Deficit Hyperactivity Disorder', or just plain 'fucking mental' according to Mum, the more she toiled, the more I took her side and began to despise and disown my younger brother.

But then Mum showed signs of her own illness when I was eleven, and Martin was ten. She complained of being tired and her arms would continually have fresh bruises on them. She spent hours in bed, grumbling about being too hot or too cold. I, in turn, would go to Martin's room and tell him it was all his fault. One day, when Mum had barely surfaced from her room for over forty-eight hours, I told Martin she would get better if he wasn't around. Later, he was rushed to hospital after Mum found him on his bed alongside an empty packet of paracetamol. Of course, I denied any knowledge, and he was allowed home the next day. I knew he wouldn't say anything, though.

Three painful years later, Mum died peacefully in a rest home. I was by her side, only fourteen years of age, but she had nobody else. I told her Martin didn't want to come because he was too scared. Mum nodded as I secretly smiled to myself. Unbeknownst to her, I'd threatened Martin not to come anywhere near us.

After her funeral in our local town, social services found us a foster home in Lincolnshire. It was miles from where we lived and I considered our new environment flat and boring. We were both enrolled at Ridgeview Grammar School, and from the very first morning, I instructed Martin to walk behind me and never tell anybody he was my brother. As I say, we had different surnames. Mum never told me why she kept Martin's dad's surname, but that suited me just fine. If he kept his mouth shut, nobody would ever know we were related.

From the first day at Ridgeview, Martin was bullied. Will Parry and his mates saw to that. A new kid, half fucking crazy as well. Martin was easy pickings. To begin with, he looked at me for help, but I'd just glare, daring him to say something as Will shoved another clump of grass into his mouth.

Things changed in the second year – my final year – and Martin finally befriended somebody. And not just any old body, our bloody history teacher, no less. Miss Young must have taken pity on him. The constant bullying, the tantrums, the threatening to take his own life. She took him under her wing, even took him back to her house for tea after school. Martin told me all about it one night when I asked where he'd been. He talked of how much he liked her and of her horrible husband, who he was sure used to beat her, and how one day he would 'deal with' him. I laughed, although I knew he was serious.

I kept my mouth shut. He said if I told anybody about his special friendship with Joyce, then he would tell everybody he was my brother. So, we both had our secrets.

At seventeen, I left our foster home and moved in with a friend who I met at work. It was the last time I saw Martin, well, until last year.

Two days after my twenty-first birthday, I'd saved enough money and relocated to Ireland. Six years later, I bought my cottage, where I've worked and lived ever since. That's when I wrote my first novel, 'The Unwanted Child'. The words flowed, as the subject matter was just a case of recollections.

I know who this book is about...

I never found out who left me that note, but Joyce was my favourite. Or perhaps Charlie? Nonetheless, whoever did it cemented in my mind why I arranged the whole damn reunion in the first place; to ensure nobody left that island alive.

The book sold well, was picked up by a major publisher and, as a result, sold even better. Within two years, I'd saved a very healthy nest egg, suitable for a rainy day – including enough to pay for two flights home from France – and all at the expense of my crazy half-brother.

Everything was fine. I kept myself to myself, although loneliness had its side effects. I drank more, a lot more, and my moods changed as a result. Often, I found myself in a confrontation at the pub or even whilst queuing at the supermarket. Road rage was another of my traits, 'effing and blinding at any passer-by who dared to cross me. And as the years passed by, the more unreliable I became. Perhaps it's in our genes?

And then the phone call late last year. Martin had somehow tracked me down and said he needed to see me. He said it was urgent, and however much I protested, he told me it would be in my best interests. Two days later, I reluctantly boarded a flight from Shannon Airport to Stansted and caught a train to Peterborough.

Martin's address was a hospice, but before I arrived, I hadn't put two and two together. It was stupid, considering I'd been through exactly the same with Mum all those years ago. He looked like shit. So much so, I thought the nurse had sent me to the wrong room. His face was so gaunt it looked as though he was sucking his cheeks in. He only had tufts of hair and his arms lay on top of the woven blanket like two twigs fallen from a tree. It took my breath away and the immediate onset of guilt hit me so hard, I had to grab the back of a blue plastic chair, sat in the corner.

For the next hour, we talked, albeit, in Martin's case, extremely slowly. But he made me listen to every last detail of what he'd been through since I walked out on him the day I turned seventeen. And shit, my little brother had been to hell and never come back.

They expelled him from Ridgeview Grammar after somebody informed the authorities he was having an affair with a teacher. Martin swore it was never like that. She just befriended him, looked after him, especially the year after I left school. I couldn't decipher if it was the truth or not, but I could detect how upset he was.

"She was everything to me, Ed," he said, choking back tears.

"Who told the authorities?" I asked, trying to move the conversation on. I couldn't handle him crying as the self-reproach threatened to overwhelm me.

"Do you remember Charlie Green and Mel Edmunds?" he replied. I nodded, recalling the 'golden couple' from the year below. "Well, after they grassed on me, on us, Joyce blamed me for giving us away. I promise I never said a word, Ed. She was so good to me." He stopped to compose himself once more. I found his recollection difficult to hear. "She told me to stay away from her. Said I'd ruined her entire life."

He explained that after she left Ridgeview, she separated from Tony, too. "He punched her the day she came home and told him she'd lost her job," he continued. "Fortunately, he's had a real bad time of things ever since. In and out of prison for a multitude of minor offences, and I found out recently that he's living in some squat."

It sounded like karma to me.

After a few sips of water, Martin told me he dossed around for a while, taking crap jobs for crap money, but a couple of years later, he heard of a company who specialised in travel. Without disclosing how he found his contact; Martin informed me he wrote to someone called Hazel Dunn. "She went to Ridgeview, so I thought it would be the perfect introduction," he said. Finally, she gave into him and offered him a role. "Things were on the up," he continued. "Not only did I get a new job, but I also met a girl there. We started dating," he added with a grin. "Chloe Jones was her name."

But things soon spiralled again and Martin found himself in a dark place. A year later, this Hazel Dunn had him fired and, to add to his misery, a few months afterward, some guy called Oliver Ramsey stole his girlfriend. "I fucking loved her, Ed. We had plans, so many plans. I couldn't believe she went off with him."

However, Martin left the real bombshell until last. The real reason he'd asked to see Ed.

"Dad died last year. My real dad. Harry Pell. He might be your dad too, but I guess we'll never know, will we?" My face must have conveyed all he needed to know. "He found me. Three, four years ago. Said he wanted to make up for all the lost years. So, we spent a lot of time together, Ed. It meant so much to me, to have a proper dad for the first time." Martin was choking up again, and I had to do everything in my power not to show any sign of weakness. For the first time in my life, I so wanted to protect my younger brother and cursed myself over and over for being such a hideous individual during his early life. I'd even stopped him from saying goodbye to Mum. "But last year, he had a massive heart attack. In a bloody restaurant, of all places."

"I'm so sorry, mate," I responded, reaching out and taking his hand in mine. It felt so fragile, so tiny and oh so bony. But he was *my bloody brother. The guy I blocked from my life years before. And there he was, laying on a bed, thirty-one years of age and dying right before my eyes.*

"There is a silver lining though," he added, a mischievous smile stretching across his face. "He left me a fucking great big house on some island in France."

MEL SAT in shock as Ed relayed the story of his younger brother. She could physically detect the colour drain from her cheeks and the knots in her stomach tighten on his every word. She'd had her doubts, but still, to actually hear it in person made her feel wretched to the core.

Martin Pell was Ed Lawson's half-brother. The boy who Joyce Young had an affair with. The affair she and Charlie told the authorities about. They knew who the pupil was, but they never knew the teacher involved. Mel recalled the day the invitation arrived and Charlie claiming their innocence.

"…and what did we do wrong? Nothing. Absolutely nothing."

"That's not entirely true, is it, darling?"

Following her discovery online of who lay in that grave, Mel had phoned the police in France. They confirmed her worst fears by telling her not to worry, but they still hadn't caught anybody in relation to what happened on the island. Ed hadn't received a call from them at all. He'd lied to her. Covered his own tracks.

"It was you?" was all Mel could muster. "You?" She sat in her chair, knowing she should run but somehow unable to move. "You set up the entire thing to get revenge on the people who made your brother's life hell?"

Ed stood and paced the room before downing the contents of his latest glass of wine. Within moments, he returned from the kitchen with a fresh bottle.

"Yes, Mel," he eventually retorted. "I owed him. But more than that, I owed my mum." He paused. "*Our* mum."

Mel sat perplexed as Ed told her of his mum's dying wish that he looked after his younger brother. But he never kept his promise. He despised Martin, blamed him for their mother's death, and eventually blanked him from his memory. It wasn't until that phone call a year earlier that Ed gave him a moment's thought. But when he saw him, listened about the life he'd laughingly held, all of Ed's guilt came rushing to the surface. He said he couldn't stop thinking of his mum, looking down, cursing him, loathing him for not looking out for Martin. Ever since his brother's funeral, Ed had nightmare after nightmare. Self-condemnation to the extent of ending it all would be his only way out.

But then the deeds of the château arrived, and Ed took a flight from Shannon to Nantes. He spent a week locked up alone on the island and did nothing but think, contemplating retribution on his brother's behalf. Seek revenge on all the people who made his life a hell. But Ed not only did it for Martin, he also did it for his mum.

. . .

First, he coaxed Joyce into hosting the entire charade in return for twenty thousand pounds. *'It came from a name I didn't recognise,'* she'd said to Mel. *'My knight in shining armour'*. Joyce was flat broke, living on handouts from food banks. Ed found out where she lived and, unbeknown to her, visited her house. Although he resisted knocking on her door, he knew he'd hit the jackpot straight away.

As with all the invitees, Ed set up a spurious email account, logged on via some VPN to hide his IP address, and sent her an offer she couldn't refuse. She jumped at the opportunity. Joyce had already explained to Mel the contents of her email were different, but Ed confirmed the strict set of instructions she had to follow. He sent her a list of names, which she "stupidly wrote in a little black book," he added. "She even crossed Will Parry out once I told her he wouldn't be going."

It hit Mel like a hammer blow.

"Fuck. You killed Will Parry."

Ed smiled and nodded. "Yeah, I took a flight over and paid him a visit. Like all of you, I had to get him in a position where he couldn't refuse my offer."

He explained how he'd followed him after work to an address which was part of his postal round. After a couple of conversations with fellow workers, Ed soon discovered Parry was having an affair with a married woman. He made further enquiries. "… and to cut a long story short, I contacted her husband and got him to return home unexpectedly. He caught them at it like a pair of rabbits," he chuckled.

"But he still turned down your invitation?" Mel asked, uncertain where she was finding the actual words from.

"Yep. Bloody idiot," Ed smiled, formidably. "So I paid him another visit, a month before the reunion."

He slit his damn throat.

Mel sat dumbstruck as Ed moved on and explained how he'd contacted Mel and Charlie's biggest customers. Informed them they were in serious financial trouble and they should go elsewhere for their printing needs. "They fell for it so easily, I couldn't believe my luck," he added with a grin.

Ed then revealed how he convinced Hazel's company. He sent emails, allegedly from clients, describing how she'd been acting inappropriately whilst abroad. As a result, they threatened to look elsewhere if they continued to send her to inspect their properties. "I don't think they even checked," he concluded. Finally, he spiked Ollie's drinks when he foolishly stopped at a pub on the way home in his delivery van. It had been the very day Ed chose to follow him. "It was all so simple, as if it was meant to be. A sign from Mum. All I had to do was bide my time until your money troubles hit home, and I clicked 'Send' on my invitations and waited until you all said yes."

The smile on his face made Mel want to be sick. He sat down opposite her. He was acting as though everything he said was perfectly acceptable behaviour and she would continually nod and agree.

He killed your husband, Mel. It's why you're here.

"Oh," he added, by now loving the exchange, "I also popped off Ollie's wife."

Mel gasped and attempted to push herself further back into her chair. *He's fucking crazy.* "How?" she asked without even realising she'd spoken.

"Hit and run. She wasn't even looking. Although it was dark." *Is he actually smiling?* "That'll teach Ollie to go pinching my brother's girlfriend. He bloody loved that Chloe Jones. Did you know her?" he added chirpily.

Although realising she was in deep trouble, Mel wanted to know more. As if she needed every detail before it was her turn. She shook her head at his latest incredulous question and moved the conversation on, all the time thinking of how the hell she could escape.

"So, when you got us to the island, you always knew you would kill us, one by one?" Mel couldn't believe the words she was actually saying. They were coming out like she was chatting over a coffee at her local café. Leaning forward, without taking her eyes off Ed, she gingerly placed her glass of wine on the table, ready to run. Ed stood quickly, making her flinch. Fortunately, he stepped to the window overlooking the wild Atlantic Ocean and Mel looked for something to defend herself with, but there was nothing to hand. Ed spoke without turning, occasionally taking a sip of his wine. She could see he'd drank most of his next glass.

"No, not to begin with. I guessed I'd just scare you all." He paused, as if lost in thought, before eventually turning to face her, the sick grin still spread across his face. "You see, I didn't really know what to do," he added matter-of-factly, "but I realised if I got you all on a deserted island, I could bide my time until I decided." He took another drink. "I wanted you all to stew, fall out with one another." He outstretched his arm and pointed his glass towards her. "That was your fault, that was," he added, grinning.

"My fault? How?" It was like car crash television. Mel didn't want to watch but couldn't stop herself.

"Waiting to walk with me at the bloody airport," he grinned. "Sneaking into my room on the first night we were there." Despite her predicament, Mel couldn't help but redden. "I must admit, Melanie Edmunds, I fell for you."

She felt sick. Sick to the core. Mel needed to move the conversation on. The thoughts of her intimate times with a madman on the island, whilst her husband lay comatose in the next room, made her stomach churn.

"But you didn't wait long." She realised her tone might make him even more volatile, but Mel was beyond trying to find ways of expressing herself. Jeez, it wasn't as though she was well practiced in such a situation.

"What do you mean?"

"Tony. That's what I mean. You killed him on the Monday evening. We'd only been there three bloody days."

Unbelievably, Ed laughed loudly. "Oh yeah. It was only three days, wasn't it?" He sat down again, an expression of sheer shamelessness written across his face. "Oh, come on, Mel. *Everybody* hated Tony. Remember that argument he had with Joyce the night Hazel screamed out? Both Charlie and Ollie told him to piss off. And after he'd gone, nobody batted a bloody eyelid." Unfortunately, Mel realised he had a point where Tony was concerned. He had given her the creeps, too. "I did that one for Joyce more than Martin, though," he continued. "Bloody bully. Apparently, he used to beat her pretty badly…"

Ed left his words hanging and stood again, stepping back into the kitchen. Mel contemplated making a move, but terror weighed her to the chair. Terror and not having a clue what to do or where to run. It was pitch black outside, and the mist ensured she wouldn't see beyond the end of her nose. Moments later, Ed returned with a refill. His wine glass was full to the brim.

"And it was you who stood at the foot of Hazel's bed,

I presume?" she asked, watching him spill his drink over the edge of his glass.

"Yeah. I took some of Martin's clothes from his house after his funeral. I remembered them from when we were in our late teens. He was forever wearing that bloody waistcoat. They didn't fit me very well, but in the dark, it was enough to scare the living shits out of her."

"And the message in my mirror?" Mel asked without requiring a reply. "The PE kit?"

Ed didn't even need to answer. Instead, he took another drink. Mel then recalled Joyce's story of tipping Hazel from the boat.

"So, how did you kill Hazel?"

Ed took another huge gulp of his wine and almost finished the glass. He held it up as if he couldn't work out where the contents had gone.

"Didn't have to," he replied with another slur. "Stupid bitch fell out of the boat. Joyce told me."

He doesn't know. Joyce didn't tell him.

"But you pushed Ollie out of his window and you killed my Charlie, didn't you?" Her voice caught. The first mention of Charlie for a while sent her emotions spiralling. This man sat six feet in front of her murdered her husband with his bare hands. For the first time in a while, Mel's inner hatred threatened to overwhelm her sheer fright.

It's why you're here.

"Yeah," Ed said, smiling and necking his drink. "You remember when the police said they found the ride-on mower near the bench?" She reluctantly nodded. "Well, halfway back to the house, I turned around, went back, finished your Charlie off with one more blow. I loaded him up next to Ollie, drove up to the clearing and rolled them into the sea." He smiled. "Thought it was quite fitting, really."

"Let me refill that for you," she said, standing. Her legs felt wobbly, and she thought she may fall straight into his arms.

"Ah, good girl," Ed replied sardonically.

As she stood in the kitchen, Ed continued his boasting from the living room. "Had to hit your Charlie with a fucking brick to finish him off. I couldn't believe it. He fell into the water, hit his fucking head on the boat and still came out smiling." She could hear him laughing at his own story, lost in his own world.

"What about Ollie?" she shouted, desperate to keep him talking and spare her any further details about her husband.

"Ha! Now that was the most fun. You see, I went outside one night and walked up and down the gravel outside his room." He paused, and Mel's heart sank. Has he moved? "Can you remember when he said somebody was walking outside his room?" he eventually shouted.

"Yeah," Mel called over her shoulder.

"Well, I walked up and down, just to scare him, but then I did the same again, you know, to get him to look out the window. But first, I got a ladder and put a blue toy car on his windowsill and stapled a note to the wood."

"Okay," she said, not quite believing he wasn't demanding where his next drink was. "Why did you do that?"

"So he knew Martin was behind it all, of course. Wanted him to know he'd killed his damn wife, too. The note and the little blue car saw to that."

He's absolutely insane.

"Then, I sneaked back upstairs, watched him from his bedroom door, ran across the room and gave him an almighty shove in the back. When I looked down at him, I thought his bloody head had snapped off."

Mel felt bile rising in her chest once more as Ed giggled from the other room. "So you never got a call from the French police? The day you called me and said they'd arrested someone?" Silence. "And I suppose Joyce killing herself saved you that one too?"

But still Ed didn't reply. Instead, everything remained deathly silent. Even the wind outside abated, and Mel could hear the distinct sound of waves crashing against the shoreline in the distance. And then she heard footsteps. One, two, three. Coming from the living room towards the kitchen.

Standing still, Ed's breathing was the next thing she heard. He could only be a step or two behind her.

"And what about you?" he asked, his voice lower, the joviality gone. "How are we going to end all of this, Melanie Green?"

Mel was unsure if she could do it. Her hands gripped the work surface, the bread knife trapped in between. Ed took another step closer until she could physically feel his breath on her neck. Every single nerve in her body tensed, leaving her feeling paralysed. But as soon as she felt his hand brush the back of her hair, she summoned the strength to move.

Turning slowly, as if to reciprocate, she kept her hands behind her back. Unsure how she ever plucked up the courage, Mel smiled at Ed, his face inches from her own. Ed returned the look, his lips and teeth crimson from the wine, but as she leant forward to kiss him, Ed took a step backwards.

"It would be more romantic if you put the knife down, Melanie," he said casually.

Fuck. How long has he been standing there?

Whilst Ed had been boasting of his exploits from the other room, Mel had opened the kitchen door leading into the garden, ready to run for her life. She glanced towards it over Ed's shoulder and his eyes followed hers. Quickly, she lifted her arm and pulled the blade down with all her energy. Ed screamed in agony as the knife penetrated just below his shoulder. He grabbed the handle, pulling and wriggling to free it from his muscle. And he shrieked and cursed before eventually releasing it with a sickening slicing sound.

But Mel had made her move and found herself outside in Ed's garden. She couldn't see a thing, darkness suffocating her whilst the sea mist immediately clung to her body. However, as soon as the screaming subsided from the kitchen, Mel took one deep breath and began walking, counting every step as she went.

She had to concentrate once Ed joined her outside. She knew he couldn't see her, already twenty paces from the house, so she consented to maintain the identical stride, the same as she had done six or seven times that afternoon. Ed bellowed her name, over and over, and she could hear him scrambling somewhere behind, all so close yet safe in the knowledge he would have to be physically by her side to actually see her.

At fifty-five steps, Mel Green stood, knowing the cliff edge was only a leap away. A vault away from joining her husband. A quick death, relatively painless, washed out to sea, never to be found. Instead, she turned.

"Over here, Ed," she shouted and immediately detected him stop still. "Come to me. I can't see a thing."

"Where?" he called, his footsteps slowly growing closer.

"Here," she said again. "Over here."

He was getting nearer, and she prayed she had

counted the steps correctly. *Fifty-five*, she said in her head, *and it's fifty-seven to the edge*. If the cliff edge wasn't directly behind her, Mel knew she was in deep trouble.

"Where?" he shouted, his anger rising now that she had stopped talking. "Where the fuck are you, Mel?"

Not until he could only be two or three paces away did Mel move again. "Just here," she said quietly, taking a step to her left. She didn't see Ed until he was barely a stride from her side.

In one swift movement, Mel jumped behind, and with every ounce of strength left within her, shoved Ed in the middle of his back. Initially, she believed she had made an error in her calculation. He took two unsteady steps forward with his arms flailing, but his feet remained firmly planted on the ground. However, his third step hit fresh air and Mel listened as he screamed in obvious recognition of what had happened. But the scream lasted only a second as the sound was replaced by a sickening thud of body against rocks. Then two more muffled bangs before what sounded like rolling and eventually the distinct noise of something hitting water.

Mel outstretched her arms; the sea mist having now soaked her to the skin. And she screamed too. As loud as she could. And she continued to scream, contemplating jumping herself, until she heard voices from behind. But they weren't threatening voices. Instead, friendly, reassuring, calming voices, quickly followed by a powerful beam of light from a torch piercing the spray and the gloom. Finally, Mel felt the comforting arms of Ed's neighbour wrapping gently around her.

And so she closed her eyes and imagined that when she turned, Charlie would be there, smiling, but also angry that his hair was getting messed up by the wind.

THREE WEEKS LATER

Mel stood at her sixth funeral in as many weeks. Ed Lawson's. She had thought long and hard about attending. Her mum said she was crazy to contemplate going and the police and even her doctor said it wouldn't be wise.

But Mel Green needed conclusion and felt it quite fitting that his was the last.

The final chapter, she thought with a wry smile, as they laid his coffin effortlessly into the ground, next to the grave of his younger brother.

'The Family' Psychological Thriller Trilogy

Have you read the series everybody is talking about?

Available in both eBook and Print Versions

*EACH BOOK AVAILABLE SEPARATELY OR AS A
BUNDLE - Just search for 'Jack Stainton Books'*

⭐⭐⭐⭐⭐ *'I was amazed at the twists and turns in these
books… brilliant... impossible to put down'*

⭐⭐⭐⭐⭐ *'Had to finish it quickly so I could get my heart
rate back to normal...'*

⭐⭐⭐⭐⭐ *'I love a good psychological thriller and I have
just found my new favourite author!!'*

⭐⭐⭐⭐⭐ *'I like to think I read enough thrillers to be able
to suss them out before finishing, but this one kept me
guessing until the very last sentence!'*

'THE BOSS'S WIFE'

A compelling narrative that delves into the complex dynamics of ambition, power, and desire. Explore the depths Adam must navigate to safeguard his dream job while unravelling the captivating mysteries surrounding his enigmatic Boss's Wife.

How far would you be willing to tread the thin line between ambition and consequence?

COMING VERY SOON!
The BRAND NEW Novel by Jack Stainton

FROM THE AUTHOR

Thank you for reading 'He Is Here'—I hope you enjoyed it. If you've followed my previous works, you may have noticed a shift in direction with this novel. It marks the first time I've adopted a third-person narrative, and I must say, navigating multiple third-person perspectives proved both complex and refreshing.

The feedback from my Advanced Readers Club was overwhelmingly positive, and I'm sincerely grateful to each of you for catching even the intentional mistakes—like when Joyce called for help despite the absence of phones on the island!

One prevalent comment was that none of the characters were particularly *likeable*. This was intentional! Midway through, I realised I didn't like them either, but that was precisely the point—they weren't meant to be *likeable*. It's why they found themselves on the island in the first place. And, as you no doubt discovered, each of them received their comeuppance—a part I thoroughly enjoyed writing :)

I'd also like to express my gratitude to my editor and cover designer (my favourite cover to date). However, most importantly, I want to thank you—the readers. This novel is dedicated to you. You've turned my dream into a reality, and without your support, I'd merely be sitting at my desk, typing words for my own enjoyment. Although, I must admit, it wouldn't stop me!

Thank you once more, and keep an eye out for my next novel, 'The Boss's Wife', set to be published early in 2024!

To learn more about me and my books, please sign up to my FREE newsletter below…

www.jackstainton.com/newsletter

 facebook.com/jackstaintonbooks

 x.com/jack_stainton

 instagram.com/jackstaintonbooks

REVIEWS

Enjoy this book? You can make a big difference

Honest reviews of my books help bring them to the attention of other readers.

If you've enjoyed this novel I would be very grateful if you could spend just a few minutes leaving a review (it can be as short as you like).

Thank you very much.

A GUEST TO DIE FOR

Jack Stainton's debut Psychological Thriller

Available online in both eBook and Print Versions

…I bought the book and read it in two sittings. Very good, lots of twists and red herrings.

This does exactly what a thriller should; it keeps you guessing until the end…

Excellent book full of twists and turns. The characters are brilliant… The ending was totally unexpected…

Sucking you in with a dreamy hope of a better start, the fear of what might happen next will keep you turning the pages!

A fantastic, gripping debut!

Made in the USA
Monee, IL
24 March 2024